The Hauntings of
Hood Canal

The Hauntings of Hood Canal

Jack Cady

St. Martin's Press ✹ *New York*

www.stmartins.com

ISBN 0-312-28079-3

First Edition: October 2001

10 9 8 7 6 5 4 3 2 1

For Stephen Becker (1927–1999)
Great man, great friend, great writer

And then the headman turns to the bones. For the bones a platform has been built of oak; and a stout tanned hide shelters the bones from wind and rain. The bones are of several small people, perhaps children, perhaps the smaller forefathers that figure in ceremonial tales of the ancient hot green land to the south. Thirty years ago, when these bones were taken, the headman declared that they were old, indeed, older than any bones yet seen by him, older than any head taken by the Wild Wa; perhaps even older than the headman's grandfather's grandfather's grandfather. In those days men and gods roamed the earth together, and copulated freely; these bones are surely the relics of living gods.

Stephen Becker, *The Blue-Eyed Shan*

The Hauntings of
Hood Canal

The Road

The road beside the Hood Canal runs snaky, the Canal branching from dark waters of Puget Sound and growing even darker as it runs a black furrow east of the Olympic Mountain range. The Canal was carved by the last ice age. It is dolomite and granite-walled; wider than the Mississippi, and darker than a bad man's thoughts. It runs with geologic indifference before trailer parks, boat moorings, bars, bait shops, and villages. Cresting waves break wild as oceans when our world lies flogged by storms, although on windless days the Canal holds the calm of a black and nigh bottomless lake.

In daylight the road carries locals who are easy in their minds and tourists who are tight-lipped and white-knuckled. Since tourists are accustomed to freeways the road seems to them a narrow path beside a watery hell. There are no guard rails.

Locals know the road and stay off after midnight. Bars and roadhouses close at eleven P.M. Men pack up pool cues, or put away their darts. Wives or girlfriends bundle up against the wind. Everyone gets home before the road "turns ugly".

During long night hours when the road is ugly a few trucks pass this way, or a traveling salesman, or a tourist who has ventured too far from cities. If the Canal reaches out and swallows a car, or if the road dumps a truck into those cold waters, the people who perish are strangers.

And, sometimes, people turn ugly. More than a few "sensitives" have roamed these parts:

Chantrell George once wore visions at his throat, having made necklaces of hallucinogenic mushrooms.

Sugar Bear Smith had a girl's pretty looks, and a girl's gentle ways, but those things slipped after he killed a man.

Greek Annie is a witch who talks to frogs and reptiles, and who lately called down storms.

Petey Mullholland and *Bertha*, of Bertha's Beer and Bait Shoppe, resemble pool sharks.

And *Miscellaneous*, which is to say, there's a scatter of beer drinkers, top fallers, wharf rats, loggers, and other humble but possibly sainted folk; the most inconspicuous being a thoughtful character known as *the fisherman*, the youngest being a truck driver called *the tow-truck kid*.

Even some animals act better than they should. *Jubal Jim Johnson*, who runs with Petey, and who is a blue tick hound, likes to bay cuss words across dark water, raising his snout toward a clouded moon while pretending he is a wolf.

There wasn't a dangerous one among them. Even Sugar Bear was angelic. He only killed a man because that man messed with children. If Sugar Bear hadn't, someone else would feel obliged.

So, when the road and Canal seemed to get ambition, and took more cars than usual, folks first looked to see if anyone had "gone ugly". During last summer and fall thirteen cars—at least thirteen we know about—got swallowed by the waters. That was different. Always before the Canal only took one car a year, or at most, two. The wholesale dunking began after Sugar Bear killed the man.

Police divers came up from the state capital. Police, who knew nothing of the murder, swarmed that road, held roadblocks for testing booze, and before it was over lost one of their own.

The best cop of the lot, a nice guy, seemed fated. He was swallowed by darkness; and we learned it was not a person or the road that pulled cars into the Canal and caused drownings.

But, it took a long time to learn that. Everybody waited while traffic experts measured sight distances. Engineers found the only way to put up guard rails would be to sink pilings along the entire road, a job too expensive for dreaming. Then cars stopped drowning willy-nilly and concentrated in one spot.

A crane worked full time. It snaked cars like lifeless fish when divers found them. The cars held bodies, mostly, although two people got free of the cars; a mixed blessing. The Canal is not only cold; it's hungry.

Petey and Bertha
. . . and the Fisherman

Petey Mullholland generally hangs out at Bertha's Beer and Bait Shoppe where pool tables are famous for being level. Beer and Bait is a dandy building fronting the road with the Canal running at its back. There's a small finger-pier with fuel pumps. The parking lot is large, graveled, and well-drained, which is generally the way we build them in Washington state.

It was on a sunny day in that dark summer that Petey entered, knocked back a glass of lemonade and stared through an open window. The Canal lay tranquil as the mind of a monk, although beneath the surface anything could be going on. Beyond a back window, but before the Canal, Jubal Jim Johnson dozed in full sun, his nose twitching from dog dreams of chasing varmints. Petey wrinkled his own nose and seemed pleased with the way it worked. He turned to Bertha.

"I bin up and down the road. Everything looks the same except for some people we don't want to know. State cops, mostly." He unpacked his cue stick, screwed it together, and checked the premises for "live ones". A fisherman sat in a far corner of the large room. He nursed his beer and cared nothing at all for a joust at pool with Petey.

"I know a girl who dated a cop, once. It was more-or-less an

4

education." Bertha, who is thirtyish and taller than Petey, sat at the end of the long bar. Her blond hair is nicely streaked with grayish tint, her eyes are blue and canny, her tones sound mostly gentle; although Bertha has never hired a bouncer, having seen no need to pay others for work she enjoys. Still, men along the road dream fond dreams of her. Simply told, Bertha is gorgeous.

"It's either good or bad for business," she said about the police and divers and the drowned. "Hard to tell which just yet." She looked toward the Canal, then to the front door and the road. "But I see no business now." She pulled her favorite cue from its place behind the bar.

They've shot pool for a real long time, this blond Norwegian, and Petey, who owns less pedigree than his dog. Petey is sort of Indian and sort of Spanish, both in the darker traditions; but his bald spot is English, his artistic hands no doubt Italian, or probably Portuguese. He's maybe ten years older than Bertha. The two shoot a game so complicated only they understand rules they've made up. All standard pool games are too easy.

Jubal Jim Johnson snoozed beyond the windows, then gave a quick yip. A cloud ran across the sun. Jubal Jim came dashing through the doorway like a sudden shower. He looked real uneasy.

"Bear?" Bertha chalked her cue, talking to Jubal Jim, getting ready to razz him.

"Maybe." Petey walked to the doorway, watched a passing Dodge, looked toward the mountains and forest and then stepped onto the porch. Jubal Jim sat behind the screen door pretending to be brave, which, if it was a bear, was possible.

The cloud cleared the sun. The world brightened. Petey walked toward the Canal. Water swirled near the shore. The water sort of humped up, then spread, then turned to wavelets. Petey

5

shrugged, walked back inside, picked up his cue. "Better sleep on the porch," he said to Jubal Jim. "And watch that show-off mouth."

"Break," Bertha said to Petey, "unless fear holds you back." Her smile denied her words and her fingers touched her hair, pushing it back across her shoulder. Bertha looked like a teenage girl practicing seduction moves before a mirror.

Petey set the cueball beside the racked balls, gently popped it three rails to come back and tap the head ball. The rack broke a little, the one, two, and three balls drifting off a couple inches. The cueball nestled against the four, freezing the board.

"If I was a dog," Petey said, like he talked to no one in particular, "I'd hire a cat to sleep out there by the water."

"If you was a dog," Bertha told him, "you could shoot pool better." She fired a shot two rails. The cueball danced down on the one-ball, tapping it into a corner pocket. The cueball drifted across and freed up the seven. "Cops," Bertha said, "lead snoopy lives. Sniyn' worse than hounds." She looked at Jubal Jim. "You'll forgive it."

"Mom always told me the policeman was my friend." Petey chalked his cue with moves delicate as a girl. He never rubs the chalk or smears it. It's just dab, dab, dab until he gets a level surface. "Of course, Mom always claimed my daddy was my daddy."

Sometimes his mouth gets ahead of his good sense. He turned to watch the Canal and hide his embarrassment. A yacht slid down the eastern shore, outward bound. Petey blushed red as a faded three ball.

They dance around each other, this blond Norwegian and her too-shy pool partner. For a while people took bets on how long it would take them to conjugate, but time ran on and the bets ran out. Then there was talk that neither one knows what themselves

6

look like naked, being too shy to stand in front of a looking glass. Considering all the razzle-dazzle that goes on in beds around here, we find Bertha and Petey sort of endearing.

"Safety," Bertha said in pool language and tapped the two ball one rail. The cueball touched the three ball, then sat solid as a stump behind racked balls. The three ball fled to the other end of the table and nestled against the rail like two-part harmony.

"These are state cops." Petey tried to sound detached. "They're different than city cops. Take my word." Petey knows as much as a man needs about city cops. He has to journey to Seattle or Portland or Vancouver when his money runs low. He hustles pool, then returns to the Canal. He keeps his skills honed at Beer and Bait.

"Cops are cops." Bertha watched Petey's shot. He cued from behind the rack, heavy right-hand English, and the ball went two rails to end up maybe three-quarters of an inch from the three. Petey muttered something under his breath, something poolish.

"Gotcha," Bertha said, "or at least I got a little run." She set to work and it was a dazzler. Showtime. Balls falling, thump. Ringling Bros.

"Take my word," Petey told her. "These cops are different." He sat on a bar stool watching Bertha loosen that rack, peel off a ball, sink it while loosening another. Sunlight set Beer and Bait aglow. The three pool tables stood like spectators beside a hardwood dance floor large enough for twenty couples smooched together tight; plus a bandstand large enough for piano, drums, and a couple guitars. Chairs and small tables surrounded the dance floor, the tables now sitting in gloom. Sunlight only stretched so far before petering off into shadow.

The fisherman stood, stretched, scratched, then walked to a window. He moved fisherman-smelly through late afternoon, a man home from a month's work, walking easy and slouched with tiredness. He was not about to ask Bertha for another beer while she was in the middle of a run.

"It mostly happens nights," he said. He continued to look through the window onto the Canal. "It's humping again. Putting on quite a show." Beyond the window a hump beneath the water moved toward the channel like the burp from a giant carp, a carp bigger than a walrus or a whale, bigger than a blimp. Water spread across the calm surface, roiled, and nothing showed—no fin, no rolling body. The fisherman turned to where Bertha knocked down the last of the run. He carried his empty beer bottle. Bertha stays friendly when you bus your own table. Beer and Bait is a nice place for people who are polite.

"And you're right about those cops," the fisherman said to Petey. Whereas Petey is about forty and sharp, this fisherman was mid-thirties and qualified as the thoughtful type. He carried wrinkles on his forehead and his face was craggy; like it claimed first cousin to a sea eagle. "These boys act like they know what they're doing. Makes a nice change, copwise."

The cops we know are generally not bright, and the cops we know enjoy being nosy. They like to pack .357 magnums, pistols so big that if they ever went off, would scare the living christmas out of their owners. Our cops like to pull pretty girl tourists over, give them a ten minute talking-to, then let them off with a warning. Our cops draw weekly pay and treat the locals like people in custody even when we aren't. Our cops are country boys, plain and simple, who got jobs on the cops because their talents led them away from honest work.

"I could be wrong," Bertha admitted. "I was wrong once before. When I bought into a mortgage." She looked over the premises and her look was sweet. She checked out chipped Formica on the tables, looked at the polished sweep of the solid oak bar, at the twirly advertising hung here and there by beer salesmen. She counted herself lucky, as anyone could see, and even sunlight which showed certain imperfections—scratches on the dance floor—a bullet hole in the bandstand—did not take away her vision of the place.

Jubal Jim snored and gave a little woof as he dreamed of chasing varmints, then poked his nose farther between his paws and kept snoozing. The fisherman, thoughtful, watched him with envy. Petey murmured something low and doggy. Jubal Jim opened one eye, licked his nose, and went back to sleep. A beam of sunlight warmed his fur. Everybody felt pretty dreamy, thinking how it must be if you are a hound hanging out at a nice bar where you are obliged to sleep all day and run all night.

Of course, during the night you meet every kind of creature from rabbit to wolverine, and you learn to use good judgment. More than likely, you also run into whatever it is, out there, that makes the road turn ugly.

"Customers," Bertha said as tires crunched gravel beyond the open doorway. "Go ahead and rack 'em," she told Petey. "It's an hour before things get busy." Bertha did another flip at her hair, smiled broad as only a Norwegian can, and turned to greet whoever was just then slamming the door of a truck.

A Kid Arrives

Footsteps danced on the porch, then a young man who seemed filled with promise came through the doorway and blinked as his eyes adjusted to inside. He stood no taller than Petey but as muscular, and he moved like a kid practicing ballet or karate. Nothing about him suggested anything but a deep thirst, plus a regular dose of young lust. He looked around for girls, saw none, and figured thirst was the only itch he could scratch. He seemed polite, hazel-eyed, dishwater blond, only a little dense, possibly shy. He said, "Howdy."

The fisherman sat at one end of the bar pretending to ignore the kid. Petey leaned against a pool table waiting for the next game. Bertha smiled, drew the kid a beer, and for some motherly reason stayed to talk.

"You've not been in before," Bertha said. "Passing through?"

"Hauling wrecks," the kid said. "Wet ones." He tried to say it conversational but it was a failure. Bertha gave him credit for trying.

"One of them fish they're pulling from the creek?" Bertha looked toward the Canal but stayed rooted behind that bar. She was absolutely, completely, one-hundred-percent not going to be first to head out and look at the wreck. The fisherman did not budge. Petey stroked the cueball two rails into a corner pocket while whistling a show tune. The kid, being a kid, expected more. He took a lick of the beer. "Nice dog," he said. Jubal Jim opened one eye, growled, returned to snoozing.

"Pretty busted up?" Bertha pretended nobody's feet were on fire to tear out for a look at the tragedy.

"I've towed worse, but nothin' this weird." The kid stepped to the doorway, looked toward his truck, and the kid wasn't faking. He might be a little scared, but he was really and truly sad. "Two people," he claimed. "A guy and a lady. Hell of a thing to do to a Buick." The kid really was light on his feet, like a boxer or tumbler. "Folks from north of here," he said to Bertha. "Up at the development."

He talked about a housing project, and about how the road is situated. Bertha's Beer and Bait, with pool tables and fuel dock, sits like a fulcrum for the road. Beer and Bait lies almost exactly halfway along the Canal, and the Canal runs from the head of Puget Sound to the state capitol in Olympia.

At the north end of the road, thirty miles from Beer and Bait sits Al's Dock, known locally as the Rough and Randy. Just north of Rough and Randy, where the dead people came from, sits a high-priced housing project for retired presidents, white-collar criminals, stock market types, and other folk for whom no one on the Canal has any time. "Because," as Sugar Bear Smith often explained, "if you got morals you might as well use 'em."

About thirty-five miles south of Beer and Bait, near the Capitol building in Olympia, Lee's China Bay Taverna flaunts pinballs, fantan, cribbage, tap beer, a bartender who is wise, and Lee, as wily an Oriental as can be found in any moving picture. For a number of reasons that will later appear, a sense of magic and mystery always hovers around China Bay.

To the west stand mountains, to the east the Canal, and every-thing not road or water is covered by trees. Rain keeps things nicely washed nine months out of twelve, and skies turn blue for tourist season. On clear nights Greek Annie looks to the stars and puts curses on satellites sailing high above; curses indiscrimi-nate toward nationality or economic belief. Through most of the year the skies seep gray rain, or fill with low-flying cloud scud.

"A' course it's busted up a little," the kid said about the Buick. The kid was not going to be denied the reputation he had com-ing. The fisherman, kinder than required, took a final pull at his beer. "Got to git," he said. "Still got some cleanup on the boat." He walked casual to the door like a man reluctant to go back to work, and he was worth admiring. The kid remained unsure, but hope just oozed from his pores. The fisherman hesitated in the doorway and reflected on the view. He said to no one in particu-lar, "Better come look at this." Charity, the preacher tells us, is the greatest of the virtues.

The kid was off the hook. Petey moved so casual anyone could see why he is such a good hustler. Bertha came from behind the bar and she carried a bar rag. That rag kind of advertised that she was too busy attending to the wreck to pretend she wasn't.

There are some who claim a Buick is a pretty sorry sight to begin with, though none of them are Republicans. This Buick threw a chill across the sunlit afternoon. It sat on a trailer, being impossible to tow from a harness because the wheels could never, ever track. The car was not quite twisted into a corkscrew, but twisted it was; twisted so the gleamy grill had broken loose and dangled from one small bolt. The roof bulged, as though raised from within by a hydraulic jack; or it might be the bulge came from some sort of awful suction on the outside. The windshield had popped out and must now lie at the bottom of the Canal. The trunk lid stood half-raised, and two deep scratches ran the length of the car, like it had slid away from something that grasped it with iron fingernails. Beneath sunlight, streaks of mud dried on royal purple paint.

The wreck would make the bravest man feel timid. When that windshield popped, water would have crashed in like a cold and suffocating hand. Those people would not have seen a thing, and maybe that was the only lucky part.

And, when it comes to the imagination, this wreck worked different from other wrecks where body metal shears, or glass shatters, or fires leave their imprints on paint. This wreck had done nothing to itself, no crash, no burn, no damage from hitting tree or telephone pole. This wreck had been done unto.

"You hear about it and it don't seem real." Bertha shuddered and looked at the Canal. "It's real." She spoke to the kid. "Did you see those folks?"

". . . talked to a guy who did." The kid had lost all his brass. He didn't even pretend he wasn't scared. "They were kind of blank. That's all the guy said. Just kind of blank. . . I don't know what that means. . . they weren't in the water more than a couple days."

"I'd be fearful just towing that thing," Bertha said. "I give you credit."

"It sure don't beat a dish of ice cream," the kid said. "It durn near don't beat walking."

Petey climbed on the trailer and looked through the window on the driver's side. "Nothing broke. Sopping wet. Air conditioner switch on high. Headlight switch on. They were cruisin'."

"I've got work on the boat but this drives me towards another beer." The fisherman walked back into Beer and Bait.

"Me too," the kid said. "One more beer won't bust a Breathalyzer."

The Wrecks—Three Views

The kid became a regular at Beer and Bait as he averaged a tow a week. His truck, all lights and hook, looked almost cautious as he hauled wrecks on a trailer. The wrecks still caused people's hearts to go dull with fear and wonder.

The kid worked up a routine of two beers and talk at Bertha's, because Beer and Bait is friendly. Then he hauled to the police lot outside the Capitol. Then he finished off with a beer or two at Lee's China Bay Taverna. The kid became a kind of newspaper. He connected the south end of the road with the middle. Messages went back and forth.

"Lee's bartender says the Canal's no different than ever," the kid confided to Bertha. "If something's different, it's not made of water. That's a smart bartender." The kid looked uneasy.

". . . smart enough to stay away from here, anyway." Bertha, who figures herself for smart, claimed people at the south end had no right judging what went on toward the middle. "Next we'll hear from up north. Al's Rough and Randy will form a posse."

"Nothing too sober," Petey told the kid. "Al's is more randy than rough."

While Bertha took to the kid in a motherly way, Petey hustled him like a father teaching a son about hazards. The kid proved brighter than he looked, catching on to Petey's hustle in under fifty bucks. The kid, and everyone else, still shivered when looking at the wrecks.

Meanwhile, worry spread up and down the road as more local people saw more drowned cars:

Greek Annie found herself at the site of the biggest haul which was not even a car. A drowned tractor-trailer was pulled glowing like a red sunrise from beneath the water. Annie, who at twenty-two is young for a witch, and actually pretty gorgeous when she brushes her hair, watched from the woods where she gathered herbs. She muttered and promised to take a lesson about who and what she cursed. This was a wholesale grocery truck, and, while Annie could never remember cursing groceries, she thought she might have once said a word or two on behalf of trucks or truck drivers. She watched as the silver trailer slid back into dark water where it remains. She watched as the red tractor got pulled ashore. The fiberglass cab squashed inward, like someone ran it through a giant garbage compactor. When the coroner's men pried the truck door Annie discovered that she had been watching about thirty seconds too long. She headed for Bertha's Beer and Bait at a slow trudge, which is not her nature. Her elfin face can ordinarily find a smile, and her lithe body is that of a runner. She is often seen trotting like a college girl who jogs, hoping to impress a quarterback.

And Chantrell George, whose visions are sometimes induced and sometimes not, took no lessons; that being his nature. He walked his bike along the shoulder of the road as a little foreign car was pulled ashore, squashed like the middle part of a sandwich. Chantrell stopped to watch while keeping fast hold on his bicycle. The bike has no chain because Chantrell doesn't ride, but it has nice baskets front and rear. He pushes it along the shoulder as he peddles legal mushrooms, saving the other kind for himself and a select group of consumers. He sometimes comes up with a stone tool, or other Indian relic, scrounged from the forest. A village lies back there beneath an ancient mudslide. The relics bring a couple of bucks. Chantrell George just misses being a deadbeat, but scrapes by on small bills and change. Plus, some nights he tends bar.

Chantrell watched the car, this one orange, and as usual he looked like a raggedy scarecrow. His long brown hair lies greasy over thin shoulders, framing a thin face that carries amber eyes alight with things that to other people are unseen.

Visions lie behind those eyes, and in a vision Chantrell saw the orange car stewing in subterranean fires of an undersea volcano. Then the car rose through dark waters as it was trailed by pink sea lions. The orange and pink caused darkness to turn to sunrise, and sunrise changed the car into a chariot pulled by giant pigeons. The pigeons gradually tired and the chariot fell toward the sun. Chantrell George pushed his bicycle away from the scene as he analyzed the vision. He walked right past two state cops. He was too busy to have time for them, and they were too busy to notice the illegal merchandise riding openly in the front basket of the bike.

Still, Sugar Bear Smith, who is pretty as his name, and as big, had it worst. Sugar Bear stumped his toe on a wreck scene as he meandered toward Bear and Bait. Sugar Bear arrived during late afternoon on one of those miserable northwest days when the thermometer hits seventy-five and proposes to go higher. Sugar Bear, whose beard and mustache are brown and furry, and whose hands can bend steel rebar, closed down his blacksmith forge, closed up his tool repair shop, and went on strike against the weather. He shambled from the woods as easy-going and smiley as a satisfied saint.

The police crane stood waiting. It snaked out a small, red-with-top-down sports car. The car came up empty. The driver's spirit dwelt no doubt in heaven, or possibly elsewhere, but the driver's remains were forever below in the Canal, along with all other mistakes people make in the presence of deep water.

Sugar Bear tsked, said a few prayerful words, hummed a couple bars of a hymn and felt he'd done his duty. His shamble turned into a stroll as he resumed his trip to Beer and Bait. Then his stroll ended.

A nice looking man, and an attractive woman watched the red car dangle from the crane like a sea creature that has been hooked for so long it's dead. The two were in their fifties, well-dressed, and the woman clung to her husband like someone about to slide from a cliff. He held her as close as love or fear can cause. His eyes blinked, his face ran with tears. He murmured to his wife, consoling words that did not console. Other people stood in a group, gawking. The gawkers watched the sorrow and took pleasure in sensation, like people reading headlines on papers at the grocery.

"Cheaters," Sugar Bear said to himself about the gawkers. "Gyppers." Sugar Bear walked quickly from the couple's sorrow. He knows when he can help and when he can't. If those people mourned a son or daughter lost forever in that dark water, their mourning deserved privacy. Sugar Bear walked quickly, because, while it takes a good bit to make him mad, he doesn't like himself when he is mad. Vulgarity sometimes makes him explode. The cheaters probably didn't know they were vulgar, and they sure didn't know they were in danger; even if cops were present.

The Murder

Not all fishermen are thoughtful, or at least not around here, but the one thoughtful fisherman we do have would put it this way: "If a tree falls in the forest, and there is no one around to hear, there may not be any sound. It follows then, if a corpse gets pitched into the Canal when there are no witnesses, maybe there has been no murder." This particular fisherman says stuff like this all the time, because, while he is thoughtful, most folks claim he isn't very bright.

And then, there is Sugar Bear. Not all blacksmiths are dear men, but Sugar Bear is; a man who lives in a fairy tale or a poem. His blacksmith shop and tool repair sit in a mossy glade. If his small house sported a little gingerbread it would fit nicely in a children's book. Or, if in a poem, Sugar Bear would fit with Longfellow's, "Under a spreading chestnut-tree/The village smithy stands;/The smith, a mighty man is he,/With large and sinewy hands. . . ."

Of Sugar Bear's transgression, if it was a transgression, a few things need saying. There were no witnesses to the dumping of the body but there were three witnesses to the transgression: Chantrell George, Greek Annie, and Jubal Jim, a combination that would make any defense lawyer believe in providence.

One other piece of business needs saying: this road, these trees, these mountains, and the Canal form a setting for people who forgive most mistakes, cut slack for others' dumb opinions, but who will not budge the thickness of a sheet of paper when it comes to essentials. Some things here are not done, or if they are, the doer had best run to the nearest cop.

When it developed that a man who messed with children started hanging around the school, and when one kid came home crying, no one said a word to Sugar Bear because that's the kind of thing Sugar Bear can't stand. No one said anything to Bertha because everyone is fond of her. Besides, if she went to jail who would tend to Beer and Bait?

Talk happened among the men. The kid's father was told to stay away and establish an alibi. The mother was told to say nothing. A couple of loggers cornered the guy in the woods behind the school. They managed to keep most of the bruises from showing. The loggers told the guy to get out of town or they'd set his pant cuffs on fire and watch the sparks rise upward. That should have done it. End of story. But, the man didn't have a dab of sense. He enjoyed the attention, and kept hanging around the school.

This sort of thing had not happened here since days when the state was still a territory. Always before, bad men took the hint. This bad guy couldn't get it through his head that boats leave these parts for open ocean every day, and he had a one-way ticket to the waters off Cape Flattery.

He lived in a never-never land more goofy than Chantrell's visions. The guy was chubby of face, red of permed hair, skinny of frame, and survived by running his mouth. No vacuum cleaner salesman ever born had such confidence in a talent for weaving in and out of tight places. This guy's mouth motored about a thousand miles an hour.

On the fatal day, and two days before his scheduled cruise, the guy sat in Beer and Bait complaining about loggers. Petey and a fisherman shot pool, and Sugar Bear sat drinking a bottle of pop while waiting for the next pool game. Light music played from a radio. Beyond the windows rain patted on the Canal which lay black as macadam. Trees seem darker on such days, conifers nearly ebony, and alders brushed with streaks of darkest gray. The guy nursed a beer, heckled the pool game, and spun fantastic scenes. His puffy face swelled and his mouth looked pouty. His imagination included complaints for assault, loggers busted, entire logging operations shut down, media attention, police photographs in evidence of scrapes and bruises, lawsuits; he was having a dandy time. He acted like an exhibitionist dropping his drawers in front of a Sunday school class.

Bertha stood confused as Bertha ever gets. This customer talked about something she knew she should have heard about, but hadn't. Bertha knows guys do not get roughed up around here for things like bank robbery, so it had to be something serious. She turned on more lights against grayness of the day. She turned volume on the radio to a murmur.

The guy sparked and fizzed. He threw up roman candles of speech and skyrockets of self pity. His chubby face reddened with indignation. He spoke of how wronged he felt, and all because . . . at which point Petey stepped in with a busted pool cue and suggested the guy take a walk. The guy took one look at Petey's face, and skedaddled.

"You just run off a customer," Bertha said to Petey. "I expect you had a reason." Her voice carried a hint of indignation. Bertha is not used to being kept in the dark about important stuff. She leaned on the bar, elbows firmly planted, and ready for a scrap.

"Tell me."

It turned into a great moment for both of them. It was, at least, Petey's second-to-greatest moment in his whole life, probably. Bertha and Petey had danced around each other so long they had settled into a warm groove of friendship. Both had about given up hope of ever becoming lovers.

"We need you here," Petey said, and his voice carried warmth that surprised Bertha, and Sugar Bear, and the fisherman; and it especially surprised Petey. "This is a tough one. This ain't jail stuff, this is prison stuff. It's not too tough for you. I don't mean that, but it's already handled." The warm tone, the truly loving tone, sounded in his own ears and the magic stopped as his blush started; but, had Bertha been asked, she'd have said the blush was what she'd expected. ". . . tell you when it's over," Petey said, and, by heaven, there were still remnants of warmth in his voice. It seemed like he couldn't shake 'em.

"I wanta talk to you," Sugar Bear said to Petey.

"You don't," Petey told him. "Go home and bend some rebar, or weld something, or build a windmill. . . ."

"Outside," Sugar Bear said. "I wanta talk to you now."

"C'mon," Petey said to the fisherman. "Maybe the two of us can handle him."

Bertha, who by rights should have insisted on coming along, just stood behind the bar and glowed. Tough as she is, Bertha still has warm feelings, and Petey had just brought hope back into her world. If matters with Sugar Bear had not been so serious, Bertha and Petey might have gotten together, right then. It would have saved a world of trouble. As it was, Bertha stood and glowed. For the moment she was a woman first, a bar owner second.

Gravel in the parking lot lay polished with rain and puddles collected in low spots. On the Canal a Navy minesweeper poked along, heading seaward. Drizzle glistened in Sugar Bear's hair and beard because he never has enough sense to wear a sock hat. As the fisherman explained the situation, Sugar Bear started to heat up.

"Leave it be," Petey said. "It's dirty business. The fishermen can handle it." Petey is a hustler, but this was a day when his hustle gave way to deeper feelings. "You got this bad temper," he told Sugar Bear. "Save it for some time we're gonna need it." Sensible advice. Respectful, too.

"Go home and stay home," the fisherman said. "If you need groceries or beer give me a call." This was the fisherman who looks like a sea eagle, the thoughtful one. "And keep quiet as a dead mouse. The fewer who know, the better."

"Because," Petey said, "cops got no sense of humor."

"If Bertha gets to asking," Sugar Bear said, "we gotta think up something good to tell. Say the guy's been robbing crab pots." Then he stopped to think. "The guy ain't the type. Tell her it's not a mushroom kind of deal. Tell her he's pushing bad stuff."

"That'll work," the fisherman said. "Stay on ice. Do nothin' indiscreet. Someday this will all be just a sea story."

The fisherman would have been right except the victim interfered, which with him was a main talent. Either that, or he had an instinct for saving time. Instead of being seasick for a day and a night, and drowning after a cold, fifteen minute swim, he walked right up to Sugar Bear like a bunny strolling in front of headlights.

During midafternoon on the day of transgression, the weather turned deep gray. Chantrell George showed up at Sugar Bear's place to see if anything could be mooched. Sugar Bear sometimes comes up with completely worn out lawnmowers, or nicked up bars from chainsaws. He lays back a store of rusted and broken bolts, gears with stripped teeth, and odds and ends of the blacksmith business. Chantrell sells them for scrap, sometimes earning as much as six bits to a dollar.

And Greek Annie was there as well, accompanied by Jubal Jim who often tags along. Annie is more interesting than Sugar Bear's transgression, because the transgression turned into one of those ragtime affairs that are over before everyone has taken seats.

Annie, whose rich parents live in the housing project, migrated to the Canal shortly after high school. She appears, and winsomely, at the blacksmith shop some days. Even witches need a social life beyond reptiles and spiders. A joke around here says that when Annie wants a date she kisses a frog, and that, in fact, Chantrell George is one of Annie's frogs who never changed back.

Such jokes are cruel. As lonely men know, and especially if those men are also scared of Annie, there's more to Annie than there is to most witches. Her black hair falls long and almost Indian as it covers thin but prettily rounded shoulders. Her form is slender, mildly athletic, and her face, when smiling, makes men think thoughts warm and sweet. When her face clouds, or is puzzled, men wish they could make things right for her, but she's the one with special knowledge. If she can't fix her confusion, others can't.

For another thing, there are weeks and weeks, sometimes, when nothing weird happens in her presence. A tourist once asked if she was a white witch or a dark one, but no one, maybe even Annie, knows.

So Annie shows up at Sugar Bear's place. She hangs out, bakes cookies, sweeps the floor, sits in the shop and weaves spells; but none of her spells work on Sugar Bear who can't get motivated.

On the day when the bad man went west, a gentle scene progressed at Sugar Bear's shop. Sugar Bear fiddled around changing a magneto. Outside, mist sailed in the trees and the temperature dropped, but inside, what with woodstove and forge, felt warm as mittens. Tools hung along the walls. Pots and pans hung from rafters. Sheets of boiler plate stood on edge like books between bookends. Annie sat on a bar stool salvaged from Beer and Bait back when Bertha remodeled, and Annie discussed world and local news with a spider. Chantrell George polished a busted piston from a rototiller on his sleeve. Jubal Jim snoozed beside the woodstove, but, asleep or awake, Jubal Jim has a hound's nose and a hound's sensitivity. He raised his head. Growled.

The guy came in without knocking. He looked around, concentrated on Annie, licked his lips. His hair glowed permed and red. His lips remained pouty as he checked the premises, pretended to hide a sneer, then stopped dead as Jubal Jim growled and Chantrell began trembling. Chantrell fought for control. He rubbed the piston against his cheek and whispered something untranslatable.

"Get out," Sugar Bear said, and he spoke soft as a man can when he's trying to stay in control.

"Or what?" The guy spoke halfway between a sneer and a giggle. He looked at Annie. "You open for business, or is this what I think it is?"

Sugar Bear's gaze stayed fixed on the guy, but his hand searched around a tabletop as he felt for tools. "Get out or I'll kill you."

The guy had probably heard that line too many times before. "I got a loose bumper on the car," he said. "Let's you get your welder-thing and *do* it."

"Please," Annie said to the guy because she caught Sugar Bear's tone of voice, "go away quick. This is serious."

The guy looked at Annie, rubbed thumb and forefinger together. ". . . while I take care of the shop . . ." and those were the guy's last words. Sugar Bear let drive and put a ballpeen hammer deep into the guy's skull. The guy's eyes didn't even have time to flicker. He didn't even know he was dead before he was dead. The body fell just inside the doorway and Chantrell screamed. The body twitched a little, lay silent. The head had a hole that sort of oozed, but nothing spectacular.

In Chantrell's vision a cartoon hammer started tap, tap, tapping around the room. The hammer did a song and dance, humming to itself, then began squashing spiders. Spiders appeared from everywhere, and little splashes of spider-goo sizzled on the woodstove. Sugar Bear dashed madly about the room attempting to capture the hammer, but the hammer jumped through an open window and escaped into the world.

"It'll rust out there," Chantrell moaned. "You just know it's gonna rust." He fell silent, his head down and eyes closed. He turned and leaned against the wall.

Jubal Jim strolled over, sniffed the body, and sat on his haunches as much as if to say "What the hell?" Sugar Bear stood above the body. His shoulders tensed, his hands trembled, and tears spread down his cheeks. He brushed tears, got under control. "You okay?" he asked Annie.

"Of course not," she said. "I'm scared. I don't know what's going on. Are you okay?"

"I'll get past it. Can you take care of the mushroom kid? I'll be back in a minute and explain." Sugar Bear picked the body up by its belt, like he carried a suitcase. "I'll stick him in the trunk of his car. Think of what to do next. . . ."

That night Sugar Bear drove car and corpse to the Canal. The only way anyone ever knows the Canal has taken a car is through skid marks on the road, or broken shrubbery along the roadside. Sugar Bear picked a place where the grade is steep and with few plants. He set it in gear and let it cruise into the dark waters. Bubbles rose as the car sank, and as Sugar Bear bowed his head and said a few words. Then Sugar Bear walked away, down the dark road beside the dark water. He did not see the Canal start humping, the swell moving just beneath the surface, moving toward the burial site and then quickly away; spreading like the burp from a giant carp.

Early Summer Girl Talk

Sugar Bear's iniquity became a sea story long before even a thoughtful fisherman could predict. Rumor extended south to Lee's China Bay Taverna where the bartender, in spite of being wise, could not keep word from spreading. Original rumor said some guy with hot pants hassled Bertha then disappeared. In that form it didn't amount to much.

There are some awful sinners down at China Bay. By the time the story got elaborated, told and retold for a couple weeks, it bloomed like a lawn full of dandelions. By the time the story faded it included conspiracies and agents from the FBI, plus unofficial execution(s) by noose. The body/bodies (depending on the stage of the story) was/were hanging from its/their neck(s) back in the mountains where ravens pecked out eyes.

Hardly any guy who attends Saturday evening services at Beer and Bait did not get credited for the execution. Suspicion largely ignored Sugar Bear who has the reputation for being a sweetie. The suspect who received the most attention was Chantrell George because he is weird. That caused Chantrell to feel both guilty and glad, which was a bad thing for a story to do. When that version drifted north from China Bay, every other man at Beer and Bait felt indignant and rejected.

Then people further north got into it. At Rough and Randy

the story claimed all credit for some unknown warrior up in that direction. Rough and Randy tried to steal the Beer and Bait story. For a few days nobody laughed.

All of this happened in early summer. Through the summer, other stuff happened, some normal, some not. Anyone who is thoughtful would just naturally make a list:

a. Dead guy gets dumped and cars start drowning in the Canal.

b. A lot of fishermen went north to Alaska, or stayed offshore hassling Canadian boats while the Canadians hassled them.

c. Tourists puttered ahead of logging trucks and logging drivers cussed like blue flame. Those Kenworths cost over a hundred thousand, and owners get paid by the trip. Every r.p.m. they drop makes it that much harder to meet the truck payment.

d. The main thing that happened was that Petey went to Seattle looking sort of dreamlike, but not so dreamy he couldn't make a stake. He won a big tournament, did a bit of hustling, and dealt with other little odds and ends that came to hand. In mystical terms you could say he followed The Way of the Hustler.

e. Bertha stayed behind and took care of Jubal Jim. Since business was good Bertha continued to carry warmth in her heart and a glad look in her eyes. No one had ever known Bertha to act so kindly for such a long stretch, and everyone felt concerned.

f. Chantrell grew more ethereal. He knew himself well enough to question if he had really killed anyone, but the story said otherwise. It was only after some weeks of meditation that he grew reconciled. Pictures of a flying hammer remained with him, and the thunk of a hammer hitting bone sounded in his dreams. Chantrell fought for control. This was his first fatal vision. Always before, even rowdy visions ended with no one dead. This vision marked a fearsome new departure. Chantrell had probably never heard of the crossing of the Rubicon, and would not give a sniff if told of it (for it was a very small river), but the fact remains that the flavors of life were Changing.

Chantrell rolled his bike along the road in an increasingly timid manner. He did not exactly lose touch with reality, although reality had never been a big priority. He retreated into innocence, becoming more childlike.

Men are not supposed to cry, and, of course, Sugar Bear did not after that first early shock. He grew more quiet. He sang softly and sad when at the forge, whereas before the murder his voice rang lusty and flat and joyous and obnoxious. Nighttime often found him wandering near the Canal where the dead guy doubtless still curled in the trunk of his drowned car. Sugar Bear spent late afternoons or early evenings at Beer and Bait. He brooded, became depressed and considered religion. He confided to Bertha that he thought of joining the Baptists, because the Baptist version of hell seemed more friendly than anything the Adventists had to offer.

And Annie spent more and more time in the woods. In her less-than-twenty-three years Annie had seen a lot of natural violence; spiders trapping bugs, owls catching mice, and a couple of bar fights that went nowhere. A flying hammer changed her world view. She spent even more time thinking about Sugar Bear, worrying about him. For a time she could not decide if she wanted to run away from him because of fear, or run to him and try to help. Annie, had she been told of the Rubicon, would have made a mental note.

Although Navy ships, submarines, yachts, and sailboats dotted the Canal, no one reported movement beneath the water. It seemed like the creature, or spirit, or whatever it was that moved out there reserved itself for local residents. In other words, things went on as usual until Annie made a decision. Sugar Bear was kind, and nice, and gentle when it came to everything except perverts and boiler plate.

Annie experienced a problem peculiar to her sex. She needed another woman to talk to, someone who knew the score. A man would not do. Annie thought Bertha the smartest person around. On more than one occasion Annie had watched with interest as Bertha escorted a logger to the doorway, usually by firmly grasping his ear. If Bertha could bounce a logger there seemed no limit to her knowledge. Annie felt that, to Bertha, men were simple creatures easily tamed. Annie headed for Beer and Bait.

Rain covered the forest and patted on the Canal. Beer and Bait sat as restful as Jubal Jim who snoozed before the bar. Early afternoons are generally quiet. A boat or two may nose up to fuel pumps at the finger pier, or a tourist may stop for directions. Bertha uses those hours to sharpen up the joint—furniture polish on the piano, glass polish on the mirror behind the bar, wax on the dance floor, or play pool with Petey. Petey, though, had not yet returned from hustling the lower and middle elements of Seattle.

Bertha looked up to see the slim figure of a woman standing in the doorway. The woman stood framed in gray light from the chilly day. Bertha, were she less practical, would say the woman materialized out of mist. The light being what it was, Bertha could only see a slim figure with long hair, a figure wearing a dress far too stylish for early afternoon. To Bertha, wise in the ways of other women's seductions even if her own did not work, the woman looked like a lady on the hunt. Either that or a hooker.

"We're open," Bertha said. "You just passing through?"

Annie stepped into bar light and away from grayness of the day. When Bertha recognized her Bertha played at being miffed. "Don't ever cut the clowning. It's too amusin'. Where's your jeans and sweatshirt?" Bertha looked Annie up and down, saw hair washed and glistening and nearly silky. She saw a greeny-silky dress hitting an inch below the knee, and a face nicely washed and pretty without benefit of makeup.

"You're a good-looking kid." Bertha did not try to hide her astonishment. "You ought to do something with it. Make a name for yourself."

"I gotta talk to you." Annie's voice sounded like a confused girl, not like an attractive young woman. "I'd love to talk about lots of stuff but I'm afraid somebody will come in and interrupt. I got man problems. . . ."

"Who hasn't?" Bertha grinned. "Hell, men have got man problems, what with chainsaws and pickups and marriage." Bertha swiped at the bar with a bar rag and looked Annie over very, very carefully. "You preggers?"

"No."

"You ain't wet, either. How can you walk in here out of the rain and not be wet?"

"It happens sometimes," Annie told her in a vague way. "Something to do with weather satellites I expect. . . . How do you get a man to like you?"

If Bertha figured this would be the blind leading the blind she did not let on. "Depends on the man. If he's like most of the bums who come in here you just show a little cleavage."

"Sugar Bear," Annie said, her voice shy. "He needs help . . . or something . . . I don't know."

"Sugar Bear," Bertha mused. "You won't get anywhere helping him, not if he knows it. Times when a man like that needs help

31

are the same times he resents it."

"You help without him knowing it?" Confusion deepened Annie's voice. "I've tried spells."

". . . and you're not trying to help him, anyway," Bertha told her. "Get honest. You're trying to get him interested."

"That's helping. I'm sure it would help."

"Tell it to a frog." Bertha grinned and Jubal Jim thumped his tail. Then Jubal Jim eased onto a warm spot where breezes blow from the heater. His hound ears spread perfectly flat along the floor. He snuffled once, then dozed.

"Besides," Bertha said, "sooner or later Sugar Bear will get busted. Too many people are talking. The talk will keep up until one of our jock cops decides to play like he's on television."

"They wouldn't . . . they would. They really would." Annie looked toward the Canal. In the distance water swelled, moved like the burp from a giant carp. "He can't get busted."

"Anybody can," Bertha told her. "He'll convict himself because he's green when it comes to lying." She also looked at the Canal. "It's humping again. It must mean something."

"It's a Fury," Annie said absent-mindedly, "maybe the only Water Fury in the whole world. It's not even a very good one."

"Child," Bertha said, "it's time for you to settle down."

"That's the plan," Annie said. "As soon as I get him interested."

"There's lots of men," Bertha told her. "You haven't lived long enough to know all the kinds of men there are."

"Maybe if I fixed my hair different, or got a cut. . . ."

"Clean up your act," Bertha told her. "You look real pretty. Try that first, and hope the stories stop before cops get interested."

Inspiration shone in Annie's eyes. "If they have something else to talk about they'll forget to talk about Sugar Bear." She reached to touch Bertha's hand. "You're so smart. I never would have thought of that."

"Somebody did," Bertha admitted, "but I can't remember doin' it."

Determination can be a scary thing. When Annie left, her narrow shoulders were squared. She would make the world a better place by getting it to talk about something besides Sugar Bear. Also, she felt prepared to wear dresses and ribbons.

Mystery Women and Butterflies

Thinking back on last summer it's easy to see how confusion spread up and down the road. While it takes no time at all for news to spread, it does take time for gossip to change ordinary news into facts that count as satisfying information. It's only natural to review happenings in order to stay sane:

Sugar Bear did his hammer toss in early summer, along about mid-June. Annie decided to set her cap for him a week later while Petey left to hustle the good folk of Seattle. Cars started to dunk in late June, but state cops did not really show up with their crane until very near the end of July. It must have been mid-August, then, that the forest dried out; by which time, of course, Petey was back. Stories, mostly caused by Annie, were running from the top of the Canal to its bottom with all three beer joints involved. Part of the information rode with the kid who drove the wrecker.

Annie tried to push bar talk away from Sugar Bear the third week of June. She first tried whipping up a plague of locusts, but something went sour with the enchantment and only a few showed up; and seagulls got them. Then she tried a rumor saying the Navy aimed to move its base to the west side of the Canal, which was senseless, stupid, and governmental, thus likely. Most people yawned, but it seemed, at the time, the rumor caused speculation in building lots.

Later on, everyone became wiser, but that was later. All during the summer, "for sale" signs for real estate came down almost before they went up. In a three-mile stretch surrounding Beer and Bait, somebody bought every stitch of land.

Sugar Bear brooded all through June. People talked. Up north at Rough and Randy a betting pool started with guys making choices about who, at Beer and Bait, would be the next guy busted.

Annie fought back and had a stroke of luck, because Annie is not old enough to be truly humorous. She bought women's things at a distant thrift shop, sneaked to the post office before midnight, and ran the stuff up the flagpole. As luck would have it the outfit would fit a lady sumo wrestler, and there came wind. Daylight saw a display of giant pink balloons. Talk temporarily turned to the postmaster who cussed and protested, but seemed privately proud. Annie, too young to understand cheap shots, regarded her work and thought it good.

Then Annie conjured up a spell of silence that misfired. For a couple of days people walked around with their ears ringing. Then Annie scored big. She wore her nicest dress, hitched a ride to Rough and Randy where she demurely sipped iced tea. She sat at a table, legs crossed, but with one patent leather slipper dangling from her toes and claimed she waited to meet a guy. Annie is not too young to know how to handle the bad, bad boys at Rough and Randy. The guy she claimed to be meeting is a local cop, famous in these parts for breaking heads. Annie flirted and made certain she would be known as a mystery woman, then pretended she had been stood up and took her leave. She disappeared, maybe into the woods, but at any rate disappeared, and made it back home before midnight.

Next day, talk of the mystery woman swept up and down the road. General opinion said she must be someone from the development up north. At the same time, opinion said, she could not be from that housing project because she claimed to wait for a local cop. The mystery woman had the kind of class usually wasted on rich bozos, not on bozo cops.

Sugar Bear drew further into himself. It is all very well to know that bad men must be stopped. To kill a man, though, is not something Sugar Bear's morals can alibi. Sugar Bear did not then understand that in some less-than-sublime situations all choices are wrong.

He became testy with his work and testy with Chantrell. On some afternoons Sugar Bear closed shop, retreated into a nap, then woke toward evening. He walked through the night, or at least until just before clocks struck twelve. People driving home from Beer and Bait would see him shambling beside the road, or standing beside the Canal as he looked across its dark waters. When they offered him a lift he refused in low and kindly voice. On the following day, having snapped at Chantrell the day before, he would be gentle and sad; slipping Chantrell a couple of bucks which eased both their feelings.

When Annie began wearing dresses and being an absolute knockout, it seemed to soothe Sugar Bear. The reaction was not what Annie hoped for, but better than nothing.

"I don't know what to think," she admitted to Bertha on one chill and drizzly summer afternoon. "I don't even know much about the guy who got dead. It happened so quick it's like it didn't happen."

"The guy was city, and city ways don't work here. At least not those ways." Behind Bertha's shoulder, and mounted high up, a television, usually off—but turned on sometimes in afternoons or during ballgames—broadcast soap . . . somebody's psychiatrist was boffing the teenage daughter of his patient's deranged third-cousin twice removed . . . something like that.

"I get lonesome for him," Annie said. "We've never so much as hugged, but I get lonesome. It was never this way before, even back in high school." She reached to pet Jubal Jim who was about to settle in for a snooze. He licked her hand.

"It's called a nesting instinct." Bertha's voice betrayed the same confusion Annie felt. "I don't know if you ever get over it."

"Spiffing up seems to work a little, but it's working mighty slow."

"It don't pay to rush," Bertha told her. "Sugar Bear's a long way from being in the clear. Just hope he put that car in deep, deep water."

The muted sound of tires crunching on parking lot gravel seemed to Annie like an invasion of privacy. "I'm really sad," she whispered quickly. "I'm scared. When I get sad I do things that are really, really stupid."

"Who don't?" Bertha told her. "Take a strain. Customers."

". . . which of course," a woman said as she opened the door for two other women, "is why she got in such a tiz. Gregory is an attentive man, but no hair dresser." The women were clearly from the housing project up north, and clearly in the wrong pew. Bertha waited. A customer is a customer until the time comes when a bouncer is called for.

All three women were manicured, slim, in their fifties-going-on-thirty-five. Annie, accustomed to magic that only worked when it felt like it, didn't give them a second thought. The women headed for a table in back.

"Ladies' day," Bertha called to them. "You kids can set at the bar. Saves steps."

There came a hurried consultation, like the buzzing of a disturbed hive. The word "hopeless" clawed the air. Then thirst

37

overcame indignation and the three turned, tried to stroll to the bar; although it is impossible to stroll at Beer and Bait. Walk or stagger, yes.

"It's certainly not the country club," one said. This one was the scrawniest of the lot, a tough little number wearing a purple dress. She spoke to the others as if Bertha and Annie were not there.

"Yes it is." Bertha's voice sounded pushy, cheerful, and brisk. "Limited seating."

"Pleased to meet you," Annie said.

"They're from New York." The scrawny one's voice held admiration. She turned to the other women. "New York humor is special."

To this day no one can explain that afternoon. Some sort of magic kept logging trucks from stopping, and boats away from the fuel pumps. The only male present, as far as any lady could tell, was Jubal Jim who napped mightily.

But, if a man had been sitting at a table in shadows, forgotten, and looking toward the bar; and if he was a man of depth, he would have imagined an assembly of butterflies on bar stools. Colors glowed orange and purple and green and tan; dresses and skirts as aery as wings, and Annie gorgeous in blue pastel. The ladies from the housing project gradually let down well-coifed hair, once they got their noses into their second round. There's something extra relaxing about Beer and Bait on drizzly afternoons.

"This actually is lovely. A Grandma Moses sort of place." This, from the green butterfly who was tallest, and seemed kindly. She spoke to the orange butterfly whose wings seemed wide above the bar top because she leaned on elbows; enjoying a place where no consultant on good manners would ever visit.

"I only wash the windows twice a year," Bertha lied. "There's stuff happens on that water you really don't want to see." Bertha decided to experiment. "Potato chips," she told them, "are on the house. Stay off the pool tables unless you know what you're doing."

Annie suppressed a giggle. The purple butterfly blinked. "It's a man's game," she said. "One of the curses of our existence." She turned to the other butterflies, picking up a conversation that must have gone on before they entered the joint. "And then, my dear, in the very midst of playing house, you can just imagine who phoned her from the airport. . . ."

"Explain about men," Annie said, because, although Annie stayed with lemonade, Annie felt confused and out of sorts.

"Men are sorta unusual," Bertha told her. "They come and go and do stuff they claim is important, and most of it amounts to diddly. Men are absolute suckers for feeling important. Men stumble around, do something major dumb, then claim they had the whole thing planned from the beginning."

"Men play at being noble." The purple butterfly took a healthy belt of her drink, then sniffed suspiciously, then giggled. "I've never drank with a dog before. Unusual." She seemed about ready to wake Jubal Jim and offer him a sip.

"The last guy that tried to get that dog bombed is still on crutches," Bertha said.

"Noble," the purple butterfly repeated. "Men play at being noble. You can take that to the bank."

"If I'd known what trouble the second one was going to be," the orange butterfly said, "I wouldn't have been in such a hurry to divorce the first one."

"You can hustle a man at pool when you can't hustle a woman," Bertha said, "'cause a woman don't feel like her reputation's on the line. A woman gets her reputation from interesting stuff."

"Do you hustle, dear?" The purple butterfly emptied her glass, looked toward the doorway and probably thought of the chilly afternoon. She shivered. Pushed her glass forward for another. "I mean pool. Of course I mean pool."

Bertha ought to be a good hustler, because good hustlers are unflappable. She grinned. "I do tournaments sometimes because I'm good. But hustle, nope, though some *ladies* enjoy the risk."

"Count on men being disorganized." The green butterfly already sipped deep into her second drink.

"You got that right," Bertha said. "Men will drive around hell-and-half-of-Georgia looking for a spare part. They could do the same thing faster and cheaper with a phone."

"Is this important? Tell me something I can use." Annie figured herself in the midst of experts, and figured the experts talked over her head.

"Kiddo, you wanta know about men. . . ." The purple one, the scrawny one, seemed to change from butterfly to beetle. "There's two kinds. One kind owns underwear, the other doesn't. The kind that owns underwear acts more civilized, but don't let that fool you."

"There's actually three kinds," the orange one said. "Some of them play golf. The trick is to find one with underwear that don't play golf."

"Or pool," the beetle-lady said, and glared at the pool tables, displeased, sorting through barely mentionable memories. "Planned community," she said about the housing project. "I'd like to find the sonovabitch that planned the recreation."

"We have a problem," the orange one told Annie. "Our men are so competitive. For the last year they've been mad about the game."

"They didn't even go sport fishing last fall," the green one said. "They stayed sober on New Year."

"What the hell," the beetle-lady said, "they stayed sober on

Easter Sunday."

"Our world is not exactly crumbling," the green one confided to Annie, "but try living with one when he is constantly cold sober." The butterfly giggled, which is unusual in a butterfly. "Impossible to make social plans. In addition, his sex drive becomes invigorated." The butterfly did not blush, but Bertha did.

"It sounds ideal," Annie murmured. ". . . of course, I only guess from what I've heard."

Bertha tried to appear unruffled. "Send 'em down this way," she muttered. "Tell 'em humility don't hurt once you get numb."

A light of interest crossed the purple one's face. "Are people here very good? Our gentlemen have worked for better than a year developing skills." Her voice sounded only a little phony.

"Around here," Annie said, "boys learn pool about the time they learn to drive, and they learn to drive at age nine."

The beetle looked intrigued, and also looked ready to do business. "We can solve our problem," she said to the butterflies, "or at least we can try." To Bertha, she said, "Play would have to happen on our tables. Our men are not accustomed to losing. A loss may cause them to quit the game."

"Our guys don't play for love," Bertha told her. "I've seen titles pass to pickup trucks, and the guy who lost the truck didn't even get a ride home."

"Give me your card," the beetle said.

"My cards ain't returned from the printer. Phone number's in the book."

"Some spiders eat their mates," Annie explained, but only Jubal Jim paid attention. Jubal Jim stood, yawned, stretched, and trotted to the doorway. When Bertha let him out he walked to the only car on the lot, a Lincoln Continental, raised his leg and anointed a tire. He was soon joined by the butterflies. Jubal Jim sniffed the air for the familiar scent of booze, and the unfamiliar scent of truly expensive perfume. Then he trotted back to the door and scratched.

"I did something stupid, didn't I?" Annie let Jubal Jim inside, watched the Lincoln pull away, then sighed.

"Nope," Bertha told her. "You did okay. I did something stupid."

The Way of the Hustler

Petey followed The Way of the Hustler through late June and a good piece of July. It takes time to make a stake because loafing is part of the hustle. Petey's old Plymouth, also part of his hustle, parked outside poolrooms or before cheap motels on Highway 99 in Seattle. Petey would not attend a good hotel if someone paid his admission. Image counts. Some hustlers go for Cadillacs and class, because showy stuff challenges punks who own more pride than skill.

Petey, on the other hand, likes the "aw shucks" approach. With his stripey shirt and creased pants he looks like a small town tinhorn. He talks like a small town tinhorn, and waits like a loaded bear trap for city boys who fondly believe they know something. If asked about The Way of the Hustler, Petey would doubtless clam up because The Way requires great purity of mind.

It was tough to leave home, and even tougher because love bloomed and all of Petey's senses told him it was wrong to go. Yet, if a guy sees zeros coming up in the money stash he must make another stake. Without money Petey would be too embarrassed to hang out at Beer and Bait; and Petey believed his presence there would, sooner or later, present a perfect opportunity to cuddle up and marry Bertha. Sometimes he dreamed of snow blowing in over mountains, piling so deep only he and Jubal Jim could break trail. Bertha would be stranded, alone, listening to soft music on the tape deck; at which point the dream changed from heroic to sensual and is really Petey's business and no one else's.

The hustler is not exactly a nobleman, although a few have been rumored to show occasional twinges of kindness. The hustler is a man, or sometimes a lady, who lives by wit and skill. That the hustler can shoot nine-ball better than most other humans may be assumed, but no hustler is a superior shot in every game. Even Willie Musconi was known to shank shots, and the legendary Minnesota Fats was not technically as good as Musconi. Willie Hoppe, whose reputation echoes through the halls of time, sparked a phrase among generations of players. When faced with a truly complex layout, players will scratch their heads, sigh deeply, and mutter, "Now what would Willie do?" The answer is: "You damn fool, Willie would miss. Because he screwed up."

Because of the "screw-up" factor no hustler can depend on technical superiority to carry each and every day. Hustlers can win big when they're hot. They win when suckering novices. They win by placing bets on trick shots. They win in tournaments. They win most of all when they play guys who have some slim chance of winning.

A hustler is a fifteen percent gambler, which means that any game he enters will be no more than fifteen percent luck and eighty-five percent skill. If he plays blackjack he counts the cards and sits to the right of the dealer. If he's in a game where the deal passes, he measures the amount of his bet accordingly. When working a new bar or poolroom the hustler makes only small bets until he learns flaws of the pool table. He hangs his jacket where he can keep an eye on it.

It's a solitary life; a life of rented rooms, sandwiches, coffee, and pop. The hustlers who last, drink about as much beer during a night's work as it would take to float a ping pong ball in a saucer.

When engaged in making a stake hustlers have no time for social graces, which is why, when Petey is on his home turf he finds himself inexperienced with women. Thoughts of love can be expensive to the hustle because they break the concentration. And, time itself stands against intimacy. Mornings are for sleep. Noon to two A.M. requires attendance at the tables. Only Sunday is open for prayer or a bath, and even then the pool halls open in early afternoon. Most hustlers settle for a shower.

And finally, the game itself is an exercise in purity. No one realized how pure the game is until computer jocks, having a sporting nature of their own, calculated the possible combinations on a pool table at slightly over sixty-five quadrillion. The changing face of the game fascinates beginning players who do not understand how a good hustler can shape that face in pretty much the same way a sculptor shapes clay.

Petey worked the Seattle scene for a couple of weeks. It's a scene most lucrative because, a few years ago, the game became so popular that "pool schools" appeared. Bright young men who wished to impress young women, or wished to appear in beer commercials, attended school with diligence. A lot of hot rock players appeared, short mileage guys who look good for an hour, then fade.

Petey's old jeans-jacket hung floppity, blue and stained, on a hanger beside suit jackets with expensive labels. Petey's blue baseball cap, this one reading "Ace Fish Processing" was in stark contrast to fancy green eyeshades and tinted glasses of other players. Petey's cue looked like a plain stick beside the pearl inlaid cues of the newly initiated, but Petey's cue is a sleeper. A thousand bucks would not buy one as good.

When Seattle tired of him Petey dropped down to Tacoma, a drive that takes less than an hour. Petey took three days. He checked the action in bars, poolrooms, back rooms, and card rooms. A fifteen percenter, he treated small timers in kindly manner and picked up another thousand over expenses.

Very promising, especially since the big money lay untapped. In Portland it is sometimes possible to gain entrance to a gentleman's club. In Portland all play is methodical, because in Portland patience is a virtue. Politics excepted, Portland does not deal wild cards or loaded cueballs, never has. Portland was originally settled by New England churchmen and thus suffers. Portland believes that Four Roses refers to a garden show. Seattle, on the other hand, does not believe that at all. Seattle was originally settled by bums.

Petey adhered to the purity of The Way, and the last week of July saw him pulling out of Portland. His Plymouth groaned beneath the weight of his wallet; but the Plymouth was not about to pass up any good thing. It headed for Lee's China Bay Taverna at the foot of the Hood Canal.

Only the hand of the artist, and an Oriental hand at that, could take concrete blocks, stack them in a fifty-by-seventy rectangle, put a roof over them and make the whole mess beautiful. Dark pines soar above China Bay's golden, twisty, roof. Its doors shine Dragon-Lady-red. The paved parking lot has a grade dropping toward a roadside ditch. That grade, together with rain, keeps the macadam nicely shined and free of gum wrappers, cigarette butts, combs with missing teeth; all the ragtag and clutter of happily wasted lives.

China Bay is a smiling place, and only occasionally scary. The bartender is renowned for wisdom, and the owner, Lee, has the Buddha's tolerance for occasional imbalances between yin and yang. Lee and the bartender have been together for more years than most folks can imagine, although no two people could seem more mismatched. Together, though, they give China Bay Taverna a reputation for good sense in an area where good sense is at a premium; an area that cares nothing for yin and yang, because abstract stuff is hard to steal.

The state Capitol sits nearby. As Petey's Plymouth pulled onto the paved lot, Petey could see the Capitol dome rising like an ambitious hamburger above a low range of hills. Petey pulled into a parking space beside a new Chev pickup. He looked the lot over, saw one frowsy Jaguar, one Japanese rice grinder, and two old hang-and-rattle dump trucks. The Jag belonged to the bartender, the pickup, Petey figured, belonged to Lee. The junk dump trucks spelled working men. The rice grinder could be anything. Petey scratched his bald spot and felt the way a guy does, when that guy has been too long away and sees the first signs of home.

Petey told himself he must be getting old. It was not that his joints ached, or that he felt bored. He just felt a little too pleased to be back on familiar ground. In a man born to hustle that seemed worrisome. But, although he worried over being happy, he would not have to worry long. He did not know about developments back home.

Petey did not then know, and would be surprised to learn, that Sugar Bear brooded. He did not know that Annie had changed from a lithesome shadow flicking between trees in the forest, to a vital and beautiful young lady.

Nor did Petey know that cars were dunking with great regularity, or that Bertha had spoken to women from the housing project. Most of the regulars at China Bay knew nothing of these things, either, but accurate information has never been a requirement for bar talk.

Petey eased from the Plymouth, walked to the Dragon-Lady-red doors. The doors opened to a view of four pool tables, a twenty-five-foot bar with polished top, and a front of black and green enamel. Three exceedingly fat goldfish swam in a tank big enough for ten. The tank had a top fastened with clamps, thus keeping twenty-one-year-old alcoholics from showing-off as they tried to swallow the fish. A carved dragon sat beside a halltree on which hung tinsel left over from some now-forgotten holiday. Tables and chairs staggered across the room in happy confusion. Two retired gents played cribbage at the fish-tank end of the bar. From the storeroom behind the bar Lee's voice consulted with itself in Chinese.

"Petey," the bartender said. "Long time."

"Petey," a guy said. "I get first shot at you. Five bucks, bank the eight." The gent unwrapped himself from a bar stool. He was thin to the point of gangly and moved with the grace of someone who mostly lives outdoors. He smelled of loam, which meant he worked with plants and grades and trees; and loam must be what he carried in his junk dump truck.

"Working or drinking?" the bartender asked. This bartender, of all bartenders anywhere, could keep a joint under control by voice alone. This bartender's eyes were golden, or sometimes gray, or sometimes blue. This bartender had a young girl's moves and a strong man's assurance.

"Bottle-a-pop," Petey said. "Strawberry if you got it."

"I'll watch the show," the other truck driver said about the coming pool game. "If you can't stop a massacre you might as well enjoy it."

At the far end of the bar a guy wearing a dirty suit sat staring into a beer glass as he puzzled the meaning of life. Everyone politely ignored him. This guy would doubtless get skunked a little further, somehow make it back to the rented room, sleep it off, and then try to listen to his lawyer. In a year or less he'd be married again; that sort of guy.

"You don't wanta play for five," Petey advised the first guy.

"I'm on a roll. I'm making 'em overhand from center court. Play for a buck."

"Ten," the guy said. "I know you're bulling me but get in line. Lemmie do it to myself." The guy racked for eight-ball.

"We could still do a little work this afternoon." The truck driver who was not playing was also skinny, but not so tall. He looked into his beer glass. "When I die I'm gonna get myself cremated. I raked so damn much dirt in my life I can't bring myself to be buried in it."

"Petey don't come by here all that much," the first guy said. "How often do you get a chance to hustle a hustler?"

". . . trying to decide on a long or short afternoon," the shorter guy explained. "Which means do I plan on one more beer, or what?"

"The electrical system on Jaguars," the bartender mused, "is like playing solitaire with wild cards. I presently have one headlight that winks like a hussy picking up Pontiacs." The bartender turned as the sound of Lee's voice rose in the back room. Lee cussed, sincerely, heartfelt, deep in his own problems; the cussing like fundamental curses from prophets of olden days, but all in patriarchal Chinese. "Pearl of the Orient," the bartender called, "Petey's here."

Petey broke the rack, made a solid, ran four balls, then failed to break a little cluster that covered the other solids. "Run 'em,"

49

he said to the dump-truck driver, and the driver did. Petey tossed ten bucks on the table, gave a tight little grin like he was in pain and had planned nothing. "Next time," he muttered and began to rack the balls. The tall driver stood as proud as if he'd accomplished something. "You think you're doing me but I ain't going to let it happen."

"It's what I like about you. . . ," Lee came from the back room and talked to the truck driver. Lee tried to look inscrutable, and not advisory, which is easy enough for the average Chinaman. Lee, however, is far from average. ". . . you're easy money. Let me sell you a damn tavern."

No one can guess Lee's age, but in the very long-ago he must have stood five-nine and weighed one-thirty. Now he's shrunk to five-seven and gained to one-sixty. His color fades with age, so he's almost bleached. He sat at the end of the bar. "Petey," he said, "what's news from the home front?" Lee wears black suits, gray shirts, orange ties.

"Can't say," Petey told him. "I'm just coming off the road." He watched the truck driver break. The guy popped the rack head on, the way they do late at night in small joints throughout Montana. Nothing dropped.

"Don't spend that ten," Petey told the guy, and Petey set to work. To Lee he said, "Haven't been home in six or seven weeks."

"Then you don't know about the mystery girls," Lee said. "The woods up your way are supposed to be full of them. Our guys keep drifting up that way and looking. I'm losing customers."

"The woods may be filled with something," the bartender said, "but not with mystery girls. Rumor is a dreadful thing. Our boys will soon return and again consort with local trollops."

"Lot of wrecks going on up your way," the shorter driver said.

"A guy at the truck stop told me."

"I'm thinking about that problem," the bartender mused. "Something up there isn't square."

"You could square up this table," Petey said. "The right corner on the breaking end backs up like a plugged drain."

"Mystery women up that way don't make sense," Lee said. "There's nothing up that way except a few stores and Bertha's joint. Good-looking babes, my kiester," and that's where he scratched himself. Lee's hands are chubby with short fingers, while the bartender's hands are slim and reachy; and it isn't only the hands. Those two are different in about every way, although they've worked side by side for a long long time.

"Plus you've got that serial murderer," the shorter driver said. "What's all that bull about lynchings?"

"What's the bull about the wrecks?" Petey worked the table, his face shadowed beneath the baseball hat. He seemed sort-of Italian, but too relaxed to be Mafia; a nice deception. He ran six of seven, left the other guy completely hooked. As planned. The guy missed. Petey cued and missed. As planned.

"Somebody's forcing cars into the water," Lee said. "It's gotta be that. There's too many for a coincidence. The road hasn't changed, the Canal hasn't changed. Somebody's gone ugly."

"Anybody we know? I mean the wrecks." Petey watched the other guy make a little run. "You ought to give lessons," he said to the guy. He watched the guy run the table. As planned. Petey threw down a ten. "I got a lonesome twenty says you won't do three in a row."

"Rack 'em," the guy said. "I'm on a roll."

"A lot of cars," Lee told him. "I haven't heard any familiar names. No one we know."

The tall driver broke the rack. Nothing dropped. Petey dropped a stripe, pulled the cueball to kick a little cluster, and had his table set. He ran the table while the other guy stood helpless.

"Play for a buck."

"Twenty," the guy said. "I got a feeling."

A low moan sounded from the far end of the bar where a tortured soul wore a dirty suit and stared through a beer glass toward the far end of eternity. The moan sounded adolescent, like the guy had no experience with the suffering that occurs for pool hustlers, bar owners, Jaguar drivers, or poets. The moan sounded sincere but inexperienced.

"We have ninety seconds," the bartender whispered. "There will be a revelation concerning someone's infidelity. It will end in a full confession and/or indictment. Perhaps there will be excuses. We may see manly tears."

"Her name was Georgia," the voice quavered from the far end of the bar.

"Oooopsy," the bartender said, "I was off by sixty seconds."

"Gray," the guy said. "Georgia Gray. It was a sort of a joke." The guy looked at himself in the mirror behind the bar. He straightened his tie. Sniffed back snot. Squared his shoulders like a good soldier.

"You gonna rack 'em or what?" Petey could see his hustle fading. A hustle depends on the undivided attention of the party being hustled.

The tall player racked, but his thoughts clearly drifted elsewhere. Petey had to figure that a mildly promising hustle was going to end in no more than a twenty buck profit.

"Women sure can do it to ya, can't they?" The tall player lifted the rack and waited for Petey's break. "You'd think a guy would learn." He ground chalk onto his cue tip and looked hopeless as a man writing alimony checks.

"I'm glad I'm settled in," Lee said. "What with all the society diseases running around. It must be a real crapshoot out there."

"I miss Pinky, too." The guy in the suit turned on his barstool and his voice held indignation. "Naturally, I do not miss the sad bastard all that much."

"We're playing twenty-bucks-a-game pool here." The driver who was not playing sensed an opportunity. "To make it friendly I'll play you for ten."

"Mistake," the bartender whispered. "Now you've extended an invitation. We will endure a tale of hanky-pank between lonesome Georgia and loathsome Pinky. Imagine, if you can, a lover named Pinky."

"With tax and license," the drunk guy said, "she came to a little over sixty-seven thou. The shop can do a dry-out and rebuild, but it'll never be the same. Never." He belched, then moved along the bar in a plausible imitation of W. C. Fields. "Naturally, they're all having a good laugh at the office."

"As grandma used to say," the bartender mused, " 'I swan to glory.' He's talking about machinery."

"I'm now driving," the drunk explained. ". . . a little Japanese rental thing with vinyl seats for God's sake . . ." He looked at Lee, at Lee's eyefolds. "The Japanese are a great people."

"The Japanese are assholes," Lee told him. "And you're taking a cab, if we have to club you to get the car keys."

"I got to quit drinking," the pool-playing driver complained. "I thought we were talking about women."

"You were," the bartender told him. "He wasn't." The bartender looked the guy over; gray suit, school tie to a school he likely never attended, high-priced haircut. "For a number of reasons," the bartender told him, "you may be drinking in the wrong bar. Who, may I ask, is Pinky?" The bartender moved to the phone behind the bar and punched in the number of a cab company.

The guy made it to a barstool, planked his rear, and leaned on the bar. He fished in his pocket for car keys. "Some of my best friends are Japanese." He put the keys on the bar.

"Pinky," Lee said. "You have a friend named Pinky."

"Had," the guy said, and almost yelled. "Had, had, had! Until he got his stupid self drowned." The guy teetered on the barstool, and spoke in what amounted to shorthand. ". . . big golf weekend up north . . . business deal . . . lots and lots of real estate . . . big hairy emergency at the office . . . caught a quick flight back in a puddle jumper . . . big hush hush . . . Pinky follows with the car and golf clubs. Splash. Bye bye Pinky." The guy weaved, which is not that hard to do on a barstool. "Bastard was a liability from the get-go."

"This is interesting," Lee said to the other guys. "I never saw crap stacked so high it could wear a suit."

Petey, his hustle busted, as surely as he busted the rack of balls, almost indifferently ran the table. He banked the eight ball with no real satisfaction and picked up the driver's twenty. "I reckon it's time to travel." He looked at the driver. "Unless you're still hot and want healing."

"Forget it," the driver said. "And thanks. I needed the practice." A very cool head, that driver.

Petey turned to the drunk, maybe because "Petey" and "Pinky" sound similar. "You attend the funeral?"

"Dead people shouldn't look that calm," the drunk said. "Like all the meanness had been sucked out of him."

"Was he as nasty as you?" The bartender pretended interest. "Because perhaps we've discovered a cure."

"He was vice president of a mortgage company." Then the

drunk realized he'd been insulted. "Suppose it was your car?"

"If it were my car," the bartender told him, "and we're talking authentic Jaguar here, I would erect a shrine in their mutual memory."

"There must be something to all that bull about accidents," Petey said. "I reckon I'd better get on home." Then he paused. "You think somebody's gone ugly?"

"Something isn't square," the bartender said. "I'm thinking about the problem. When I figure it out I'll send word."

"Avoid hustlers," Lee told Petey, as Petey headed for the door. "I worry about you kids."

The Complications of Love

On sunny days the Canal glosses over with a sheen of darkest green, and islands in the flooded landscape rise like wet clumps of moss above the darkness. The Canal covers all sorts of things acquired from the land: automobiles, boats, ships, tools, beer bottles, drowned kittens, corpses, crashed airplanes, sunken buoys, stolen electronics, wedding rings cast by the divorced and depressed, incriminating evidence, pistols, shotguns, rifles, hypodermics, butcher knives, as well as great numbers of other by-products of the greatest civilization ever seen in all the history of the universe.

In the Canal's depths, and they are deep, tumble more wrecks than we know. On the surface fishing boats cluster near tidal beaches where salmon runs grow thinner with each passing year, and where, in their seasons, shrimp and crabs and bottom fish are dragged flopping and gasping to the surface.

On dark days the Canal seems more itself. Waters ruffle before the wind, and breakers pound against the Hood Canal Bridge, against the shores, against the islands. Ships come down the Canal, Coast Guard icebreakers, Navy frigates, and atomic powered submarines. The Navy tells us a single sub carries more firepower than has been discharged by all the navies in all of history. Hard to believe, and sort of meaningless. Any boy on a schoolyard can tell you that it ain't how much you swing, but where do you hit?

By the time Petey pulled onto the gravel lot at Beer and Bait, the westering sun stood smack dab on the mountain tops. On the last day of July that means a little after eight P.M. Cars and pickups filled the lot, and from inside came the lonesome sound of guitars. The tape deck in the bar broadcast a country singer mourning loss; and perhaps the loss was a Cadillac, or maybe only a lover. Petey sat in his Plymouth, listened to imitation sorrow from the tape deck, and became aware that he had changed. For years, having made his living in the presence of fiddles that sounded like scalded cats, he did not even hear bar music. Now, though, he wished for nothing but silence, Bertha, and his dog. Petey asked himself if it was time to settle down, buy a little store or something, and pull a few hustles on the side. In other days such an idea would fill him with revulsion. Now the idea seemed almost smart. He told himself he was going through a phase. The road takes something out of a man.

Across the lot, two figures sat on the hood of a pickup as they soaked up last rays of sunlight. One appeared to be a fisherman, and the other bulked too big to be anyone but Sugar Bear. Petey climbed from the Plymouth and trudged toward them. He figured Sugar Bear would catch him up on the news and the fisherman would try, although fishermen are definitely at a disadvantage:

Fishermen, like hustlers, are often away for a month at a pop. While they are away news gets elaborated. While there's not much time for talk on a fishing boat, there's plenty of time for folks to misinform poor fishermen when the boat hails into port. Then, of course, the fishermen have to revise everything by asking questions. A new round of embroidered news lies waiting to greet the next returning boat. After a few boats arrive, the stories get as confused as trail mix. When blank spaces appear in a story, even an honest fisherman has to make things up.

This fisherman turned out to be the thoughtful one, and he scooched over to make a spot on the hood of the truck. "Petey," the fisherman said, "do I just keep missing you, or the other way around?" The fisherman had been ashore for a while. His hair shone clean and he did not smell all that bad.

"I bin to the big city," Petey told him. "I'm glad nobody's revoked your bail." Petey eased up onto the hood, looked across the fisherman to Sugar Bear, and realized he'd screwed up with his crack about bail. "Things steady out your way?"

"The usual," Sugar Bear said, but didn't sound like he meant it. He looked at the last sunlight like a man headed for eternal darkness. His huge shoulders slumped. His hair, furry and curly, brown and thick, fluffed over his ears. His beard curled beneath a furry mustache, and his brown eyes filled with sorrow. He watched the sunlight like a man who sees it for the last time.

"You're a smart guy," the fisherman said to Petey. "We were just discussing women."

"Actually, not exactly women," Sugar Bear said. "It's more like a what-the-hell-do-I-do-next discussion."

"Because Sugar Bear has a thing for Annie," the fisherman explained.

"And Sugar Bear is headed for jail sure as a bear craps in the woods." Sugar Bear squinched up his face, which meant that a lot of hair moved around and his eyes blinked. "Suppose I tell her," he said, "and suppose she likes me, which maybe that could happen, but maybe not. Then, when I make the slammer, she's left behind. That wouldn't be right. Everybody knows that. Hell, I know that."

"I wouldn't own your conscience if they gave me a winning lottery ticket," the fisherman told him. "I wouldn't keep your conscience unless I owned thirty damn churches."

"Even if somebody gets shouting-drunk, and blabs, the cops would only have a b.s. story," Petey said. "The cops don't know the dead guy and the car are there. You're hustling yourself."

"You did that punk a favor," the fisherman told Sugar Bear. "He didn't suffer. You saved a fishing boat some trouble. The guy was a goner no matter how you slice it."

"The cops will find the car," Sugar Bear told Petey. "You ain't bin here. The cops got divers pulling out wrecks. They're going through that water like you run tranny fluid through a strainer." Music moaned through the open doorway of Beer and Bait, something about love letters stashed behind a commode. "Besides," Sugar Bear said, "that's not exactly the problem. I got to live with this."

"You ought to talk to Annie," Petey told him. "It looks like she has a stake."

"Annie talks to bugs," Sugar Bear said, as if he were explaining something.

"In other words," the fisherman said thoughtfully, "we're talking about you having a case of the hots. I figured we talked long term." He made a motion to slide off the hood of the pickup, then decided to wait for an answer. On the Canal the first suggestion of mist hovered on the surface.

"You don't get it," Sugar Bear told him. "I *like* it that she talks to bugs. I *like* it that she's a nut. That stuff don't bother me. It's actually kind of cute."

"Long term?"

"Sure, long term. But girls who talk to bugs must be conning themselves, because you sure can't con a bug. If I ask her, she'll maybe con herself. Then I get busted. . . ."

"I bin missing my dog," Petey said. "Is he okay?"

"What the hell does that mean?" Sugar Bear seemed ready to apologize, or fight, or run and hide.

"You can't predict what will happen ten minutes from now," Petey told him. "You're trying to arrange her whole life, and your whole life forever. And I thought I could hustle."

The fisherman slid off the hood of the truck. "Get off your back pockets and propose, or take her to a movie, or something." Music from Beer and Bait sobbed, lonesome as a lost man in a desert, sitting beside his dying horse.

"I'm feeling sort of fatalistic."

"I'm not sure," the fisherman said thoughtfully, "that Annie's the biggest kid in these parts. And you, a full grown man."

The three men watched the forest go dark, while at their backs a little light still lay across the Canal; light reflected from high clouds, and from trees and buildings on the far side. A couple of outboards piddled along like moving specks, but the surface of the Canal lay otherwise deserted and calm. Sugar Bear slid from the hood of the pickup, seemed uncertain whether to go inside Beer and Bait, or head for home. Petey slid down to stand beside him. "I really do miss my dog," he said to Sugar Bear. To the fisherman he said, "You comin' in?"

"I'll be there directly," the fisherman told him. The fisherman watched as Petey and Sugar Bear trudged across the lot, and the fisherman thought neither one looked like a man with a happy thirst. If he had to choose a word to describe them, he thought, that word would be "beleaguered".

And no doubt the fisherman felt beleaguered as well. As Petey and Sugar Bear disappeared through the open doorway of Beer and Bait, and as the music changed to twanging sobs because some guy's lady ran off in some other guy's Peterbilt, the fisherman walked to the side of Beer and Bait, hesitated, then moved slowly to the bank of the Canal.

Perhaps he only came to watch the show, as water humped and carried on. It may be he wondered why the thing that humped out there never bothered with anything on the surface, and he surely wondered why it did not bother police divers. As darkness slowly descended over the face of the Canal, the fisherman, accustomed to deep water, and accustomed to not thinking of their depths—because sailors don't—surprised himself by thoughts of coldness, darkness; the eternal night lying at the bottom of the Canal.

He shivered, but not with cold or fear. He knew about cold, having spent a good deal of his life offshore. He knew about fear, because there are things that happen offshore so scary that no witchery on the Canal could equal them. In his day, the fisher-man's long lines had brought from the depths colorful creatures, gasping and strange. The lines snagged an occasional carcass, sea lion, or seal, or other things. Since much of this happened in mist, and since mist is ghostly, the fisherman (like most of his clan) had seen many-a-thing walking across the water, some of those things vaguely human. A little problem like water humping on the Canal would not occupy this fisherman for long.

Something bothered him, though. It may be . . . it just might be, that although Annie scared him, this fisherman also had a thing for Annie. It might be that the studly talk that goes on aboard boats or in bars does not actually tell much about the boldness of the average guy; although, of course, this fisherman thought of himself as higher-than-average.

And so he probably asked himself why, if weird things of the sea did not scare him, and the thing in the Canal did not scare him, how come a pretty girl had him tied in fearful knots?

Because, he told himself, the whole deal was hopeless. Even if he had a "sort of a thing" for Annie, he somehow knew Annie was infatuated with Sugar Bear. Besides, the fisherman told himself, he was probably too old for her, anyway. Still, the whole deal made him about as sad as a cynical guy can allow himself to get.

He turned toward Beer and Bait, while at his back, water began to hump and spread. He figured everything was working out about the way it should. Annie was almost surely a stay-at-home type, and would rather hang around boiler plate in a warm shop, than sit in a small house waiting for a man who made his living at sea.

Annie

During the first two weeks of August a heat wave descended. Temperatures of eighty degrees cooked the forest, and while eighty is thought mild in many places, we're not acclimated. Around here, summer visitors from the midwest usually wear sweaters, talk polite, and shake their heads in private. Sixty-five degrees and drizzling is considered ideal.

Heat brings dryness. Moss on roofs turns from green to black, and shrinks into little patches. Dust gathers golden on windshields because people aren't in the habit of washing them. As hot day follows hot day, steam from the forest diminishes. Conifers take a grayish, sick look, and leaves of maple and alder show patches of yellow. Trees do not drop leaves until October, but drought speeds them up. When Annie walked in the forest, as she often did in August, the mat of needles from fir and pine no longer felt spongy.

She watched from behind the cover of trees like a small girl playing hide-and-seek. Police patrolled the road. One cop—who looked like a movie actor dressed up to play a cop—seemed to run the show. This cop cruised the road until divers found another wreck. Then he hustled in more cops and a crane. The cops closed one lane and shuffled traffic past in the other. Cars backed up, drivers sweating and disgusted. Little kids, who couldn't hold it any longer, had to make quick dashes into the forest. People were kept from work, or from errands. The amount of cussing that went on would peel the paint off a steeple.

In the midst of it, Annie felt unsettled. She did not know that Petey thought of himself as going through a phase, but she knew she was. Vague thoughts never bothered Annie. Vague emotions did. Vague dreams made her scared. She felt, somehow, that life passed her by. She felt aimless, adrift, and with nebulous hankering to be of use to the world.

True, she battled satellites. The things flew overhead with never a by-your-leave. They interrupted the natural flow of the heavens, so when you first looked up and thought you had discovered a new star, it was only a peeping piece of tin.

Since leaving high school, and retiring in the woods, to the relief of her well-to-do family that lived in the housing project, Annie could look back on a few years of accomplishment. Certain herbs in the forest needed weeding to survive. When baby birds awkwardly left their nests in the spring someone needed to keep an eye on them, because housecats roamed the forest. Annie cast enchantments on submarines, and the enchantments worked since the subs always returned to base without discharging missiles. And sometimes, when no one was around to see, Annie arranged leaves and sticks and ferns in small displays, like artworks in a closed museum: for art is necessary even if not understood, and especially necessary if no one knows to look.

That Annie possesses talent cannot be denied. It is her loss, and ours, that her talent was never liberated through training. The talent came through the genes of a Greek grandmother, who, when Annie was a little girl, talked to trees. The trees always answered, and held odd, tree-like opinions; but Annie never really learned the language.

Annie was vaguely aware, in early August, that if she wanted a man, she could have her pick from half the unmarried guys in the neighborhood, and ninety percent of the married ones. The problem was not getting a man, but getting the right man; and the right one was Sugar Bear. In her imagination she saw herself in Sugar Bear's kitchen which she knew well, and which would now be their's. She saw herself weeding the garden, or sitting in the warm shop while Sugar Bear worked. Sometimes an occupied cradle sat nearby. At other times she thrilled with the thought of the two of them hiking to the crest of a high ridge, and looking onto the Canal while feeling alive and free.

These imaginings had something to do with being of use to the world. Annie would not be the first young person to become flustered because life refused to take a proper shape. Annie didn't know that. Perhaps it's just as well. Had she known, she might have tried to help.

She was aware Sugar Bear liked her, sort of. She just couldn't tell how much. She also knew Sugar Bear worried, and that the dead guy no doubt walked through Sugar Bear's dreams. Annie may have been a kid, and accustomed to nebulous thoughts, but Annie can never be thought of as dumb. It seemed wrong that a good man should be in danger, just because the world spat forth a guy who should have gone out with the garbage.

And, because she had her cap set for Sugar Bear, she tried, really tried, to understand him. She told herself she was more practical, but in a way she understood. It must be awful to do something really, really, really bad, and not be able to undo it. It must be even worse to be the kind of person who could not shove the blame off on someone else; and it must be pretty bad to dis-cover a streak in yourself so ugly it caused you to smash someone.

She thought over the problem, and watched from the forest as backed-up traffic drew a colorful line along the dark road. Stink of exhaust swirled among dry smells of the forest. On the north side of trees, where moisture still lingered, roll-y bugs, little snails, slugs, and earwigs hid, and, buglike, did things to each other.

Sometimes Annie showed the knowledge owned by the Ancients, even if she was not very old and knew little of them. When, for example, she told Bertha that the thing in the Canal was a Fury, she was fairly sure she spoke true. Annie was not exactly clear about what a Fury was, but made a mental note.

Meantime, she showed the wisdom of the Ancients. For two days and nights she remained silent and listened to the sounds of Canal and forest. She cloaked herself in silence, and let the voice of wind, the lap of water, the snap of twigs and rustle of leaves speak their pieces. She heard flutters of wings, the birds long past mating season, and soon to fly south. Her mind could feel fingers of mist touching the Canal when sunlight faded and the forest grew black as shoal.

Solutions presented themselves. Some solutions made her hopeful, and some sad. She was urgently aware that police divers steadily moved closer to the dead guy. She understood that if she was going to do something, she had better do it right away.

The problem with spells is some worked, some didn't, and some went off half-cocked. With time to experiment, she could learn what worked. There was no time. Plus, she felt sort of sad, and that made it possible to do something dumb.

She saw these options:

Move the dead guy's car, and the dead guy, to deep, deep water where the divers would never find him.

Or, just move the dead guy.

Or, cause a distraction and shut down the whole operation.

"It will take time," she whispered to the forest. "I'll have to stall for time." Those, her first words in two days, dropped into the silence of the forest like an echoing voice from long ago. The forest remained silent, tranquil, and possibly as tired as August; and August is the tiredest month.

On the road a state cop who looked like a movie actor hassled traffic. He seemed really official out there. When he halted traffic with his hand, he wore his don't-screw-around-with-me cop look. He also looked like a cop who needed a drink, and Annie thought—if he were not a cop—she would take him some lemonade.

She also thought she had better figure out a pretty good stall. It would take at least a couple of days to see if she could move the car, or the dead guy. Or whatever.

Concerning Real Estate and Cops

Wind picked up during afternoon, gusting at first, then changing to a steady blow. The Canal ruffled with heavy chop, and the chop turned to waves that crashed along the shore. A few fishing boats headed to sea as Navy ships fled into port, heavy weather being tiresome to the Navy.

As wind continued, police divers shut up shop. Cops took down orange barriers blocking one lane, and the yellow crane parked. The crane looked like a heron hovering over a fishing spot, and its color matched yellow dive gear being packed into a police van. Turbulence along the shore shifted remains of fallen trees as it churned water. Divers could not see a foot ahead of them. Whether the wind and wave action was enough to tumble wrecked cars was anybody's guess, but folks hanging out at Beer and Bait argued the possibility. Everyone figured the blow would drop when the tide changed.

Afternoon progressed toward evening, the tide turned, and wind, if anything, picked up. The parking lot at Beer and Bait came alive with rumbles of diesels as log truck drivers understood there was no other place to go, except home. The trucks are rarely fancy. They occasionally display a snazzy striping job, or an extra smidgen of chrome, but for the most part are working machines; bulky, sort of beautiful like a herd of colorful metal bison. The trucks congregated because drivers knew, what with wind, all logging operations would shut down. The forest rapidly turned to tinder where even the spark from a chainsaw could spell catastrophe. Drivers relaxed at Beer and Bait, grumbled, and were secretly glad to take a break, though everyone worried. It was no longer a question of: will there be a forest fire? That seemed certain as an owl hoots. The only way out was miracles or magic.

As a good crowd gathered, Chantrell George wandered toward Beer and Bait. Wind snatched at his raggedy orange shirt and his equally raggedy green pants. His shoes in summer are aerated, allowing breathing space for toes. Before entering Beer and Bait he used his sleeve to make sure his nose didn't drip. He combed his hair with his fingers. Bertha, who sensed a big night, put Chantrell to work right away. She figured he would be pretty well cleaned up, for a junkie. What with the heat, his mushroom source was temporarily closed. The shy creatures prefer lots of moisture and a muted sky.

Sugar Bear sat at a table in the exact center of the room, looking like a mountain of sorrow rising above foothills of routine cares. A few fisherman scattered among loggers, and beefed about wind. A few tradesmen clustered near windows and talked shop. Wives and girlfriends chatted, laughed, or patted the backs of their men's hands, as the men worried over truck payments.

After the first dust got washed from throats, and the first beer-buzz made the world more palatable to most, Bertha turned the whole show over to Chantrell. She sat at the far end of the bar, the end away from the door. She hassled pool games and tried to figure if it was time to give up on Petey, because he'd made no big moves since coming home.

As wind continued to crash, Bertha turned the tape deck

down instead of up. Chatter competing with music did not ordinarily cause her to bat an ear, but today seemed different. She felt an edge of impatience—not the best sort of feeling for the owner of a joint; impatient with herself, impatient with Petey, plus the weather was enough to make a preacher cuss. What with wind and general unrest, Bertha suffered a bout of melancholy.

That afternoon she and Petey had been playing their first truly private game of pool since Petey's return. The only other soul present was Jubal Jim, a-snooze on the floor. Or, it might be someone sat outside on the front steps, relaxing in the sun, and listening. If that "someone" was there, he probably made bets with himself on how far the line of traffic would stack up.

Part of Bertha's frustration came from want of privacy. Since Petey's return they hardly had a single moment. What with cars backing up halfway to Timbuctoo, and with the usual run of tourists who managed to feel lost on a road where you couldn't get lost; and what with logging drivers mildly suicidal and longing for a beer to settle nerves, privacy became a memory. Quiet afternoons playing pool with Petey belonged to a past so remote somebody should have written books about it.

That afternoon Petey almost got something said. Now, with the lengthening shadows of evening, Bertha sat at the end of the bar watching him run a routine hustle on a logger. She had to admit Petey was not the handsomest man in the room. He was not, for example, as pretty as his dog. On the other hand, he had appeal no other man could touch. Bertha, a Scandinavian descended from Norsemen, held an appreciation for piracy . . . she hesitated . . . suddenly remembering the women from the housing project. Those women really might start something poolish.

It didn't figure. Women like that generally competed against each other, but might gang up for revenge or profit. Or, they

70

70

might let that beetle-lady run a number just for the fun of seeing somebody get burned. And . . . what were those women doing in a beer joint in the first place? That never happened before.

Bertha knew her joint and knew her guys. Most acted like civilians until placed behind a pool cue. The majority of men at Beer and Bait were not particularly courageous, and not good at fighting, even when pumped up by adrenalin and beer. Put them behind a pool cue, though, and they wouldn't leave two sticks nailed together when it came to dismantling bank accounts of rich guys at the development. Behind a pool cue Bertha's boys turned into a bunch of heathen savages.

She figured the development could not handle savages. If her boys romped too freely it would eventually mean cops. Rich guys had a way of getting back. Rich guys were not a hell of a lot different than regular guys. They took themselves serious.

She did not know which part of life was the biggest mess. She looked at Petey, and, to give him credit, knew he suffered from the same problems of privacy. That afternoon, alone and studying a complicated lay-out on the table, he muttered, "Thinking of settling down a little. Go into business, maybe." His voice had nearly been a whisper, and he blushed. Since there was nothing to blush about when it came to going into business, he had to be blushing about something else.

"A business can be fun." Bertha had spoken carefully, although she couldn't picture Petey behind a bar or a counter. Her head was telling her "Go Slow" and her heart was saying "This is *it*. This is the big *It*."

"Because," Petey whispered, "this bein' on the road gets to a guy." He hid behind his shot, banking three rails on the seven ball that sat like a purple blush two inches off the pocket. The ball fell with a little click, an itsy sigh, and a thump.

71

"What kind of business?" Bertha made a point of keeping her back to him. She stepped behind the bar where she picked up a fresh piece of pool chalk.

"I dunno," Petey said, and then almost choked. "I figured maybe we could talk about it." He sounded, to Bertha, like a man strangling.

"We can do just that," she whispered. "I know about business stuff. . . ."

That was as far as she got. They were so concentrated on each other they did not hear tires crunching gravel in the parking lot.

Heels clicked on the front steps and a stranger appeared. He was slick-haired, suited, vested, shoe-polished, wearing a red tie and a smile so cheery as to brand him severely retarded, or a phony. He stood taller than Petey, tried to appear languid, and could not even look relaxed. Everything about him said "failed hustler".

Bertha figured him for an electronics guy, pinballs and videos. She wiped the counter, ready to say that she called the tunes in Beer and Bait; not some drunk with a buck for a jukebox.

"Passing through?" she asked.

"Business in the area." He tried to sound reasonable, but still looked like someone peddling pukey-green refrigerators to Eskimos. He passed Bertha his card. Real estate.

"I have a buyer. Wants to retire. Looking for a small business in a quiet place."

"Cemetery lots in Miami," Bertha told him. "Big market. Lots of quiet." She said it, but sounded mildly interested.

". . . thinks a bar would do nicely. We're talking money in front." The real estate guy named a figure only slightly higher than reasonable.

"Whose shot?" Bertha asked Petey. To the guy she said, "I

make my mortgage." She turned to the table and looked at a reasonably easy shot. Instead, she chose to show off. She popped the cueball between the eight and nine, a really narrow space. The cueball Englished its way two rails off the corner, ran the length of the table, caromed off the ten and tapped the eleven into the pocket. "Suppose I sell the joint for a wad," she told the guy. "I have to move someplace, buy another joint, and joints don't come cheap. There's no profit in it."

"I might come up with a deal on the other end."

"Do that." Bertha said. "Make it a major, major deal, or give it to your retired guy."

"You've got my card." The guy sort of slithered from the barstool and disappeared into the dry and windy day. Bertha turned to Petey, and she saw Petey was lost in some kind of Hustler's Revelation. Their magic moment was lost as Petey put together plans.

"One of the problems with business," Bertha said to Petey, "is you got no privacy. We'll talk." She said it just as gravel crunched in the parking lot. Two guys from the phone company arrived, guys on their third lunch hour of the day.

Now she sat in early evening and listened to wind bang and holler against windows. She wondered why she had been dumb enough to say something dumb about business. Then she wondered if she still felt good about Petey, or if he was just habit. She did not wonder about her own shyness, because Bertha, being of the Norwegians, prided herself on being "old school". Some things are done, some things are not. It was up to the gentleman to get matters started. Bertha knew little of the last twelve centuries of Norwegian history, but she knew a lot about Lutheran guilt.

She did not exactly trust her premonitions, but she did not

distrust them. It seemed like all the bad stuff that got tossed up in the air since last spring was about to land. Cops closed in on Sugar Bear's little problem. Annie was acting her age, which was dangerous. A forest fire would drive away tourists, and while she might joust with a real estate guy, it was true that bank balances got thin during slow seasons. And, if a pool tournament took place at the development, all hell would pop. She looked toward the open doorway while keeping an eye on Chantrell, or rather, on how Chantrell handled the cash register. Sunlight still lay behind the western ridges, so shadows crossed the road before running into a line of golden light reflected from high clouds. The tape deck played pop tunes of the '40s and '50s. A couple stood in the middle of the dance floor, swaying somewhat, mostly rubbing, while swirling light from a beer sign crossed their married faces; married, but not to each other.

Bertha became aware of unrest near the doorway. At her elbow Petey studied a shot and said something to a logger.

"The police radio," Petey said to the logger, as Petey made a little run and the logger cussed, "claims another car dunked. Hambone radio."

"That won't do nothin' to the baseball standings, either way," the logger said. "This late in the season . . ."

"A Mariners fan," Petey told him, "is the hopefulest damn fool in the nation. Tell me you ain't a Mariners fan."

"If a car has dunked," the logger said, "that makes number eight or nine. I'm losing count."

The disturbance near the door increased as people searched for places at tables, and got as far away from that end of the bar as they could without looking too guilty. They scattered like a flock of sparrows before a cat, but what stepped through the doorway was no kitty.

A state cop, who had to know he was where he wasn't wanted, took a seat near the door. Bertha reacted; shocked, then angry, then ready for a scrap. She quietly reviewed her own transgressions. None of them seemed serious enough to warrant a state cop. She looked over the house, saw customers shrinking into shadows, and a few obscene gestures waving toward the cop's back. This, the best crowd of the summer, was about to be chased home, or up to Rough and Randy, by a cop who obviously had not been raised to know his place.

Think of it as a dance, even while being surprised about who is dancing. Into Beer and Bait walks a thirsty man in a cop suit. The poor fellow can't have a beer because of the suit, but he's almost dry as the forest. He perches near the doorway, looks around, and orders lemonade from a visionary bartender—and the cop has enough experience to guess where those visions come from. This cop knows that every mother's son and daughter in that bar is guilty of something, because all of us doubtless are; but the cop doesn't know what, and doesn't give a flush. When he wants is to drink and be left alone. Which doesn't work. The dance begins, because the cop sees Bertha and things start happening like it's daytime television.

The cop sees a lady who, if she wished, could shake out a six-by-nine carpet like it was a rag rug. Bertha tops six feet, has blond hair with sexy streaks, and a figure that causes despair among the average run of housewives. Bertha's Norwegian blue eyes are smiley above a full and smiley mouth (most days). She has artistic hands. Bertha, in other words, is a knockout when a man is sober, and the stuff of mooshy dreams when a man is not.

And what did our second dancer, Bertha, see?

The cop, were he not a cop, was himself not indistinct. The

cop bulked big as Sugar Bear, but without Sugar Bear's easy ways. This cop had been up and down a few roads. He turned a little too far east on his bar stool, and looked into the mirror in back of the bar. This cop, Bertha admitted, would be mighty attractive as a TV repairman, or a garage door installer. He might do as a farmer, a house painter, or a dentist. As a cop, though, he amounted to just one more pretty-boy. He watched her with that sideways, indifferent look guys use when they pretend they aren't interested. Man or woman, there wasn't a good-looking bartender in all of history who had not picked up on that look; maybe even that wiseass at China Bay.

This cop looked filled with fantasies of moonlight, but Bertha could see he should not even think of women, at least not now. He looked tired to the point of exhaustion, hot, miserable, ready to tell the state to take its cop-job, and its traffic, and its political pizazz, and shove it all in a sunless place. Bertha also knew if the guy got a good night's sleep, and woke in time for an extra cup of coffee, he'd be right back on top of matters. He'd put in another day. If Bertha knew anything at all, it was certain she knew working men. Meanwhile, matters in Bear and Bait grew tippy.

"We got a cop," the logger muttered to himself, "and I got a hot chainsaw in back of the pickup." He looked at Petey. "Your dog gonna allow this?" Jubal Jim was nowhere seen.

"This ain't strictly a dog type of problem." Petey looked toward the cop. "He wants somebody, but I ain't done nothing. Lately." Petey checked himself for violations. He wore his going-to-town clothes, stripey shirt, narrow pants—you can hardly get good sharkskin anymore—and a baseball cap reading "Alaska Tours and Travel". He cued and missed an easy shot. The logger saw an opening and seemed somewhat cheered.

Sugar Bear sat unmoving. His shoulders slumped. He seemed fatalistic, resigned. He obviously did not even think of running, or hiding, or digging foxholes.

Chantrell gave a little moan. His eyes widened, the way eyes do in animated cartoons. A fine tremble developed in his hands. Bertha did her best to steady him.

"Nothing's wrong," she whispered. "It ain't got a thing to do with you. . . or does it? Do we need an alibi?"

Chantrell plucked aimless as a dying man at the front of his shirt. A necklace of illegal stuff might be soaking up sweat beneath that shirt. Chantrell looked guilty enough to hang, to have precise hallucinations when it came to jail.

Bertha glanced toward the cop, listened to whispers and the click of pool balls at her back, and Bertha gave a little giggle, then felt calm. The cop was still checking her out. Her giggle was not enough to get rid of her anger, but enough to keep her from doing something idiotic.

"He don't care a thing about you," she told Chantrell. "Act normal as you can. All he knows is you're a health violation."

She turned from Chantrell and looked over the crowd. People would drift away if the cop did not leave. For one horrible second Bertha imagined a gloomy and empty bar, the windows beaten by a dry wind, and no one to cast away the gloom. She imagined Sugar Bear sitting alone in the center of gloom while carnival music danced from the tape deck and across an empty dance floor. Bertha shuddered, turned back to the bar. The cop had knocked back his first lemonade. Now he motioned to Chantrell for another. Matters were getting serious.

She paused, thinking if the joint emptied she could get Petey to stay. They could have the privacy they needed . . . then Bertha told herself she must be nuts. She was not going to drive away the best crowd of the summer just so Petey could practice some line he learned from a movie. Nesting instinct or not, business was business. She changed the tape deck, discarding pop music in favor of guitars and country-boys.

She stepped behind the bar, trying to look official but not too tough. If the cop did a number on himself it would be dumb to break the spell. Every eye in the house was on her. It was like being on stage.

"Missing children?" she asked the cop. Up close this cop was more interesting. From a distance she had not seen little crow's feet around his eyes, or beginning wrinkles on his forehead. His mouth didn't really seem cop-like, being a little on the smiley side; crinkles in the right places. He looked like he should be a forest ranger, or a fifth grade teacher . . . something to do with wildlife.

"Tough afternoon," the cop said, then went into a sort of explanation, and his explanation was mostly a crock. Bertha watched him check out her ring finger. She began to feel a teensy bit warm.

"You got a nice place."

"Plain folks," Bertha said. "Just hard working folks." She leaned forward, like this was intimate, and whispered, "Folks will feel more comfy when you ditch the suit."

The cop was only mildly dense. He picked up on what he figured was an invitation, while Bertha silently wondered if she should cuss herself.

"Got to get moving," the cop said. "I've done a hand of work in my day."

"Just plain honest folks," Bertha said, and watched the cop "show off" as he stood in the doorway with his back to the crowd. When the cop walked toward his car, Bertha went to the door and watched. He climbed in, tired as a winded horse; an outcast driven from among his own kind, but, Bertha mused, the damn fool brought it on himself. No one asked him to be a cop.

Nobody asked her to extend an invitation, either. She announced that the cop was gone, then returned to her seat. The three pool tables began clicking. Murmurs started to liven as Bertha turned up the hick music. She told herself to take a couple minutes and figure things out.

She should have told the cop that lemonade at China Bay was the way to go. Instead, she somehow managed to tell him to come back when he ditched the cop suit.

She sat, vaguely aware that Petey leaned on his cue and whispered, and Petey looked like a hustler who had been hustled. He whiffed another shot. The logger watched in cynical disbelief, because Petey does not shank easy shots unless he's hustling.

"Gotcha," the logger said, "or at least I gotcha if I don't screw up."

"Run 'em out," Petey told him about the game. "That cop . . . ," and Petey nearly strangled on the words, "that cop is gonna be back. That cop saw something interesting."

"As long as it wasn't my hot chainsaw," the logger said. "This is the last time I do business with teenagers. They ain't discreet."

"He seen the bartender," Petey said in a tentative way, like he wondered if he could trust the logger.

"Chantrell's been busted before," the logger said, "it's not like he's a virgin."

Petey shut up, because he wasn't talking about Chantrell, and the idea of virgins makes him break out in hives.

"Maybe," Petey said and changed the subject, "this wind will put that car to the bottom of the ditch. Maybe it will clean the whole shoreline."

"Cars weigh a helluva lot," the logger said, his voice a little tense because he was in the middle of a run.

"They don't weigh much under water," Petey said. "The water lifts 'em, sort of."

Bertha listened in a half-hearted way, being not-a-little distracted. Bertha generally thinks honesty is the best policy when dealing with yourself, so figured she must be lonesome. The first fine-looking man who came along, and who smiled at her . . . and she fell for it. She acted as innocent and dumb as Annie. She told herself, sure as the wind blew, if that cop came back wearing work clothes she'd forget he was a cop. She would not lie to herself and say she felt a little too warm just because of a warm evening.

"And if the shoreline gets cleaned," Petey said, "some problems around here might get cleaned up too." He glanced toward Sugar Bear who sat in the center of the room like a mountain of sadness.

"He sure is takin' it good," the logger said, and his voice filled with admiration. "Sugar Bear just sat there and faced that cop down. He didn't run away, or nothin'."

The Dead Guy Disappears

It wasn't twenty-four hours before news of Sugar Bear's standoff with the cop spread along the Canal. The story started with the simple mistake that Sugar Bear had the moxie to face down a cop. By the time the story hit Rough and Randy, it bloomed into a titanic struggle between a giant cop and a giant blacksmith. Accusations were said to have passed back and forth. Blows were struck. Sugar Bear prevailed, but now had a big price on his head. Guys at Rough and Randy took pride in loudly claiming they would not turn a buddy in, even for a million bucks, but some looked sneaky when they said it. By the time the story was twenty-four hours old, it claimed the Canal was about to be over-run by a task force composed of National Guard, Marine MPs, and every state cop west of the Cascade Mountains.

As the story spread south it grew more sophisticated. Storytellers know the bartender at China Bay. That bartender can spot a snow job faster than Jubal Jim can spot a barroom sausage. The story claimed Sugar Bear had something on the cop, or the cop and Sugar Bear exchanged looks that said they were in cahoots. Maybe (the story said) the cop shacked up with a rich lady from the development, a lady whose husband spent time doing business in far places. The story figured the cop had enough evidence to hang Sugar Bear, but Sugar Bear had so much evidence the cop could not make a move. This story went for quiet drama. Rough and Randy adores John Wayne. China Bay discusses *Casablanca*.

Meanwhile, the dry wind blew. Weather forecasters on TV puzzled over a high pressure zone camped above the Canal, while on either side of the Canal rain pizzled in typical northwest manner. As dry wind blew, needles on firs browned and dropped. Chop on the Canal rose, became waves, and churned against the shores. The entire Puget Sound area between Olympic Mountains and the Cascades range was once covered by a mile-thick sheet of ice. The Canal is a giant trench plowed over millions of years by three separate glaciations. It's shallow near the shore, then plunges to deep, deep water. Wave action against the shore moves debris. Banks and shores are glacial moraine and will collapse with little more than a whim. People build houses near the shore, but not too near.

Above the shores stand third growth trees, or blackberry bushes, or, sometimes, nothing. There are stretches of rock shingle where even a cactus would feel deprived. It is along these shingles that cars usually go in. It was along one of these shingles that Sugar Bear dunked the dead guy. And, it was to this place that Sugar Bear, on late nights, visited. He came rain or shine, calm or raging storm.

Darkness covered the forest as Sugar Bear left his small house and drifted along a familiar path. He carried a flashlight. Wind swept the sky of clouds. Up high, wind hollered and yelled, blowing even harder than on the surface. Sugar Bear's hair and beard and mustache blew all curly, sometimes in his eyes. Sugar Bear told himself he had seen some wind in his day, and, telling himself that, felt experienced and old.

And it is true he was older than Annie, but younger than a fisherman who also sometimes strolled through dark hours. The fisherman wended his solitary way because he was a man who thought too much, although folks claimed that what he thought wasn't worth the time it took to think it. The fisherman occasionally encountered Sugar Bear. Sometimes they walked together, silent, each engaged with matters he did not care to discuss.

At other times, Sugar Bear, or the fisherman, might encounter Jubal Jim Johnson whose specialty is to run all night. Except for those three, and for whatever it was that made the road turn ugly, night seemed untouched except for the pounce of owls, the squeak of doomed mice, the eternal wash, and shush; the liquidly speaking voice of the Canal.

On this night of brilliant moon when waves crashed against the shore, and wind sucked moisture from the forest like soda pop up a straw, Sugar Bear stood at the site of the dead guy in the dunked car. He believed himself alone, but was not. Annie crouched nearby. Annie was on her own errand, plus the fisherman walked somewhere in the neighborhood.

There being no one around to talk to, or at least no one Sugar Bear knew about, it seemed natural to talk to the dead guy; since, by then, Sugar Bear was sick of talking to himself.

"All this had to happen," Sugar Bear explained toward the water. "There's stuff that's gonna happen no matter what anybody does, and this was some of that stuff. That don't mean it's right." His voice, which after this much time should have been steady, trembled with grief.

"When I was a kid," Sugar Bear explained to the Canal, or the dead guy, or maybe to the wind that snatched his tired words, his sad words, and blew them over the forest and out to sea, "I seen some bad stuff. Then I grew up and there was more bad stuff."

On the Canal, a running-light, red-right-returning, showed a fishing boat beating its wet way home. Overhead, stars shone so clear it seemed they might start to click, and movement among the stars showed a satellite that no doubt broadcast weather, or TV pictures of clowns in dressy paint, dancing before trained poodles in a cosmic circus.

"So maybe you saw bad stuff, too," Sugar Bear said to the dead guy. "Only how come you acted one way and I acted the other? And, now look at the mess."

Water boiled at Sugar Bear's feet, and wind took tops off waves so the Canal lay like churned milk beneath the moon.

"There ain't no way to make this right," Sugar Bear said to the dead guy. "I can't alibi you. I can't alibi me. I don't like either one of us, you sonovabitch, but I'm sorry."

The fisherman, standing silent nearby, told himself he would-be-damn. He knew Sugar Bear took stuff too serious, but never believed Sugar Bear took it this serious. The fisherman figured he'd better make some noise.

"I said it before." The fisherman spoke casual as if they sat among folks at Beer and Bait. "This was gonna happen. The guy was a goner. If you blame yourself, it's like blaming yourself for earthquakes."

"I figured you might be out here tonight." Sugar Bear did not turn around. He kept watching the Canal. "It's one of them no-sleep deals, ain't it?"

"The souls of fish," the fisherman said. "On my conscience I got the souls of maybe a million fish. That includes some championship halibut."

Sugar Bear slumped. Starlight and moonlight lay so intense that shadows of trees ran blackly toward the water. Waves broke against the shingle. "I got a problem with you," Sugar Bear told the fisherman. "I never know when you're flipping b.s. and when you're actually talking."

"I got the same problem," the fisherman admitted, "but I think right now I'm talking." He stepped from shadows to stand beside

Sugar Bear. "I ain't never killed a fish, not even a dogfish or a shark, that wasn't more important than that guy."

"You can't compare."

"You can," the fisherman insisted. "A shark does what sharks do, because sharks don't know any better. They got no choice." The fisherman put his hand on Sugar Bear's shoulder. "Man, you've got to get past it. This is messing you up."

"If it don't rain real quick," Sugar Bear said, "we're going to lose the forest. I shouldn't of built the shop in the middle of all them trees."

"And you accuse me of b.s."

"It'll be a punishment, I reckon," Sugar Bear told him. "I'm not exactly changing the subject."

"Sure," the fisherman said. "In order to punish you, the whole damn forest will burn. That's getting pretty universal." The fisherman stepped toward the shoreline, looked into the surf, looked farther along the shoreline. "You got a bigger problem," he said quietly, "or else you got no problem at all. Bring that flashlight." He walked across the shingle and into a small stand of trees. Sugar Bear followed.

The car had either been washed or dragged sideways. It sat in surf a good forty yards from the original dunk site. Under starlight strong as beacons, the car sat like a small, steel stain in churning water. Its hood stood buried beneath surf, but its rear end rose above water level. The rear end looked like a clamp had twisted against the fenders until the trunk lid popped open. The trunk lid stood above the surf like a small imitation of the police crane, like a shore bird fishing.

"Let's hope that trunk is empty," the fisherman said, "because otherwise this job is running overtime." He worked his way through trees and small brush. The car trembled as surf crashed against its front end. Nothing, except the rear end, seemed bent or squashed.

"Flashlight," the fisherman said. He took it from Sugar Bear. "Empty," he said about the car's trunk. He ran the beam of light up and down the shore. Nothing tumbled in the surf, not log or flotsam or corpse.

"I'll be honest," the fisherman admitted, "this is scaring the living crap out of me."

"I think," Sugar Bear said, "I'm going home and wait until this plays out. I almost wish the sonovabitch was there, or maybe I don't." He stood quiet for a moment, watching boiling water, watching whitecaps and stars and moon. "You're a good friend," he said to the fisherman. "Better than I've got coming, probably."

"I keep feeling like somebody's watching us," the fisherman said. "Maybe that's why this is scary." He backed away, passed the flashlight to Sugar Bear, and made his way through brush and trees to the road. As he did, there was small movement among the trees where Annie still hid.

She crouched, not wanting to be seen, but wanting to help. As the two men stepped onto the road and parted company, Annie told herself everything was going to work out. Some part of her spell had meshed. The dead guy was gone.

She felt the wind move through trees, and felt, really felt, the starlight. Then she told herself not to get feeling too smart, because there was still plenty to worry about. Maybe she had done something dumb, because wind might cause the forest to burn. It seemed that work only caused more work, because now attention must be paid to knocking down wind and bringing rain. As she stepped onto the road, and headed for home, she shivered because of an unaccustomed feeling. She had the feeling that something or someone was watching.

Interlude—Jubal Jim
Smells Something Dreadful

Night holds the mountains like darkness is welded to rock. Night clasps roots of trees and rhododendron and blackberry, and the bug-running litter beneath fallen leaves. Night defeats a brilliant moon where shadows fall. Owl-light, as it fades to darkest dark, signals a time for night-creatures to scurry, glide, tramp, or scatter. It is time for hounds to run.

Jubal Jim Johnson, who, during the day could be taken for a goldbrick, oozes serpent-like from the porch of Beer and Bait. The Canal lies black as tunket behind him, and mountains stand bountiful and dark with smells. It's a smorgasbord for the nose out there, at least if one is a hound.

In light from neon, Jubal Jim looks like a black-saddled, but otherwise white apparition fading into the forest. His ordinarily smiley face with its little brown eye patches, and the blue ticking on his brisket, can't be seen. His eighty pound body stretches long, lithe, muscular, and he can run twenty miles in a night.

Hound sense being what it is, Jubal Jim makes do with half-a-hunt, for he has no hunter following. Jubal Jim can run a fox to ground, make a raccoon wish he was in Topeka, and tussle a bear in a manner that leaves both parties bloody and unsatisfied. If he had a hunter, or had a pack to run with, Jubal Jim would be a fulfilled hound. As it is, he has vague longings.

Of sin he is innocent because he doesn't know what it is; or gives a smidgen. In his doggish way he understands that men stand around pool tables and things go click. He understands that brown paper bags sometimes contain interesting things to eat. Dog-like, he knows some humans can be trusted, and some cannot, and he knows the bar smells of sweat and beer like he knows the back of his paw. In the field of crime Jubal Jim is innocent, although he once secretly peed behind the piano, possibly through a whim, or possibly because during winter months Bertha keeps the doors shut and forgets to let him out.

Of crimes of passion Jubal Jim has no knowledge. He obeys the laws of dogs when in the forest, and manages to sleep past the laws of men during daylight. In the forest he learns from doing things. It sounds like fun, for example, to tangle with an adolescent cougar, but the experience is such that you generally ignore the next one.

Of history, Jubal Jim is proud heir. His bloodline traces back to the time of the Phoenicians, or at least part of it does. His sire lived a vigorous life of twelve years, his dam lived thirteen. Jubal Jim, at age seven, already moves toward that passing show where, if there is a heaven, and if that heaven comes up to advance notices, all humans who are worthy will be allowed to rejoin their dogs.

Jubal Jim runs through a windy, moonstruck night in a place where humans have lived for twenty thousand years. He runs past an extinct Indian village covered by an ancient mudslide, from which, occasionally, appears a stone or ivory tool that Chantrell George scrounges and sells. Jubal Jim runs past sites of ancient massacres, slave-trading, bone-breaking, and lodge fires where echoes of dance and chant are long since washed into the soil by millenniums of rain. And who is to say, in those prehistoric days, whether bone-breaking did not amount to cultural amity?

As Jubal Jim follows his nose past scents of drying needles beneath firs, of mice, and shrews, and chipmunks (small bait, these, for the attentions of a hound), past the smell of a two-week-old bear trail, past the smell of a campfire extinguished two years previous, he passes down an avenue of smells as a human might walk an avenue of advertising signs and art.

A hound's nose is one of the exquisite instruments of creation. Relatives of Jubal Jim, the bloodhounds, can follow a week-old scent across a highway on which cars have been running. A hound's eyes can handle darkness better than a human's, but a hound's nose is as keen as the eyes of an owl.

And, as with humans in a city, a hound often runs on sensory overload. As humans come to a blessed state where ears no longer register sounds of sirens, so Jubal Jim's nose ignores unimportant smells. For deer poop he cares not at all, but will note the scat of weasel, martin, or wolverine. He will pick up the scent of humans, of the lingering smell of chainsaws, and the fresh smell of wood chips flung by saws. His nose discards the comforting salt-smell of the Canal as it flows on the strong night wind, although his nose picks up the smells of carrion along the shore where lies an occasional gull or seal whose luck went bad. If Jubal Jim were human he would say he had lived a long life, had seen it all, and what is more, smelled it all. Yet now, trotting beneath moonlight, he stops, attentive, ready for fight or flight. There is a new thing under the moon.

Stirring on the Canal, a hump moves languidly, then disappears in the milk-white froth of breaking water. Wind fades beneath a fading moon as clouds cloak the scene, and from the Canal comes an ancient smell, like the musty scent of two-thousand-year-old tombs, of camphorwood and olives.

The smell passes on the back of a dying wind, and the milk-froth begins to fade. Something Jubal Jim has never seen before—or has anyone else—begins slight movement. Jubal Jim watches a figure rise near the shore, a figure seemingly born of surf. The thing stands with the unsteadiness of a drunken man, and it vaguely resembles human form. The thing is pale as rapid-flying clouds that obscure the moon. Jubal Jim hesitates, tests the dying wind, the smells, and stands ready to bolt.

Stench flows ashore in a wave that would sicken gulls. Stench flows like rotten meat turned liquid, like dread odors from musty graves.

The thing staggers, makes movement toward the beach, then slowly sinks; gradually fading into depths like an empty beer can filling with water. Stench blows away into forest. The thing seems weak, not yet strong enough to walk the earth.

Jubal Jim sniffs the wind, noses out an approaching storm, and begins an easy trot toward home. Drivers in occasional cars see a white and black-saddled dog cruising the side of the road. None of the drivers recognize Jubal Jim, because all of the drivers are strangers. Perhaps there is a squalling of brakes as another car disappears beneath water, perhaps not; because when Jubal Jim turns his easy run into a full dash, water overfloods and slickens the road as a mighty rain hurls against forest and Canal.

Amid Rain, Chantrell Puzzles

Dawn woke beneath the pounding force of rain. Water beat on dry leaves, poured into the forest, and drained bare slopes. Rain pretended it was Biblical, a Noah-type flood, or punishment for sins committed in places like Indiana and Kansas. Rain danced an east-coast number on roofs accustomed to west-coast mist and drizzle. Little balls of dried moss, black as sorrow, turned green and washed into gutters. Water filled ditches, flooded the road, and formed major puddles in parking lots, school yards, ball fields, golf courses; as human rejoicing filled the land.

No more charming scene exists than that which happens in the Pacific Northwest when rain follows drought. While people in other places keep their children inside, we take the kids outdoors so everyone can sop it up. People are known to pack picnics, or wash their cars and dogs. A light rain is good, a medium rain is excellent, and a heavy rain—a real gully washer, flavors our world with colorful umbrellas.

Moods change. Aggravations caused by constant sun magically disappear. We shed purgatories of small responsibilities, of small sins, of unrequited lusts. All of these falter before joy smeared with optimism like fudge on a two-year-old.

And for those who love the forest, or for those who live by it, rain is a special dispensation. It is the enemy of fire. To the uninitiated, a forest fire is a grand show that takes out a few hundred or a few thousand acres. To the initiated, a forest fire spells destruction fearsome as bombs.

Chantrell George, who is next to worthless in the eyes of nearly everyone except his guardian angel, spent morning in the forest. Rain penetrated the thick cover of trees. Chantrell's hair hung wet and stringy about his shoulders. His feet soaked in dilapidated shoes, until he took the shoes and tied them to sling over his shoulder. He moved quickly, at least quickly for a man of visions. Chantrell knows that if you don't keep moving you catch a chill.

Mushrooms would not bloom until after dark, but mushrooms were not Chantrell's only reason for cruising beneath sweeping branches of cedar. In the forest, sometimes, his mind clears in the same way the Canal lies tranquil on a windless day. In the forest, sometimes, Chantrell George can nearly recall what it felt like to be straight; for, unlike some unfortunate others, Chantrell was not born a junkie.

A man of visions sees infinity in small things: the smile of a gopher, the scorn of a water faucet, the shifting patterns of light on the forest floor, or in artificial bait which also smiles; but with hooks. A man of visions sees things as they really are, and not the way they look to folks who are only high on booze or religion or business.

On some days Chantrell searched the forest looking for the flying hammer that killed the dead guy. Chantrell sought the hammer because he needed a witness. He clearly remembered how the hammer hopped around Sugar Bear's shop, then fled through a window. That the hammer had been a cartoon hammer, and one seen in a vision, did not spoil its reality. Chantrell would point out that life more often resembles cartoons, than cartoons resemble life.

He pressed his search because he wanted the hammer to testify. Early stories, after the dead guy became dead, passed up and down the Canal. Men worth admiring, because of their positive voices and positive opinions, had given Chantrell George credit for killing the dead guy. They did it because Chantrell seemed the most likely suspect. To people who think of themselves as normal, weird people appear capable of anything.

It had been a golden time, the first time in many years anyone paid attention to Chantrell. The glow of it mixed in his mind with a cold little spot of uncertainty. At first he was not sure he actually deserved credit. Since Sugar Bear did not want to talk, and since there was only one other person Chantrell trusted, he turned to that person: his bike.

As he wheeled the bike along the road, conversations turned to arguments, then turned back, and arguments were often resolved. So were doubts.

"Did I do something wrong?" he asked the bike. "I maybe did something bad."

"I kinda doubt it," the bicycle told him. "The way guys talk, I reckon you're a hero."

"The hammer actually did it," Chantrell explained. "You weren't there. You were parked outside."

"Don't tell anybody," the bicycle advised. "That hammer don't want any credit."

As the story shifted back and forth, from China Bay, to Beer and Bait, to Rough and Randy, it gradually became known that Sugar Bear was the man behind the tragedy. People stopped talking about Chantrell. Chantrell knew the story was wrong, and he felt hurt. He experienced moments when he resented Sugar Bear.

"That's the way it goes," the bicycle explained. "A guy gets blamed for everything when bad stuff happens. Then he does something big, and crooks rush in to claim the credit."

"It's the way it goes," Chantrell agreed. "A guy don't hardly know what to do."

"Get high," the bicycle kindly advised. "That's always worked before."

Chantrell's summer progressed with visits to the hiding places of mushrooms, with a little pick-up work at Beer and Bait, and with helping Sugar Bear by selling off his scrap metal. On two occasions Chantrell, who, out of a keen sense of self preservation never poaches items locally, chanced on tourist cars containing orphan goods; radios, cameras, golf clubs. Adoptions took place. He peddled the adoptees to guys at Rough and Randy. Summer spread its wealth around him, and life was splendid.

Then August arrived. Tourists became testy and unreliable. Traffic backed up. The forest dried. The world turned dreary as nighttime music at Beer and Bait. Without many funds, it became harder and harder to score a decent high. Then a cop showed up at Beer and Bait, and life was hell.

"It all changes because of rain," he told his bicycle, as he hid it among trees. "This day is gonna work."

"Luck always turns," the bicycle assured him. "You got to ride out a bad streak, and you really got to ride a good one." The bicycle did not explain what it meant.

Chantrell hesitated before walking in the forest. As rain penetrated the thick cover of leaves and needles, he could see glimpses of the road. Traffic was not backing up, not yet. Something went on, though. Chantrell peered through brush.

It looked like more bad driving. The back end of a car showed itself, with the trunk lid sprung and the hood buried beneath water. Chantrell could not remember where he had seen the car, but knew he had.

A couple of cop cars parked alongside the road, plus an unmarked car, plus three cops. One of the cops looked familiar, and Chantrell shivered. It was the cop who drank lemonade at Beer and Bait. The three cops wore rain slickers and hats. They looked discouraged, like guys who came to work, found that overnight somebody trashed their job; like guys who have to do a cleanup before they can even get back to work. Rain pounded. Nobody was going to hook that car out until the rain shunted off a little. Nobody could even move the crane.

Chantrell moaned. Across the fecund field of his inner vision danced a chorus line of policemen holding giant mushrooms before them like balloons of bubble dancers. The police danced on the dark waters of the Canal, and as their feet hit, little splashes flicked forward wetting the tip of Chantrell's nose. The nose grew and became two noses, one smiling, and one with teeth. . . .

"Not here," the bicycle advised. "Strictly speaking, you ain't high and there ain't no evidence. Get a grip."

"You got it," Chantrell moaned. "Uh-huh. It figures. Yep. On the other hand . . ." He forced himself to pay attention, vaguely aware of rain pounding on the forest. He watched the cops.

The tallest cop looked kind of stoned, or his mind was somewhere else. He got in the unmarked car. He just sat there, maybe listening to cop radio, or maybe just cussing and wishing he could bust somebody.

As Chantrell faded into the forest, the cop started the car, turned it around, and headed back in the direction of Beer and Bait.

Petey Plays Cupid

Those happy folk who have never owned a bar may feel surprised to learn that reliable and honest bartenders are harder to find than a cat's belly-button. Reliable bartenders are one of the world's diminishing resources, a valuable commodity, and Bertha would hire one in an instant if she could afford it. As it is, Bertha opens early, stays late, and exhibits the Norwegian's ability to work herself to death. Bertha needs a man to help, and no one on the Canal would deny that, especially Bertha.

Most mornings at Beer and Bait remain quiet. The joint opens at eleven. This early in the day the parking lot usually holds a couple of cars or pickups, guys taking a break for coffee, or sport fisherman after frozen herring. On most mornings Bertha has plenty of time to sweep floors, brush down pool tables, and restock coolers. On some mornings, though, routine shatters; a water heater busts, or half of the house cues need new tips, or a cop drags in out of the rain.

When Petey pulled onto the water-logged parking lot at Beer and Bait, a cold chill grabbed the back of his neck, while hot fury entered his heart. The cop was back. The cop that checked out Bertha, and who Petey knew was going to run a scam on Bertha, was, right now, inside making all kind of important noises. Petey could feel it happening.

He sat in his old Plymouth and looked over the parking lot. An unmarked cop car sat beside a red wrecker, all lights and hook, but towing a flat bed trailer. The kid who hauled wrecks was also inside. If the kid showed up it meant a car had dunked. By now, maybe two or three had dunked.

A deep sigh came from the back seat. Jubal Jim lay snugged up, his nose propped on an armrest. His wet fur placed a comforting but doggy smell in the steamy car. As rain pounded on puddles in the parking lot, and danced on the hood of the Plymouth, Petey felt grateful for the tow-truck kid. The kid had a sense of humor. He would help keep the cop humble.

Sitting beside the cop car and the wrecker, two local cars showed a guy who owned a grocery, and a guy who sold insurance were inside tanking up on coffee. Petey cussed, and tried to decide whether to go in, or turn around and go home. He told himself he needed a cop like he needed his head drilled for more nostrils.

Then he told himself he'd better go in. Bertha was smart, but Bertha did not have much experience with cops. In Petey's world experience counted. A slick cop could run the best hustle in the world if that cop wanted to talk you out of something. A slick cop would tell you somebody else's life story, pretending the story was his own. He'd seem like such a good guy that innocent people confessed to stuff so they could also sound like good guys.

Still, Petey sat. Rain turned the Canal into a surface every bit as pebbled as sharkskin, and gray light lay over the water so close it was hard to tell where air ended and water began. He told himself that, if he went in there with hatred in his heart and fury in his gut, something real, real wrong would happen. He sat listening to rain, to Jubal Jim's light snoring, and the sound of a truck engine somewhere behind him. Petey reached for the calmness of the hustler, the patience a guy needs to drop a half dozen games while waiting for the right opening.

A knock sounded on the window of the passenger side, the door opened, and Sugar Bear edged into the car. Sugar Bear's hair hung matted and straight. He wore ratty old rain gear, and he dripped.

"Feel free," Petey said. "The seat covers are plastic."

"Makes a guy feel better." Sugar Bear's voice sounded hoarse as the flu. He looked at the unmarked car. "I mean the rain, not mister cop." Then he sort of giggled as Jubal Jim sat up, looked around, and licked Sugar Bear behind the ear.

"If I was you," Petey told him, "I'd bail out of here and take a vacation. If you need a beer get one at China Bay. Even with all that hair you got a guilty look."

"This dog ain't made for serious conversation." Sugar Bear reached back over his shoulder to rub Jubal Jim's ears. "I'm feeling scary. That guy's car washed ashore."

"For hellssake . . . " Petey drummed his fingers against the steering wheel. "Lay off," he said to Jubal Jim, but said it quiet. Jubal Jim stretched, yawned, lay down and once more began to snooze. Rain pounded puddles. "When did this happen?"

"Last night. Late."

"And you did what?" Petey sounded like he spoke to someone hopelessly retarded. "That's a different kind of cop in there."

"Nothing to do," Sugar Bear told him, and said it sad. "The body ain't in the trunk. Trunk's sprung open. Car is mangled like those others."

"At least," Petey said in disgust, "it's raining."

"That's supposed to mean something?"

"You've seen what things look like after a couple of months in the water. That guy is mush, if crabs and fish have even left mush. Maybe cops can connect him to the car, but not to you."

"I dunno," Sugar Bear said. "I can't quite get wrapped around the idea of getting away with it. If I turn myself in and explain what happened. . . ."

"You ain't never bin in jail," Petey told him. "Did you ever go to jail you'd sing different."

"Have you ever?"

"Assault," Petey told him. "I bopped a guy with a pool cue. About to do it again." He grinned. "Get out of here. Take Annie on a trip. Barring that, go to Olympia and get your ashes hauled. They got nice hookers when the legislature sits." Petey figured he gave good advice, and gave it easily. For some things, like giving advice, experience can be a hindrance.

"I'm trying to get straight on this," Sugar Bear said. "What I did is wrong."

"If you say so."

"It's serious," Sugar Bear said.

"I agree," Petey told him. "It's wrong and it's serious. So what?" He looked at the unmarked car. Jubal Jim gave a little snore. Rain increased, pounding, driving, obscuring the windshield so the cop car looked vague and fuzzy. If raindrops are the tears of heaven, then heaven had a case of blue miseries. "You're a guy who wanders," Petey said. "You stay around here, and you'll wander right into that cop's lockup."

"Seems like there's a price on everything," Sugar Bear said. "I might go along for a while, but sooner or later it'll cost."

"So does going to jail," Petey advised. Then he thought about it. "A big guy like you could probably run the whole damn prison, up until you got stabbed." He again drummed fingers on the steering wheel. "Nope," he said, "do your time outside the walls." He turned to Jubal Jim. "That's the way they talk in Chicago."

Jubal Jim snored. Rain pounded. Sugar Bear sat solid as a lug nut. Petey fretted about what went on in Beer and Bait. He told himself he was too smart to smack a cop, but something better happen.

Sugar Bear sounded pensive, but a little bit hopeful. He sniffed, rubbed his forehead, "I think I'm coming down with something. You really think I should get out of town?"

"Either that, or get invisible. Go with Annie, or without."

"Without," Sugar Bear said quickly. "She's not part of this. The cops would think she was in on it." He searched around in his beard, found his nose, rubbed it, then gave a little sneeze. "Olympia," he said. "I know a place to crash. I'll check into China Bay from time to time. Let me know what happens, willya?" He cracked open the door, slid into the rain, and walked toward his truck. Through misted windows he looked like a real bear hulking through gray light. Petey sighed, thinking of his own problems and only resenting Sugar Bear a little. Petey once more reached for his hustler's calm. Jubal Jim, sensing something joyful, gave a happy little woof.

A knock sounded on the passenger side. The door opened and Annie stepped from the driving rain and snugged into the seat. Annie wasn't even mildly damp, and her long hair gleamed and smelled pretty. Jubal Jim bounced like a pup. Petey told himself he sat in Grand Central Station, or was attending somebody's old home week, or maybe a murderer's convention.

"You just missed Sugar Bear," he told Annie.

"I know." Annie turned around in the seat, leaned over the back, and rubbed Jubal Jim's nose against her nose. There seemed to be some communication. Jubal Jim quieted, wagged his tail, controlled his impulses.

"Down to Olympia," Petey told her. "Down to China Bay. That car washed up."

"I know about the car." Annie's voice sounded like she tried to stay neutral. "The dead guy's gone. They'll never find him. Probably."

"I think so too," Petey told her. "That don't seem to be the problem. The problem is we've got a guy who takes this too hard, and a cop who'll spot him." He looked at Annie. and responded to her fear. Her lips trembled. "If it was me," he told her, "I don't know how I'd feel. Not good, probably, but not that damn bad."

"I can help him. That's one thing I know." Annie pursed her lips, making decisions, wondering, maybe, if she could trust Petey. "Nobody except Bertha knows this. But, I like Sugar Bear a lot. A whole lot."

"This is getting comical," Petey told her. "Sugar Bear is driving every guy he knows completely nuts because he's sweating over you. He's can't propose for fear he gets busted. You're both living in a sitcom."

Her eyes widened. Her lips trembled. She touched her hair, held her fingers to her mouth, took three quick breaths. "I got to go to him. Got to do it now."

Jubal Jim, responding to all the action, gave three quick woofs.

"I gotta catch a ride," Annie said. "Nope. I got to go home and pack some stuff. Nope. I gotta catch a ride."

"Go home and pack," Petey told her. "You'll have to sooner or later."

"Later," Annie said. "I gotta catch a ride." She reached to touch Petey's hand. "You're such a good guy. You really, really are."

Petey told himself that when someone called him a "good guy" the world was warped. "You can't catch a ride from me," he told her. "I got a little problem of my own. Go on inside."

"That's the trick," Annie told him. "There's always someone driving south. It's the quickest way." She opened the car door, whistled, and Jubal Jim jumped across the back of the seat and into the rain. Petey watched them head for Beer and Bait. Petey felt about ready to follow. He did not have his hustler's calm in place, but Annie might cause enough stir that he could get by without slugging a cop. He reached for the door handle, then paused. From the passenger's side, there came another knock on the door.

The Cop and the Hustler

The fleet was in. A fisherman, wearing worn rain gear, opened the door. He brushed water before climbing into the Plymouth. This fisherman was either deep in thought, or else needed sleep. His hair looked a rat's nest, his eyes swollen. He sat like a man who tries to stay on top of things after having spent one of those nights a guy tries to forget.

"You're looking good," Petey told him. "Who was she? Or is it truck problems?"

The fisherman looked injured. "My stuff always runs," he told Petey. "Keep the oil changed regular. Tune 'em up."

"You got no woman problem. You got no truck problem. You got no problem." Petey, in spite of wanting to get into Beer and Bait, told himself this day looked sort of interesting.

"I bin up all night thinking," the fisherman said. "It keeps a guy occupied." The fisherman looked across the lot. "Cops," he said sadly. "They don't have enough to do. It makes them nosy." His voice became apologetic. "Maybe that's not true. Maybe they just notice different things."

"You bin thinking," Petey said. "Am I supposed to be surprised?"

"The dead guy's car washed ashore."

"I know about it," Petey told him. "I talked to Sugar Bear."

"Annie just went inside Beer and Bait," the fisherman reflected. "Neither of you said anything to Annie. Right?"

"She already knew."

The fisherman sat silent as a frozen fillet while studying. "Sugar Bear told her?"

"Nope."

"We were not alone," the fisherman murmured. "Likely, very likely, that's the reason I felt someone was watching."

"You'd better slow down," Petey told him. "You're talking to yourself."

"Sugar Bear went to the beach. I followed. We saw the car, then came away. It felt like someone was watching. Then it turns out Annie already knows, so Annie had to have been watching. It don't figure she was watching me." The fisherman sighed, a man grieving, a man who had just seen the last bright tailfeather of hope fly over the horizon. "I guess she really is nuts about him," the fisherman said, his voice sad, perplexed, a little hostile. "Of course, Sugar Bear's a sweet guy, and Annie could do worse." The fisherman drooped like a bucket of stale bait. "She could do a good bit better." He said this in a whisper, but with conviction.

A beat-up International pickup turned from the road and splashed across the parking lot. Rust mingled with pale blue paint, and orange marker buoys tangled among crab pots. The guy parked, got out, and hiked into Beer and Bait with the reluctant step of a drinker who knows he's getting a too-early start on the day.

"There will never be a second American Revolution," the fisherman mused, "until we have a beer shortage."

"We got a cop," Petey said. "I got to go inside." He picked up his cue case, then reconsidered. "So Sugar Bear went to the beach. What'n hell was he doing on the beach?"

"The dead guy . . . I'm not happy with the way the world runs," the fisherman said. "That dead guy causes as much trouble now as when he was breathing." The fisherman looked toward the Canal, looked at rain, dropped his gaze to his hands. The hands showed long scars from hotly running lines, from hooks that know a life of their own; and the hands held calluses, thick and stubby nails, blunt from labor. "That dead guy shouldn't have been let to put foot to ground, and especially not around here. We ain't geared for this."

"What's the problem? The guy wasn't worth a popcorn poot."

"Only two guys don't believe that," the fisherman told him. "The guy who's dead and the guy who killed him. We can say Sugar Bear did just right, and Sugar Bear did do just right, but how would we feel if it were us?"

"Not so hot, I'm guessing." Petey turned the notion over in his mind. "Maybe I'm guessing wrong. I'd feel great." He thought some more. "I see what you mean."

"This is gonna end ugly," the fisherman mourned. "I don't know why bad guys always win." He stretched, looked toward the Canal. "Of course, you can't exactly say being dead is winning."

"Annie wants a ride south," Petey said. "Sugar Bear is holing up someplace near China Bay."

"This is getting morbid," the fisherman said. "I'll be the guy who gets to deliver her to China Bay. It's pre-frigging-destined. People act stage plays about stuff like this."

He opened the car door and edged out to stand with bowed head in the rain. His lips moved, talking to himself, then did an ounce or two of cussing. "Let's do it." He walked toward Beer and Bait. Petey followed. Neither man was prepared for one more situation, but extra situations have a way of happening.

•

Inside, and back before Annie and Jubal Jim showed up, two small groups sat at opposite ends of the bar pretending to ignore each other. Two local business guys, plus the local drinker, sat at the end farthest the door. The cop and the tow-truck kid sat at the end near the door. Bertha, flustered by the early action, and a little breathless because of the return of the cop, hovered behind the bar and midway between groups. The cop wore a rain slicker he unzipped but did not remove. The slicker hid his cop suit. Bertha wore Scandinavian stuff, skirt and blouse modest as church, and well-pressed as a politician's morals. Bertha actually looked kind of starchy. It seemed to impress the cop.

The kid fooled with a cup of coffee, had thoughts about the pool tables, decided to wait further developments. Not much seemed likely to happen for the kid until the crane got a car snaked out.

Bertha fussed with her hair. She told herself the cop was there to see her and that was good. All she usually got was a collection of stiffs. Then, with her luck, an interesting man finally came along, and the stiffs got in the way.

What everyone else in the bar saw was a tall blond woman and a tall blond cop, who, should anyone think about it further, could, with luck, get harmonic. They could do things that would increase the population. There are already more Norwegians in America than in Norway. This pair could keep the trend alive.

Then Annie and Jubal Jim stepped through the doorway, Jubal Jim in a state of happy relaxation, Annie in a tiz. Jubal Jim headed for a nap beneath a pool table. Annie headed for Bertha.

The tow-truck kid, still young enough to be in that tempestuous stage of life, took one look at Annie and figured that if the good Lord had created anything better, the good Lord was keeping it for Himself. The kid blushed, squared his shoulders, breathed about three reams of bad song lyrics under his breath, and fell tonsils over toenails in love.

By the time Petey and the fisherman arrived, Annie stood leaning over the bar whispering to Bertha. Because it's a wide bar, and because Annie leaned close, her bottom became an item of interest to six pairs of men's eyes, while the cop's eyes remained with Bertha. This early in the day only half of the beer signs were lighted. Twirly glow in the gray morning struggled to make a point that, under these conditions, the best that could be expected was an exercise in pastels.

Annie wore a greeny-bluey dress designed to evoke lust in men named Sugar Bear, but there was a certain amount of spill-over. The tow-truck kid saw other guys watching and became possessive. The business jocks and the drinker rubbed their noses, tugged at ear lobes, looked thoughtful, and sucked in their guts.

Annie, meanwhile, experienced throes of anxiety. She whispered to Bertha, bounced in a way she really didn't mean, and completely ignored the guys.

"She needs a ride," Bertha said to the bar in general. "Are any of you deadbeats driving south?"

"Me," the fisherman mourned, and stepped up to the bar beside Annie.

"Me," the tow-truck kid said. "All the way to Texas if that's what it takes." Then the kid turned red. Ah, youth.

"Actually you're not," the cop said quietly to the kid. "What you're actually going to do is load a wreck." The cop's voice sounded firm, but not unkind. He seemed about to chuckle.

The kid got redder, that being a correct response for youth when made a fool of in front of a girl.

"Are you my boss?" the kid said. "You're not my boss."

Attention shifted from Annie to the kid. It takes passion, or stupidity, or reckless abandonment of reason, to sass a cop. The kid tried to turn even redder, but was already red as his truck. He made movement to stand, then realized standing up might be pushing his luck. He wiggled on the bar stool.

"Not exactly your boss," the cop said, "but in a manner of speaking, yep. I'm a friend of your boss. Your boss is in the towing business. I got a couple of cars need towing." This time he actually smiled. He held his hand up like he stopped a line of children at a crosswalk. He turned to the rest of the bar. "You should watch him with that towing gear," he said about the kid. "I've never seen a man handle a tow truck any slicker, and I've seen a lot of tows."

The kid sat before his coffee, gulped, but not the coffee. The cop had him cut-from-under. Somehow the cop made the kid into a big hero while the kid was making himself into a hind end. The kid's face looked like it was going to turn inside-out as he tried to figure what in the rainy world had happened.

"Thanks anyway," Annie said to the kid. "I already got a ride." She touched the fisherman's hand. "Could we drop by my place for a couple minutes?"

"Sure," he told Annie. He followed her toward the door, Annie still in a tiz, the fisherman slumping. ". . . talk about getting your hull scraped," the fisherman murmured to himself, or possibly to the Fates.

"Eight-ball," Petey said to the kid, and actually said it kind. Even Petey wondered, probably, why he tried to take the kid off the hook. As the kid walked to the table Petey whispered, "Don't let it getcha down. She's already spoken for."

That just messed the kid up worse. Beyond the windows, while the kid tried to decide whether to fight or play pool, rain pounded on the Canal and water humped. Something out there moved slow, like it was tired, or lazy, or just waking up. The kid didn't see it, the cop didn't see it, and Petey had other things on his mind. The cop kept busy looking at Bertha.

Petey, who is copwise, understood that a pool game amounts to invisibility. No one pays attention to pool players, although sometimes people pay attention to the games. If Petey shot pool, and kept his hustle quiet, he could keep eye and ear on the cop without being noticed.

"Your boss is a pal of mine." The kid mimicked the cop, but in a whisper. The kid tested the house cues. "Talk about police corruption. . . ." He found a cue that suited. "Play for a buck," he said under his breath. The kid knew Petey had him out-classed. The kid seemed suicidal. On the other hand, the kid had to redeem his manly self.

Word passes fast up and down the Canal. On the evening of that same day, and while he was almost sober at China Bay, the fisherman heard a story about Petey. The story claimed the tow-truck kid hustled a hustler. The kid rode in like the mythical hero Parsifal, slaying dragons with a cue stick that glowed with ancient charms, while mystery maidens scattered begonias at his feet . . . something like that.

At any rate, the story said, the kid hustled Petey for a young fortune. The kid, the story claimed, would use the money to start his own towing business. It was a good story, maybe a noble story, and possibly held Freudian symbols.

The fisherman had enough experience with Canal stories to know that somewhere in the bull lay a small seed of truth. By the time the story began to circulate with complete abandon, and grow, the fisherman had his own problems. Later, though, he wished he'd been around to see the show.

Because that morning, with rain pounding on the Canal and bar-light glowing, the kid got on a roll. Petey paid attention to the cop, and not much attention to his game. His hustler's calm slipped toward quiet agitation. He dropped a game, dropped another. The kid, with an attention span somewhat better than a tree squirrel's, sensed an opportunity. The kid upped the ante. In the excitement of the chase the kid forgot trucks, beautiful women, and bossy cops. By the time the kid hustled Petey for a hundred bucks, the story started taking form. When that much money changes hands before noon, people talk.

All during the hustle the cop did his quiet best to impress Bertha. The cop exhibited charity, because he knew betting went on, and that took money away from the state gambling commission. The cop sipped coffee, ignored the pool game, and stayed friendly.

This cop was no social giant, but Bertha knew working men. If you want a working man to spill don't ask about his line of work. Ask about his current job. Before he gets done cussing, he'll tell you about his line of work; and the time, when as a kid, his uncle took him fishing. He'll tell about his big project— restoring a '53 Pontiac, or redesigning his front porch. If he is the lower class of working man, he'll sink to the level of bankers, professors, and surgeons by suggesting he is good in the sack.

"You said a 'couple of cars'." Bertha wiped the bar in front of the cop, although the bar didn't need it. Bertha often keeps control by acting official. That, together with modest clothes, stops most guys from messing up. She tried a sad smile and succeeded. "Nothing like this ever happened before. How many is it?"

"Nine. Maybe ten." The cop looked toward the Canal where rain raised sheets of mist. "Another one just came ashore. It don't look fresh. Plus, it looks like someone went in last night." The cop sounded unhappy. "You'd think you'd get used to it. Some guys do. Other guys look for better work." Then, realizing he was confidential and uncoplike, "We thought we had this job buttoned up. Then one washes in and another goes down."

"People are starting to wonder," Bertha said, and spoke the truth.

"Worst stretch of road in the state," the cop told her. "Not a fast road. It's technically not unusual. Except, it's making a name for itself."

"Folks are scared." Bertha once more spoke the truth.

"So far it's a problem for the state investigative unit," the cop said. "Of course, the officer on the scene has some responsibility. More than that I'd hate to say." He looked toward the Canal. "Some things you can't know," he said, and it seemed almost like he talked only to himself. "That night road is different . . . sometimes you can find out." By now he definitely talked to himself, and Bertha waited in reluctant admiration. This cop was turning out to be a thoughtful guy; almost unheard of in a cop. Bertha felt warmth rising in her cheeks and elsewhere; this from a woman, who, if quizzed, would say that anyone who experienced racing hormones before eight P.M. was sicko.

"The coroner handles the hard part." The cop looked at the rain. "You'd think it would stop. It never rains this heavy this long."

No one, except Annie, believes Annie has a blessed thing to do with weather. Still, at the time Annie was preoccupied. She would not think to turn off the faucet. Of course, nobody believes Annie has anything to do with causing sun or rain.

"You must put in quite a few hours," the cop said to Bertha. "Hard work."

"It keeps a girl busy." Bertha smiled what she hoped was a brave smile. She felt a little shiver, because Bertha can smell a lead-in a mile off.

"Your bartender comes on nights?"

Bertha told herself that this—this—this was just exactly what she deserved for not having decent help. The cop wanted to know if she was free, evenings. The cop wanted to take her to dinner, or a show. The cop looked serious.

Bertha, being poor at lying, and knowing it, decided to stick with the truth. "Know of anyone honest? I use pick-up help, or none."

"I get around." The cop sounded disappointed. "Could be I'll run across somebody."

"Do it quick," Bertha said, then blushed. When a Norwegian blushes the room sort of lights up. Bertha had enough sense to look away, shy; and that is about as promiscuous as Norwegians get. "I'm grounded," Bertha admitted. "It's a pretty good business, though. The problem with running a bar is you sometimes put up with drunks."

"That's a common police complaint." The cop chuckled. "I had one the other day who tried to trade a DWI for the name of a murderer." The cop's voice sounded not unkindly. "You hear all sorts of stories. . . ." He was interrupted as a cueball hopped a rail, bounced high in the air, then hit the floor and rolled quite a-ways. Jubal Jim gave a yip from beneath the pool table, and dashed to Petey for comfort. Petey stood, red as a tow truck, embarrassed down to his pool-player socks. Hustlers do not hop pool balls. . . unless, a'course, they want to. The shame of it.

"That'll be a buck," Bertha said, her tone merciless. Hopped pool balls at Beer and Bait are costly. The buck goes in a tin can. When somebody makes the eight ball on the break, he gets what's in the can.

Petey patted Jubal Jim, fished a dollar from his shirt pocket. He walked to the bar, still blushing. "Don't believe everything you hear," he whispered to the cop, but the whisper was so loud everyone in the bar took notes. For some reason, maybe the hopped cueball, Petey looked guilty enough to hang. He kept his eyes downcast. When he raised his head he looked shifty.

"There's a problem on the road," the cop told him. "Something has changed with the sight-distance, or the grade. The slide-rule boys can figure it." The cop pretended Petey acted normal, but the cop obviously took notes. "There's another problem."

"Oh, yes sir." Petey backed away, made a movement like he would return to the pool table, then thought better about turning his back on a cop. He stood, looking sort of hangdog. Bertha smacked the bar with a damp bar rag, and Bertha was disgusted.

"Something strange happens when cars hit the water, and that's why people talk about murder." The cop sounded real positive, which meant he felt confused as everyone else.

"I got it figured out about the cars," the beer guy said from the other end of the bar. "The Navy's got a sub fitted with grapples. The CIA forces stuff into the water so the Navy can practice grappling." The guy gave a polite hiccup.

"You'd better have another," Bertha advised. "You sound like a man who's dangerous when he's sober."

"There's something mechanical down there," the cop admitted. "It must be like a clamp or a grapnel." The cop smiled. "Does the CIA have that much imagination?" He stood, and motioned to the tow-truck kid. "Rain or not, we've got to give it a try." To the beer guy he said, "If you come up with something more let me know." He checked Petey out, turned to Bertha and smiled, this time sort of shy.

"Don't make yourself too scarce," Bertha said, while wondering if she was nuts. She watched the cop leave, then turned to Petey, gave a little sniff and got busy restocking a beer case.

"In case I ever have to punch him," Petey said apologetically, "I want a sucker punch. Right now he thinks he's got me running." Petey absent-mindedly set up a four-ball combination and tapped it home.

"I believe it," Bertha said. "Why wouldn't I believe it?" Her voice held a small edge of contempt, and Bertha was not happy.

"You're runnin' behind on the work," Petey said. "I'll give you a hand."

"I can take care of my own," Bertha told him, and Bertha sounded colder than ice cubes.

A story circulated along the Canal. By the time the fisherman, who was practically sober, heard it while sitting at China Bay that same evening; the story said Petey not only lost a fortune, but Bertha kicked him out. The story also said some traitor tried to sell out Sugar Bear in exchange for a free pass on a charge of driving while under the influence. There's always a slight germ of truth in every Canal story.

Happenings at China Bay

Bar light at Lee's China Bay Taverna is less twirly than at Beer and Bait, and, although goldfish swim happily in their tank, conversations rarely deal with fish. The bartender is allergic.

Subjects include Canal stories as well as opinions about the "nose" and "body" of varietal grocery wines. Talk often centers on the exact curve of the front fenders on '57 Dodge trucks, or wanders back to the good-old-days of revolution when people danced somewhat naked in the streets while throwing flowers at police. From that subject will surely rise observations about the indolence of today's youth, the immorality of teenagers, and tales of remembered passion in the back seats of Studebakers—which, as anyone who ever owned a Studebaker knows—is a damnable lie.

It is, in fact, a tough job to even begin to capture the atmosphere and thoughtful gravity of China Bay. However, a certain fisherman sits there, so there's no way out of it.

He arrived at China Bay after a thoroughly depressing drive alongside the Canal. Rain rumbled, sloshed, flooded. Annie, beside him, alternated between chirping optimism and downright gloom. She went from anticipatory giggles to low sighs, from chatter to silence; then back to chatter. The fisherman kept his hands ten-two on the steering wheel as the pickup seemed to float. He could not tell if there was more rain in the road or the shy. The road seemed puzzling the best way to persuade the truck into the Canal. The fisherman expressed vile opinions of rain gods, thunderbirds, low pressure systems, and whatever else might cruise the heavens.

Annie blushed, concentrated, and rain started to slacken. When the fisherman pulled in beside Sugar Bear's truck at China Bay, sunlight overflooded the landscape and steam rose from roads and roofs.

China Bay sat well attended in early afternoon. The parking lot displayed a concrete mixer, a delivery van, a pristine '53 Packard, three or four econo-boxes, a few pickups, the bartender's Jag, and a tanker truck from a dairy region. The silver trailer of the tanker truck carried the picture of a fulfilled cow.

"The milk run," the fisherman muttered to no one in particular. "Next it will be jam and peanut butter. The world is headed for perdition, I promise you." He watched as Annie, three times more lovely than ever, hopped from his truck. She fussed at her hair, moistened her lips, and stood poised and impatient. The forlorn fisherman climbed from the truck.

As Annie and the fisherman walked to the Dragon-Lady-red doors the fisherman had one of those queasy feelings that come just before reality alters forever. It was the sort of feeling a guy gets eighty miles offshore, with a thumping piston in his engine, as he discovers a serious leak in the hull. It was the sort of feeling a lady would get who chases a fire truck to a major fire, and the truck pulls up in front of her house. One of those feelings.

When they stepped through the doorway the fisherman paused while Annie headed for Sugar Bear. The fisherman took his time and looked the place over, because this particular fisherman knew enough to keep his back to the wall in bars.

•

Three fat goldfish at Lee's China Bay Taverna live on the cutting edge of social commentary. As they cruise their protected fish tank, emitting carp-like burps among weaving fronds of underwater plants, faces and situations pass before them like a TV documentary. Along the bar ranges an assortment of working gents.

At the fish-tank end of the bar a cribbage game generally occupies two elderly persons. These ancients are greatly valued for stories that carry a frosting of facts exotic and droll. One claims himself an ex-Navy man; and that is probably the case since he wears many-a-tattoo. The other claims a former career as a diplomat, and perhaps that is true as well; for he always wears a clean and pressed hankie in his jacket pocket. Neither claims to spread anything but pure veracity, although some listeners have doubts as to whether gold can be panned from coal mines, or African headhunters infiltrate the coroner's office in Chicago, or Argentine cowboys use motor scooters for chasing steers. In the idiom of the Canal, these geriatric lads are suspected of being "full of it".

On this day at China Bay the bar was attended by these two old gents, and by the Packard guy who had a forlorn look and a dab of grease on his nose. Alongside the Packard guy sat the milk-truck guy. He worked at getting snockered, and wore a baseball cap that read "Dairy Doings". Next to him were three other gents who only looked confused.

In this early afternoon the fisherman saw China Bay a-click with pool games and under tidy control. It held a beer-drinking crowd. Later on, legislators from the Capitol would arrive after a day of organized b.s. and gather to hear random varieties. They would be joined by rich guys from up north, and by an interesting group of young women desiring to understand legislative and economic processes if they were paid; but for now, yep, a beer-drinking crowd.

Then the fisherman looked at Sugar Bear, and wished himself elsewhere.

He looked poorly, did Sugar Bear. He sat like a large and liquid lump on the barstool farthest from the fish tank. He had a nearly full glass of flat beer before him, and as he listened to impassioned whispers from Annie, he dripped. It was also clear Sugar Bear had been dripping quite awhile longer than anyone else, because every other soul in the crowd was either dry or mildly soggy.

The fisherman then regarded the bartender, who, it is understood, knows the ways of the universe; and knew enough to be interested by Sugar Bear's condition, but not awed. The bartender had a mop leaning against the far end of the bar. It was clear the bartender occasionally mopped around Sugar Bear the way one mops around a leaky refrigerator.

"It has something called a load-leveler," the Packard guy said about his Packard. "Just a little forked hydraulic lift that pushes the fanny up when you put too much load in the trunk. The rebuild shop won't touch it." The guy sighed. The milk-truck guy burped politely.

". . . and strictly speaking," said one of the oldsters (the diplomat with the hanky in his pocket), "there is no New Zealand ordinance against catnapping, so the charge was broadened to feloniously assaulting a feline. . . ."

"They are reviewing previous conversations," the bartender said in a low voice to the fisherman. "Your man has them confused, and the young lady has them stunned. They will shortly revive." The bartender placed a glass of beer before the fisherman. Then the bartender gave something sounding nearly like a giggle.

"We have a pool on how long it takes your man to stop drip-ping," the bartender added. "Costs you one semoleon."

At China Bay large windows face the Canal, and tall trees rise between China Bay and the beach. On the walls hang Chinese tapestry, beer signs, and pictures of gorgeous Chinese girls, the pictures torn from calendars. These pictures rest comfortably beside calendar pictures of Athens scenes and Greek dancers. One set of pictures belongs to Lee, the other to the bartender.

"Ten minutes," the fisherman said sadly. "He'll stop dripping in ten minutes, but I don't want the bet."

"You seem to know your man very well."

"I know the young lady," the fisherman said. He figured Annie would cast a spell of dryness, and it would take ten minutes to catch hold.

This time the bartender actually did giggle. "Numbers of our lads have journeyed north to search for mystery women. Is she one?"

"She's only a sweet kid," the fisherman explained. "And he's a sweet guy. It's just that things are sorta star-crossed." The fisher-man's voice sounded so mournful he felt ashamed. He obviously felt sorry for himself.

"A certain amount of tension will shortly appear," the bar-tender said in low but normal voice. "Please do your part by remaining seated. The young lady will be as safe as one can in this troubled and uncertain world."

And the bartender had that one taped. With Annie's appear-ance bartalk slowed, stumbled, fell into temporary silence. Then talk gradually sounded as a whisper, a suppressed murmur, a wave of lonesome expostulation. The amused bartender switched the tape deck to something containing violins and moonbeams. The two old gents dealt cribbage, looked dreamy, and the one who claimed a Navy career spoke of Paris after World War II. He mentioned girls named Nanette and Babette.

Pool games sounded differently, the click of balls sharper as guys took heat in their pants and put it behind their cues. Subdued cussing dwelt around tables, because passion and pool do not mix, not if you want to make the shot. The only sane member present was the bartender.

"It isn't what you think," the fisherman said. "It's worse."

"I believe the term is murder." This time the bartender actually did whisper. "During the past weeks our boys have dissected cause and effect on the demise of a child molester. They concluded they understood and approved. Now the killer sits among them, and is attended by a girl who is a daisy." The bartender, who is slim and who moves liquidly, tugged gently at one earlobe. "Our laddies are confused."

"She's from up to Beer and Bait. One of Bertha's loveydovies." A guy spoke a little too loudly, drummed fingers on the counter, took a rapid and healthy gulp of suds. This was the milk-truck driver, and when it came to genes the poor fellow sat shortchanged. His receding chin drooped toward a skinny chest that rode above a pot belly. He looked sadly in need of protein.

As the fisherman began to slip from his barstool with gladness in his heart, because he finally owned good reason to smack somebody, the bartender looked him back onto his seat. "It seems," said the bartender, "we are to have a dramatic moment." The bartender did not exactly say, "Sit, Stay, Good Boy," but the look did. The fisherman sat.

The goldfish, who have seen a lot through the eyeglass of their tank, hovered just above fronds behind which they might easily dart and hide. The two old gents, as experienced as the fish, smiled to themselves in anticipation. The Packard guy froze, not understanding that something nasty had been said, but feeling fixed by the slow and inexorable movement of the bartender. One pool game paused as men stood watching, then another, and yet a third, and then a fourth. Silence descended. The bar might have been peopled by monks with vows of muteness. The bartender moved slowly, nearly dreamy. The milk-truck guy sat pinioned but indignant before his beer. From the far distance on the Canal came the hoot of a ship's horn.

Bar rag in hand, the bartender arrived before the milk-truck driver, and the bartender gave one of those smiles of regret so often seen among folks who run mortuaries. The bartender picked up the driver's beer glass, mopped the counter with the rag. The bartender dumped the beer in a sink, then leaned forward, and in a voice as gentle as the fingers of a loving hand, said, "Moo."

Silence. Each man present heard his own heartbeat. Each man thought about excesses in his own speech, and thought of guilts and misunderstandings. And, each man, as if in defense of sanity, reached for his beer.

"What'n. . . .", the Packard guy said.

"Moo," one of the oldsters chuckled. "Pass it on."

The other oldster gave a low moo. He sat surprised and pleased. He gave another moo. It is amazing how many different ways there are to say "moo".

It became the thing to do. As moos spread along the bar like a crashing wave, and as guys really got into it, pool players resumed their games. The moos crescendoed, then faded as the milk-truck guy headed for the doorway, never again to be seen at China Bay or Beer and Bait. As the milk-truck guy departed the fisherman sat with a load of adrenalin, and no place to put it. Plus, a Canal story began.

The story worked its way north. By the time it arrived at

Rough and Randy the story said China Bay was overrun by cows. The cows were brought in for demonstration purposes by the ice-cream lobby. A new law by the legislature mandated a milk bar in every beer joint, and because of this riots covered the southern part of the state. The poor cows were caught in the middle, and a great barbecue was even then being held on the front steps of the state senate. The leader of the demonstration would run for governor, and Lee's China Bay Taverna was also overrun with mystery women.

. . . But that was later. As the milk-truck driver disappeared, and as talk returned to normal along the bar, the fisherman reluctantly turned his attention to Annie and Sugar Bear. It seemed Sugar Bear resisted. It also seemed that Sugar Bear was bound to lose, because no man born was gonna pass up a confession of love and lust by a Greek goddess; or maybe, the fisherman wondered, did the ancient Greeks have angels? Because no man born . . .

Because, because. Because Annie, still wearing that greeny-bluey dress, now sat on a barstool beside Sugar Bear. She whispered earnestly, reached to touch Sugar Bear's wrist with her fingertips, and that caused every other man in the bar to die a little. Gloom began. Daylight through large windows grew dull gray. Even pictures on the walls seemed saddened. Talk once more faltered, although pool games still clicked. The bartender, as wry as any bartender who ever drew suds, changed music on the tape deck to something with lots of french horns.

"There is a very good chance the young lady is mistaken," the bartender said, and wiped an imaginary spot of crud from the bar. The bartender spoke mostly to the fisherman. "Because a Fury, should such a thing exist, would be a dangerous and dismal creature. A lone Fury would feel lost and doubtless haunted, because Furies traditionally run in packs." The bartender dwelt so deep in reflection that bar light actually dimmed.

"Of course," the bartender said, "we speak of creatures from more than two thousand years in the past. Further, we speak with knowledge that evolution is inevitable." The bartender became so absorbed that guys along the bar actually began to pay attention. "It would make sense, then," the bartender explained, "that back in the days of spectacular copulations, mating of various gods with Greeks and Romans and Persians, with Abyssinians and Ethiops, would produce mighty curious spawn. Perhaps an underwater Fury is not impossible."

It was the first time the fisherman had ever heard of a Fury. Later, it would develop that Annie had once mentioned the subject to Bertha, but even that knowledge would never persuade the fisherman he had not been in the presence of magical stuff. Of course, it's true bartenders generally know everything that's happening.

"There's not a soul here who understands what you're talking about," an oldster said to the bartender. "Except, of course, yours truly." This was the retired diplomat, the one with the hanky. The oldster fiddled with a cribbage peg. He looked interested. Also, somewhat alarmed. "Creatures of revenge," he explained to the bar. "They were remorseless."

The bartender drew another beer for the fisherman. "Perhaps 'retribution' is a better word. At any rate, Furies punished crimes, even when the criminal acted for the common good." The bartender looked toward the Canal, absorbed in thought. "I have my doubts . . . though doubtless there is some meaning . . . ," and then the bartender waxed philosophic, but no one followed the train of thought except, possibly, the guy who was once a diplomat.

The oldster regarded the bartender with awe. "I take it you

believe a Fury, or some such, infests the neighborhood. If true, I'm moving to Iowa."

"That guy just stopped dripping," the Packard guy said. "I win the pool."

And even later that evening, as the fisherman sat practically sober beside the Packard guy who was in no shape to drive, events swirled in the fisherman's mind like flotsam in a whirlpool. Because, by eventide of that dreadful day, Sugar Bear had been led away by Annie, or rescued by Annie; no one could say for sure. A story worked its way down the Canal. The story said Petey had been kicked out of Beer and Bait after losing a fortune to the tow-truck kid. Plus, a rumor said Bertha and a state cop had a case of the hots for each other. It was also said that a great number of cars had gone in the drink, but the fisherman, who knew Canal stories, figured the number would amount to no more than one or two. Plus, there was the sell-out story about the DWI.

And if all this were not bad enough, it seemed whatever patrolled the Canal was not a normal monster. The fisherman recalled talk about Furies that carried on for quite a while before the bartender went off shift at six P.M., and Lee took over in his Chinese sort of way.

The fisherman, in the first stage of slight fuzziness, the way a guy gets after a beer or so, could easily understand that—what with Furies and chinamen—he stood at a brink . . . some sort of brink or other . . . like maybe the decline and fall of western civilization . . . something like that . . . something big time, anyway.

And the bartender had sort of suggested that. When the bartender turned philosophic, part of the rap had been about the rise and decline of nations.

And Lee, who represented the mysterious east, ran the bar with aplomb as he manipulated legislators, teased their lady friends, and ran a number on rich guys who had driven south to buy legislation; the rich guys glad of heart because there were enough lady-friends to go around.

And Lee heckled pool games, while sturdily backed up by three goldfish who, it appeared, suddenly developed eyefolds. The fisherman saw that the Fury in the Canal really did mean the destruction of the western world. It was clear the Orient was about to take over, and more luck to it.

Then the fisherman talked more with the Packard guy about rebuilding hydraulic lifts. Then he watched drunken legislators and rich guys from up north with high-priced lady friends. Then he thought of Annie and grieved. Then he worried about Sugar Bear without exactly knowing why.

Then Lee, for no good reason the fisherman could see, cut him off. Lee did it in that skillful way the Chinese have so nobody feels bad about getting separated from a beer.

And then the fisherman remembered that, when a guy goes fishing, the best part comes when you get so far out that land sinks below the horizon. At that moment you feel this great sense of relief, because a man at sea no longer has land responsibilities . . . there not being a damn thing he can do to change anything ashore. When he thought about that, the fisherman understood it was time to go back to sea.

Except for a Mouse,
No One Is Happy

A satisfied mouse, plumpish, generally well-intended, and curious, lives in the shack to which Sugar Bear and Annie repaired. It is not a vacationer's paradise, but a hunter's shack; a crude shelter of unfinished boards and shake roof. A glassless window allows ingress and egress of bugs, bats in season; but the place is not classy enough to lodge a barn owl. For a mouse who has enough sense to appreciate advantages the place is home-sweet-home-with-a-view.

The view is of a copse of madrona, vine maple, and alder. Leaves float through autumn air, or, in the case of the madronas, all year. Small flowers in their season, and edible mushrooms sprout from a thick layer of loam accumulated through centuries. The ground gives beneath one's feet as the buildup of broken leaves, twigs, and moisture combine and cover the forest floor like a plush rug. Among, around, and in this forest-rug are bugs, seeds, and edible shoots. A mouse, patrolling the perimeter of the shack, cruises his domain with all the confidence of a well-heeled lady in a specialty grocery store.

And, because the mouse had no experience with humans and had shelter from most predators, it sat fearless on the single crossbeam of the ten-by-ten shack and watched as two creatures, one furry and enormous, the other greeny-blue, opened the door.

They entered, saw bunkbeds, a chair, a small woodstove, fire-wood, a bucket, a kerosene lamp, and stubs of a half-dozen candles, unchewed, having been scorned by a mouse who was filthy rich.

"You're gonna have to move," the greeny-blue creature said to a huge spider who webbed the space between upper and lower bunks. "I know it's a pain but we've got a problem."

The spider shrugged, climbed the bed frame, swung by filament to the wall, and began spinning in the upper corner of the room. "And you," the greeny-blue creature said to the mouse, "will need to mind your manners. It looks like we'll be here for a while."

The mouse, who heretofore had never learned a word of English, or, for that matter, Greek, understood and accepted the situation. He gave a chirp of welcome. In mouse terms, the greeny-blue creature looked interesting.

"Get that stove going," Annie said to Sugar Bear, "and then get into that sleeping bag. I've got a little work outside." Annie's voice, which in days past had been either vague or demure, sounded positive as fire trucks. She felt Sugar Bear's forehead, tsked, felt inside his shirt. "You're sweating pretty good." She picked up the bucket. "Cold sweat. Where's the spring?"

In the week that followed, a week of rain on mossy shakes of the roof, the mouse watched as the window was repaired with plastic film. The mouse sniffed as the shack filled with odors. Burbles of herbal potion steamed on the stove top, mattresses of piled cedar-tips lay beneath colorful sleeping bags while the great-big creature wheezed, grumbled, moaned, sniffed, apologized, and wondered what the hell went on back home. When, after a couple of days, the creature grew comatose, peace and quiet entered the shack, and when the creature began choking it kept the mouse awake. Steam filled the shack. The greeny-blue creature applied hot cloths, rubbed smelly concoctions onto chest, throat, and held breathable but stinky stuff beneath the nose. Sometimes the creature cried, but she did not stop working. When the crisis passed, sunlight of Indian summer shone through the plastic window. The shack became uncomfortably warm.

"You're gonna be all right," Annie told a very weak Sugar Bear, "but don't do that again."

"I didn't plan it," Sugar Bear whispered. "Are we gonna stay here, or what?"

"You're gonna stay," Annie told him. "I'm hitching a ride north to see what's going on. I'll be back day after." She hugged him, kissed him on the ear. "Don't wander off."

With Annie gone, the mouse felt uneasy because of the language barrier. No mouse ever born could fail to understand Annie, but no mouse ever born could fully understand Sugar Bear; at least not without a bit of magic. The mouse did not head for his hidey-hole, but no longer assumed he could hop from the beam, scamper along a chair back, and nibble at spilled crumbs of bread and crackers. The mouse awaited developments.

Sugar Bear sat, yawned, stood, stretched, lay on the bed, scratched, stood up, said, "Dammit", opened the door and looked into the sunstruck copse. A light breeze sent leaves in a slanting, yellowly shower. He started to take a chair outside, then sat on the door sill instead.

"I got a little problem," he confided to the mouse. "She thinks this sicky-business is over, but maybe it ain't. A certain amount of crap circles the universe. Sometimes it drops on a guy's head."

The mouse, clearly sympathetic, but no more philosophic than your average mouse, remained silent. Perhaps on some level of mouse wisdom it knew there are times when a guy just needs a good listener.

"Because maybe my worst problem ain't cops. I felt okay until that last night at the dunk site . . . felt like something tried to crawl all over me. Felt like I was being watched."

Sugar Bear spent the rest of the day, and all of the next, painfully gathering and chopping firewood. He no longer moved like a big man with confidence in his strength, but like a man with a body too large for his spirit. Illness hindered him. Worry hindered him. Although dragging firewood takes time, it does not take much concentration. He had plenty of time to imagine horrible things that might happen at Beer and Bait. He feared Annie might walk into the middle of a mess, and he would not be there to protect her.

As it turned out, by the time Annie stepped into the middle of a real mess she was the last person who needed protecting. The mess had built over the past week. By the time the mess played out, Annie felt like she'd taken a course in history. She guessed the whole thing started with Petey.

During that week Petey drifted from Rough and Randy, to China Bay, with only occasional stop-offs at Beer and Bait. His route seemed erratic. The Plymouth parked in odd places, outside of courthouses, mostly.

And history, as far as Petey was concerned, turned to bunk. His slumping figure hunched over the steering wheel of the Plymouth, or leaned against pool tables where guys rushed to take advantage. Guys figured Petey swam through depths of despair; which was sad but good, because that meant Petey was losing his hustle. Without hustle Petey became a man not feared, but nearly scorned. Guys played him for bucks, hustled him, and Petey generally managed to break even, or a few bucks ahead, although his heart was not in his game. He no longer showed up at Beer and Bait during mornings. During evenings he remained distant with Bertha, and sad, and his baseball cap read Bob's Used Truck Parts.

And almost always, during mornings, the Plymouth parked not far from dunk sites where police divers remained busy, and where cops directed traffic and hassled taxpayers. The cop who looked like a movie actor pretended indifference to Petey, but coplike, made mental notes. Petey was present on the day the cops pulled out the dead guy's car, and it seemed that Petey also made notes.

The car dangled from the crane like a guppy on a boat hook. When the crane eased it onto the tow-truck kid's trailer it sat like small change. It was one of those imported things, painted orangey-pink, a monument to miniaturization; that if you sat in it you couldn't cuss a cat without getting a mouthful of fur.

The front end sported a loose bumper. The fenders were unscratched. The trunk lid popped up where the back end had been squeezed, but, when compared to other drowned cars this one hadn't been squeezed much. This car looked like a piece of spit-out gum.

"And Petey just stood there," the tow-truck kid confided to Bertha when he stopped for a going-home beer. ". . . like he's worried the cop will blame him for something." The kid now enjoyed the status of a regular at Beer and Bait. A regular can leave his change on the bar when he goes to the john. The bartender keeps an eye on it.

"He's a good guy, too," the tow-truck kid said about Petey, "even if his game is over-rated." The tow-truck kid rode high and wide as he made a name for himself. His red truck and dread trailer parked before Beer and Bait, or China Bay. The kid gained muscle in arms and shoulders, and shone with manly pride; but only enough to be slightly obnoxious. Men who were brave, and men who hoped they were brave, made room for him at the bar.

Because, out there in that parking lot, one more doomed piece of machinery sat chained to the trailer; helpless as a crab in a crab pot. Guys looked at the wreck, felt emptiness in their minds at the sight of violated metal.

Because, while anyone can regard a wreck with dismal satisfaction if that wreck is not his own, these wrecks went to scary places in mind and soul where even bad people do not want to visit. Men privately told themselves the tow-truck kid was courageous, or, more likely, so damn dumb he didn't know what he fooled with. Still, you had to treat a guy like that with some respect.

And if credit for courage was not enough, the kid also rode the wave of a Canal story that turned him into a pool hero. Since hustling Petey for a hundred bucks, the kid's game improved. He began wearing shirts with loose sleeves, a bolo tie, and lightly, very lightly, tinted sunglasses. Winning builds confidence, and confidence lets a guy relax. Relaxed guys win at pool.

"Petey's game is better than you think," Bertha told the kid on a morning when the bar was otherwise empty. In the parking lot a twisted station wagon sat chained to the kid's trailer.

"Maybe once-upon-a-time." The kid looked across the green felt of the pool tables like a farm-guy gazing at his fields. His voice sounded kindly.

"I guess you gotta learn on your own." Bertha's words were more positive than her voice, which carried echoes of dismay. Petey had chickened out before a cop. He ran road and lost at pool.

"How's that cop to work with?"

The kid studied the problem. "Somebody's gonna get busted." The kid turned on his bar stool, looked toward the Canal, and his voice got louder. "He's a loner. He's not even buddy-buddy with other cops." The kid tried to lower his voice and still sound positive. "I think somebody has the guy in their sights, like dangerous. The cops are scared. Who would've ever thought?" The kid gulped the last of his beer. "I gotta admit. I'm almost scared. I got to git."

"Petey's game is better than you think," Bertha repeated as the kid left. "If you back into a buzz saw don't say you ain't been told."

When the kid left, Bertha faced an empty joint, and suddenly, an empty life. She could not admit that Petey was half the reason she loved her bar.

As days passed dismay tried to replace love, because Beer and Bait still had to be opened even though the world turned dreary. Mornings saw no pool games. The whole notion of pool brought worries about the butterflies from up north, and the beetle-lady. And, since Jubal Jim rode with Petey, there was not even a tail-wag of greeting when Bertha arrived through chill mist to an empty bar. Added to that, Annie and Sugar Bear were way-the-hell-and-gone off somewhere at China Bay. What with no Petey, and no girl-talk with Annie, and poolish worry, life became gray as the weather.

Bertha, being Norwegian, turned her considerable energy toward improvements. The bar mirrors sparkled, reflecting dull faces of morning customers mumbling hangover talk. The dance floor gleamed with wax, and anything that could handle polish, did. When folks looked through windows onto the Canal they felt wind would blow through the room because, while the windows were there, they were so clean you couldn't see them. If the joint suddenly turned into a burden, Bertha admitted nothing.

And the cop, what of him?

"The state police have an investigative unit," the cop admitted wistfully to Bertha during one afternoon when the bar held only two tourists and an inveterate drinker. The cop wore his cop suit, stayed near the door, and pretended he caught a quick lemonade before leaving to intimidate the populace. "It's an elite unit," the cop confided, "and I can honestly say my chances are good. I've seen a little too much road." The cop did not actually say he wanted to become a detective and settle down, but Bertha caught his drift. She blushed a smidgen, then blushed a lot because she'd been caught blushing.

And, there was no denying the cop turned snoopy. Instead of attending to busted cars, he spent time investigating the shore-line.

"We run the license numbers of the wrecks," he confided to Bertha.

Bertha waited, wanted to ask questions, and knew enough to keep her lips firmly closed.

Thus did life continue with wet roads, dunked cars, and grow-ing fear among regulars at Beer and Bait. Regulars figured it might be a good notion to drink elsewhere, because a cop in a bar is as welcome as a horse on a houseboat.

True, the cop drove south each evening because he lived in that direction, but a taint of copness seemed to linger in the parking lot of Beer and Bait. A timid Canal story claimed Bertha was in collusion with the cop, but the story didn't fly. Even the hardiest men were not willing to take a chance on dealing with Bertha's wrath.

General unease caused business to decline. As autumn rains swept the Canal, Bertha began to worry that she would soon have money-worries. She no long wanted a bartender, not even part time. She no longer needed Chantrell George for pick-up work. That was tough on Chantrell, who was about to make the mess even messier.

Chantrell wheeled his bike along the road, an abandoned waif looking for a handout and a home. He could not mooch from Sugar Bear, because Sugar Bear holed up down south. True, mushrooms blossomed in fall rains and that was sorta good, because a guy could stay sorta high all the time, but abundance proved a problem because Chantrell's customers could easily pick their own. Tourist cars virtually disappeared, so no adoptions of orphan cameras and golf clubs could take place. Chantrell had seen economic downturns before, but, as he confided to his bike, "This one is a slam-banger."

"A guy don't hardly know what to do," he told the bike as they walked along the road. During fall rain Chantrell's hair dripped even more than his nose and his bike was feeling rusty.

"There's always wholesale," the bike kindly advised. "You gotta get new connections, maybe go into export." The bike dreamed of mushroom shipments to Canada and Mexico.

"That ain't jail stuff," Chantrell murmured. "That's more like . . . feds."

"And it ain't fair," the bike said. "Sugar Bear dumped you and took all the credit."

The bike had a point. Chantrell remembered a time, and that time not long ago, when he had been a hero. Guys worth admiring, because they sounded positive and loud, had given Chantrell credit for killing the dead guy. In Chantrell's memory, which was rarely clouded with reality, it had been a golden time. Bar work had been available. Tourist cars crowded the scene. The mushroom market had been at a premium, and Sugar Bear contributed saleable scrap-iron plus a few bucks.

"It all started downhill when Sugar Bear took the credit." The bike sounded so sad its front wheel squeaked.

"We could get reliable," Chantrell muttered. "Bertha wants somebody reliable."

"Naw," the bike told him. "How much can a guy put up with?"

Their discussion turned, returned, explored avenues crowded with remembered visions as they neared the parking lot of Beer and Bait. In the parking lot sat an unmarked cop car, and beside the cop car sat a Lincoln Continental. Beside the Lincoln sat the red tow truck, and on a far corner of the lot sat a couple of gyppo log trucks. At the edge of the lot, beside the road, a busted-up Ford pickup pulled over, stopped, and Annie stepped out. She dressed in jeans, plaid shirt, practical shoes, and her long hair was braided and piled like the soul of practicality. Chantrell did a flashback. A vision of Annie discussing world events with a spider flooded his mind. A cartoon hammer tapped, tapped, tapped, as it flew around a room where the dead guy lay. Then the hammer started squishing spiders. Little splashes of spider goo popped and sizzled on Sugar Bear's forge. The dead guy lay oozing a little blood before the doorway of Sugar Bear's shop while an entire bar-full of fishermen and loggers watched. The hammer tapped, tapped, tapped, then escaped through an open window while Sugar Bear stepped forward, hands raised above his head in victory, as guys clapped and stomped and cheered.

Chantrell and the bike moved steadily across the parking lot as Annie disappeared through the doorway of Beer and Bait. Then Chantrell and the bike mourned their unhappy situation, and that took a little while. Then they discussed options.

"The trick," the bicycle advised, "is to let guys know Sugar

Bear swiped the credit. But don't admit to nothin'. Guys can figure it out."

Chantrell parked the bike and stepped toward the doorway of Beer and Bait. Neither Chantrell or the bike had never heard of the Rubicon, and would not be impressed if they had. It was, after all, a very small river.

All Hell Breaks Loose

The brief Indian summer hung around long enough to illuminate Beer and Bait like a stage as Annie entered; a stage flooded with light through windows so clean you couldn't see them. On the Canal fishing boats swam through autumn light and a hump in the water moved lazily. Inside Beer and Bait, light reflected from mirrors and polished surfaces of piano and chairs. The joint, which has seen so much drama in forms of real hopes and real pain, now seemed a stage set for a surreal play.

At center stage sat the main hallucination. She was manicured and enameled, tough as old leather, fifty-going-on-thirty-five, who resembled a purple beetle, not a butterfly. Her purple dress swirled around an active little body. She wore a necklace that did not come from a dimestore. Her fingers tapped the bar, and were ornamented with fancy rings. No one, except Bertha and Annie, had ever seen anything close to the beetle-lady, at least not in Beer and Bait. Every soul in attendance pretended to ignore her, and every single soul paid strict attention.

In addition, things were about to get delicate, whether or not the beetle-lady strode center stage. No one could possibly guess how delicate.

At the end of the bar nearest the Canal, two gyppo loggers sat before beer glasses from which they occasionally sipped, there being no reason any sensible man would want a cop to see him guzzle. When Annie took a seat beside the two loggers, the atmosphere lightened at that end of the bar, grew chilly toward the middle, and confused at the other end where cop and tow-truck kid sat near the door. Behind the bar, Bertha stood perplexed by mixed tenses; because Annie and loggers represented the past, the kid and the cop represented the present, and the beetle-lady presented a most alarming future.

"What's happening?" Annie whispered to one of the loggers, the one with wide red suspenders.

"Some kinda pool tourney," the logger whispered as he studied the front of Annie's shirt.

"Up to the project," the other logger whispered. This was the logger with the Kenworth belt buckle. "Looks like there might be bucks involved." The logger glanced toward the cop. "A 'course, with mister cop around, nobody's talking straight."

"I doubt our guys can do it," Bertha told the beetle-lady. "They got a lot going on right now." Bertha, standing behind her own bar, sounded defensive. Unbelievable. Bertha wore her starchiest shirt, her baggiest jeans, and her hair piled and braided the same as Annie's. To those who love and fear her, Bertha seemed unreal.

The beetle-lady ignored Bertha. "We'll make it a team affair. With prizes." She looked at the loggers like a shopper poking a chicken to see if it is fresh. "Those two look adequate. We'll need six more." She turned to examine the cop and the kid. This time she looked like a consumer examining pork. "It's a late afternoon, evening affair," she said. "That makes four. We'll need four more."

The cop smiled and said nothing, having just heard such overwhelming b.s. his entire belief system temporarily went aground on rocks. Then his smile vanished.

The kid looked insulted, but financially interested. "Prizes?" he said. Then the kid, who proved a little less dense than expected, caught on. He pushed his lightly tinted sunglasses to his forehead, shook out the loose sleeves of his shirt, and fingered his bolo tie. "Tell me where and when," he announced with authority. "I can furnish a team." All of this while Bertha looked ready to scream.

"Step over here young man." The woman pointed to a table. The kid sat. The beetle-lady sat. The two conversed in low tones.

"Some spiders eat their mates," Annie murmured, but no one understood what she meant.

Wordless, Bertha placed a lemonade before Annie. Bertha gave no sign of recognition or friendliness.

Annie caught on. She said not a word, but turned to the loggers. "You guys working north or south?" She listened to the bull and kept an eye on the far end of the bar. It was then that Chantrell entered, looking furtive, and took a chair at a table away from the bar. Chantrell's eyes were wider than usual, and his nose was sorta liquid. Bertha gave a low moan, practically inaudible. The cop picked up on it. A look of charity crossed his features as he ignored the obvious.

Annie sat stricken with sudden worry. At the time Annie could not have known of Bertha's isolation, or her uncertainty, or her fears about the beetle-lady. All Annie knew was that in other days, Chantrell, in stoned condition, would be kicked out the minute he opened the door. Annie, in a burst of absolute dismay, understood that Bertha had lost control of the bar.

Those socially deprived people who have little experience with bars will be hard put to understand how scary it is when a bartender loses control. Uncertainty causes men to pull change toward them, furtively check back pockets for billfolds, and turn sullen. The noise level increases. If a bladder contest is underway, the contest usually breaks as one guy gives up and heads for the can to pee. Of course, those who have little experience in bars probably do not know that bladder contests, as extensions of male pride, even exist.

When a bartender loses control, bravado steps forward among guys guilty of misdemeanors, in other words, everybody. That's one reason for an increased noise level. Another reason arrives because if something truly stinky is about to happen, it will come without warning.

Bertha's nearly inaudible moan was answered by a thoroughly audible sigh from Chantrell. He sprawled in a chair, arms and legs floppity as Raggedy Andy. He gazed at the ceiling. On the ceiling, a vision unseen by everyone except Chantrell, showed a huge party. Fishermen and loggers and girlfriends toasted Sugar Bear, while a pinky-orangey car sped across the sky towed by pigeons. Chantrell traded his sigh for a moan.

"The hammer did it," he announced in the general direction of the loggers who paid not the least attention. "That hammer don't want any credit." Then Chantrell's voice became secretive, coy. "That dead guy knows who gets the credit. . . ."

A flurry. A flash of yellow as a twelve ounce can of lemonade described a flat line between Annie's throwing arm and Chantrell's nose. No one, not even Annie, believed Annie could put one over the plate with that kind of accuracy. As lemonade splashed in one direction and a bloody nose spewed in the other, Chantrell went over backward; tipping slowly, almost glacially, arms wide-spread, eyes rolling toward heaven, feet gradually rising above shoulders as he backwardly crashed; all of this while a further flash of colors, bluejeans and plaid shirt, flew across the room. Annie landed on Chantrell as Chantrell landed on the floor, and Annie had hands around Chantrell's throat intent on choking him into the graveyard.

Bertha came around the logger-end of the bar, while the cop, at the other end stood momentarily amazed. The cop, being only a traffic officer and thus largely unaware, had not the least chance of keeping up with Bertha's bar fight experience.

"Back off." Bertha grabbed Annie's arm. "I got him." Bertha sounded unbearably happy. The misery of the last week fled on the joyous occasion of regaining control of her bar. If Chantrell had not been so stoned and snotty and bloody she would have hugged him.

"Back off," Bertha told the cop, who by now had arrived. The cop was not having a good day. He stood momentarily stunned, then further stunned as Annie dashed to the cue rack, pulled down a twenty-one ouncer, and came back wielding it as a club. The cop was aware that on the periphery two tough and experienced loggers sat completely intimidated. He may have been aware that the startled tow-truck kid reminded himself to act manly; while the beetle-lady could not have been more pleased at the quality of help she believed she was hiring.

"That's a house cue," Bertha growled at Annie. "Twenty bucks if you bust it." She took the cue from Annie, then patted Annie on the cheek. She pulled Chantrell to his feet, grabbed him by the ear, and marched.

The cop stood even more amazed. Instead of heading for the doorway, Bertha marched Chantrell to the rear of the room. To applause and snickers from the loggers, Bertha stood Chantrell in a corner. "Move one inch before I come to get you," Bertha whispered, "and you're the deadest man around." The happiness in

Bertha's voice got through to Chantrell. He faced the corner while doing flashbacks of third grade. Something had gone terribly wrong with his plan, and he had no bicycle to discuss this with. His nose dripped blood on his shirt, the loggers laughed at him, and Chantrell was afraid to so much as moan.

The cop, wondering if he should bust Annie for assault, hesitated just long enough to save himself. The cop realized he looked at one black-haired Greek, one blond-haired Norwegian, and they both had their hair put up and were cat-spitting mad. No traffic officer was going to step into the middle of that. That was big city cop stuff.

Spatters of blood and a pool of lemonade soiled the immaculate floor of Beer and Bait. Bertha turned to Annie who stood breathless with anger. Annie looked ready to cast one of those spells that destroy junkies.

"Lay off," Bertha told her. "If that guy bursts into flame it will be because I strike the match." Bertha looked at the tipped-over chair, the spatters of blood leading from the scene to Chantrell. "You know where I keep the mop." Bertha headed back to the bar, once more in full command.

The tow-truck kid, torn between greed and lust, did himself credit and opted for lust. "I'll give you a hand," he told Annie.

"Stay seated, young man." The beetle-lady now paid strict attention to the kid's muscles and broad shoulders. "Are you familiar with common brawls?"

"That was a friendly brawl," Bertha said to the beetle-lady. "Nothing here is common except customers who don't know their place."

A low whimper came from Chantrell. A logger chuckled. A second logger belched. Annie reluctantly headed for bucket, rags, and mop. "This is the absolute last time I ever, ever, ever *pick up after you,"* she spit in Chantrell's direction. Her words, which seemed innocuous, were loaded with awful promise. No one who knows Annie's witchery would give Chantrell an old dog's chance in the city pound.

The cop took a lick of lemonade and looked at Bertha with the standard mixture of love and fear. No one quite understood what propelled the cop, but it was probably the desire to become a detective, settle down with Bertha, and breed small, blond cops. The poor man had to start somewhere, and solving a murder must have seemed like fine credentials.

"Talk continues about a murder." The cop mused, but in a way calculated to impress Bertha. He certainly sounded sincere. "It's almost like the road, itself, is a murderer . . . on the other hand. . . ." The cop pretended he was not using the bar mirror to watch Chantrell and Annie.

"Don't waste your time," Bertha told him. "Around here a junkie's word is zilch." She smacked the bar with a bar rag and turned to the two loggers. "Thanks for the big help, gents." The loggers, aware they were supposed to feel guilt-ridden, only felt confused as Bertha placed fresh beer before them. "On the house." The loggers looked at each other, shrugged, clearly worried.

"We've recovered the bodies of all the drowned except two. One was lost from a top down sports car," the cop said. "The other cars have been about the same except for one . . ." He looked at the tow-truck kid ". . . that was a little odd."

"More like weird." The tow-truck kid did not give a hang for solving murders. He was torn between pool arrangements and his concentration on Annie. The kid sat beside the beetle-lady, and the beetle-lady seemed absolutely consumed by admiration for Bertha.

"We run the plates," the cop said. "The people who drowned

have all been solid citizens. All of them have been losses to the community . . . ," the cop paused long enough to let the bar empty of all sound except a tiny whimper from Chantrell, "except one. You'd think a missing persons would have been filed, but on that one dead man no one seems to care." The cop stood, looked in Chantrell's direction. Then he looked at Bertha. "I can take him off your hands. I'd like to have some conversation."

Bertha glanced at the bar clock. "He's still got a half hour of corner."

"In that case," the cop said, most innocently, "I'll get back to the job."

"I'll meet you there," the kid told the cop. "Ten minutes." The kid talked to the cop like a partner, or like a guy with a sure-fire poker hand. He turned back to the beetle-lady.

"Ten minutes." The cop stepped through the doorway into Indian summer. Silence held until the starter of the cop car whirred. It took only that long for a Canal story to form.

The story said the kid sassed the cop because he was now *Captain Tow-Truck Kid* who, together with *Surreal Beetle-Lady*, organized international pool tournaments in Monaco which was outside the cop's jurisdiction; pool tournaments worth tens of thousands.

And, the story added, Chantrell had tried to finger Sugar Bear for killing the dead guy. Annie leveled Chantrell with a lightning bolt hurled by sheer magic, and Chantrell was presently in flight to Canada; which would do no good because Chantrell was clearly headed for a cold and watery grave.

And the best part, the story said, was that Bertha had got past her case of the blues.

Bertha stood in the doorway, watched the cop car disappear, and turned to the beetle-lady. ". . . you want to do any more business," she told the lady, "take it outside." Bertha looked at the kid and decided he was too young and dumb to be trusted with private stuff. "You too," she told the kid.

"I gotta git," the kid said. "I got a bunch of stuff to do."

"You're in over your head," Bertha told the beetle-lady. "How much dough can you afford to lose?"

The lady, still stricken with admiration for Bertha, strove to get past her plans and learn something. She failed. "Our gentlemen have taken care of themselves for many years. One supposes they can handle a contest."

"They can't handle hustlers," Bertha said. "Believe it." She pointed to the door. "Come back when you're sane." She looked at the loggers. "You deadbeats stay where you are."

When the kid and lady stepped into sunlight Bertha turned back to the bar. To Annie she said, "Quit moppin' and get over here." To Chantrell she said, "C'mere."

Chantrell cowered in the corner, snotty and sobbing.

"Yard 'em," Bertha told the loggers.

The loggers, glad of heart, crossed the room.

"If you blow snot on me," one of them said in a quiet voice, "you lose both legs. I got a chainsaw in the truck."

Chantrell cowered. He blubbered. Something had gone bad, bad wrong, and he couldn't figure out why.

"And if you bleed on me," the other logger said, "I feed your nuts to chipmunks."

Chantrell, knowing something of loggers, understood that what he heard was true. He trudged slowly to the bar, head down, scared nearly straight.

"You shut up," Bertha told Annie. "I'll handle this."

"Do it right," Annie said, "or I will."

Bertha leaned across the bar as Chantrell stood sniffling.

"Major screwup," Bertha said. "What should we do with you?"

"I think maybe break his jaw," the Kenworth logger said. "That keeps a guy quiet for a good, long time."

"Not a bad idea," the second logger said, "but there's mister cop. If we mess this guy up too bad the cop comes looking."

"You're not worth jail time," Bertha told Chantrell. "But you're dangerous. So you've got a ride with the next guy who goes to Seattle. In Seattle you're just another bum."

Annie made movement to protest.

"He won't last ten minutes," Bertha told Annie. "He's about done, anyway. Let him do it on city streets."

She turned back to Chantrell. "You poor sap," she said, "I don't know why you had to do it, but don't come back. If you come back you go in the Canal. That dead guy is down there. Just think of what that dead guy would do to you."

The Kid Visits Rough and Randy

Petey made his rounds in Indian summer. His worn Plymouth cruised through green foothills as he mostly ran north and west; or parked near the dunk site where Petey sad-eyed the cop while acting suspicious.

The Plymouth also parked outside of lawyer's offices, and before remote joints on the Washington Peninsula; in Port Angeles where the game of nine-ball is king, and in Forks where eight-ball-slop is about the best a guy can expect. Petey laid a mild hustle on guys who, having heard of his reputation, expected trouble. Guys played him, won or lost a few bucks, and were greatly impressed with themselves.

On every third or fourth evening Petey dropped into Beer and Bait where he hung out at the pool table farthest from the bar. His visits, though glum, were nice for Jubal Jim who received big welcomes and scored a few potato chips. Petey, on the other hand, barely broke even. When he left before midnight, and before the road turned ugly, Petey would pack his cue then stand irresolute while glancing covertly at Bertha.

And, during those visits, Bertha slapped the bar with a wet bar rag more often than necessary. Bertha was not about to admit that Petey meant a blessed thing to her, but Bertha's countenance grew bleak. When a Norwegian is bleak the atmosphere turns cloudy. At closing time, Bertha would pretend indifference as her crowd drifted to the door, and Petey drifted with it. For a few days the crowd passed a junk bicycle that leaned against the building. It stayed there until a well-juiced guy tripped over it, stood up cussing, and threw the bike into the Canal.

And, during that short spell of good weather the tow-truck kid found himself in one of those anxious situations that plague the young. The kid needed to assemble a pool team, and he had to "get everybody organized", and the kid had "gotta have the hottest cues around"; and that meant Petey, a guy who drove the kid nuts because of the Plymouth's wandering ways.

During the day the kid drove the tow truck, but took it to the company yard at dusk. Then the kid hopped in his own outfit, the cherry '57 Ranchero with snazzy mudflaps, and checked out joints along the Canal as nighttime crowded the road. When the kid finally caught up with Petey it was not at Beer and Bait, but at Al's Dock, known locally as Rough and Randy.

Rough and Randy sits beneath buzzing mercury lights mounted high on fir trees. Forest as black as midnight stands on each side, though the joint, itself, faces a backwater of the Canal. The parking lot drains well because it holds yards and yards of crushed limestone mixed with clam and oyster shells. Through the years rain concreted the lime to form a base that handles anything including bulldozers.

Rough and Randy's origins lie in the far distant past when an elderly gent, towing a ten-wide-fifty house trailer, parked, and fished. When he returned with a couple rock cod, he found flat tires on one side of the trailer. He said, "to hell with it," and settled down. In those days land went for next to nothing. It only cost two bucks to jack up the trailer. The elderly gent, after a productive retirement spent drinking and fishing, passed to his reward. Al bought the outfit. He lived in back of the trailer and opened a bait shop in front.

The rest is ramshackle history. Through the years Al added beer coolers, a shed to house a kitchen, a concrete slab for pool tables and dancing, then put walls and a roof over the entire outfit; including the trailer. Rough and Randy is low-ceilinged, and three times longer than it is wide. The joint caters to guys who carry shotguns behind their truck seats, and argue the virtues of pit bulls as opposed to dobermans. They do this in a joint where pool tables are level because of concrete, but where otherwise, the floor sags.

In the whitely-lighted parking lot, as the kid pulled in, sat a dozen experienced pickups, three Harley hogs, Petey's Plymouth, and Al's treasured '53 Kaiser acquired from a suicidal patron who believed he could beat Al at poker.

The kid knew Rough and Randy only by reputation. He took a deep breath. He climbed from his truck, walked across the light-stricken parking lot, and heard, beyond the buzz of lights, shushing and slooshing of the Canal. In the forest an owl hooted. A disgruntled woof came from inside the Plymouth where Jubal Jim stood guard.

The kid slowed. The joint was too quiet. There should be chainsaw music going on in there. There should be voices, the click of cueballs, laughter and cussing.

The kid took a deep breath and reminded himself that he was just as tough as the next guy. Besides, he had just gotta talk to Petey. When he stepped inside he stood for a moment deciding whether to run or stay.

The bar at Rough and Randy is a long and skinny oval. It looks like the letter O would look, if the letter O had been run over by a Kenworth. Al walks on the inside of the oval where sit beer cases, beer taps, sinks, and a billy club. Customers sit on bar stools around the oval. They look across the oval at each other. On one side sit guys from a nearby paper mill, on the other are guys from a sawmill. At the ends are a scatter of bikers, shade tree mechanics, retired alcoholics, and an occasional survivalist. Few ladies attend services at Rough and Randy, and those who do are not artful.

Guns are checked-in the minute you walk through the door, because Al will supply a stern lesson to any dope who believes he can pack and drink. In this, Al is backed by his customers. Any guy found with a gun gets kicked soft and forever banished. Rough and Randy knows that .357 caliber illusions are just lovely, but when .357 turns to reality, that reality is too heavy-duty for Rough and Randy.

The kid tip-toed to the bar and saw the reason for silence. At the far end, two giants sat locked in an arm wrestle. One giant looked sorta Japanese mixed with Indian, or prob'ly Filipino, and the other looked like the biggest gawdawful Hawaiian that ever rode a surfboard to the mainland. The Japanese-Indian-Flip had a forearm like old growth timber, and the Hawaiian's arm looked like sculpted steel. Both guys were black-haired, sorta tan-like, with hands big as shovels and shoulders purely rowdy. It was hard to tell which guy's eyes popped most, but the truly scary thing was neither breathed very hard.

No sound came from the bar where sat mill-rats with spikey and unwashed hair, bikers, a red-hair lady wearing a real tight sweater, an ancient gent who looked kinda loaded but smart, and a mean-looking guy wearing a camouflage jumpsuit.

Al moved toward the kid. Al looked like a ship of war; an aircraft carrier or at least a cruiser. Al's full beard is not curly like

Sugar Bear's, and his eyes are not gentle like Sugar Bear's, but his hands can bend rebar. Al was not quite as big as the arm-wrestle guys, but nearly.

"Beer," the kid whispered, and searched the room for Petey. A guy along the bar blew his nose. Other guys turned toward him, sneered, turned back to watch the contest. The kid saw Petey standing beside a pool table toward the darkest corner of the room. The kid carried his beer in that direction, and he walked quiet as a mouse on velvet.

Petey yawned, scratched his bottom, looked bored. The kid, who knew just enough about hustling to be dangerous, understood he was welcome.

"How long?" the kid whispered about the arm wrestle.

"Maybe half an hour." Petey sounded indifferent, but he kept an eye on the Hawaiian's forearm, which meant Petey's dough rode with the Hawaiian.

"Rack 'em?" the kid whispered, because the kid figured if you were gonna talk to Petey it better be while doing a game. Petey, without a pool cue, was an unknown quantity.

"If you wanna get kilt," Petey told the kid, "go ahead and rack 'em. Otherwise . . . ," Pete yawned, ". . . hang onto your beer and wait."

Along the bar men silently drank, watched, silently pushed empty glasses toward Al for refills. On the paper-mill side of the bar the mill-smell rose like dark perfume, and on the lumber side the smell of fresh wood chips mixed with the sour smell of wet bark. Al cruised silent as a forest weasel between customers and beer taps.

The kid, without understanding why, felt like a child in church . . . something about devotion or devotionals . . . about being bored spitless . . . something like that. The kid would not have been surprised if organ music burst across the room. You didn't talk in church, and sure as stink you didn't talk during an arm wrestle. Church or not, the kid still had enough sense to check for exits.

He stood in the best possible place. The cone of light over the table hid him from the bar.

The long oval held the quality of a painting, like it ought to hang in a museum alongside faded ships' logs, pioneer tools, Indian trade-trinkets, iron-shod wagon wheels, moth-eaten buffalo robes; a museum of the wild-wild west without the gloss of movieland. The kid, who knew just enough history to believe the world was made ten minutes before he was born, found that he felt itchy; like maybe he caught a case of fleas, or maybe hepatitis.

Petey gave a small tap with his toe as the Hawaiian's arm gained a degree off center. The Hawaiian looked at the Japanesey-sorta guy, looked at his eyes. Mauna Loa hatred flared, blazed, seemed ready to crackle. The Japanese looked back, samurai violence like cold light mixed with the swish of swords; and veins stood out on arms like they would bust, like blood would spurt through skin, fountains of it. The Japanese guy's arm moved back one degree.

The red-hair lady pushed an empty glass toward Al. A mill-rat pushed some bucks alongside the empty glass. The red-hair lady turned to the mill guy, smiled, and even the kid could tell matters in that direction were settled for at least one night. A skinny biker, hopes vanquished (for at least one night) stood, knocked back the rest of his beer, and headed for the door. He gave a backward wave to Al. In less than a minute the Harley barked its open-throat song, and the bike moved away like sad talkin' and slow walkin'.

Now the arm-wrestle guys entered the heavy-sweat stage of

the wrestle. They dripped from foreheads, and neither had a Second who could wield a hanky. They started to breathe heavy, and each stared at the other's face. The Hawaiian grunted, sweated, gave an extra heavy grunt, and sudden as a squall, nailed the other guy's hand to the bar while cheers erupted from the sawmill guys. The paper mill guys sat ticked-off and ready to holler that the fix was in. Al distributed winnings.

"Hot work," the Japanese guy said to the Hawaiian with affection in his voice. "I'll get your scrawny butt next time."

"Winner buys." The Hawaiian yawned. He spoke to Al. "Give my man a beer."

"Rack 'em." Petey came from the bar with his winnings. "We got time for a game or two."

Noise filled the bar. Guys joked, bulled, thanked the losers for their donations, and Al turned up the tape deck. The sound of molested guitars thumped beneath the low ceiling. Windows facing the Canal, washed only when the health inspector made unbribable threats, showed a full moon shining dimly over tranquil water.

"I got a deal," the kid told Petey. "It's a real deal."

"I heard the bull," Petey told him. Petey popped the rack a little too gentle and failed to hide the cueball. "Run 'em," he said. "I wish you luck."

The kid ran three balls, then shanked an easy shot. "This ain't bull," he told Petey. "This is major money. This is a damn gold rush." He watched the cueball end up in the middle of the table, naked as a centerfold.

"Lemme ask you something." Petey took his time running the table. He checked his watch. "Do rich bastards get rich by being nice?" Petey tapped a three-way combo on the nine ball, picked up the fiver the kid had laid out. "We got time for one more game."

"I figure easy in, easy out," the kid said. "One hot night, and leave 'em stew in their own crap."

"You're talkin' younger than usual." Petey watched the kid rack. "Which means you won't listen. But, it's your education. Sometimes it costs to learn things." Petey broke the rack, hid the cueball while making nothing, messing with the kid's brain.

The kid tried to dig out of the hole and left an opening. Petey shanked the shot and hid the cueball. It dawned on the kid that Petey played mind stuff.

"If you go to that tournament," Petey told the kid, "win, but win polite, and don't win big. This is Petey tellin' you." He checked his watch. "The road is gonna heat up." He ran the table. "The worst damfool is the guy who wins big in front of the other guy's woman." Petey picked up another five, unscrewed his cue. "See ya."

The bar emptied as guys shrugged into jackets, and eased through the doorway while carrying six-packs. Loud music faded as Al turned down the tape deck. Al picked up beer glasses, mopped the bar, emptied ashtrays and pitched them in the sink. Al looked like a bear hulking behind the bar, but not a Sugar Bear. Al looked like one of those bad, bad bears that rule the forest, and, as guys attest, crap where they want.

The kid packed his cue, then stood irresolute. He was a good, long drive from home. He had work tomorrow, and guys were leaving before the road heated up. Worse, even, was Petey's big advice. The kid wondered what kind of hustle Petey was running.

Al pointed toward the door. Then Al yawned, grunted, leaned over to work the kinks out of his back. "Sleep in your truck. Use the parking lot if you wanta." Al reached beneath the counter. Switches clicked. Lights went out. The kid, who had not recruited a star pool player in Petey, and who still had to put a team together, walked to the door. The only light came from a couple beer signs. When he stepped outside, the only light came from the moon riding high and full above the Canal.

In spots where light shone unblocked by tree-shadow the road lay like a silver strip beneath the moon. Headlights of the Ranchero picked up greenly-and-redly glowing eyes of possum, raccoon, and housecat. The kid drove rapid but not fast, and he turned up the FM band because nothin' AM was gonna come in this far from the big city. Electronic music, the bass-beat thumping heavy as a fat pile driver, filled the cab and spilled through partly open windows. Forest creatures fled, or watched flaring headlights, and if they had opinions, kept those opinions to themselves.

The road does not always adhere to the Canal. Sometimes it takes short excursions into little valleys between mountains. In one spot it runs through national forest and is often littered with roadkill, mostly deer, mostly dumb deer. Then, when a guy least expects it, the road bends back and follows the Canal real single-minded. It eases close to dark waters. Moonlight that lies in a strip across the water seems to climb right off the surface and halve the road like a silver knife.

It was in just such a spot the dunked cars were going in, the same spot where the kid loaded wrecks onto the trailer of the tow truck. As he approached the dunk site a whiff of good sense, or maybe only a beer belch, caused the kid to come off the gas. Caution seized him. The kid tapped brakes, slowed in the curve leading to the dunk site, then braked further as the electronic bass thumped from the radio. The Ranchero crawled forward with less speed than a bumper-car in an amusement park.

At first it seemed that the truck skidded sideways. Movement caused a little fishtail, and as the kid steered into it he realized it actually was the road, and not the Ranchero that was going twisty. His rig moved slowly, inexorably, sideways, like on an icy grade and pulled by its own weight. Headlights slowly twisted away from the road as the rear end sorta fell toward the Canal. Headlights shone into the forest and were swallowed by trees as the Ranchero moved back-bumper-first into the Canal; moving like on a tow cable wound to a slow winch.

The kid bailed. He slipped on the rock shingle as he jumped. The open door of the Ranchero clipped him. He fell. Scrambled toward the road. Slipped again. Scrambled to the road and turned, blinded by headlights of his own rig. Then the headlights pointed to the sky as the rear end sank into the Canal. Bubbles rose. Electronic music thumped, thumped, stilled. For a moment headlights shone underwater, then shorted out and only moon and kid stood witness to the demise of a classic.

Because no guy, even guys who just escaped drowning, and prob'ly worse, are gonna lose a '57 Ranchero without a lot of mourning. The damn things only get ten miles to a gallon when heading downhill with a tail wind, but when guys have got the best they gotta expect it's gonna cost.

The kid, scared silly, watched the little truck disappear. He watched the moon take over, the silver path indifferent, like nothing cosmic or tragic had been goin' on. Then the kid scrambled to the far side of the road, crossed the ditch, and actually hugged a tree while kneeling. He told himself if the Canal meant to take him, it had to get him tree-'n-all.

The path of moonlight showed a little ruffle near the shore, something stirring just beneath water, something sort of dead-fish pale, white, bloodless, cold as a corpse; a shimmer of white beneath the silver path of moon, a stir of water. The form slowly broke the surface. It shimmered, coalesced into a hulking, almost human shape, and struggled toward land. A wave of cold, and a stink of decay drifted across the road. The thing was more than apparition, but less than solid, and it made no sound although it had a sort-of face, a sort-of mouth. It stood, not even half-formed, grasping toward land; and then slowly sank backward into dark water.

The kid held to the tree and found he could not think. He trembled with cold. He retched from the stench. His arms shook with cold, like changing a tire in winter. The stench passed but the cold did not, and he felt it reaching toward him. He feared he could no longer hold onto the tree. He watched water close over the what-ever-it-was. The kid was barely conscious that a hump moved just beneath the surface of the Canal, moved pretty quick toward the drowned truck, seemed to pause, then slowly moved away. The hump headed toward the darkest and deepest trench of the Hood Canal.

The kid found himself a long, long way from home, without wheels, and not a chance of anything coming by 'til morning. He shivered. He still held onto the tree. Nothing pulled at him. He took a step onto the road, took another. He began walking slowly along the berm, ready to jump for another tree in case the Canal tried to take him. As confidence increased he speeded up. He warmed as he got further from the dunk site. The kid figured to sleep under the porch of Beer and Bait, then catch a ride going south. He kept shivering, but not with cold. Considering everything that had been goin' on, shivering was no more than a guy would have to expect.

Short Bulletins as Bertha Hustles

Three weeks, only three little weeks. Three weeks that brought to his boat one daddy-rabbit halibut of 230 pounds, one junior-achievement halibut of seventy pounds, plus the usual suspects; black cod, snapper, and redfish. Three weeks of gulls circling in mist, squawking and ready to slurp cleaned fish guts. Three weeks of fog horns from enormous ships plying main trade routes, of bell buoys a-clank, of trips to the fish factory through wind and mist; while back on shore everything went fish-belly-up.

It was well into September by the time the fisherman returned to the Canal where enough bull waited to make a man want to stay offshore a year. As the fisherman cleaned the boat, other fishermen gossiped, loafed, advised. By the time he secured the boat, stopped by home for shower, shave, and shore-legs, the fisherman knew it would be smart to stay away from Beer and Bait. That knowledge, naturally, compelled him toward Beer and Bait with all despatch. He pulled into the parking lot suspecting that, although he'd been offshore three weeks, he needed an iron-clad alibi.

Because bull said Chantrell was history, Petey was about to get his mast restepped, Sugar Bear and Annie had returned and were hiding out, the tow-truck kid caused seventeen tons of perdition during a pool joust at the housing project, and the kid, during off-hours, pushed a new Dodge pickup, V10, tot-ally loaded, a foreman's truck; while the state cop circled Beer and Bait like a vulture, and Bertha was wearing her hair "done up".

There's always a slight germ of truth in every Canal story. Thus, the fisherman felt drawn to Beer and Bait because, being thoughtful, this particular fisherman loved truth.

In mid-afternoon the parking lot held a '63 Jimmy pickup, a fried-out Rambler station wagon, a red tow truck, a 600 Ford with cattle racks, and a gleamy new Cadillac that, as anyone with brains could see, had not the least business on the premises. The fisherman sighed, pretended he was brave, and reminded himself that the smartest guys are the ones who keep their traps shut.

When he stepped inside Beer and Bait he saw that Bertha looked lonesome but didn't know it. Bertha's mouth seemed a little tight, her formality stiffer than necessary, and yes, her hair was done-up. When she mopped with a bar rag her hands did not carry any snap.

Along the bar ranged a select group of Canal citizens, plus a couple outsiders; a rich guy playing pool, and a sorta scruffy organic lady; the kind who is always just "passing through", who wears granny skirts, shoots up yogurt, drops granola, snorts carrot juice, and drives ragged-out Ramblers. She sat next to the gyypo electrician who owned the Jimmy, and on her other side sat a pig farmer, the only soul in the joint with a light outlook. The tow-truck kid stood at a pool table where he hustled the rich guy, and, while no one at the bar paid attention to the game, Bertha made notes. It was clear when the kid finished hustling he would answer to Bertha. Big time.

The fisherman took the stool nearest the door. It had the advantage of a view plus rapid egress.

"Long time," Bertha said, and put a beer before him.

"Double-halibut," the fisherman said.

"That long?" Bertha tried to sound interested, but her eyes kept shifting to the pool game.

"And Jennifer," the pig farmer said to the organic lady, "sadly enough, has turned into a tramp." He rolled his eyes and sighed. This pig farmer was lanky, darker than Petey but not quite Mexican, and he wore a red flannel shirt and a ball cap reading "Pedigreed Porkers". He allowed himself a gentle smile as he hustled the organic lady.

"Jennifer is a pig," the electrician explained.

"It's what she's become." The farmer chuckled.

The organic lady sipped at a chablis while weighing choices. She could drive on down the road and spend the night in the Rambler. On the other hand, the pig farmer had a sense of humor, and he certainly smelled organic.

"I heard something about Chantrell," the fisherman murmured to Bertha.

Bertha dabbed with a bar rag, cast a look of Scandinavian scorn at the organic lady, leaned across the bar. "He emigrated. Ask Sugar Bear. Ask Annie." Bertha's tone told the fisherman that no public discussion would happen. She looked toward the pool game where the tow-truck kid pulled a routine combo on the nine ball. "You've missed quite a bit," she told the fisherman, her voice grim.

"It's a little known fact," the pig farmer told the organic lady, "that the I.Q. of your average pig exceeds that of your average . . ." He looked at Bertha, grinned, shrugged, and did not say "Cop," and didn't have to. "Electrician," the pig farmer said.

"And some sod-busters are dumb enough to name their pigs." The electrician sipped at his suds. The men were obviously buddies, and that made the organic lady possessive. She touched the pig farmer's hand.

"Pool tournament?" It was hard for the fisherman to catch up on bull because there was lots of it. Where did a guy start?

"We got a problem," Bertha admitted, and she did not lower her voice. "We got a kid getting way too big for his britches."

"And with a new truck?"

"Half paid for," the kid said. He stood at the pool table trying to look sharkish, but for some reason the fisherman couldn't fathom, the kid looked scared. The kid turned back to the table. The rich guy, who was plump, shanked a shot. "What?" he said to the kid.

"Like this," the kid said, and the fisherman saw the kid was not hustling. The kid gave lessons.

"He got a new truck because of bad driving," Bertha said about the kid, "because he dunked his other truck."

The fisherman watched the kid stiffen. The kid shanked a shot. He looked ready to say something sharp, looked afraid, then turned and stomped toward the can.

"It was halfway amusing," the pig farmer said to the fisherman. "The kid got to haul his junk Ranchero to impound, got to haul his own truck. Wet as wet could be."

"Without a scratch on it," the electrician mused. "Tot-ally different from all them others. All them others were scratched and twisted."

The rich guy stood listening. His golf shirt spread across his tummy like a cuddly layer of wealth. The organic lady didn't understand the discussion and seemed resentful. The pig farmer studied the situation and tried to figure whether he wanted to tangle with the organic lady, or maybe not. The electrician stood ready to take over in case the pig farmer decided against.

"That's too different," the fisherman murmured. "No scratches. It's scary when something ought to happen, and doesn't."

161

"What will certainly happen," the rich guy said in a quiet voice, "is another pool tournament." The rich guy sounded sincere, and that was also scary.

"It's a game." Bertha touched the bar with her fingertips, maybe reminding herself that she controlled the joint. "Being good at pool is like being good at nothing special. What's wrong with guys?" Her voice held small, nearly concealed pain. There was no bull, and there was definite sorrow.

The fisherman started to explain about guys, then shut up. Matters do not generally get intimate at Beer and Bait, except physically. True, an occasional drunk may talk valentine talk, or something equally sloppy, but sincerity? On the Canal? At Beer and Bait?

The rich guy leaned on his pool cue. He stared across the tip, then glanced around the joint like he owned it. "It is only a game," he admitted quietly. "Trouble is, games ask to be won." The rich guy didn't explain that he was used to winning. A new Cadillac sat in the parking lot.

Bertha leaned against the backbar. She studied the rich guy the way the rich guy maybe studied a business proposition. It was clear Bertha was ready to deal, though no one could figure why, or what.

"Your aim's okay," she told the rich guy, "and your feel for the table ain't bad, but your little finger is coming up on the cue when you stroke. You got little-finger problems."

"Happens to me all the time," the electrician murmured. He turned his right hand palm upward, squinched his eyes, and gave a deep sigh.

"One of my main sorrows." The pig farmer chuckled.

"Tape your little finger to the next finger and practice that-a-way," the fisherman told the rich guy. "You're losing about one degree on every shot."

The rich guy actually looked at his little finger like he thought of amputation. "Are you folks serious."

"Try it," the electrician said. "Stroke normal and feel what your hand is doing."

The rich guy stroked. "I see what you mean," he said quietly. He tried not to look like a man who has just struck gold. "You have a real nice place," he said to Bertha, and it was clear he tried to pay for good advice. He turned as the kid came from the can. "Why didn't you say something about this little-finger stuff?"

"Little-finger stuff?"

"I will be damn. . . . " The rich guy leaned against the table, struck by a combination of disgust and admiration. "You've been setting me up for another hustle," he said to the kid. "You should study law." The rich guy unscrewed his cue. "Because we got a lawyer-shortage. Meanwhile, you're fired." The rich guy packed up his cue as the kid stuttered.

"A very nice place," the rich guy told Bertha as he left. "You are an exceptional businesswoman, and we must talk some business soon." The rich guy sounded like a preacher giving a blessing.

"Little-finger stuff?" Then the kid realized everyone at the bar faced away from him, and four sets of shoulders shook as guys and Bertha tried to control laughter.

"That," said the pig farmer, "was educational. I'm gonna teach that move to my stud boar." He giggled, turned to look at the kid, and bust out laughing.

The fisherman, who had just witnessed a hustle delivered with total finesse, nearly choked on his beer.

"The rich bastard actually bought it. He felt his finger coming up even when it couldn't." The electrician looked at Bertha like he saw her for the first time. "I'm gonna camp here forever. This is a good, safe place to get bombed."

Bertha, temporarily happy, looked toward the kid. "Next time you set up in the pool-teaching business, pick another bar. Or, help me pay my mortgage." Bertha sounded serious. "You just made an enemy. That guy knows you were setting him up."

"While chargin' for the lessons," the kid said. "Gimmie a little credit here. That guy's wife, the one who wears purple, set up that first tournament; and the guy still comes back for more. Gimmie a little credit." Then confusion mixed with brashness, and through the mixture shone an edge of fear. "Little finger?"

"Truck payments," the pig farmer mused. "And on a damn Dodge. And aught but b.s. for a backhaul." Sympathy mixed with amusement as he watched the kid. He shook his head, turned to the organic lady, ". . . takes quite a while to grow up. . . ," looked at the electrician, "and some never do. . . ," and then to the kid, he said, "Thanks, I needed that." He stood, patted the organic lady on the shoulder, tugged at the bill of his cap, smiled in a general way at everyone, and left.

"He's flighty," the electrician assured the organic lady who sat totally steamed. "Been that way since kindergarten. Dropped on his head as a baby."

The organic lady smiled, turned to the electrician, pouted only a little, then smiled some more.

"And Annie and Sugar Bear are back?" The fisherman recalled that awful afternoon at China Bay, nearly a month ago, when Annie led a very moist Sugar Bear away; and when he, the fisherman, had probably had one or two jars of suds too many.

"At Sugar Bear's place, but I doubt he's open for business." Bertha watched the kid and seemed real worried. She at least forgot the load she planned to dump. "They haven't been in, Annie or Sugar Bear. You're his best friend."

"Phone?"

"I ought to go over there," Bertha said apologetically. "I ought to take time off." Then she brightened. "You really are his best friend." She turned to the beer case. "Take a six-pack."

The Adventures of
Chantrell George

Consider the Salvation Army. Consider, especially, the concept of Grace. Think of hymns played on big city street corners; cornets and clarinets and snare drums nearer to God than we, playing beneath eyes of storm; no pay for players, a new pair of shoes, the love of fellow man behind the blat of spiritual messages.

Consider also the customers: the junkies, alkies, down-and-outers, the hookers, run-aways, the insane and the sick, the confused; the tired people beat-to-hell because of excess by themselves or by a system that thrives not on Grace.

Because there is a difference between charity and Grace (Grace is not deductible). Grace flies free and without deserving as it rises from Sally's Army and other armies of the street that snag the occasional bum, the one, who, with a stirring of soul, would choose (if he could) not to be a bum. . . . For it is true that a bum who holds glimmers of hope, and ability to offer a little trust, can be floored when encountering Grace.

Consider also, that Chantrell George, being a country boy, knows nothing of Sally's Army, and certainly nothing of Grace. As he wanders, confused, past drug deals on Second Ave. in Seattle, past drunks and hookers, his shoulders slump and his belly is so empty he's sure his throat has been cut. His straggledy hair hangs limp, and his eyes see only the pavement in front of his feet. He steps timidly as he approaches the sound of a cornet; "Amazing Grace," and, as he steps toward this new experience we may back away from consideration of this whole deal—while experiencing a glimmer of hope.

Recent Pooler History

Sugar Bear's gingerbread house and voluminous workshop nestle among firs and cedars. A cliff stands behind the house, and above that, land rises in a sharp slope to forested mountainside. Swallows nest in the cliff, hawks float overhead, owls pounce during owl light, a few gold-bricking sparrows hang out at a bird feeder, and a house wren blesses the place with the flash of red on her tummy.

Inside the house, after the fisherman knocked and entered, matters looked pretty thin. The fisherman set the six-pack on the kitchen table, popped beers, and passed them. "You'll forgive it," he said to Sugar Bear, "I've seen days when you looked better."

"Some kind of crap is happening," Sugar Bear said. "We can't figure it." Sugar Bear looked furry as ever, but there were gray streaks in his beard and wrinkles around his eyes. ". . . like trying to punch a hole in fog."

"Slowly, slowly." The fisherman looked around the place, saw it immaculate in a way too pure for a Sugar-Bear-happy-go-sloppy life, and figured Annie was to blame. Next there would be chintz curtains and salt shakers shaped like little duckies. . . . "You've brightened the place," he said to Annie.

She sat, more beautiful than ever. Her face seemed thinner which accented her dark eyes. Long hair framed her face. Her hands, always beautiful, always one of the pretty things about her also seemed thinner; hands streamlined and practical, hands that could make everyday magic along with other magics. Annie, who the fisherman knew was fond of him in a sisterly way, was clearly on defense as she tried to figure out who she could trust.

"Tell me," he said to Annie.

It was, the fisherman would later muse, like one of those dark and improbable Russian plays where everybody does right things for wrong reasons, and wrong things for stupid reasons; and then stands hollering in the wind, or kneeling broken and bent before one or another altar. A 'course, the fisherman would also later reflect, this wasn't Russia. Besides, Annie was Greek, and Sugar Bear was a mongrel.

The part about Chantrell was easy. Nobody would want to hurt the poor sap, but a scorpion, even of innocent intent, was still a scorpion.

The part about Petey wasn't easy. It looked like Petey and the cop had a date with destiny. Instead of the cop chasing Petey, Petey chased the cop.

"Not, a 'course, like anything real obvious." Sugar Bear puzzled, looked around the immaculate house that made him even more puzzled. "But wherever the cop shows up, Petey shows up. Like he's checking the cop out. Could be the cop is getting nervous."

"And that's good," Annie murmured without explaining why. As near as the fisherman could tell, Annie ran a number on herself. She didn't look unhappy, but she didn't look particularly happy.

"Makes 'police harassment' take on new meaning," the fisherman mused. Then the fisherman realized something. He brightened. "It's a hustle. Petey's a hustler. He's running a hustle on the cop."

Sugar Bear had probably not smiled in a long time. Now he looked delighted. Annie giggled, but the giggle was tense. The fisherman realized matters were just a little less than hysteric. He tried to take advantage of what cheer existed.

"So what's his hustle?"

"Hustlers got a world of their own, so there ain't no way of telling." Part of Sugar Bear's delight came because he could think of somebody else's troubles.

"A hustle depends on letting the other guy believe he'll get what he wants."

"So what does a cop want?"

"He wants to hurt somebody. He wants to solve a case. What does a cop ever want?" Annie, the fisherman realized, was not as subdued as she seemed. Anyone who came after Sugar Bear would have to deal with Greek thunder. Big time.

"Easy answer," the fisherman told Annie. "Sooner or later we'll think it through." He looked at Sugar Bear. "And there was a pool tournament?"

"I shoulda gone," Sugar Bear said. "The cash-stash is running a little low."

To the fisherman it seemed Sugar Bear was large as ever, but if you looked close his clothes hung a little loose. If he did not have that faceful of fur, he might even look thin.

"As well you didn't," Annie told Sugar Bear, then looked to the fisherman. "I know those people."

And yes, the fisherman recalled, Annie had emigrated from the development, so, yes, she knew those people. He listened as the sordid story unfolded.

It was clear that, in the case of the tow-truck kid, only the optimism of youth could possibly have walked into that poolish situation and driven away with a half-paid-for Dodge pickup, driving toward doom and utter darkness; or, maybe, at least, coasting toward perdition. Plus, a 'course, a Canal story went with it.

The story said the kid showed up with a team of beetle-lady-champions wearing purple bowling shirts. The champions were a mixture of Beer and Bait, and Rough and Randy regulars. Under the beetle-lady's tutelage some of them actually learned to speak words instead of grunts.

Arrayed on the other side, and clad in pastel golfing togs, a team of business jocks wielded seven-hundred-dollar pool cues above a pair of tables so big they looked like soccer fields. Standard plastic balls rolled on the table, but a classic set of ivory balls, yellowed with age, and under lock and key, nestled like diamonds in a small case on the wall. They seemed like memories of antique conquest, of the white man's burden, and of jolly excursions up dark and exotic rivers.

A well-stocked bar sat at one end of the room, and around the bar sat gowned ladies who wore the colors of butterflies. Subdued music, sorta churchy, or opera-type, came from the tape deck. Autographed pictures of Republican presidents and secretaries of state hung on the walls. Cigar smoke from hundred-buck havannas magically whirled away on warm air circulated through a filter system. Drinks were on the house.

Free booze caused the boys of Rough and Randy to experience sweat in their armpits, and wonder into what type of cow-plop they had just stepped. Free booze was the oldest hustle in the book. Either these rich guys were secret hustlers, or so damn dumb it made a fella's mouth water just to think about it.

The whole deal, the story continued, turned into that kind of cuss-and-cream-soda-hustle you'd expect from a smarty-type kid backed by frowsy regulars. That is to say: indelicate.

The rich guys actually held their own for an hour. The rich guys were gracious. They complimented the bar guys on good shots. The rich guys whispered like co-conspirators, and even demonstrated a little know-how when it came to setting their partners up. As the rich guys settled into their game they pulled off some pretty showy action.

Meanwhile, the butterflies did not actually do handsprings, stand on each other's shoulders, or any cheerleader-type stuff, but they grew pretty boisterous for butterflies. As Mr. Jack Daniels lowered inhibitions, clapping and smiles increased. By the end of an hour the butterflies turned from a flock of flowers into a howling wolfpack—which, as anyone has gotta admit, is mixing a couple metaphors, but that generally happens in Canal stories.

At the end of an hour the rich guys began to fade. They started forcing their shots. Their cues no longer hung loose in their hands, and sweat in their palms asked for increasing amounts of talcum. Little wrinkles around eyes deepened, and eyes narrowed and looked snarly. The whole show did a one-eighty as rich guys began missing shots. If the butterflies had turned into a wolfpack, the bar guys now turned into wolverines.

The rest is Canal history. The bar guys did their best as they tried for a sophisticated hustle. It didn't work. They still sounded like a used car salesman urging a reluctant customer toward something that needs a valve job. The rich guys put up with it, because the rich guys knew the hustle had started. And, being rich, the rich guys could not believe they could lose. As matters grew serious, the tow-truck kid made out best. He was so damn dumb he played for the whole pot every time, and got on a roll.

At the end of it, as butterflies drifted off with great indifference, the rich guys managed to remain civil. The bar guys tried not to act like the kind of boys they are. Still, it turned into a long night, and the worst part was the indifference of the butter-flies; indifference worse than scorn. The bar guys departed the premises with no small amount of cash, but with feelings most uneasy.

"And that's where it stands," Annie explained. "Now we're waiting for the other shoe to drop."

The fisherman, mildly alarmed, told of the rich guy at Beer and Bait, and how that guy fired the tow-truck kid. He told how the rich guy and the beetle-lady were married. The fisherman told about little-finger stuff, and as he talked he felt scary because rich guy promised another joust at pool.

"He's running true to form," Annie murmured. "That kid thought he was hustling, but rich guy pulled the hustle."

Annie was, the fisherman told himself, either sharper than he was, or else talking to herself.

"Bait and switch," Annie explained. "The kid thinks this deal is about pool. It's about something else. Hard to say what." She looked through the kitchen window into the forest. Shadows lay deep, and moisture feathered the needles of trees like silver. If Annie saw important stuff out there she did not say. Instead she talked about the housing project.

"It's a game to them. They'll spend two thousand dollars and two months planning a way to cheat their brother out of a hundred bucks. Then they'll spend a thousand dollars more on a party in their brother's honor." She looked back into the forest where shadows lay deep. "I don't know enough," she whispered. "I should of paid more attention." She sounded sad, and she definitely was not speaking to the fisherman or Sugar Bear.

"Maybe all this is good," Sugar Bear said. "If we get a lot of flak then everybody worries about the flak. They'll talk about other stuff. The cop snoops someplace else."

"Don't get too hopeful," the fisherman said. "How come you're looking poorly?"

"I can't work," Sugar Bear told him. "That's the deal. I go along for a while, get to feeling good, do a little work, and get sicky. I piddle around, get to feeling good again, fire up the forge and get sicky." He looked at Annie, his look sweet as his name and gentle as his nature. He was clearly smitten. "The best thing in the world happens, and here I am, breaking down. I can't work."

And that, the fisherman thought, had to be the worst possible thing that could happen. Even the biggest goldbrick in the world did something buildable. True, some guys built, and some tore down, but *doing* was a damn infliction. Even poor dopey old Chantrell had built visions.

"The dead guy . . ." Sugar Bear began, and was interrupted.

"Forget the dead guy. He's zip. Gone. Take care of what's here, right now." Annie turned to the fisherman. She did not exactly ask for anything, not exactly; but her look asked for help he wanted to give and couldn't. He didn't see how to get a handhold on the problem.

The fisherman absentmindedly tapped a finger against his beer can and tried to look encouraging. This was the woman he loved and lost, but he'd already spent nearly a month learning to handle that. And, he told himself, he was sorta handling it.

Plus, Sugar Bear was his best friend. A thoughtful guy ought to come up with something. Then, for no reason he could see, the fisherman thought of the tow-truck kid. The kid had looked scared in spite of his smart mouth.

"The key to the cop might be the kid," the fisherman mused. "They work together."

"Cops ain't that mysterious." Sugar Bear studied the problem like a man about to take a test for a seaman's ticket. "If mystery stuff is happening, I don't see how a cop plays any part."

"The cop is lonesome. I do know that." Annie told how, on one hot day, she watched the cop from the forest. He looked lonesome then, and hot, and miserable. If he hadn't been a cop she would have taken him a lemonade.

"So is Bertha," the fisherman said. "Lonesome. But she don't know it."

The three people looked at each other in disbelief. "Naw," Sugar Bear said. "Can't happen."

"Anything can," Annie told him. She once more turned to the fisherman. "I don't see how this feeds into our problem."

"Maybe it doesn't, but it's one thing we don't know about. And, the kid knows something. I'll quiz the kid."

"Or the cop," Sugar Bear said. "But who's gonna do discussion group with a cop?"

"Me, maybe," Annie told him. "Also with Bertha. Bartenders know everything that's going on."

Petey Hustles and
the Fisherman Shudders

Next day the fisherman visited the dunk site. With sun behind mountains and pink mist across water, state cops leaned against their cars. They did not make conversation. A 911 ambulance pulled away carrying two dead people. The yellow crane whirred into silence, having deposited its burden. The fisherman approached the kid.

"The cops are scared." The tow-truck kid worked rapidly as he talked to the fisherman. The kid's dishwater blond hair had grown movie-star shaggy. He moved muscular and brisk, but kept his head down. On his trailer sat a Ford crummy-wagon, one of those new-type outfits with fancy interior, now soggy. It looked like a twisted and stomped, squashed beer can. The purr of the yellow crane speeded as cable and harness lifted up, up, and away, having deposited the wreck on the kid's trailer.

This first week of October showed little traffic. Only one cop played beckon-and-whistle, or stop-or-I'll-bust-you. Petey stood on the other side of the road beside his parked Plymouth, pretending to watch traffic while doing his "aw shucks" act. Petey looked guilty enough to hang.

The fisherman leaned against the kid's trailer. The kid rigged tie-downs, racheted them tight, moving around the trailer with the efficiency of a guy doing the job right, even though scared.

"The beer-and-bait cop is spookiest," the kid said. "Other cops talk but that guy just watches. He's primed for something. I think the guy's in trouble, and so dumb he don't know it." The kid moved quick. It was clear he didn't like to get anywhere near the wreck, but was bein' brave because he must.

"The job is getting to everybody," the fisherman suggested.

"Not everybody," the kid told him. "Some of these cops get their hots off it. They find it fascinatin'."

"And the beer-and-bait cop?"

"The guy's a damn Crusader Rabbit," the kid said. "Bertha better watch out."

"Bertha is smart."

The kid looked along the shore, looked at the now silent crane. The fisherman watched while pretending to look elsewhere. He told himself he would-be-damn. The kid actually shuddered.

"I figure it this way," the kid said. "Petey's gonna get busted. Petey's gonna spread enough bull that cops screw up and spill over on other guys . . . you confuse a cop, the cop busts every-body. Guys will get grilled like steak. Bertha better choose up sides because guys talk. She'll never sell another beer."

"There's something more," the fisherman suggested. "When you get that heap secured I'll stand for suds. I need to talk." The fisherman told himself he sounded like a weenie, but it was in a good cause. "I spend a lot of time on the water," he told the kid. "And it's getting ten-past-scary out there. You know what I mean?" He tried to make his voice sound timid, and was surprised because it sounded more timid than he tried for.

The kid was startled, but tried not to show it. His shoulders came up a bit. He rubbed muscles in his upper arm, gave an extra rachet to a tie-down. The wrecked Ford squeaked. The fisherman was treating the kid like a full-grown man. This wasn't pool table stuff, this was real stuff. It took the kid a minute to get a handle on it, and another minute to feel proud.

". . . know what you mean," he told the fisherman. The kid looked toward the beer-and-bait cop. "He's gonna hassle and hassle and hassle." The kid sounded nearly scornful. "He ain't gonna solve nothing, not if he goes home every night." The kid moved toward the cab of his truck. "I got something to talk over. I'll meet you down to Bertha's."

The parking lot of Beer and Bait showed that a few Canal citizens had knocked off work early. Loggers, house painters, carpenters, and bug exterminators would be nuzzling the bar. Enough bull would fly to serve as cover for serious conversation. The fisherman had that "halibut feeling", like he just put a line onto a big one.

When the tow-truck kid pulled into the lot a few guys gathered to view the wrecked Ford. The kid had to stay out there and act modest. The fisherman staked out a table in back, and went for a pitcher. By the time the kid got done, the fisherman was halfway to the bottom of his first glass.

The kid sorta strutted from the front door to the fisherman's table, but stopped showing off the minute he sat. He lowered his voice. "I bin catching crap about losing that Ranchero." Then, remembering he was being treated like a man, and not like a kid, he started talking like a man. "Prob-ly deserve it, too. I knew to stay off that road after closing time."

This was, the fisherman realized, a pretty good kid. The guy was no older than Annie, which meant he knew a lot about being young and how to run tow trucks, but still had to get the world figured out. Whatever scared him might be nothing, or it might be so big the kid didn't know enough to be tot-ally terrified.

"You're too good of a driver," the fisherman suggested. "You're not the kind that dunks a pickup after a couple beers."

"I told the cops I went to sleep but that ain't true. Something's bending the road." The kid talked so low he could hardly be heard because of musical groans from the tape deck. He sounded apologetic. "I know that sounds nuts."

"Something's humping in the Canal," the fisherman said. "If you want 'nuts', that's nuts."

"This is worse." The kid looked halfway ready to fight, halfway ready to cry.

The fisherman first thought he heard more bull but got rid of that. He next thought the kid was crazy but that didn't play. Then he thought of the sea, and of stuff walking across water during fog. He thought of shapeless blocks of meat snagged by long-lines, hooked off the bottom.

". . . looked almost like a person," the kid said. "You couldn't stand the smell did you live with it for ten minutes." The kid's voice was now apologetic. He expected to be called a liar. The kid took a chance with the fisherman, and the fisherman appreciated that.

". . . sounds crazy," the kid said, "but if you go there after closing time. . . ."

"You're right," the fisherman said. "If that's what happens the cop isn't gonna solve anything, because he goes home every night." The fisherman started to pour another beer.

The kid stopped him. "I gotta git. It's Friday. The yard closes at six, and I don't want to take that wreck home with me." He stood, suddenly shy. "You won't say nothing, willya?"

"You're a good man," the fisherman told him. "Not a word."

The kid left, proud but not cocky. He walked with confidence and not a bit of strut. The fisherman sat, reflected, and asked himself if he was actually dumb enough to go to that dunk site after closing. He told himself, naw, nope, uh-uh, hell no. Well, maybe not.

Then he admitted he had to do something. Like, maybe take company. But who? If he took Sugar Bear, he'd sure as whiskers-on-a-catfish have to take Annie. And Annie, sure as whiskers, would do something magical . . . the fisherman shuddered. If magic misfired, all the dead things that ever tumbled on the bottom of the sea might rise to walk the land. Nope. Nope. Nope.

Because, a 'course, what scared the tow-truck kid had to be the dead guy. It was just like the little show-off. That dead guy demanded attention even when he was bait. But, killing people for no profit?

Still, the great wrongness, the ugliness, caused such sorrow. Something had to change. People kept getting lost. The fisherman told himself he should never have questioned the kid. He understood that he had just acquired a heap of responsibility.

As shadows deepened a few wives and girlfriends started showing up at Beer and Bait. The ladies put a little color into a scatter of guys still wearing work clothes. Male voices grew louder as occasional girlish laughter came from surrounding tables. At the bar men turned and watched the women while pretending to watch pool games. A couple guys talked positive and dumb. The fisherman watched Bertha.

She was more-or-less on top of matters. She had much of her lippiness back. She razzed guys, hassled the pool games, drew beer from taps running so fast and clear you knew they'd just been cleaned. Her smile, though, looked like a slightly bent, freeze-dried-herring. Bertha pretended to have a good time, but bein' Norwegian, couldn't fake it.

Folks came and went. Most dropped in for conversation and one drink before heading home. Some might return. The fisherman figured Petey wouldn't pass up a chance to hustle on Friday night. When Jubal Jim bounded into the room with his hound-happy manner, it seemed Petey ought to be next through the doorway. Instead, a postal guy who delivered rural routes slipped in like mail through a slot. Jubal Jim scored a couple potato chips along the bar, then went to Bertha who seemed suddenly joyous. Bertha found a pickled egg. Jubal Jim snarfed the egg whilst wagging tail, then headed for a nap in his favorite spot beneath the space heater. Bertha looked lots better. It was almost like she'd made some kind of decision.

As time passed the crowd changed. Guys headed home to supper. Guys without wives or girlfriends sat lonesome before pitchers of beer. Among the pool players the ante rose to ten bucks a game and hovered. Jubal Jim snoozed. Bertha mopped the bar and hoped for a big evening. By eight o'clock a thin Friday night crowd danced, hollered, and tried to make out. The fisherman felt happy for everybody but himself, plus he worried over what to do about the dead guy. Before the fisherman realized it the clock started knocking against eleven P.M.

It wouldn't hurt to walk and clear the head. He bussed his table and waved good-bye to Bertha who, it seemed, now looked sort of tenuous.

In the October night a three-quarter moon hung wispy behind thin clouds. He meandered between parked pickups and headed for the road. The dunk site lay a ways off, but no more than he, or for that matter, Sugar Bear, had walked many-a-time. Plus, this was just a walk to clear the head.

The night road carried a few cars, bright lights whipping against roadside undergrowth, making eyes of varmints glow red or green; the glows dropping into darkness as headlights passed. The roadside felt alive with wildlife movements in a symphony of nature. The Canal lay black, except where wheyish October moonlight cast thin gleams.

The fisherman hoofed right along, not hardly weaving at all. A gull squawked and slid through night air like a spirit. The fisherman thought of dark depths, imagined the dead guy walking down there poking through debris, or maybe getting chawed on by crabs. The fisherman shook his head, took deep breaths, and told himself this was no time for getting morbid. He told himself only a damn fool or drunk would be here this close to closing time.

His watch read eleven-thirty when he arrived. The yellow crane stood to one side and the site lay stripped of vegetation. The Canal licked away at a slickery grade of rock and rubble. If a guy didn't know what had been going on the scene might look peaceful. The fisherman leaned against the crane. He tried to figure should he leave? A 'course, it didn't make sense to leave if things were about to heat up.

Headlights rounded the curve from north. An approaching car slowed and nearly crept toward the dunk site. The fisherman hid behind the crane. Anybody driving that slow looked for a place to do a deed, probably illegal, or else knew about danger.

The car crept to a stop. Thin moonlight showed make and model. The fisherman gasped, actually gasped, actually couldn't, could not believe it. Then he did believe it.

"Part of the hustle," he whispered, and watched Petey climb from the Plymouth. The window on the driver's side was rolled down, and Petey left the door open. He checked the road in both directions, patted the car on its roof. Petey looked like he tried to comfort a horse he must shoot. He reached in and put the car in drive. It moved slowly into the Canal. Bubbles rose, and dark water closed over the Plymouth. Petey stood for a minute, talking under his breath, then walked away.

Bubbles did not rise for long. Lights turned the water green, then shorted out as darkness closed in. Little wavelets made expanding circles, and the Canal once more lapped against the land. The three-quarter moon reflected on the Canal like a ghost of a ghost. A hump in the water moved fast enough to show a wake. It drew a straight line to the dunked car. Then, as if the creature had brakes, the line stopped, water swirled, and the hump disappeared. For two seconds the Canal knew only silence. Then the hump circled, moving slowly away.

Later, the fisherman would tell himself he had been sober. Not absolutely, tot-ally, cold sober, maybe, but sober. Later, he remembered standing beside the yellow crane, both hands hanging onto a grab bar, while fighting to stay sane.

A flurry of water beneath the moon. Silence. Something like a hand clawed toward moonlight. Stubs on the hand showed where fingers were forming. An arm followed, then head, shoulders; a figure slowly rose from depths beside Petey's drowned Plymouth.

A low sound, like the sigh of wind among leaves, though no wind blew. The thing moved slow, deliberate, looking a lot more like a person than the tow-truck kid had claimed. This thing had a sort-of-a mouth, almost had eyes, or at least places where eyes might grow.

The tow-truck kid had reported smell, and smell rolled across the water and onto land. It was rotten-fish smell, rancid-poultry smell, spoiled-beef smell . . . the smell of moderate decay . . . stuff for the gullets of gulls. A guy could stand it if he had to.

The thing moved forward, like it waded from Canal to shore. It seemed struggling, maybe inching one foot ahead of the other; assuming it had feet. Sighs increased. The thing sank backward into darkness. Wavelets moved on the surface. The Canal lay calm beneath thinish moonlight.

Why, the Creature?

Night clasps the Canal in layers of darkness as wisps of mist flicker ghostly in starlight. In the depths, night-swimmers drift, dart, eat and are eaten. It is a grand feast of chomping and biting and flight; the sting of jellyfish, the rush of small shark. Octopus hover in drowned cars, or in discarded refrigerators that lie on the bottom like open coffins. Octopus dart forward to make a meal or become one.

The Creature (one dare not yet call it a monster) floats high above the carnage. If, as Annie attests, the creature is a Fury, it was spawned in the Mediterranean Sea these twenty-five hundred years past. At its spawning (poor crippled thing) it bore the mark, nay the Curse, of immortality. For these aching years it has moved beneath the watery surface of the planet. As centuries passed, so must have also passed the vibrancy of youth as life turned to dull aches.

But Annie, whose magic only works when it wants, is only partly right. This creature came into being at the dawn of western civilization. It is surely less than a myth, but also much more. Like most everyone else on the Canal, Annie knows as much about the rise of the western world as a cat knows about Croesus.

Because what humps out there cannot be a Fury. It is without pedigree, some remnant of bizarre mating left over when elder

Gods and Goddesses abandoned this world to step with immortal feet across the doorsill of eternity. Perhaps in the Creature's self are strains of fury, but there may also be sorrow, even charity. After all, it has seen a lot.

Through the span of weary and slow-moving years its ancient memory recalls the downward march of civilizations, for it has viewed the decline of Greece, Rome, Spain, France, the decline of Empires. It has seen legends revised for expediency. It has even seen mountains grow shorter.

At present it moves differently at different times. Beneath the moon it rushes toward the sites of drowned cars. At other times it cruises slowly and communes with itself. A creature of the sea, it has for centuries held an offshore view of land. In olden days it watched lands illuminated by moonlight and occasional watchfires.

These days, though, it has (momentarily at least) abandoned the sea and moved to inland waters. These days it views other lights; headlights, running lights, pink glows of neon signs, blue lights vaporing above barnyards and parking lots, red warning signs atop radio towers. Something in the Creature's mind has surely changed, some lonely "something" must have persuaded it that loneliness may be only the habit of centuries. Poor crippled thing, drawing smooth and liquid lines across the water, poor crippled thing: is there something; or perhaps someone here you want, someone who, if only for a small space in the unremitting stretch of eternity, could be your companion, your friend?

Petey Deceased

On the morning after, a Saturday, and before news of Petey arrived, worlds looked a tad off-kilter. A new Cadillac sat in the parking lot of Beer and Bait and a chubby rich guy spoke with Bertha. He was gone before opening time. Guys slurped coffee at Beer and Bait, talked in low voices, and watched Bertha. She moved quiet but happy, well, happier; well, not gloomy. Jubal Jim lay beneath warm waves from the heater. Nobody, nowhere, relaxes like a snoozing hound.

Gray light in the windows showed October rain pattering the Canal. Beer and Bait glowed slightly pink because of a couple beer signs. As midmorning marched toward noon the cop showed up looking grim.

His cop suit held spatters of mud, and he looked ready to bust everybody in the bar: a fisherman, two loggers, a masonry guy, a port-a-pot guy, and a used car salesman riding unemployment. The men crouched like scared kittens.

Something was up. Somebody was gonna swing. The fisherman kept his big yap shut. He watched developments while remaining one of the throng. He watched Bertha move along the bar with the grace of a young girl. At the same time she looked sorta practical. Her greeting was friendly but nothing special, because she greeted truck drivers the same way. Bertha's hair no longer piled and braided. It swung long and full, softening a face that had been solemn for far too long.

The cop seemed puzzled because Bertha's greeting was not as warm as expected. She treated him like he was temporary, a guy just passing through. Later, in the wake of grimness and misery, the fisherman would think that the cop had already looked lost.

The cop turned from puzzled to solemn. He had to figure Petey meant something to Bertha. He spoke so low only Bertha heard. She leaned across the bar as he told about Petey. He whispered, but words "car" "Canal" "missing" were like echoes along the bar. Bertha's face lost happiness, lost all expression, and then showed sudden sorrow; the kind that breaks hearts just watching it. The fisherman sipped coffee and experienced total admiration.

The cop also looked stricken. Jealous, actually. He checked out everybody in the house, like he memorized faces. He turned back to Bertha, whispered, and received a sad smile that pretended to be a bright smile; the whole thing fake. The cop seemed confused, then sorta ticked-off. He tapped the bar a couple of times, brushed a little spot of mud on his sleeve, turned toward the doorway. He paused, like he was about to deliver a parting shot, then shrugged and went out to his car. He must have stood beside it and watched the Canal for a minute or two; maybe cussing. The door of the cop car finally slammed, but the engine did not start for a couple minutes. The cop must have sat there wondering.

Bertha turned toward the bar and delivered the next-to-greatest-moment of her life. Probably. She sniffed, wiped moist eyes, squared shoulders; she turned to the backbar, touching things, like she tried to convince herself the world was still real. She did not face the bar when she told about Petey, but her face reflected in the bar mirror. Guys saw enormous grief, did not know what to say, and sat abashed. The fisherman sat absolutely stunned with admiration, because, while he could not always spot a hustle, he spotted this one.

He told himself to get away from the bar because he was about to get droll. He told himself to stay away from sober, serious guys, because he might bust out laughing. Maybe, he thought, he ought to go see Sugar Bear. Maybe he ought to ride on down to China Bay.

He eased off his barstool whilst feeling slick as a dose of cod liver oil. He gave a sad little wave to Bertha and managed to keep from tossing in a wink.

He left wondering how Bertha could get through the day with a straight face. Only the greatest kind of actress could pull it off. And, only a born hustler would recognize that Petey pulled a hustle. Of course, Bertha had advance information.

Bertha had to have known, the night before, that a hustle was underway. When Jubal Jim showed up the game began. Jubal Jim arrived relaxed and happy. No hound, nowhere, and especially Jubal Jim, would snooze at peace if someone valuable was dead. Ergo, Petey was alive. Ergo, Petey hustled. Hounds knew about this kind of stuff.

The fisherman told himself that Irish wakes were gonna come of this, despite nobody was Irish. Memorials would come of this. Plus, this was genesis of Canal stories that would make recent history look like pale pink pudding. The fisherman vowed to give himself twenty-four hours before making any moves. There was always work that needed doing on the boat.

Canal stories began right away. From Rough and Randy, all the way south to China Bay, guys sat at bars and remembered classic games of pool. No man among them had not been cleaned and pressed by Petey, sometimes scorched. Men told stories in which they were almost-heroes, except where they had to admit Petey outgunned them. Canal stories started by being sentimental. Somebody even wrote in the men's can at Beer and Bait, "Petey the Pooler, I miss you slugger"; that was the only truly sloppy thing that happened.

As hours passed, Petey became a legendary hero who had been snuffed by a power-crazed cop. Petey grew in stature, so guys who showed-off at pool tables bragged to strangers that they had known Petey, had actually teamed with him many-a-time. They remembered Petey's forceful presence and stature: seven foot tall, blond hair, cool blue eyes with a steely look, and a dimple on his chin.

The stories turned complicated when the tow-truck kid pulled Petey's drowned Plymouth past Beer and Bait without stopping. The kid was delicate enough to wait for suds and bull until he got to China Bay. Word spread from China Bay saying there wasn't a scratch on that Plymouth, or at least no scratches not put on by Petey. Then the story turned sad.

The story claimed cops pulled a fancy pool cue from beneath the seat. When they opened the trunk out came a cloud of blue; water swirling bluey-blue where a stash of cue chalk melted. Except for a spare tire, and a cue-tip repair kit, the trunk lay empty. In the glove box Petey had stashed a flashlight, a clutter of papers, road maps, and a worn baseball cap reading "Kennel Club of Cambridge".

That was when the story took on weight. The story claimed Petey was not dead at all, but was at rest in a marble tomb hidden far back in the mountains. On some future day when people along the Canal needed a champion, Petey would rise from the fog and mist of valleys. He would slay all transgressors; senators and cops. A new social order would rise. Downtrodden masses would gain a place in the sun, and the meek would prosper. This story started at China Bay where an amused bartender proved, once for all, that you can sell anything if the price is too dear and the pitch is sincere.

As Saturday morning worked toward afternoon, then into evening, and finally into night, situations occurred. The first situation spelled "cops".

Guys were stopped for weaving, stopped for not weaving, stopped for 46-in-a-45 zone, stopped for holding up traffic doin' 34-in-a-35 zone, stopped for dirty tail lights, stopped for windshield-wiper-checks, stopped for the hell of it.

And, when guys were stopped, guys were hassled. "Where have you been? Where haven't you been? Is this woman your wife? Why not? Have you ever heard of missing persons? Are you one? . . ." Guys wore themselves out trying to remember every smidgen of hassle. The cops wanted something or somebody, or else cops were steamed. Guys walked through doorways of joints, talking to themselves. Nobody could figure what was wrong, and almost everybody stayed away from Beer and Bait.

And, all Saturday night, when he should-a been home in bed, the Beer and Bait cop seemed connected to the hassle. He stayed in the background, quiet, parked not far from Bertha's joint, like he waited for something to happen that he knew was gonna happen. Bull claimed the cop went from polite to palooka because he lost his prime suspect, what with Petey underwater laughing his dead self silly. It was a bitter little story, and no one told it in front of Bertha.

Another story surfaced on Sunday afternoon when Bertha announced that Beer and Bait would close for twenty-four hours as a memorial. Starting Monday. The story claimed Bertha was crushed, was gonna sell Beer and Bait, and move to some crazed place like, maybe, Peoria.

Bertha did not say that a service was planned. It would take place at Sugar Bear's house. Only a few select folk would attend. Bertha did not say, because she was dubious and a little scared, that something else, something seriously-serious, was in the works. She had made a deal.

A rotund rich guy showed up at Beer and Bait. He screwed around the pool tables for a few games, and the little finger on his right hand looked sorta rigid as he held it away from his cue. He lost twenty or thirty bucks, then announced a pool tournament. A grand prize of ten thousand dollars was the stake, plus side-bets a 'course, and with an entry fee of only ten semoleons . . . a deal too good to pass up. Still, a bunch of bikers, plus loggers, plus mill guys, shuddered and felt scary.

An Awful Attack
Leads to Girl Talk

October along the Canal weeps maple leaves. November storms lie a month in the future, but in October we feel occasional pops and puffs of promissory wind. The Canal remains its own dark self, and on a map may not resemble a fishhook after all. It may resemble a fractured arm, an injury, something unhealed and unhealing. Leaves float like loosened kites, or on wet days plane toward ground in a liquid slide. The leaves are yellow-y and orange-y.

October is respite for most men who go to sea. A few guys who didn't make a stake during the season take one last dash to the fishing grounds. Others, the diligent and lucky ones, work on their boats and look forward to five months of horsing around. They patch roofs on their houses, or rebuild engines on old pickups. They have plenty of time to think.

And, they have plenty of time to attend memorial services for the drowned, even if the memorial is only a mask to conceal Petey's hustle.

Maple leaves drifted in piles around Sugar Bear's shop, and around his fairy-tale house. The fisherman parked beside Bertha's Chrysler and Sugar Bear's pickup. He foresaw problems. Bertha would talk, Sugar Bear would puzzle, Annie would ask questions, and the fisherman was either gonna tell the truth or lie like a member of congress.

Still, people were dying. He had to do something. Cops could hassle 'til hell froze, but this was not a cop-type mystery. The fisherman slammed the pickup door so as to announce himself, then walked.

In Sugar Bear's kitchen stood two beautiful women, and one of them made the fisherman feel sick-y. Annie stood before the cookstove waiting for water to boil. Her long hair held no gleam or sparkle. Her smile did not conceal nervousness, or a small tremble on her lips. She did not slump, exactly, but that healthy, athletic look was gone. The fisherman felt shock, then sorrow, finally anger. Wrong stuff, like all evil and ugliness, crowded in on that small house. The fisherman couldn't actually reach and touch the wrongness, but he felt it.

Bertha, on the other hand, looked fair, considering: but Jubal Jim looked poorly. Under sane conditions he would nap beneath the table. Now he sat close to Annie. No one is more mournful than a mournful hound.

This was a wake, all right, but not a wake for Petey. "Tell me," the fisherman said to Bertha. He took a chair, watched Annie make coffee, waited for somebody to say something. Nobody did.

"I got weird news," the fisherman said, "and I ain't sweating Petey. He can take care of himself. Somebody talk."

"Off the top," Bertha told him, "I've hassled myself. I should of known Petey was running a number. I should of known Petey wouldn't really back down from a cop." Bertha sounded lonesome and ready to sniffle. At the same time her voice carried envy, also a touch of admiration. ". . . almost feel sorry for the cop. You got to guess it's a major hustle."

The fisherman told himself to be mighty, mighty careful. He wanted to remind Bertha the cop had been sorta welcome. Instead, he kept his flapper shut.

"Plus there's this other mess," Sugar Bear said. "There ain't a guy on that road that's not pulled over." Sugar Bear watched Annie, looked at Bertha, seemed totally discouraged. "Except me. I stay off the road."

"They're shaking trees," Annie said, "to see what falls out." She reached to pat Jubal Jim. "Something might. People talk."

Bertha motioned toward Annie and Sugar Bear. "These two should run a mortuary." She looked at the fisherman. "You're supposed to be thinking this through."

"You'd be surprised."

Jubal Jim shivered along his spine, then shook like a dog coming out of the rain. He gave a low growl. The growl changed to a snarl. Jubal Jim sniffed at air, turned real slow, catching a scent but trying to discover a direction. Then, like he picked up something from afar, he braced and sent a howl that should have broken crockery. The howl was not mournful, but challenge. Jubal Jim's nose pointed in the direction of the Canal, and he looked for a fight.

"If I was smart as that dog . . . ," Sugar Bear began.

Annie knelt beside Jubal Jim. She didn't touch him, didn't break his concentration. Instead she listened. Jubal Jim had something to say in ways only Annie understood.

The fisherman turned to check the wood stove because chill entered the room. It was like somebody left a door open; but this was January chill, not something a guy expects in October. The feeling of wrongness grew so strong it poured from the very walls of the house. Curtains decorated with rabbit-pictures moved slightly as cold became glacial, corpse-cold.

"Not here." Annie's voice sounded thin, nearly frightened. Her voice almost quavered. Then her voice firmed up and became harsh, ready to fight. She still knelt beside Jubal Jim. "Not here. Not in this house. Not ever." Who, or what, she spoke to, the fisherman could not say.

Jubal Jim growled as the feeling of wrongness grew even stronger. In brittle cold, a light stench infested the air. It was no more than the smell of spoiled flesh, not yet rotten, only a little high.

"All right," Annie said, her voice becoming calm. "If that's how it's got to be. . . ." She remained kneeling beside Jubal Jim. She was focused. Concentrating. Jubal Jim wagged his tail, then thumped.

Beyond the windows trees awakened as wind moved in their tops, and as golden leaves skidded through air. Showers of gold slapped against the windows, and the forest seemed to dance. A squirrel ran across the clearing and crows cawed in indignation. Without knowing how or why it happened, the fisherman felt a surge of small warmth, of security; the kind that comes from fireplaces, big suppers, and snoozing dogs.

A sound, almost a gasp, came from somewhere in the room. Then came movement of air like a rush of frightened wind. Heat returned to the room as stench and cold and wrongness fled. Jubal Jim gave a small bark, kind of happy, and licked Annie's cheek.

"I thought," Bertha said to Annie, "you planned to settle down." She watched Annie, and the fisherman thought no one, not even Bertha, could say whether Bertha was happy. He could say Bertha was impressed, and that did not happen real often.

"I don't know what it was, but it's awful." Annie now touched Jubal Jim, flopped his ears, rubbed him between the shoulders.

She caused wiggles from a happy hound. "Even the most horrible people usually have something going. This has nothing. It's foul and filthy, but it's hollow."

"I guess," the fisherman admitted, and he was reluctant, "I've got stuff to tell."

The story didn't come easy. He apologized as he went along, telling what the tow-truck kid said, telling about watching Petey, and then telling about the rush through water of whatever it was that moved in the Canal. Then he told about the shape rising from water, struggling toward shore, and sinking.

"The tow-truck kid said you couldn't stand the smell," he explained, "but I've got this educated nose. A guy could stand it. . . ." He knew his story sounded lame, but considering what had just happened. . . .

"If Petey dunked his car, Petey would've had to walk home, and that's a good hike. That means a major hustle." Bertha murmured, mostly to herself. "He couldn't hitch a ride." Then she brightened. "Petey had another car stashed somewhere."

"It was like what we just smelled, only moreso," the fisherman explained.

"It's gotta be the dead guy." Sugar Bear suddenly looked a little better.

"Because," Bertha spoke to the room in general, "it has to be major. Any hustle with this much set up has to be bigtime."

"It might be the dead guy," Annie told Sugar Bear. "I don't rule him out, exactly." She turned to Bertha, and Annie was major-displeased. "We're talking serious stuff here."

And then, either because she was too young to know better, or because she was steamed, Annie took on Bertha; and in a direct way no one but lunatics would try. "What's with the cop? And don't tell me it's a hustle."

The fisherman almost wanted to shield his groin. He figured he had exactly three and seven-sixteenths seconds before the big explosion.

A pause. A blush from Bertha. A bigger blush. Jubal Jim snuggled up beneath the table, ears spread wide on the floor, immediately a-snooze. Bertha turned, but not on Annie. She looked at Sugar Bear, at the fisherman. "You guys take off for a spell. Catch a fish or fix a saw or something." Her voice was quiet, not angry. Maybe her voice was only sad. "Girl talk," she explained, and her blush maybe faded, maybe a little.

Much later, after tons of such 'n such, it developed that Bertha turned to Annie for advice. The switch made sense. After all, Annie had once set her cap for Sugar Bear. For better or worse she fulfilled a dream. Bertha, equally gorgeous, could get plenty of men but not the man she wanted.

It was clearly one of those girl problems . . . although, as the fisherman mused much later, it was the sort of thing he and Sugar Bear had sorta discussed one time or another. But, all of this came out much, much later.

At the time, the two men stepped from the fairy-tale house into a clearing that lay beneath a cliff where in springtime swallows would dance. On the cliff, forest stood dark beneath a sky of mixed cloud and sun. The forest reached far back into the mountains where roamed bear and cougar and mountain goats, plus varmints without number.

In the other direction lay the death-dealing road, and the Canal filled with mystery-stuff. The fisherman was unsurprised to hear Sugar Bear muttering.

"How do you kill a dead guy?" Sugar Bear stomped toward his shop, but paused beside piles of firewood. "Bring an armful.

Hard to tell how long we're kicked out."

The fisherman figured they had a guy-thing going, and it would go sour because Sugar Bear owned that bad temper. Sugar Bear snapped some scrap 2 x 2s for kindling, so he still had plenty strength left. He tossed in shavings, got the fire licking away, but even getting "something done" didn't stave off his temper. When he turned to the fisherman, Sugar Bear looked a whole lot healthier than he had for quite awhile. Temper sometimes brings out good stuff.

"I had enough," Sugar Bear said. "I got a bellyful." He managed to hold onto control. He looked through the shop window toward the fairy-tale house. "I figured I had it coming," he said by way of explanation. "I kill the guy, the guy comes back at me. I get sick-y. Okay. But, now he's going after her. The sonovabitch was in our house."

There was, the fisherman figured, not a whole lot to discuss. Still, Sugar Bear was his friend, and a guy don't want to help a friend self-destruct. "You don't know it's the dead guy. It could be something worse."

"What could be worse?"

"Plus, Annie handled it."

"Annie talks to bugs."

"I don't know what that means. You've said that before." The fisherman watched fire lick at kindling. Pretty soon the fire would get into chunks of fir and the stove door would get closed. The fire would flicker down. It would go hot but sullen. Right now, though, it was bright as anger. "I talk to fish. Sometimes. You cuss at engine parts. What does it mean, Annie talks to bugs?"

The question slowed Sugar Bear. It actually cooled him off; well, just a little. Sugar Bear stared into the fire like he tried to puzzle through a lesson. He seemed bigger, like in other days. His shoulders no longer slumped. His face-fur moved around. Sugar Bear was coming alive after a month of sleep-walking, or whatever had been happening.

"She's a kid. She's smart. She's magical, kinda. But she's wide open to get slammed." Sugar Bear tossed a balk of fir into the stove, then shut the door. The crackle of fire diminished to a couple dull pops.

"I repent I killed that guy," Sugar Bear said. "I understand somebody was gonna do it. I agree it needed doing. It was also wrong. There's times when doing wrong is the only choice a guy's got. This is how I figure. . . ."

The fisherman listened and told himself he would be doubly-dipped in seafood sauce. Sugar Bear might be inexperienced at thinking, but he tried.

"She's a kid. Kids don't know how bad real badness can get. They get sucker-punched. Evil stuff, really evil like that guy, goes after kids because badness is yellow. It sneaks."

The fisherman, who had been a kid once himself and lived through it, was about to point out that everybody has to grow up; sometimes the hard way. Instead, he hushed himself.

"I guess," Sugar Bear admitted, "I'm actually kind of glad the guy comes after us. Because I won't put up with this no more. It was different when it was just me."

"There's nothing wrong with protecting yourself. Protecting Annie. Nothing wrong."

"What's wrong," Sugar Bear said, "is I'll kill that sonovabitch a thousand times if that's what it takes. This scrap isn't between good and bad, it's between bad and worse. Don't think I like it."

"There's problems," Bertha was telling Annie, "and you're not to say a word." Bertha sat at the kitchen table across from Annie, coffee-klatching, looked through windows framed with green-y curtains.

"My problem is the cop." Annie still sounded ready for a scrap. "As long as he's around Sugar Bear will stay spooked. Sugar Bear can't get over it."

"The main problem is, I've hustled myself into deep water." Bertha's blush increased. Her voice sounded someplace between timid and ashamed. "I admit to liking it that the cop seemed interested."

"And now you're afraid he isn't. He's interested in something." Annie was no longer ready to fight, at least not with Bertha. "This is serious."

"I've run a few numbers in my time," Bertha whispered, "and I think I'm pretty smart. But, I led with my jaw on this one." She blushed bigtime, and kind of choked.

"I'm not sure about those curtains," Annie said. "Winter gets so gray around here you need a lot of color. But, maybe the color's wrong."

"Never figured you for bunnies." Bertha studied the curtains. "The bunnies are mighty little. When you get too many of anything it makes the place look busy."

"There's no evidence," Annie said. "Maybe there's bones lying around down there. There's nothing except the car, but there's lots of wet cars. But, Sugar Bear's not good at lying, and that's nice but scary."

"The cop's still interested, I think. But I ain't." Bertha's embarrassment turned to reddest red. Her blond hair framed a blue-eyed face only a little bit brighter than neon.

"Then where's the hustle? What's the hustle?"

Bertha's voice, her eyes, the set of her mouth were fixed in admiration. At the same time she couldn't speak above a whisper. "Petey hustled me. Petey hustled a hustler . . . I'm first to give him credit."

"I'm in over my head," Annie told her. "What in the world is going on?"

"All that sad-face stuff, all that distance." Bertha still whispered, like she couldn't rise above some kind of Norwegian economic shame. "All that running the road, and losing at pool . . . because Petey don't lose unless he wants to . . . and then he dunks a car and sends in Jubal Jim. . . ." At their feet Jubal Jim stirred, stretched, gave a couple little snurfs and resumed napping.

"Jubal Jim I understand," Annie said. "Jubal Jim is straightforward. Spit it out."

"Petey knew from the minute that cop showed up that cops and bars don't mix. He knew it from the get-go. He knew the cop would wreck business. He did that sad-face act to show about cops. I've bin acting silly." Bertha sounded like she confessed to a capital crime. "He's trying to convince me, and I'm convinced. And now he's disappeared and I can't send a message."

"And that's it? That's the all-time big deal?" Annie sat and figured angles. "Remember when I tried to get Sugar Bear interested, and he already was. Petey told me. It solved the problem. When Petey shows back up I'll talk to him. Simple."

"It might work." Bertha allowed herself to sound hopeful. She talked a little above a whisper.

"Meanwhile," Annie told her, "a whole cop-shop is shaking trees." She stood, walked to another window. "The guys have got a fire going. I figure they're sitting in the shop thinking up moves . . . which is okay as long as they don't get secret."

"Something dumb." Bertha had not lost her spirit at any rate. "Neither of those guys could hustle a chicken off a nest."

"The cop," Annie insisted. "Get him on your side or send him home. Get rid of him somehow. Shut it down."

"I can do that," Bertha said. "In fact, I gotta do that. Plus it's the right thing. There comes a time you quit defending. Sooner or later you got to commit to the game." She did not then mention that a pool tournament was only six days off.

The Cop Makes a Decision

Consider traffic officers and their awkward social position, because some operate beyond copness and try to blend with ordinary mortals. Consider, especially, the traffic officer who runs roads, not city streets.

It's a solitary life and lonely. It's a life of coffee, wet roads, lost motorists, occasional wrecks, judgment calls on who's too drunk or stoned to drive, or too reckless because of love and its ensuing insanity.

The level of b.s. is high. Bull comes from drivers, concerned citizens, newspaper editorials, your own administrators; and it arrives in the form of fibs, lies, baloney, krapola, criticism, threats, lawsuits, new rules and regulations, sudden enforcement of old rules and regulations; all to be mulled, digested, worried over along sodden roads where each car you pull over may be that tainted one on which your name is written widely.

When you stop a guy on a lonely road there are few options. If you're a state cop, a sheriff's car may be nearby, or vice versa. Light bars flash red and blue through fog and mist, guys backing guys up, but only as a luxury. Human contact is limited. Cop contact is what you hope for. Mostly you go it alone.

And alone is what you get when you walk into a store, a bar, a church. Store clerks blush with memories of petty theft, bar-folk bristle with indignation, and preachers invoke the father-confessor-fifth even before you mention the name of a parishioner.

Plus, other cops are not much fun. Small town cops suck up. Sheriff's guys brag of criminal investigation, and you, a traffic officer get social conversation with no one. What you get is one more speeder, one more drunk; silently hostile, and convinced you are about to perforate his useless hide with ordnance.

Thus, if you get stuck with a junk job that won't quit, like cars dunking, life is gonna change. You'll really learn about being alone, because the job is so tainted it causes paper-shufflers and project-proposers and dispatchers to duck and cover. Because, whoever touches the unknowable is for-sure going to get burned.

Still, the job is stuffed with mystery that would take the starch out of a sheriff's brags. Suppose you are not yet old, and are handsome, and idealistic, and lonely (thus mildly neurotic); it's easy to imagine you can solve mysteries that baffle experts. It's easy to imagine you'll drop the traffic job and become an investigative officer, this, despite the fact you've got as much chance as a hamburger in a nest of chow chows. It's even easier to hunger after the first fine-looking woman who comes along.

And further suppose, that in a string of murders, you suspect there's been an extra murder, but you have no remnant of deceased; no scrap of cloth, no tooth, shinbone, hank of hair. It's easy to think one person is behind everything. If you can find the why and who of cars dunking, it's a good guess that you can solve the whole business.

And even further suppose that among the partying populace are numbers of sell-outs and comedians. Most likely you will, on pulling them over, come up with names of murderers: Chantrell George (a likely suspect), Sugar Bear Smith (a solid citizen?) and a pool hustler name of Petey; this latter acting strange.

Given that, plus a dunked Plymouth, it pays to shake the back teeth of the community, to hear of certain whereabouts, because Petey has become prime suspect; a dunked car not evidence of a dunked guy, not when the guy is a hustler and the car is unscratched.

And, you'll naturally tell the other guys to keep lookout for a junkie, and to keep extra close watch for Petey. Judging from his past Petey will be driving something that looks rubbed-out and ain't.

And maybe, most likely, just probably, you're gonna have to loosen up; gonna spend fewer nights sitting with TV and a beer. Maybe check out a little of that night road. Because what happens in these parts always seems to come down about the time the populace heads home, and the joints turn out their lights.

A Fisherman-type Realization
And A Cop Gets Booted

Morning at China Bay begins around nine A.M. when the bartender's Jag pulls onto the well-drained parking lot where sits a car or two; abandoned after a night that saw their owners taxied home or in the slammer. The bartender, who knows the universe and wryly approves (most days) smiles in detached manner. The Jag mutters in aristocratic tones and its bumper sticker reads: "All parts falling from this auto are of genuine British manufacture".

The bartender's daily drill is largely the same: key in lock, Dragon-Lady-red doors swing inward, and before the bemused eye appears tables stacked with upside-down chairs, barstools beneath which lie hosts of cigarette butts, and floors a-scatter with candy bar wrappers, worn out ball pens, crumpled paper napkins, randomly spread small coins (the pennies winking), here and there a dropped lipstick or a legislative bill (on which is noted phone numbers), credit card receipts, berets, hair ribbons, and on pegs on the wall, occasional jackets and regimental ties.

And, of course, silence. Only the hum of refrigeration greets the ear. The bartender turns up the thermostat and tunes a radio to a classical station; working to music while emptying and washing ashtrays, sweeping floors with large gestures of push-broom; feet a-twinkle in a dance to classical themes. By 10:30 the bar is clean, the chairs arranged at tables, the goldfish fed, the till counted, the cribbage board laid out for oldsters, pool tables brushed, and the change machine refilled. The bartender drinks coffee while sitting at the bar listening to music. The free half hour before opening at eleven is a time of privacy, art, and peace (most days).

From the radio a trumpet, a bassoon, and a flute did a contrapuntal dance as the Dragon-Lady-red doors eased inward to disclose a fisherman. The guy entered timidly. He knew he pushed his luck.

The bartender recognized the guy as belonging to Bertha's joint, and reckoned how matters in that direction must be getting tippy; this particular fisherman being a cut above the usual. He would not chance a bartender's wrath unless his ailment was abstract.

". . . you could dance to it." The bartender turned the radio down a notch. "Or, you could express sorrow for the interruption."

"I gotta talk to you," the fisherman said. "Because you're still sane."

"Which is rare."

"These days," the fisherman whispered, "it's a little scarcer than rare." He remained standing, embarrassed, not presuming to take a seat.

"Random forces accumulate around joints. I sometimes leave the doors unlocked as entertainment." The bartender sipped coffee, looked through well-washed windows onto the Canal where a sky of gray and silver hovered.

"Mystery stuff," the fisherman explained. "Up our way the cops hassled everybody, then stopped on Tuesday. Guys are taking ten percent over the limit with nothing happening. But cops are parked and watching. Watching everybody."

"Do better," the bartender told him. "An interruption should at least be interesting."

"Murder," the fisherman explained. "Murder and magic and monsters. Hustles, cops, disappearances, pool tournaments; plus I got a guy setting out to kill a dead guy. Zombies; well one zombie of some kind, coming outta the Canal. The thing is growing fingers and eyes."

"Now," the bartender admitted, "you're getting somewhere." Beyond the well-washed windows a hump moved in the Canal and the fisherman looked startled. "It gets this far south?"

"Today it does," the bartender said, "but not normally. Have you tried feeding it? Cracker Jacks? Peanuts?"

"The main problem is I've got a guy who killed a guy, which you know about that and so does everybody else . . . and now the dead guy is coming outta the Canal and trying to work over the alive guy, and the alive guy has quit feeling guilty and is ready to do murder again . . . and the problem is the guy is not good at murder, so it will ruin him; and that's gonna ruin the woman he's with, unless, of course, she gets magical and ruins the whole western part of the United States . . . " The fisherman stopped, and he was shocked to hear the desperation in his voice. He had not realized just how scared he was, or how much he cared about all this. "Plus that thing out there . . . ," and he pointed to water humping on the Canal, "that thing is wrenching cars all outta shape and killing people."

"If that monster killed people we'd have heard long before this. That appears to be a long-time monster." The bartender nearly giggled, then settled for a chuckle. "There's no legend. We have no story. We have nothing to even challenge tales of Loch Ness, and the Nessie monster made a reputation without attacking anyone. Most likely your monster is a pacifist."

"Then the dead guy is killing people."

"Or the road?"

"The road bends," the fisherman admitted. "The kid who tows the wet cars told me. But roads don't bend by themselves."

"Or the Canal?"

"I'm a sailor. I know about stuff on the water. Water don't act that way. When it gets weird it acts other ways."

"When civilizations fall," the bartender smiled (only a little preacherly), "destructive forces become overwhelming. Historically, it's a slow process."

The fisherman blinked. Stood on one foot, then on the other. He took a chair (apologetically). "I don't know what that means. What does that mean?"

"It means that a civilization is dying, or worse, killing itself. Bad to worse, then worse to ugly, and then matters turn ugly. Creative ugliness. It deals not so much in horror as in triteness." The bartender, too wise to be sad, looked wry. "The murdered man could not rise from the waves unless some dark force propelled him."

"The monster?"

"You have a reputation as a thinker," the bartender said only slightly impatient. "Give this a good think, then get back to me." The bartender turned toward the Dragon-Lady-red doors where a local delivery guy entered with a handtruck load of bar supplies. "Darkness of the kind of which I speak is collective," the bartender cautioned. "Think about accumulations." To the delivery guy the bartender said, "Good morning."

"The alive guy . . . ?"

"Is most likely doomed."

The fisherman stood stunned. "Most likely?"

"Ninety-eight percent chance," the bartender said. "Unless he, or you, or someone gets extremely smart or extremely lucky." The bartender, whose eyes were sometimes silver-y and sometimes gray, smiled, enigmatic. Like the smile of an Oracle . . . assumin', of course, that Oracles do any smiling. "How's the weather up your way?" The bartender turned, walked to the back room of the bar, and disappeared.

The fisherman stood in the middle of an empty bar as the delivery guy departed. He saw a tidy world, chairs nuzzled against tables, pictures of Athens and pictures of Chinese cheesecake like lovely mash notes from far away. He saw the polished bar mirror, the polished bar, the polished glasses as goldfish burped in their lighted tank. The pool tables looked like putting greens. In this ordered world, that through the day would become disordered, chaotic, buzzed and snockered, it came to him that the bartender offered a hint.

This bar, that through the day would go sprawled and galley-west was like a picture of the world in which all of them lived. Because things just got messier and messier, even when people tried to set stuff straight.

"An existential tiz." The bartender returned from the back room. "You're beginning to see the light." The bartender, whose eyes were not always silver-y or gray, but sometimes blue or sorta tan, hummed, then actually giggled. "I have only one question," the bartender murmured. "Why are these dark forces accumulating in this small place?"

"Are you open yet?" The fisherman thought about how drinking beer spoils a day. "For a cuppa coffee?"

"This is private stock." The bartender turned off the radio and poured. "Roll it lightly on the tongue, no gulps." The bartender looked toward the doors. "It is not for juveniles."

Silence. The hum of refrigeration. The fisherman sipped and

knew he was privileged. From the parking lot came the caw of a crow. A small boat puttered on the Canal, but too far away to hear. Only silence. The fisherman figured he'd better get on towards home, his mission at China Bay about as complete as a guy could expect. He studied the Sugar-Bear-problem for minutes. Then the soft sound of a studly engine came from the parking lot.

Slam of a truck door. Dragon-Lady-red doors swinging inward. The tow-truck kid appeared, saw the fisherman, and looked glad.

"I'm putting a groove in that road." The kid slipped onto a barstool beside the fisherman. "Another one went in."

"Coffee in a moment," the bartender told the kid as an electric pot began to burble. "When Gods become ridiculous in the eyes of men, men replace Divinity with false symbols. They create imaginary charms. How's the Dodge running?"

"Championship." The kid looked tot-ally puzzled.

The fisherman paused. "Your truck isn't exactly ridiculous, but it's too snazzy to be a truck."

"I got the same feeling," the kid admitted. "But it's a helluva ride."

"Bingo." The bartender viewed the fisherman with approval. To the kid, the bartender said, "Your little truck, the one that drowned, was unscratched. Petey's Plymouth was unscratched. Is this current job a scratcher?"

"Nobody said to bring a trailer. I brought it anyway." The kid hunched over coffee as the bartender poured. "Dealing with cops you're double-durned-damned if you do, and durn-double-damned if you don't."

"I have a nudgey feeling," the bartender explained, "that you are not tending toward a scratcher." The bartender looked toward the Canal where a hump moved lazily.

The fisherman, startled by a thought, watched the hump moving on the Canal. "I got to get home. Thanks. I mean that. I gotta hurry. Could be I'm on to something."

"Could be," the bartender said. "Be sure to leave a buck for the coffee."

Light mist washed the road as the fisherman pulled over for gas. He pumped a full tank and watched the tow-truck kid pass, headed north. As the fisherman also headed north he nearly smacked a deer and told himself to pay attention. It would be a shame to get dunked just when he had things figured.

To his left rose forest and mountain, to his right the Canal lay calm and dark as a sheet of lead. It looked like a guy could walk around out there. The fisherman imagined walking up to the monster and saying, "Hi, there. I know your game, so talk to me."

But, a 'course, that wasn't going to happen. The fisherman figured he could take his workboat, motor on out there, and try to get things organized. But, a 'course, there was bound to be a language problem.

By the time he reached Beer and Bait the sun cleared the mist, and his watch read half-past one. The parking lot held a logging truck, a propane truck, and a stripped down standard Chev. It looked like Bertha wasn't busy and wasn't gonna be, which spelled a bad mood. The fisherman pulled in beside the Chev. Paperwork lay on its front seat. Punchboards and pulltabs perched on the back.

When he entered the fisherman saw two drivers snugged up at the center of the bar, Jubal Jim napping, plus a little guy who looked flighty as a sparrow but not as pretty. He flitted above a stack of punchboards, and how a guy could flit while sitting on a barstool caused real question marks.

"It's a real good deal," the sparrow chirped, pushy as a bluejay. "Twenty percent off if you take three boards. Thirty percent pay-out on the cash boards, less on the merchandise." The guy actually seemed proud, real proud. He also wore spectacles and tassels on his shoes.

"We talked this over last time you come in." Bertha drew suds for the logger who had a streak of grease on one cheek and looked spiritually bruised. "Because I can't keep track of punch-boards," she explained to the logger. "Some guys steal punches." Bertha looked short on sleep. "You're looking good," she told the logger.

"Long story," the guy said. "You don't want to hear."

"Most likely."

And then the logger went into a long and depressed story about the job getting shut down because the guy who owned the land got in a fight with the guy who bought the trees . . . and what with a truck payment overdue . . . but Bertha no longer paid attention.

Gravel crunched. A truck door slammed, and a drywall guy stepped in. He had old spots of wallboard mud on his painter's cap, and on his pants and shirt. He looked extra dusty and glum. "Tearing out old plaster," he said to no one in particular. "Putting new walls in a dump that by rights oughta burn. I gotta find a better occupation." He took the bar stool nearest the door, because if he tracked plaster he would come out on the short end with Bertha.

The propane driver (because, when slammed, propane tends to go boom) wasn't drinking. He sipped a cherry pop, pulled at a beginning mustache and tried to decide whether it was worth running a number on the punchboard guy. He decided it was.

"Next time you see your folks," he told the punchboard guy,

"tell 'em I share their disappointment in the way you turned out." He grinned as wide as the Canal, so the grin would hide the number. Beside the bar Jubal Jim snored.

Sparrows survive because they scoot the minute they spot any movement. This particular sparrow-type guy picked up his boards, wordless, and headed for the door.

"That," said the propane guy, "was no damn fun a-tall. I was just getting started."

The fisherman weighed his drinking habits as Bertha drew him a beer. "The bull says another one went in."

"I just come from up that way," the drywall guy said. "Pontiac with the driver's window knocked out, so maybe the guy got loose. Work car. Tools in the trunk. No scratches."

"I own enormous confidence in the police," the propane guy said. "They will shortly begin arresting each other."

"They busted Sugar Bear," the log guy said. "At least that was the bull before my job got canceled."

The fisherman sat stunned. Bertha nearly dropped a beer glass.

"That's bull, okay." The drywall guy sounded pleased because he had inside dope. "It wasn't exactly a bust. It was one of them 'Where were you and what were you doing last Tuesday night' deals. Like on tee-vee."

"Who?" Bertha's voice sounded real quiet, the way it gets just before her temper scorches paint from walls. "Which cop?"

As tires crunched on the gravel and as a car door slammed, the fisherman had a feeling; like the feeling a guy gets in heavy fog listening to a major-size ship's horn too close and closing. One of those feelings.

"Take a strain," he murmured to Bertha. Then he resigned himself. Bertha wasn't listening. Whatever was gonna happen, was

214

gonna.

"Him," muttered the drywall guy as the TV cop stepped through the doorway, followed by the tow-truck kid.

"Bottle-a-pop," the kid said too quickly, and that made Bertha madder. If the kid didn't have the sense to know she would not automatically draw a beer for a guy still working while in the presence of a cop . . . well, what'n the name of Norway did the kid know? Bertha shot the kid a look that sent him to the farthest pool table. He pulled down a house cue and pretended to practice.

"Easy in, easy out." The cop smiled and looked innocent of evil thought or doing. He looked so innocent he probably, actually, felt that way, and did not know he walked into a bear trap. "It dunked near the shore. We think there was a survivor." He looked at the wallboard guy who was dusty beyond a cop's belief, then took a seat three bar stools down.

"We had a problem that turned fatal once." Bertha wiped an imaginary spot from the bar in front of the cop, but she spoke to the drywall guy. "A fellow shot a hole in the bandstand. He should of gone to Rough and Randy."

The drywall guy knew he was supposed to say something. He looked hard at Bertha, saw no hints, looked betrayed. "I was workin'," he said finally. "I always miss the fun."

"Because," Bertha explained, "he might've survived at Rough and Randy."

"Is that the guy?" the fisherman asked, "you and the crowd took care of, or are we talking about the one I took for that last long boat ride?"

The propane guy looked studious. "I always hoped to get out of this world without doing mortal violence," he said, his voice sad and slow and filled with misery. "Too late. Too late." The guy took a sip of pop. ". . . a matter of timing. The unfortunate's timing placed him in the bed, not under it." The guy drummed the bartop with his fingers, looked regretful, and grandstanded beyond belief.

"You're telling me something," the cop said. His good humor had not disappeared, but he looked uncertain. He turned to toward the drywall guy. "Any confessions?"

The drywall guy actually shuddered. Little puffs of dust fluffed all around. Then he got his voice, got brave, and not a little angry. "Banks. I rob 'em. But, if I was any good at it, you think I'd be crapping plaster?"

The logger belched and took a major gulp of beer. "Hot truck parts," he said. "Me. Wow."

"How many of my customers have you given down-the-road?" Bertha still contained her anger, but was losing her skills. Hers was a mixed problem. Hustlers need total control, but Norwegians aren't good at being devious. "How many hassles? How many *interviews*?"

The cop looked puzzled. "Doing a job. What's happening here?" He sounded sincere.

"Sometimes," the propane guy explained softly, "a guy comes into a place where people run their own affairs. If something goes wrong they handle it. That's what's coming at you."

"Nobody's exactly against you," the fisherman told him, "but nobody's for you, either. If there are skeletons they rest easy in closets. Don't open doors."

The cop looked sad, then tough. He changed like a magic person. From nice to cop. "You say 'handle it'. I say 'mishandle it'. The law is the law."

"What does that mean?" The fisherman made his voice as polite as church. "Halibuts are halibuts, cats are cats." He paused.

"Traffic is traffic. Fishermen are fishermen. I don't fish for petunias."

"You're saying I'm off course." The cop was still full of copness but he paid attention. "It's possible." The guy tried to stay tough, but little cracks appeared. "This is the world's leading lousy job," he told the fisherman. "You try it pal." He looked toward the Canal. "Something is down there." His voice filled with sadness, also frustration. "It's killing people, or somebody is. Would you sit quiet and let it happen?" He looked square at the fisherman, then at everyone. He saw Bertha, shook his head real sad. "I guess so. You will sit and let it happen. You're doing it right now. People die and you tell me about your customers. What a godawful shame." He turned and left, and he was quick about it.

"Communication problem," the fisherman said to Bertha.

"I meant to send him away easy." Bertha whispered. "Now I made an enemy. When am I ever gonna learn to shut up?"

The tow-truck kid came to the bar. Bertha drew a beer. The kid blushed, actually said, "Thank you," because he had been taken back into the fold. "He's checking guys. He checked out a guy named Sugar Bear, and a couple bikers. He tried to give Al a hard time up to Rough and Randy. Al wouldn't have any part of it."

The fisherman thought about what the cop said and realized the cop was missing something. It was still possibly-possible for Sugar Bear to survive. "I think I'll drift over to the blacksmith shop," he said to Bertha. "We'll talk later."

"Take the dog," Bertha said. "He's sleeping his life away." She seemed talking mostly to herself.

"Drive careful," the logger told him. "You know who's out there."

Very Likely,
the Fisherman Acts Dumb

Guys who think to excess are naturally going to keep arranging facts, because facts get slippery when not lined up. While Jubal Jim napped on the truck seat, the fisherman drove through that October Wednesday and tried to remember everything:

Fact: Petey was the hell and gone off someplace running a hustle.

Fact: If still alive, Chantrell George was in Seattle sponging three hots and a flop from Union Gospel Mission, or maybe the Baptists.

Fact: As a pair, Bertha and the cop were history.

Fact: The cop tried to solve the car-in-the-Canal problem, and not the murder of the pervert; so Sugar Bear's name must have come up as one among many.

Fact: The monster wasn't killing people . . . the fisherman paused. At China Bay he thought he had it solved.

The understanding came to him; the monster tried to save people, but was massive. The fisherman reflected on the tragedy of good intentions combined with lack of finesse. He thought that, scary or not, he and the monster had a date.

But, since the monster wasn't trying to kill people, but save them. What? Send a message? The monster didn't squish cars without drivers. The monster didn't bother the living, like, for

218

instance, the police divers.

Which meant it wasn't the monster who twisted the road.

Fact: The dead guy came out of the Canal, but the bartender at China Bay said something made him do it; and that was going to ask for full-time thinking in the very near future.

Fact: A pool tournament would happen on Saturday, and rich guys at the housing project were going to run a number. Depend on it.

Fact: Sugar Bear was a question mark. What had Sugar Bear told the cop?

Fact: It would start raining like Mister Noah any day now, because this was the Pacific Northwest and getting on toward the end of October.

Fact: Another car, a working Pontiac, had gone in, but without driver and unsquished. Easily recovered. The fisherman wouldn't make the mistake of calling suspicion a fact, but he suspected the fine hand of Petey lay behind that little number.

Conclusion? He figured he couldn't get any good conclusion until he found out where Sugar Bear stood with the cop. Assuming things were not too bad, the whole business might turn out okay; the fisherman paused. The troubles would go away if the dead guy quit coming out of the Canal.

As the fisherman approached Sugar Bear's place Jubal Jim sat up on the truck seat, wiggled along his spine, gave a happy woof. When the fisherman pulled alongside Sugar Bear's shop Jubal Jim danced, then bailed the minute the door opened. He headed for the house and Annie. The fisherman looked the place over.

House and grounds looked extra tidy. The woodpile no longer sprawled helter-skelter. Orange light from the forge glowed through clean shop windows, accenting the gray and silver day. When the fisherman stepped from his truck he heard Sugar Bear singing a show tune in his flat, obnoxious tenor. The fisherman figured things must be okay because Sugar Bear sounded normal.

Once inside the shop the fisherman felt slight alarm. No working place, no where, except maybe a fishing boat, ought to be this well-ordered. The place was not only swept, and tools arranged. There were decorations. The smell of fried steel mixed with the odor of cedar branches; most perfumy in the nose of a working man.

"You're looking well." The fisherman took a stool and watched Sugar Bear hammer and shape steel rod. It looked like a new handle for a roto-tiller.

"I'll be along in a minute," Sugar Bear told him. "Annie wants to see you. I got to keep the heat up, here, or start the job all over." Sugar Bear's fur shone washed and curly, almost fluffy.

When the fisherman entered the kitchen he saw that bunny curtains had been exchanged for something green which reminded him of trees. Jubal Jim sat beside Annie. The two looked like the dreams of Mormons, of hearth and home and family. When he looked closer, Annie seemed better, not so drawn. Or, maybe not.

"I planned to talk to the cop," Annie said even before greeting. "But the cop came to us." She poured coffee for the fisherman, sat across the table from him, and even in mild distress could not help being beautiful. Much of the elven look had disappeared. Her face seemed a little fuller, and her dark eyes were as alive as a gypsy. Her hair was braided, but not pinned up. The fisherman felt a pang of loss, then reminded himself that Annie also sometimes scared him silly.

"He came to hassle Sugar Bear. He did. A little. Turned out, he was hassled. Now we'll never know what he thinks."

"Do I want to hear this?" The fisherman imagined that Annie had caused a coven of bears, or an attack by Greek-speaking lizards.

"He came down with a case of damp socks," Annie murmured. "It started small and stayed that way which was a real break." She looked toward the shop. "Sugar Bear is still a suspect. You have to guess that's true."

"The shop is slicked up."

"He's convincing himself everything is normal. He's working so hard he's about persuaded."

"At least he's working."

"I got a problem." For the first time, maybe ever, Annie looked at the fisherman with real trust. "That coldness still shows up like an attack. When it happens he heads for the Canal, and it mostly happens nights. He wants me to stay out of it. Is that right?"

The fisherman reflected on the problems of being young. "Up to a point. Maybe there comes a time when you step in."

"He's got a temper."

"Always has," the fisherman agreed, "but you don't need to fear."

"I know it. You know it. The birds in the trees know it. What scares me is he'll get mad and walk into something he can't handle." Annie looked in the direction of the Canal. "Something darker than night," she whispered. "Why here? Why us? What is it?"

The fisherman reflected. The bartender at China Bay had asked the same question. The bartender had spoke of accumulations, of the fall of civilizations, of creative ugliness. "Something awful old," the fisherman guessed, "but new to us." He told of his conversation at China Bay. ". . . it has something to do with cheapness, with phoniness . . . or maybe those things are only the wrappings." He knew he stumbled badly. "What does it mean?"

"It means I don't understand you." Annie flopped Jubal Jim's ears, looked toward the shop. "Sugar Bear's finished his job."

"He's no longer getting sick?"

"It's confusing." Annie watched Sugar Bear step rather too lightly toward the house. "The minute he fought back, things changed. Whatever's out there is big but cowardly."

"A comfort."

"Cowards sneak. I'm afraid he'll get sandbagged."

If he had the least smidgen of hope left about Annie, the fisherman gave it up when Sugar Bear entered the house. The two looked at each other in a way that seemed like they'd been together for years and years. He touched Annie's shoulder, she reached to touch his hand, and Jubal Jim thumped his tail. Beyond the windows sun slanted through silver mist, and the fisherman thought things were getting a little too sentimental. Then he figured things looked that way only because he was standing on the outside lookin' in.

"Maybe you're off the hook," he told Sugar Bear. "The cop doesn't think of a single murder. He's thinking of all the murders under the heading of one murderer." The fisherman told about cop-conversation at Beer and Bait. "The cop figures somebody forces cars into the Canal. The dead guy is one of many."

"He came here to hassle," Sugar Bear said. "Now I understand. He talked about road stuff."

"Something ugly is still trying to jump you?"

"There's this," Sugar Bear said, "I still feel the wrong of what I did, but the guy does me a favor. When he attacks us, he's attacking Annie. That means I don't have to feel guilty if I smash him. Which," he added, "I'm gonna do as sure as breakfast happens."

"What are you seeing? You could get jumped from behind." The fisherman watched Annie and saw her approval.

"I get to the dunk site," Sugar Bear said, "and the thing stands in the water. It's looking more and more like the dead guy. It's dark and nasty-smelling, but getting less smelly. I say, 'Try something you sonovabitch' and it backs down. It oozes back into the water."

"What happens on the night it doesn't back down?"

"I got a nice chunk of rebar," Sugar Bear said. "Better than a ballbat. It bops and slices at the same time." His voice held very un-Sugar-Bear tones. His face, normally sweet behind a mop of fur, hardened. He looked like a guy who should be getting knee-walking drunk at Rough and Randy.

Jubal Jim gave a low whine. Unusual, because Jubal Jim is a barker, a growler, a woofer. He pointed his nose toward the Canal, and he moved away from Sugar Bear. Annie reached toward him, touched his shoulder, and Jubal Jim relaxed.

"I know what you're thinking," Sugar Bear said, and his voice was still harsh. "Answer me this. What choice does a guy have. You got to fight back."

"Bad stuff makes it stronger," Annie said. "When you fight back that makes it stronger." Her voice was subdued. She did not want a disagreement with her man.

"I don't doubt it," Sugar Bear said. "But where's the choice?"

"Let Annie give it a shot," the fisherman suggested.

"I started this," Sugar Bear told him. "I'll finish it. Annie ain't to be involved."

"She already is. At least listen to her." The fisherman had a sneaky notion he was about to do something stupid. He was also afraid for Annie.

"I can listen," Sugar Bear said, "but I ain't magical."

"Tell you what," the fisherman said, while knowing he closed in on maximum-stupidity, "Let me try it. Tonight I'll go, and we'll see if it acts any different." He realized he talked stupid because he wanted Annie to love him, even if it was only sisterly. He also felt, in a way, like some kind of mythical champion . . . a dragon slayer . . . or a golden-haired knight . . . and told himself that a youth misspent reading comic books must be dictating his actions; and Lord help those who love literature.

When the fisherman departed, Jubal Jim followed. Jubal Jim couldn't stand to be around Sugar Bear.

Petey Reveals a Motive
and Two Guys Get in Trouble

On that Thursday night clouds scudded before a high wind and were cut by streaks of silver. Waters of the Canal looked like abstract painting beneath a silver moon. And while winds blew up high, on the surface no breath of wind stirred as the fisherman left Beer and Bait. For the past two hours he had sipped soft drink, listened to one line of bull after another, and watched Bertha while knowing matters moved way too fast.

Talk was of the big pool tournament. Fantasies of wealth had guys practicing at pool tables. Although a couple of cynics looked deeper into matters, most guys took the bait.

And, the bait was a ten-thousand-dollar prize, with only a ten buck entry fee, in a team tournament scheduled to last as long as it took, if it took a week. Bull said no less than three hundred guys would sign up. Three hundred guys at ten bucks a head came to three thousand dollars. Since the prize was ten thousand, somebody was buying something. The fisherman smelled dirty weather clouding over the noble game of pool.

And bull said Rough and Randy would come to Beer and Bait, and that the boys at China Bay sent challenges. Plus, every pool hall in western Washington, Oregon, and British Columbia would hear the news. The fisherman foresaw a convocation of hustlers that would make the Mafia look like prize pink piglets.

Through the layers of bull, Bertha tended bar, kept her own council, razzed pool games, stocked extra beer, and tried to make the place seem normal. Bertha looked optimistic. Part of her optimism came because news traveled fast. Everyone knew the cop was history and that Beer and Bait no longer lay off-limits. Part of Bertha's optimism came because a week of tournament meant a packed bar, and a packed bar meant cash.

And, bull said, cops were everywhere pulling back. The TV cop was nowhere seen, so maybe the whole show had ended. Maybe cars stopped dunking and the road ran clear. Still, going for a drive around midnight didn't seem the world's best idea.

As the fisherman entered that dark and silver night, his loyal companion, Jubal Jim, trotted by his side. From Beer and Bait came the lonesome sound of bashed guitars. It seemed there was /rain on the hay/ and worms in the corn/ I wish to this day/ I'd never been born/ something like that. The fisherman figured Jubal Jim felt uncertain and wanted company; which made two of them.

Through late afternoon the fisherman had perched on the pier beside his boat while Jubal Jim snoozed. The fisherman first thought of work on the boat. Then he thought of good and evil. It came to him that the business of true evil was to make nice people join its program; which explained Sugar Bear.

The fisherman thought of the bartender at China Bay who spoke of the fall of civilization. Then the fisherman thought of all the folks he knew. The fall of civilization seemed like a pretty sturdy charge to lay against folks who were only guilty of misdemeanors, or maybe teeney-weeney felonies. A' course, the bartender said the whole deal was gradual. It figured, then, that everybody was in the middle of something.

Then the fisherman thought of Sugar Bear, and especially of Annie. He finally understood about men and women. The realization came so quick he didn't trust it. Then he did. He saw that men got to run around making all kinds of noise and doing all kinds of stuff. Then women got to come in after guys were up to their armpits, and say, "Now that you've made a complete, beautiful mess of your life, let's see what we can do to fix it."

So maybe Annie could fix things, but it would not happen as long as Sugar Bear insisted she stay out. It once more came to the fisherman that Sugar Bear was too cherubic to expect long life. The fisherman shuddered.

As he stepped along in company with Jubal Jim, night seemed like a darkened stage seconds before a play begins . . . curtains already raised, stage pitch black, and footlights about to rise . . . like the world paused, ready to swing into action.

The yellow crane still hovered over the dunk site. Along the road, cops had placed wooden barriers with blinking red lights. A couple barriers were busted, but not too smashed. Red warning light cut through silver moonlight, and flashed like little puffs of fire across rubble of the well-worn shore. Nothing grew there, nothing could, what with foot and vehicle traffic. The fisherman looked from land to water, saw running lights in the channel, red where a crab boat chugged home, and green where something far-away passed to seaward. Water lay placid as a lake, but near the shore the backend of a small station wagon appeared.

The fisherman knew with awful suddenness that something dark lay in wait. Something had changed. The air seemed chilled. Of course, it was night and it was October.

As the fisherman approached the crane Jubal Jim started going crazy. He danced with joy and jumped against the tires of the crane, trying to get inside. From inside the cab came a mutter as Petey said something unprintable. The door opened. Petey looked down. Jubal Jim woofed. Petey looked ticked, but also happy as only a guy can when reunited with his dog.

"Nice work," Petey said to the fisherman. "You ain't exactly welcome. There's no room for three of us up here." He climbed down. As Petey and Jubal Jim got back together with licks and rubs, the fisherman told himself this night was lonelier than usual.

Red light made dark shadows darker, and silver streaks flashed like blades of knives. Petey and Jubal Jim looked like cut-outs against red light; moving silhouettes. The fisherman waited until man and dog regained sanity. Petey took off his belt and leashed it to Jubal Jim's collar.

"Welcome back from the dead," the fisherman told Petey. "For awhile you became a legend."

Petey pointed to shrubbery fifty feet away. "Get over there. Company's coming." He walked quickly. When the three were concealed Petey whispered, "What's the bull?"

"Everybody thinks you're dead," the fisherman told him, "except Bertha and Sugar Bear and Annie, and, a 'course, me." The fisherman paused. "Maybe that cop has questions. Plus, the bartender at China Bay always knows everything that's going on."

"How's Bertha?"

"Championship." The fisherman told how Bertha and the cop came to mutual disagreement. "As far as Beer and Bait is concerned, the cop is history."

"In that case," Petey whispered, "the cop is one up. I see I done wasted a Pontiac." He looked toward the Canal. "Plus a busted rice grinder."

"You're running a hustle?"

"I'm getting rid of a cop."

The fisherman could not see Petey's blush, but felt that he heard it.

Petey mumbled. "I was hoping for false arrest, or at least get roughed up a little. Bertha wouldn't stand for that. But that's busted. Plus, stuff comes up." Petey still sounded embarrassed. "The cop started to get smart. He started showing up here nights, but never the right time, or never on a night when anything happened. I fed him the Pontiac to keep him interested."

"Something's happening?" The fisherman pretended ignorance.

"When it happens you'll know. When the cop sees it his case is solved. When his case gets solved he'll have to explain it to the home office, and you're gonna see how he can't. Way I figure it, he'll quit, or get transferred, or marry a lady cop. The important thing is he'll get outta here."

"Which will save Sugar Bear."

"Don't bet on it," Petey said. "Sugar Bear shows up on bad nights. Sugar Bear has worse problems than cops."

"And that's the whole entire hustle, to get rid of a cop?"

"What gives on the pool tournament? I overheard some bull."

The fisherman explained.

"That'll work," Petey muttered, mostly to himself. "I gotta move quick. Mostly, it's already set up." He flopped Jubal Jim's ears. "You know me better. A 'course it's about more than getting rid of a cop. Stuff comes up. The rich guys are running a hustle. I just naturally got to work that house."

"Which? What hustle?"

"Heads up," Petey whispered. "We got some action."

Parking lights appeared as a car crept silently fifty yards away. Lights went out. There came the soft click of a door opening, but no interior light came on. The cop had taped down the switch. The door barely clicked as it was pushed back but not closed. "As sneaky as a crutch," Petey whispered, "but he thinks he's bein' mysterious." Petey hooked a finger into Jubal Jim's collar and held tight to the leash. "Can it," he told Jubal Jim.

The cop walked as discreet as a dancing elephant. Gravel crunched, the swish of cedar branches sounded like whispers as the cop pushed them aside. He took his time, but had no experience at walking silent.

The fisherman looked toward the Canal. Silver moonlight crossed the water and ended at the shore. Puffs of red danced toward the silver and turned black. The fisherman watched calm water, then saw slight movement beneath the surface; a ripple, like a sea turtle grabbing air, or a feeding cutthroat trout. Wordless, the fisherman touched Petey's arm, then pointed to the water. Petey nodded "yes," and his Portuguese-Spanish-Italian-type mouth hardened. He took tighter hold on Jubal Jim's collar, and it was clear he protected his dog because Jubal Jim was too brave.

"Something's stirring. It's getting stronger. This could get bad. Plus Sugar Bear's gonna show up," Petey whispered. "Get out of here and warn him." Water stirred. A light odor dwelt along the shore, an odor of decay. A feeling of dread rose from the stench.

"I dunno," the fisherman said about Sugar Bear, "I promised Annie . . . " He did not finish because, well, because.

"I made the offer," Petey whispered to himself. "Plus this hustle has crashed." He took a tighter grip on Jubal Jim's collar. "If things go sour I'll cause noise, then beat it." He sounded disgusted. "Sugar Bear. A cueball's got more brains."

The fisherman thought about Petey helping Sugar Bear. Some hustlers rise to nearly ordinary kindness . . . always a shock when it happens.

The cop approached the dunk site. In blinking red light he looked taller. He did not wear his uniform, just work clothes and jacket. He looked like a regular guy trying to walk off trouble. He carried one of those long, long flashlights cops use. He hid behind the crane. When he saw the busted barriers, and the rear end of the station wagon his shoulders raised, then lowered like he held back a sigh.

The fisherman remembered what Annie said. Fighting just made the thing stronger. Or maybe she talked about the right way to fight.

The fisherman asked himself if evil had gotten strong enough to challenge a cop? Then he told himself he was simple-minded. True evil wouldn't care if a guy was a cop.

Another ripple of water. For moments it seemed nothing more would happen. Either that, or decisions were being made. Then the ripple became a concentrated swirl of red and silver water as something broke the surface. The thing rose slowly, slow, taking its time, so filled with power it paid no attention to anything or anyone.

The cop gasped, and the fisherman almost did. The thing looked like a rough-cut human, like a thing turned out of a mold a little too early. It looked like a dark manikin, unwigged, splayed around shoulders, broken pieces knitting. It had fingers, a sort of nose, and eyes; eyes that in flashing red light shone red, then black, red-black-red-black, metrical. Arms raised crookedly, hands palms up and beckoning. A light smell of decay spread among surrounding trees.

The fisherman told himself he saw evil incarnate, evil walking, a work-in-progress, almost finished. He remembered that the cop thought himself alone. The fisherman reluctantly admired the cop's courage, just as the cop stepped from behind the crane.

Red light flashed across his face and his mouth firmed, cop-like, then went slack, then firmed. Darkness flashed between red and silver slashes. Fear mixed with courage. The cop stood fixed for maybe twenty seconds before he finally understood nothing human caused the wrecks. He fumbled the flashlight switch. The sense of dread filled the clearing as the cop made a couple of practice moves with his mouth, then decided to stay silent.

He pointed the flashlight and acted out his own show. The beam moved slowly along the bank, rested on the rear end of the drowned station wagon, flashed among shrubbery so Petey and the fisherman ducked lower. The beam ignored the shape in the water, like the shape was unimportant.

"If you can talk," the cop said in a pleasant voice, "better get started."

Movement of water. Decisions being made. The smell of decay increased, but only a little. The mouth moved, soundless, imperfectly shaped. A whisper. Silence. Whisper. Silver streaks of water danced like knives as light wind rippled the water. The cop, casual, steady, moved the beam of light onto the form. The light illuminated, but did not shine through. "Not a ghost," the cop said, talking to himself. "The damned thing is solid."

Behind the cop, movement. The road did not exactly twist, but seemed to flow, traveling sideways pretty quick, but not so fast that barriers tipped. The cop proved smart enough not to turn his back. He stepped sideways, flicking his light across the road, but also watching the dark creation standing in flashes of red cut with silver knives. The road continued to flow as it tried to pull the cop sideways into the Canal. The thing looked a little smaller, somehow, or maybe just tentative. The road returned to normal so smoothly it seemed nothing had happened.

"Let's see you do it again." The cop's voice remained calm, but he spoke a bit louder. He sounded pleasantly angry, but about to get less pleasant. The fisherman figured the cop thought of the many people dead, the drowned cars, the endless traffic problems, and sneers from the populace. The cop stepped forward, cop-like.

The fisherman moved, was restrained by Petey. The fisherman tried to pull away, tried to stop the cop's terrible mistake. The cop should not approach. The fisherman wanted to yell, to keep the cop away from the thing, but Petey motioned silence. Then, even Petey began to stir, and Petey was scared.

Breezes increased to wind, and the fisherman wondered if Annie was taking over. Wind gusted, and little tips of fir rained onto the road.

The cop stopped moving forward. Tried to step back. He seemed frozen, looked suddenly confused and fearful. Behind him the road moved only a little, returned to normal. The cop could not step backward. His right arm extended, like he was being pulled. His arm jerked, trying to pull away. As wind gusted on the red and silver water the thing seemed smaller, more concentrated. The cop tensed, made movements backward, but remained held in place. Whatever dark power dwelt in those depths was not strong enough to pull him forward, but the cop stood fixed, held in an ugly game of tug; caught.

The fisherman moved, ready to stand, and Petey motioned him down. "Take care of my dog," he told the fisherman. "I'll take care of Sugar Bear." He passed the leash. He patted Jubal Jim. "Sound off," he said, then disappeared.

Low growls, rising between sharp barks. Jubal Jim braced and sounded. The thing reacted, grew smaller as Jubal Jim raged. At the waterside the cop stumbled backward only a little, then was held.

The fisherman stood, holding the leash as Jubal Jim sounded. Jubal Jim tugged ahead as stronger wind began to whip the water. The cop sucked air, gasped, tried to free himself. In flashing red light the cop's face contorted as he fought for breath. Small waves began to lap the shore. The thing seemed smaller, still. It was weakening.

The fisherman steeled himself, rushed forward, and reached the cop. The fisherman grabbed the cop's arm, and pulled backward so hard both men stumbled. The cop managed to stay on his feet. The fisherman, whose shore legs were never as good as his sea legs, fell among red flashes, fell into darkness, fell yelling as his right hand went cold as death; tripping over Jubal Jim who now stood braced, growling in the direction of the Canal. The fisherman felt immersed in darkness, in cold, and even red flashes did not color the ground where he fell. He was so busy trying to rise he did not see a rapidly moving hump of water, and did not see the dark incarnation quickly sink beneath the waves.

In reddest light the cop stood dazed. Weak. Shrubbery looked withered, frozen. The cop looked at the fisherman, at Jubal Jim. He rubbed his arm and awful fear lived all across his face. Wrinkles around his eyes deepened. He looked older, lots older. His shoulders were rounded, stooped, geriatric. He gasped. Gained control.

The fisherman rubbed his own hand, the hand that did the grabbing. His hand felt cold. Not cold like pulling line at sea, but corpse-cold, lifeless. The cop continued to rub his arm. Something suspiciously like a sob sounded, followed by a deep breath. The fisherman wiggled his fingers.

"You guys are okay," the cop muttered. "Thanks," he said to the fisherman. To Jubal Jim, he said, "You got a great voice." He staggered, walked toward the crane and leaned against it, then fished in his pocket for keys. "Something's screwed up with this arm. I got a car parked. We gotta get out of here."

It occurred to the fisherman that, except for Jubal Jim, everyone was in shock. He turned toward the Canal and reckoned that wind gusted to twenty knots. Waves broke around the rear end of the dunked station wagon. He felt his cold hand, felt for returning warmth, felt none. He fumbled Jubal Jim's leash, got it free. "Go to Bertha," he told Jubal Jim. "Hang tough," he told the cop. "I'll be right back."

The Fisherman and the Creature

Along about dawn when local delivery guys checked their loads against their routes, and when newspaper guys dropped copies of the *Daily Blat* onto counters of self-serves, or in boxes before restaurants, a Canal story worked its way north from Olympia.

The story said a gang war raged north of Beer and Bait. Survivors were even now carried through doorways of hospital emergency rooms. The war was fought with knives, clubs, insults, cuss words, accusations; plus tire irons, shotguns, slingshots; all the usual stuff, plus a secret freezer-zapper that floated ten feet above the ground and, instantaneous, turned guys into corpsecicles.

News of the war erupted when a cop and a fish-guy showed up in emergency, tot-ally froze out, and not saying squat. The cop made a death-bed confession, then a minimum recovery because of a prayer session with an itinerant missionary. The confession indicted every cop and every preacher in three counties.

Because a plot was afoot to a: dump speeding tickets in return for church attendance, b: make DWI a Class-A felony, c: raze every joint along the Canal and build rich-guy condominiums in a grand cleanup of bums, deadbeats, goldbricks, freeloaders, fornicators, hustlers, and honest men.

By midmorning, when the fisherman slept exhausted across his truck seat while waiting for China Bay to open, the story reached Rough and Randy where guys toasted a wind-blown day with hair-of-the-dog, and watched each other with suspicion. Talk stayed at a minimum. Mental inventories of weapons, tactical plans, and deep, deep, deep, deep holes for hiding lay on the surface of each and every mind. If a war went on somewhere, no one could say the men of Rough and Randy were not prepared.

And, at Beer and Bait, Bertha swept floors, polished mirrors, stocked cold cases, and poured coffee while listening to one crock after the next. Guys played at being brave. They hovered above steaming cups and passed the creamer.

If a gang war was goin' on out there, where were the cops? And was it a good idea to get back on that road or what? Plus, the bull said, another car had gone in. Men talked in low voices as they pretended not to listen for gunfire; but if sounds of battle went on, the sounds were carried away by wind.

At China Bay, the fisherman slept in his truck as the bartender arrived, cleaned the joint, and got set for the day's business. The fisherman kept sleeping heavy-duty, like after a twenty-hour stretch at sea . . . it having been one helluva night . . . drive to Olympia with a badly injured cop who was hurt lots worse than it first seemed . . . and himself feeling broken and old . . . and both of them so scared they could hardly talk . . . catch a return ride north for his truck, then drive back to Olympia where he could be near hospital and bartender; all with a hand that was gonna gangrene if blood didn't start pumping pretty quick.

A dreadful dream woke him at noon. He dreamed of the cop and Sugar Bear, and coldness, and eternal night. He dreamed of his face reflected in the truck's mirrors, of wrinkles and seams, eye-pouches of age. He dreamed of the depths of the sea, and of a missionary voice, almost familiar and echoing from the bottom of the Canal, or maybe from a hospital waiting room. He heard the swish and flow of dark creatures moving monstrous above drowned men, monsters feeding on the fleeing souls of men. Impressions and memories mixed in the dream, and all through the dream sounded pain and darkness.

He woke to twenty knots of wind. And, when he woke he looked in the truck mirror and saw the face of nightmare, a face aged and aging moreso as he watched.

The parking lot displayed a lunchtime crowd, dink-commute-cars belonging to government jocks who packed in one beer, or maybe two, max, before tightening ties and heading back to make rules that molested suffering humanity. Plus, work trucks were sprinkled among the econo-boxes. A hefty crew of poolers had come aboard. The bartender's Jag sat in quiet, if rumpled, splendor.

When the fisherman stepped inside he saw all pool tables busy with guys practicing. He figured they clustered at China Bay, because Beer and Bait would already be crowded with folks arriving for tournament. He saw lunch tables surrounded by bureaucrats stuffing with gobbled cold cuts while sipping beer. He saw two retired gents playing cribbage at the fish-tank-end of the bar. One was the tattooed ex-Navy guy, the other the former diplomat with the pressed hanky.

Lee was nowhere seen, but the bartender stood behind a bar that was pretty near deserted. The fisherman took a seat three stools down from the old gents, and two stools away from a well-dressed, well-coifed, and very slender lady who sipped white wine and looked emotionally satisfied.

The bartender placed coffee before the fisherman, then, being either charitable or interested, waited.

"It's worse than serious," the fisherman said, "but you know about that." His voice trembled. He cleared his throat. Then, because he didn't really believe bartenders know everything, he told it anyway: How the dark creation had appeared, and how it acted. How maybe he would never pull a line again, because his right hand wouldn't close. He tried to talk calm about it, at least as calm as the cop had tried for.

And he told how, a cop, a guy he feared, turned into a good guy after all; and was maybe going to live. How, it seemed like something dark tried to crawl all over the cop, and how the cop had stayed mostly brave and quiet. How, no matter what, living or dead, the guy was done, hurt, looking older than old; and how doctors in emergency, doctors who saw every kind of bad thing, had been afraid and not hiding it when they found a completely dead arm on a living body.

Wind slapped the windows of China Bay, and the fisherman told how coldness, like no cold he had ever known in a life spent at sea, still deadened his fingers. He rushed with his words until fear choked him. He fell silent. Beyond the windows, water broke in gusts of froth and wind-blown spray around a hump that moved slowly on the Canal; but no one seemed to notice.

"It's little known," one of the retired gents said, his voice completely sympathetic as he studiously avoided inquisitiveness, "why Europeans prefer hairy armpits. In actual fact, they've been civilized for so long that wild armpits are all they've got left of nature." The gent moved a peg three jumps. "I speak, of course, of the more northerly latitudes." This was the former diplomat, who sometimes seemed as wry as the bartender.

The bartender's eyes, sort of hazel, showed interest in the fisherman. "You speak of dark power, yet it runs away?"

"It's getting stronger," the fisherman said. "Like it gets stronger every time it wins something, and weaker when something happens it can't handle. It attacked a cop and went smaller before a dog."

"Bingo," the bartender whispered, and could barely be heard above bureaucratic chatter and the click of pool. "It feeds. Think of what it feeds on. Because it can't handle natural forces." The bartender turned to draw beer for an approaching gov-guy. "Third one today," the bartender told the guy.

"Like I give-a- . . . " the guy looked toward the satisfied slim-lady who paid no attention. "My car is paid for, I got no wife or kids, so do I give a . . . rap?"

"Unemployment insurance," the other retired gent mentioned, "is not actually a creature of the New Deal as is generally supposed." He kept his eyes lowered, so as not to embarrass the fisherman. Discreet for a Navy man.

"I had a ten-year career plan," the gov-guy said. "I'm reducing the sucker to three more beers and fifteen minutes." He looked toward the satisfied lady who paid absolutely no attention.

The fisherman sipped coffee, awkward, his bad hand resting on the bar, his left hand fumbling the cup. "The docs didn't want me to leave, but I can still shift gears. Hang the wrist over the shift, or come up from under." He heard tears in his voice but wasn't shedding any, not yet. He imagined that coldness was moving up his wrist.

"Poor, dear, John," the satisfied lady said when the gov-guy departed. "He's ridden that slippery slope since the moment he championed public transit." The lady's delicate wrist curved as she sipped from her wine glass. To the bartender she said, "Odd people infest this bar. You'll surely lose business." She wrinkled her nose as she glanced at the fisherman, looked at his hand.

"There appears to be a problem," the bartender mentioned.

"One spends one's days with important problems," the lady said, "and wishes to relax at lunch."

The retired diplomat who knew about Europeans, and who

was conscious of bad, bad trouble, chuckled. He turned to the lady. "My dear, if you lose a couple pounds and do a little something with your hair . . . what an improvement would come to your sympathies."

"That," said the lady most grimly, "was crude, sexual, filled with filth, and amounts to harassment." She barely kept control, and clearly thought of body fat.

Wind popped in gusts against the windows, gusts that maybe hit twenty knots.

"We will now take a short break," the bartender told everyone. "Each and all will think charitable thoughts. Your happiness is at stake." The bartender did not explain, and did not have to.

"It grows when it steals life," the fisherman murmured, mostly to himself. "It's creating itself out of what it kills."

"For the moment," the bartender said, "let us put an end to this. You are sorely ridden." The bartender touched the fisherman's hand. "You are a man of the sea," the bartender said, "perhaps your answer is on the water, which is where you should now go."

The fisherman felt the tiniest tingle on one fingertip, felt a small pain in a knuckle; like the fishy-type arthritis that flogs hands in cold-weather fishing. "I do gotta go," he said, knowing he would choke up and act stupid if he stayed. He left quickly, but not so quickly he forgot to say "thanks", or leave a buck for the coffee. When he stepped outside, wind still gusted around twenty.

It blew that way as he drove north, slowed by increasingly heavy traffic as people headed for Beer and Bait. Wind continued to blow as he arrived at his home pier and got underway. His workboat carried a downeast bow that threw large spray into the wind.

The fisherman fumbled the throttle and told himself he was the luckiest man afloat. Pain flashed across his fingertips, burned his wrist and contorted his palm as the hand returned to life. It hung hooked, crooked, a claw; and maybe it would never completely close again, but a guy could re-rig the winch for working line. The hand trembled a good bit, but that might go away. He watched the hand, saw no black streaks, nothing blue or purple. Calluses flaked off, the way it does after a month ashore. Working hands, and it looked like, one way or other, they would keep working if a guy was not too feeble.

He did not know where to go or what he looked for. If answers were out here, they would have to come to him. He kept the engine running at half, the boat moving slowly into the chop, splitting waves and casting them, white and foam, above black water.

For the third time, if a guy counted the nightmare that had waked him, the fisherman thought of the depths beneath his keel. He thought of darkness and of discarded things, of darkness and the death of men; thus the death of dreams. He thought of stuff sailors don't think about, or else wear survival suits so they can think about it.

Beneath him, even lower down than the wreckage of modern boats and airplanes, of beer cans and discarded appliances, lay prehistoric bones, Indian villages, ancient echoes of lives lived and lost, century after century after century.

How much junk, he wondered, had cluttered around the ruins of Atlantis? How many busted bowls and worn-out olive presses clustered around sunken temples in Greece, Italy; how many bones of oxen lay in the muds of Burma? The sea gets it all. Eventually.

But was it the sea? Because the sea is indifferent. When worlds come apart, the sea does not care. And so it must be that Something . . . Something even uglier than spite . . . caused the clutter that overlays the fall of nations.

Wind kicked so hard he kept ten degrees left rudder to hold a straight course against the easterly. A dark sky pressed close, and only whitecaps told where wind and water met. He pointed toward the middle of the channel. Water in the middle looked flattened, but showed turmoil beneath the surface. It moved beneath winds different from the easterly.

He suddenly sailed into a place of calm, but not calm in the eye of storm. Temperature raised, hot and dry, heat that cracks rock, and sunlight that ennobles marble. Wind fell to a breeze, and carried the scent of islands, olive trees, and markets. Wind carried sounds of creaking from slowly turning windmills, their sails white beneath the sun. Wind carried the murmur of voices in hurry-scurry of trade, and wind carried other voices, calm, stating syllogism, stating enthymeme. And, lying like the foundation of the world, a crystal sea lapped against distant shores while fish of kinds he did not know flashed across the sea floor.

The fisherman slowed the engine, stopped, listened, waited. Fishing boats of a curious style were silhouetted on the horizon. A distant island glowed, a distant temple white against a sky of Mediterranean blue. The workboat drifted nearly without movement.

In the near distance, and closing as though tired, water swirled where a hump moved beneath the surface. The fisherman knew he should feel alarm, yet did not. As the creature closed, water gave a final swirl, then the surface went calm. Somewhere close the creature moved beneath a sunlit sea.

The fisherman automatically checked for ocean traffic and saw he need not worry about interruptions. He peered into deep and sunlit water. An old face peered back, his own, but now with more wrinkles, and with skin thin and stretched tight across bone. At first he did not recognize himself. Then he choked, sobbing. He wondered how old he was, if he was old as he looked. Then he commanded himself to stop blubbering.

His attention went to movement as the sea floor disappeared. At first he believed he sailed across the shadowed mouth of a cavern, one so huge it could swallow ships. Then he understood it was not a cavern but an eye. He waited. Watched. Waited.

The creature drifted beneath him, wounded, decrepit; its immortality no guard against disease and crippling, no guard against all ill things; except death.

It drifted, mountainous in sunlight, larger than temples, as large, even, as ideas. It glowed pale in places, luminescent in others; and with much of it hidden because it was huge and not alone. The fisherman thought of an island cruising beneath water, an island invaded by frenzied beings. Myriad creatures hovered, darted, swarmed, and fed on the luminescence; not a frenzy of feeding, but steadily, unhurried; grotesque creatures, unnatural, not exactly flesh and not exactly rock. Not exactly iron or bronze or wire; nebulous, ugly forms of spines and hooks and mouths; flashing, darting, black and red and blue and purple, flashes of pink, white, the color spectrum lacking green. Fins, snakelike, many mouths. Low sounds seemed to rise through water where they swarmed, sounds of chatter, mindless, babbling as they fed.

Immortality. The fisherman, who was not nearly as tough as he pretended, peered through crystal water and understood that life needs an ending. He imagined himself immortal, imagined the unending days, while all around him friends and lovers and even enemies stepped into eternity.

He thought of change, and how true things get discarded generation after generation: asking himself what did this creature know, remember; what part of this creature's wisdom had the world cast off as it giggled its way from amusement to amusement? This crippled thing, alive after twenty-five hundred years, now eternally gnawed, eternally old.

The creature moved slowly in a wide arc, rising little by little until it hung suspended at four fathoms. As it rose further, the chatter from feeding things became screeches, and the fisherman understood that the creature lived in a world of mindless sound.

It hovered, the part he could see, just beneath his keel. It's immensity and paleness, it's luminosity, spread across the sea and made crystal water glow bloodless. It rested among noise, or else it waited. Waited.

"I would help you if I could." The fisherman did not know what else to say. Waited. It seemed to him that noise diminished, but only a trifle. It seemed the gnawing slowed, but only a trifle.

The creature rose, nearly on the surface, and the fisherman thought his workboat would go aground. As the creature neared, the swarm of feeders dropped lower, still chattering, but avoiding the surface. It came to the fisherman that the creature had been alone, except for feeders, a very, very long time. The fisherman reached over the side, prepared to touch.

"I don't understand," the fisherman said. "Maybe you don't need help, but I would if I could." He sensed that something was about to happen, some communication. The noise of feeding diminished, only a little. Then startlement ran though the water, like a sea animal hit by harpoon.

He watched as the creature sank slowly into depths; then, quicker than the quickest fish or gull, spun and drove away while the sunlit sea turned darker. Water erupted, as from an underwater explosion, and the fisherman told himself nothing so huge could move so quickly, yet it did. The workboat heeled before the explosive wave, then settled onto a sea going black, like a slow fade-out in artsy movies. Distant islands and temple slowly disappeared as the workboat began to rock.

Wind kicked the workboat. Canal wind and Canal water crashed, and low clouds blew as mist. Sudden chill dwelt in the wind, and cold rose from the water. In the distance a hump closed the westward shore, moving toward the dunk site. The fisherman ported his helm, spun toward the west and opened the engine full. Wind pressed his starboard quarter, wind rising in a sudden squall bringing spume over the low rail of the boat. Whatever was happening must be happening fast. The boat kicked and stumbled through chop. Wind crashed from starboard.

Wind gusted from gale to storm. Along the shore, explosions of water rose, salt spray blowing across the road and into forest.

The fisherman cut r.p.m.s, felt the stern slide sideways, increased r.p.m.s and spun the bow to wind. He held it there and looked backward to the shore.

Dim figures moved as the forest went dark. Two people or maybe three, and two of them running. Near the shore a battle began. Water rose like geysers, paused, rose, spouted, paused, exploded. Enormous movement, challenge, fight. Waves kicked back from the shore, beat against waves blown shoreward by wind. A turmoil of water crashed before the fisherman's bow. Water rose high into the wind, was blown into the forest. Then, almost as quickly as it began, the battle stilled before a screaming wind. Whatever happened beneath the waves had happened.

The fisherman, who knew with awful certainty that he must get to Sugar Bear, imagined two exhausted and deadly enemies resting on the bottom among detritus of broken planes, cast-off junk, the bones of men, and beer cans; the two enemies no doubt also broken. Why enemies? Why battle?

He unwillingly accepted, though, that nothin' down there was dead. There was only continuation of tortured life.

A Fearsome Result

Along the Canal, motels are few and rich guys shared them with
visionaries. As poolers tended toward Beer and Bait, while being
buffeted by wind, motels also hosted several realists. The visionaries were poolers who were better'n average, but did not have a
Protestant's chance in Purgatory when it came to contests that
included hustlers.

Realists were practical folk; percentage players, real hustlers
ready to make a wage from side bets. Since only one team would
come away with top prize, the realists knew where the big money
lay.

Motel registers carried names: John Jones, L. Smith, Peter
Jones, Alexander Smith, George Smith, and Samuel Green. When
translated the registers actually said: Shi Shi John, Peanut Louise,
Issaquah Pete, Vancouver Alex, Jaybird George, and Sammy the
Snooze.

The realists' autos told tales: '78 Buick pimpmobile with leop-
ard skin seats, once the property of a Tacoma optimist who
thought he could play pool; '49 Ford pickup packing four barrels
and electric pink paint; Dodge van, at present rather weary but
once customized beyond yearly i.d.; Humber of indeterminate
age, veddy, veddy shiny, black, and British; '82 Cad reputed to
carry bulletproof glass; '47 Packard hearse with custom interior

and fold-down bed.

Along the narrow roadway, traffic crept in bursts of up to probably three m.p.h., and a fisherman managed to catch up on his cussing. Camper trucks pulled over when drivers found spaces between trees, or beside cars already parked. Tents sprouted like flowers, red, green, orange, blue, khaki, as campers hunched back-to-wind, trying to heat beans over fires that blew sideways. Here and there a child shouted, skipped, danced in the wind, and colorful baseball caps blew from heads in a happy abandon of words: "Beulah's Beagles", "Bremerton Bowl", "G.M.C. Trucks", "Kitty's Koffee Klatch", "Poulsbo A.C.", "A Rage Of Catnip", and "Feckless in Seattle".

Police cars cruised, hassled guys who parked too near the road, and cops were stone-y, unfeeling, colder'n beer in the coolers. Cops played tough, watched the Canal, and stayed close to their cars even when hassling. If cops were afraid, their fear didn't show.

Matters were otherwise festive. Some folk complained of a missionary-type who passed out pamphlets, a small annoyance; but no cop could find the guy among other opportunists who set up shop along the road: selling roasted corn, hot dogs, souvenirs: mostly plaster seagulls and shopworn pennants of Northwest sporting pride: Mariners, Seahawks, Sonics; plus colors of the greatest and most enthusiastic university in the history of football.

There were so many gorgeous things: carved totem poles, authentic, made in Japan, and pins reading "Sex Is Good, Irish Is Best", or "Cows Do It Butter". Ah, such gorgeous things. Helium balloons reading "Bankshot", "Shoot the Moon", "Pool Guy", "Corner Pocket", and "Acme Pool School and Latté Palace".

And things for kiddies: mostly dolls with nipples or erections;

and bubble gum that carried trading cards of super heroes: The Joker, Rambo, Barfman.

And of course, there was nostalgia: tie-dyed tee shirts, sticks of incense, tinkly strings of bells, clay pipes, and lids of Mary Jane. Bikers packed sand-filled socks, and Harleys barked their sainted song into the wind; wind that blew the song into the forest where deer stood puzzled, then disgusted, and where bears took the week off to go hunting in the foothills.

In the parking lot of Beer and Bait a new Cadillac sat beside Bertha's Chrysler, while California cars mixed with plates from Oregon and Idaho, a geographic cohabitation of machinery parked tight as the curl in a little pig's tail. Here and there, in the parking lot, a Kenworth loomed above cars and pickups, including the tow-truck kid's V10 Dodge.

As the fisherman inched along, stuck on the only road that led to Sugar Bear, he heard noise from Beer and Bait that mixed with blare from the tape deck. Bertha had loaded the thing with mellow stuff, tranquilizer stuff, but mighty loud. The fisherman viewed the parking lot, saw one guy checking cars for orphan goods . . . the fisherman, startled, thought of Chantrell. Then he saw it was not Chantrell but some other deadbeat. Meanwhile, from the tape deck, no fewer than a thousand violins belted "Stranger in the Night."

Traffic stalled so bad a guy had to set stakes to see it move. The fisherman could only follow a state-owned dump truck, painted orange, fulla rip-rap, driven by a guy forced into overtime without pay. In the fisherman's mirrors a Dodge crummy-wagon, muddy and glass-cracked, followed too close since it prob-ly had no brakes.

Likely, the fisherman told himself, very likely this day before pool tournament would be worst. As days wore on, optimists would fail, do sideways betting, and go home busted. Amateurs would tire and hustlers would stay until easy money ran out. Locals would be in and out, some wistful; it was hard to tell what rich guys would do.

Because oncoming traffic from the north held expensive iron, Cads and Lincs and Jags, plus campers longer than a bad girl's dreams. Rich guys were coming in for another contest, were gonna get blown out . . . the fisherman paused, watched the orange back-end of the dump truck and told himself, naw, nope, no way. Rich guys might be dumb about pool hustle, but they weren't dumb about hustle. They would not make the same mistake twice; well, with women, maybe, but not with money.

And riding beside the drivers, a butterfly perched on the passenger side of each car. The butterflies seemed confined when they should be aery. But, how colorful they were, how lovely. At least from distance.

The state dump truck showed turn signal to the right, and the fisherman realized the three-mile-an-hour crawl had brought them to the dunk site. Air brakes hissed and the truck pulled off the road. The fisherman found himself behind a new Ford pickup pulling a new utility trailer; the truck too snazzy to use as a truck, the trailer full of trashed electronics: outmoded record players, typewriters, computers, and the dead eyes of televisions.

The fisherman looked into the dunk site where a two foot hunk of rebar lay on churned ground pounded clean of vegetation. Shrubs that once concealed Petey and the fisherman looked like they had barely survived the worst storm of an unhappy year. Douglas fir stood shorn of lower branches. The yellow crane stood tilted, but not quite enough to be scary. It hovered above cuts and gullies where something had scooped or cut, like giant claws.

A 'course, the dump truck would not be here because of the

battle of a while ago. Rip-rap would have been ordered earlier. It looked like something a government would figure, rip-rap over shingle, concrete over rip-rap, and a wall rising above concrete; the whole business sliding into the Canal in the first really bad winter.

In the fisherman's mirrors the crummy-wagon began to steam as low speed caused overheating. The driver revved the engine to rush air through his radiator. Wind showered the road with fir tips. The driver gave up and pulled off the road. Behind him, the fisherman now saw a cop car. The cop pulled over. He stopped beside, and not behind, the crummy-wagon. Now, in the fisherman's mirrors, and following too close, a Volvo station wagon rolled in quiet Swedish snootiness.

The fisherman watched as the cop climbed from his car. This was an older cop, a guy who should be flying a desk and not running road. He walked to the crummy-wagon, careful to keep the junker between himself and the Canal.

With the Ford in front and the Volvo behind, the fisherman inched along like the middle part of a vehicle-sandwich. Wind continued steady at twenty. The fisherman looked at the back of his hands as they hung on the steering wheel. He tried to feel something, horror or sadness or anger, and felt nothing. He figured he must still be in shock. His hands seemed mere curiosities. They held wrinkles he could not remember. One hand twisted, cramped, but at least it was alive and painful. His wrists seemed thinner. When he finally reached the turn-off to Sugar Bear's place, he cursed himself for vanity. He actually feared being seen. Then he thought of Annie, and feared what he was about to see.

Sugar Bear's pickup stood with its front bumper hovering over the front step of the fairy tale house. Sugar Bear, or maybe Annie had at least managed to get to the front door. The fisherman pulled toward the shop, backed, got his own truck pointed back toward the road. Cut the engine. Watched.

Maple leaves large as hubcaps blew across the ground, dry and crispy, some skeletal. When rains came the leaves would slick-up, then molder and turn to soil. When the fisherman stepped from his truck, though, the leaves crunched and crackled and seemed satisfied. From the forest, where wind moved the tops, dead twigs rattled as they fell.

Windows in the shop were dark, windows in the house even darker. Light seemed blown away by wind as afternoon turned to gloaming. The fisherman rubbed his crippled hand, wondered why he felt distant from his own problems. He thought that he thought too much.

He stepped from his truck, walked to the door, knocked and entered.

Small wrinkles on her upper lip, strands of gray in hair long, flowing, but having twisted also by a turmoil of wind. Annie stood before the stove waiting for water to heat. Dim light of gloaming lay across her face as early evening marched through windows to cast dark shadows and turn solid objects gray. Annie, girl-like even now, brushed hair from her cheek with fingertips, looked apologetically at the fisherman, looked more closely. She stood mute.

"Where?" The fisherman figured Sugar Bear was still alive, or Annie would not be heating water. Annie would be weeping.

She pointed to the bedroom, turned her attention back to the stove. Her shoulders slumped, but her body tensed against fear or fatigue. Her shoulders seemed thinner.

The fisherman wished to go to her, told himself, "No." He was not an intimate part of her world. He was a shadow against larger scenery, a helping shadow maybe, but nothing about him, was, for Annie, very real.

When he walked to the bedroom he expected worse than what he first saw. Sugar Bear lay propped on pillows and one hand beckoned, while the other moved. His arms were not dead like the cop's. Sugar Bear's furry face looked nearly jovial, a man telling a joke, a guy about to deliver a punch line.

"Katzanjammers," Sugar Bear said. "Aloysius. Sardines. Bejabbers." His voice filled with laughter. Then he became serious, explaining: "Best if you fried it. Seventeen naughty miles. I gotta girl from whatchamazoo, zoo, zoom-ly." He shook a finger, like an admonishing mom, or like a teacher ticking off point one, point two. "The hunny bunny hunny hop," he said with satisfaction, as if some complex matter had been explained.

"You're full of it," the fisherman told him, hoping there was something in Sugar Bear's wrecked mind that could hear. "Quit crappin' me around."

Sugar Bear smiled broad, like the painted smile of a clown. Darkness in the room gathered around the smile, and face-fur moved like it tried to clasp the mouth shut. Sugar Bear smiled and smiled.

The fisherman returned through darkness to the kitchen. It seemed that no amount of light could fully illuminate this small house. "Tell me."

"It manifested." Annie now sat at the kitchen table. On the stove something simmered and smelled herbal. "It looked almost like the dead guy, only not quite finished." She looked at the backs of her hands, took a strand of long hair and brought it forward, studied streaks of gray, puzzled. "Why did he hafta? We could have run. Have to? What's wrong with guys? What are we going to do?"

She was aware of how she looked and wasn't exactly thinking

of it, but the girl part still reacted. She brushed tangled hair with her fingers, automatic; trying to put a shape to things, arranging life.

"Gonna do?" He stood puzzled. "We figure what we can do, or what we can't. Tell me more."

"We were attacked in daytime, right here. Coldness came into this kitchen and it was strong. It wouldn't run."

The fisherman remembered how coldness had entered the house once before, and how Annie chased it away. "It wouldn't leave?"

"So Sugar Bear went after it. I went because he feared leaving me alone. What came from the Canal made sounds that were almost words. It was red-head like the dead guy, and it simpered. Like it was happy about being awful."

The fisherman thought of Annie's fear, of his own, that Sugar Bear might tangle with something he couldn't handle. "How close were you?"

"There wasn't a fight," Annie said, "or at least not much. When Sugar Bear went after it stuff started happening in the water. Water flying everywhere." Annie studied wrinkles on the backs of her hands. "I could feel it crawling on me." She stared, almost impassive. "What has happened? What has? I just turned twenty-three."

"It steals life," the fisherman told her. He looked toward the bedroom. "Now it steals consciousness." He understood that the power of thought was what the thing needed to completely manifest.

"There's a war going on," he told Annie, "but not a bull-war, a real one. Something ugly tries to get free of the Canal and something very big and very old tries to prevent it." He told what he knew.

"Why here? Why us?" She looked toward the bedroom.

Windows darkened as gloaming faded to night. In the forest deer bedded down, cougars began to stretch and move like kings among the lesser night animals. Mice instinctively sought cover although wind kept owls from accurate flight. From the bedroom Sugar Bear hummed a show tune and spoke in clear pronouncements of the joys of root beer and cabbage.

Annie stood, walked to the stove, tasted whatever simmered there. "I don't know enough," she whispered. "I should of paid more attention."

It was the second time she had said that. The fisherman knew that Annie had learned from a grandmother. He did not know what or how much.

"This won't work," she whispered, "but it's all I know." She watched the simmering pan like she could read messages. "You got to eat something," she said to the fisherman. "So does Sugar Bear. Me too. I'll fix it." She turned to the refrigerator, not like an old, old woman, but not like a young one. "Don't leave us," she said. "It might come back. Please."

He could sleep across the truck seat. It would not be the first time. He figured nothing was going to happen. Whatever darkness dwelt in the Canal had been wounded. But, she needed him here.

"Sleep in the shop," she said. "We've got sleeping bags."

Bertha Troubled

Night blew into the northwest, wind backing and shifting as it rose from the ocean. Sleepy sailors stood watch on bows and bridges of tankers, tugs, destroyers, container ships and cutters. Sailors wore foul weather gear and thought of storms birthing out of Russia, the Aleutians, and Japan.

Along beaches tiny filaments of sand flew like mist above sturdier grains, and thin moonlight pressed through blown mist. Wind walked from beach to land, blew into cities as cops cruised three A.M. streets, and street people huddled beneath freeway overpasses.

And wind wrapped around joints. It tumbled butts and crud from the paved parking lot of China Bay. It nagged at cedar shakes roofing Beer and Bait. It salted Rough and Randy with needles of fir. At the housing project yachts rocked against fenders, and wind, as if it held dour opinions, blew on past and headed for Montana.

In the joints a few things happened. At Rough and Randy two rats nibbled spilled potato chips beneath a red night light. At China Bay an aura of luminescence appeared above the bar, maybe reflection from the moon, maybe.

At Beer and Bait, Bertha sat, sleepy, but in charge of an empty bar, that come ten A.M. would fill with poolish hopefuls. Bertha did not quite know what she felt, or why. She was tired from stocking and icing beer, storing nuts and chips and microwave sandwiches, pickled eggs and sausages to serve a mob of poolers snacking their ways hour to hour.

She ought to sleep but her mind raced with fears and problems. Talk along the road claimed the cop was dead, or if not dead, dying, or if not dying so wrecked he'd never work again. A lot of talk was bull, but Bertha knew Canal stories and this was serious.

Bull said other things. Cops were gonna rampage. Joints would be closed . . . but Bertha figured herself an expert on Canal stories and discounted all that.

In dim light from beer signs, this tall, well-formed woman, almost scandalously beautiful, not a little troubled, and only mildly mercenary, wanted a man; and had just lost what might have been a good one . . . but that was not the point.

Bertha wondered how guilty she was, and did she actually have anything to do with this? She had led the cop on and then run him off. Bertha experienced a dark night of the soul, the kind once talked about by an old-timey saint who saw dark nights as opportunities for learning something.

But, people having dark nights generally don't think of opportunity, plus they can't sleep. Beyond the windows wind whacked trees, blowing at twenty knots. Thin moonlight lay on the water. Across the shaft of light a hump moved, slower than usual, like an underwater limp.

She mourned the cop. She might've said something, or done something that would have kept bad stuff away, but she did not know what. Bertha, who was older than Annie, but not as old as the fisherman, had business experience. She did not have much experience of other kinds. This was her first brush with losing somebody who meant something, or might've meant something;

a real person hurt and gone.

And if that wasn't bad enough, Petey's hustle did not include her, because Petey would've said something by now. A 'course, Petey was still playing at being dead.

And if that wasn't bad enough, her arrangement with rich guy had her fearful. He put up prize money, she hosted the tournament and he supplied help, a secretary for himself, a couple of kid bartenders for Bertha. He paid the secretary. Bertha paid the bartenders. Plus, she was overstocked, heavily, with enough stuff to run the joint for two months and enough cash to pay for half of it.

The whole day had been confused. At opening time rich guy showed up with a secretary and two kid bartenders. The kids were quick, funny, and smart enough not to play games at the cash register. She stored stuff, then mostly sat and watched.

The secretary registered a long, long string of poolers, collecting ten bucks a pop. Guys signed up in teams, or if they had no team were assigned partners. The secretary restricted time on each pool table to fifteen minutes because poolers needed to learn the tables. Guys stood watching other guys, estimated the roll, the possible tilt, saw where one cushion was a little low which might cause the ball to hop. They ran fingertips across the mouths of pockets, feeling for ridges or declivities that might louse up a gentle shot. On this day before tournament, poolers drank beer like it was nourishment. When the tournament started beer sales would drop.

Rich guy stayed in the background. When player-lists were posted Bertha spotted part of the setup. Each rich guy was teamed with a known hustler, which meant, of course, that the winner was already decided.

Bertha did the math because she had to. She figured the rich guys invested ten thou, were taking back three from sign-ups, and would split the ten thou prize with the hustlers. That totaled an eight thousand buck take-back for rich guys. If that was the case, there remained a two thousand dollar investment that was not covered; but the hustler-factor was present. Likely, most likely, rich guys figured to split side bets with hustlers, which ought to mean a small profit. Otherwise, the only thing that made sense was revenge; but was revenge worth two thousand bucks?

In subdued light from a couple beer signs Bertha did not know whether to mourn or fear, but knew both needed doing. When the pool lists came out, the name, Petey Mulholland, was nowhere seen. It wasn't normal, it was fearful, actually . . . the all time champ hustler of the entire northwest, with a ten grand pot . . . and Bertha needed him like never before. Love had something to do with it, but not a helluva lot. In the dimness of Beer and Bait, Bertha tried to persuade herself that rich guy was not running his own hustle. She was not succeeding.

Petey would know. Maybe Petey did know. If Petey did know, Petey would maybe save her . . . or maybe Petey wouldn't. She felt such fears, even as Jubal Jim lay snoozing but protective at her feet.

Beyond the windows where wind moved tips of branches, moonlight cast a streak across water; and clouds blew past, sometimes making the streak go dark. Along the streak the hump patrolled, like it sought moonlight, or at least, light. It moved across the mile-long width of the Canal, back and forth, like a prisoner pacing a jail cell, or a caged animal; except the movement was so slow. To Bertha it seemed the entire weary world was going sour. Things had been pretty good until that monster showed up. She told herself, "Slow down. Get a grip. You're scared and blaming anything that comes along."

She watched the hump move along the path of light. It meant something, prob-ly, but it might mean nothing to her. Or maybe, like her, it mourned the cop, or, like her, felt guilty.

Or maybe it was a wake-up call telling her to keep close watch. Because, truth to tell, while she knew she was a good pool shot, she had fooled herself. She understood that pool was one thing, hustling quite another; and she was a failed hustler.

Everybody Is Doing What Everybody Does on Saturday

How gay and glorious dawned the day. What optimism ran from hearts bent to poolish competition, or corruption. And what fair chance dictated this day of sun? And everything so lovely, as traffic backed up and the last maple leaves of autumn danced before a twenty knot wind.

And, if one had been able to ride that wind, to steer it here and there, the wind would serve as a magic carpet sailing above joints where beer trucks and soft drink trucks off-loaded merchandise.

And, if one rode that magic carpet, and was thoughtful, he would just naturally note down where everybody was and what they did. Because, what with magic and wind and creatures in the Canal, plus bad stuff happening; and with some kinda hustle forming and bound to be stinky, it just made good sense if a thoughtful guy had the whole situation in view.

In a snazzy neighborhood in Olympia, a '67 Chevrolet that looked like a rolling wreck, and wasn't, eased to the curb in front of a high-priced apartment house. As if cued from off-stage, two of the fanciest hookers Olympia had to offer tripped modestly toward the Chev. The ladies were dressed to the nines, and had scarves to protect coiffured hair from wind; one head of auburn, one peachy-golden. The ladies viewed the rusty Chev, sniffed, remembered that this was a cash deal, and entered. They settled in for what was bound to be a tedious trip, what with the traffic.

In a seedy Olympia neighborhood, in a flophouse, a missionary-type rose praising a benevolent but just God, while anointing his own innards with a glass of purest water. He thanked the Lord that he could remain clean, one-day-at-a-time. He pulled a pocket mirror from his kit. With tiny sewing scissors he trimmed that part of his haircut he could see. His face was lined but hopeful. His chin was shaved. Anyone who had known him in the past would have been hard put to recognize Chantrell, now known as Brother George. He pulled on faded work pants, a thrift-shop shirt, and primed himself for another day's work among the down and out. The priming was done with a second glass of pure water.

At China Bay the bartender had not yet arrived. The huge room stood empty, or rather, peopled with memories of pool and palaver, of politics and deals (a few legal), of heartbreak and hope, of seduction and harlotry, of mysticism and myth. A faint glow dwelt behind the bar, maybe a reflection from sunlit water. Maybe.

In a low-rent but respectable area of Olympia nestled a hospital where a one-armed man lay broken, semiconscious, sedated and tied to monitors. Sanitary fluorescence cloaked the intensive care ward where a nurse moved quietly between beds. Lights suffused the man's face, lay like plastic sheen on wrappings that covered the site where once had been a shoulder. Light covered the man, but darkness pressed on his mind; darkness hovered, then increased, then dwelt.

•

In early traffic a V10 Dodge purred like a dear-kitty, and the tow-truck kid told himself he gotta hurry. Then he told himself not to get excited, 'cause excited guys don't win at pool, 'cause excited guys are tense. He watched the back end of a sheriff's car that only exceeded by maybe five m.p.h. He watched as the car slowed and took position in a hidden spot beside the road. The kid told himself that there were more local cops around than he could ever, ever remember. When he was no more than two miles from Beer and Bait, traffic backed up. The kid cussed, fretted, told himself to keep steady even if he could not afford to be late.

At the other end of the Canal, in the parking lot of Rough and Randy, a lone survivalist sat in a Land Rover as he tasted a hangover, most fearful. He waited for Al to open. The survivalist watched fancy cars heading south, and he noted one new Cadillac driven by a rotund little rich bastard. The rich guy was accompanied by a lady dressed in purple who resembled a beetle. The survivalist cussed any dumb sumbitch who would own a Cad, and hungered for that first beer of the day.

At Sugar Bear's fairy-tale house sunlight followed a woman, prematurely gray, as she moved from the house into the dimness of the forest. Annie moved awkwardly as the habits of youth tried to enforce themselves on a body that, if not elderly, was at least middle-aged.

The fisherman sat in Sugar Bear's kitchen watching Annie depart, and thinking. He understood that she had to commune with spirits of grandmother or trees. Annie was boxed, but knowing Annie as he did, he knew she would fight back. He shuddered, but continued to take care of Annie in the only way he knew; by watching Sugar Bear who sat at the table slurping coffee.

"I gotta say," Sugar Bear yelped most enthusiastic, "that all the candles and candy in the world don't make up for lignite. Try it. You'll see." Sugar Bear leaned back, as if proud to have proved a point.

The fisherman watched his friend, sorrowed, and then had a loathsome thought. Annie was gonna need lots of help with this. This was not gonna go away. Annie would sooner or later get lonesome . . . the fisherman cussed himself beneath his breath, felt terrible-ashamed, and figured he needed one full-time reality check. He told himself that when Annie returned, and assumin' he was not too old and worn to walk, some kind of real reality would be holding forth at Beer and Bait. He listened as Sugar Bear, who had never before owned a pet, made up a list of names for an imaginary walrus.

A dog can only put up with so much, even a dog who is accustomed to crowds. The glorious day saw Jubal Jim Johnson a-trot, and in one of those rare moods where doggish comments are likely. Jubal Jim made such a comment some years ago when combatting a submarine. He pointed his rear end at the Canal, put his nose to the ground so that his haunches rose, and then he lifted his tail. Thus are reputations made.

On this magic day of autumn sun Jubal Jim trotted in the forest where a dog may be unencumbered by leashes or people; where a dog can lift his leg to claim territory and bragging rights, or sniff out varmints, or dig gopher holes for the fun of it . . . there being no expectation of actually catching one. A dog can sniff trails not worth following, or stand and give voice to houndish-opinions.

And a dog may pause at the site of an ancient and forgotten Indian village where, through centuries, mud washes away revealing decayed artifacts. The mud, which slid in a foul storm five centuries ago, was once part of a foothill. When the great slide happened it brought with it trees and boulders. What a dog now sees is a rapidly rising slope on which are rooted large trees and tangles of blackberry; and where, occasionally, a stone or ivory tool, once useful, lies exposed as water drains off the hill.

And a dog may stand in the forest, apart from people, but watching them. Jubal Jim sat on a rise that overlooked a road filled with traffic. A yellow crane tilted crazily beside the Canal. As people cussed, and an occasional honk sounded because someone was desperate for a drink, water swirled along the shore.

Jubal Jim watched as a head appeared from the water, red-hair, permed, and simpering. The head was followed by a skinny body, as the guy stood watching traffic. The guy did not drip.

Jubal Jim stood separated by a good forty yards, what with road and beach, but Jubal Jim has a hound's voice. He rose to all fours, barked a harsh warning, and got the guy's attention. Jubal Jim's voice sank to a growl, threatening, loud, snarls sounding across the road from his cover of trees. The guy tried to step forward, was stopped. Jubal Jim's voice rose even louder with threat. The guy simpered, shrugged, and sank back into the Canal as drivers kept their gazes fixed on the back ends of cars in front of them.

Jubal Jim, whose nose is every bit as good as the miracle-type nose of a bear, turned as he picked up a delightful scent carried by sea wind. He headed back into the forest where Annie walked.

The Hustles Begin

The fisherman rode shank's mare to Beer and Bait, walking slow and a little painful past backed-up traffic and parked cop cars. Odd, how quickly a guy got used to being decrepit. Odd, how the mind still worked, but slower. The fisherman walked because traffic backed up to south-a-Cincinnati, and he didn't feel like putting up with it.

Something big was gonna happen. When Annie returned from the forest accompanied by Jubal Jim, she remained curiously silent. A guy could tell, though, that a decision had been made. The fisherman thought maybe he ought to go back and talk her out of what she decided was gonna be. Then he thought, no, nope, uh-uh. She deserved to take her innings. It seemed like this deal ran on rails. A smart guy just had to stay off the tracks.

Except he had not stayed off the tracks. He had walked right up to that mess with the cop; and while the cop might have learned something . . . or maybe not . . . the fisherman only learned about his own obscurity.

Annie had to know that he had been sort of brave. Or, anyway, stupid in a brave sort of way. Annie had watched him closely, saw the way he slumped with age, and he saw sympathy in Annie's eyes. It was like her. If she felt sorry for herself it didn't show, yet she pitied him. To be the object of pity . . . that he couldn't hardly bear to think about.

Annie had not looked at him with intimate thanks. She assumed he had defended Sugar Bear. It did not occur to her that he had tried to defend Annie.

Now he ached as he walked, and obscurity walked with him. If the whole rest-of-the world didn't know about the costs of love he guessed he could bear it. He could put up with being one more blip on the radar screen, one more ball cap bobbing among the crowds, one more pair of trudging feet in the passing show. Being misunderstood by the one you loved meant that finally, when your part of the passing show had passed, oblivion was the desired and logical end.

And what was so all-fired great about thinking, anyway? Look what it did for Socrates.

The parking lot of Beer and Bait was so crowded with iron a guy had to squeeze between bumpers. Beer and Bait stood with its door wide open to catch swirls of wind now gusting to maybe twenty-five knots. The wind would make life bearable, because the crowd inside would bring the place to boiling.

On the front steps a bunch of guys sat drinking beer or pop as they bulled and soaked up sunlight. Wind wrapped around Beer and Bait. It caused cigarettes to burn a little faster, beards and hair to flatten; but these were working men, outdoors guys. They knew that when sun shines, take advantage. They looked like a group picture of nineteenth-century loggers, except the beer guys automatically concealed their beer in case of cops.

The tape deck in Beer and Bait sat silent. A low murmur sounded from inside where players tried to be polite while others jousted. Serious dough was at stake. Loud mouths would get shown the door.

As he rounded the corner of a van the fisherman saw the tow-truck kid not fifty feet away. The kid sat in the cab of his pickup, doors open for the breeze, radio on but subdued. The kid sat lost in either thought or misery.

When the fisherman came near the kid looked glad. Then he looked shocked. The fisherman paused, tried to figure why, then remembered that he was older than usual.

"It's a long story," he told the kid. A realization came to him, crawling all over him, that life was shorter now. Life was gonna be brief. It came to him that if he was this much old, he ought-ta be a lot more smart. He told himself he ought to feel scared, but only felt dull, flat, toneless.

He watched fear in the kid's eyes. "Stay away from the dunk site," he said. "Have nothing more to do with this."

"I heard bull about the cop." The kid eased from his truck, and the kid was timid. "You part of that?"

As the fisherman told the story he watched the kid go stupid. The kid was getting his back up. The kid was ready to fight.

"Believe what you're seeing," the fisherman told him. "Stay out of it. You saw what's out there. Now we know what it can do." From inside Beer and Bait came a pause in the murmur, then excitement, then voices that could not hold back as someone made a genius-type shot.

"I'm teamed with a loser." The kid tried not to let his own misery get in the way of the fisherman's misery. "Might as well start some crap, might as well take a swing at it. . . ." He realized he was talking like a kid, and started over. "If there's nothing we can do, how far are we supposed to run?"

"I got no answer," the fisherman told him, and figured a change of subject was in order. "Teamed with a loser?"

"This team stuff is bull," the kid said. "One on one is the way to go. Why the team stuff?"

The fisherman had not seen the player lists. He thought for a moment. "Because rich guys need help. They probably bought help, because they can't haul their own freight." He leaned against the truck. His weight pressed against the truck, like muscles were glad to take a break, like his body tried to figure out just how tired it was. "Don't get in for more than ten bucks worth," he told the kid. "The game is rigged."

"I gotta understand this." The kid's mouth tightened. Flesh lay smooth across his face and arms, but firm, like he'd suddenly shed his baby fat. "There's not only teams. There's a sneaky guy in there, checking the action . . . looks like Deputy Dawg." He reached behind the truck seat and pulled out his cue. The cue case was getting worn. A new cue case would make a better hustle because it would yell "amateur". It would suck other players into bland assumptions.

"I'll watch that show," the fisherman said, "but I wouldn't touch it. Somebody's gonna hurt, and hurt bad."

"I got a reputation needs defending," the kid confessed. "A guy can't duck that kinda thing."

"You don't see Petey. If this was legit you'd see Petey. Take it from Petey. It's time to walk away."

The kid looked insulted, then he looked afraid, like he stood in the presence of a crazy person. "Petey's gone. Petey's drowned." The kid pointed to the Canal.

"I forgot. You don't know about that. Petey's not dead. It's a hustle." As the fisherman explained, the kid's eyes grew wider. Then he grew pale. Then he realized that he'd been brought in on a secret that almost nobody knew. He looked proud.

"I got some stuff to learn," the kid said. "Or maybe I don't want to learn it. Who would have ever thought . . ."

The fisherman looked across the tops of cars, looked at guys loafing on the steps of Beer and Bait, looked at tree tops beginning to sway as wind blew stronger up high. He figured Annie was weaving weather. He wondered idly if it was time to head for high ground. Then he stopped being idle and thought of escape routes. "Nice truck," he said to the kid.

"To tell the truth," the kid told him, "it's a pain in the keister." The kid also looked around, at high-priced iron, at junkers, at working trucks. "It's for sale," he said about the Dodge. "I got my old rig out of impound. I'm rebuilding it. I really liked that little outfit." Then the kid became shy. "Seems like I'm figuring something out. What do you reckon?"

"There's all kinds of hustles," the fisherman suggested. "Maybe you've hustled yourself."

"Prob-a-bly," the kid admitted. "Seems like I've been doing that since about first grade." He rattled his cue case, looked toward Beer and Bait. "So it's rigged. So they teamed me wrong on purpose." The kid looked toward the Canal where little wavelets danced before the wind. "I ought to be steamed, so how come I ain't?" Then he answered his own question. "In a little while I'll walk in there, shoot a hot stick, and lose. Guys will say it means something, and I'm gonna grin like it don't mean nothin', because it don't."

The fisherman privately told himself that miracles happen. This was a smart kid. In the middle of all this badness, something good. "There's no such thing as an honest hustle," the fisherman suggested. "Seems like you just made a choice."

"Seems like." The kid turned toward Beer and Bait. "You want to watch the show?"

The fisherman looked toward swaying tree tops. He thought of his boat. It was doubled up on lines long enough to handle a rise in tide. He reminded himself he had no place to go, and no way to protect who he loved. "It's gonna be illuminating," he muttered. "Why not?"

•

The crowd inside Beer and Bait seemed nearly civilized. A few loggers even used words of up to two syllables. Hustlers kept their yaps shut as cueballs clicked, and as the aromas of fresh beer, and stale beer belches swirled through cigar smoke.

Rich guys in pastel golfing togs played to a gallery of butterflies. The butterflies, gorgeous from a distance, perched at tables arranged on the bandstand. They could see over heads of a crowd seated around small tables on the dance floor. The butterflies chatted and sipped nectar. They colored the joint with tones most gorgeous; pink and mauve, orange and money-flavor, buttercup yellow, aqua-teal, and purple.

A young guy at the bar took one look at the fisherman and offered his barstool. The guy looked happy, like he'd already lost the tournament and was free to enjoy the rest of the day. A nice guy.

The fisherman felt insulted and ready to fight. Then he remembered how he looked. Not many guys were polite to old men. He said his thanks, took a place at the bar, and had a great view.

Through windows so clean you couldn't see them, the fisherman saw moderate chop rising on the Canal. To the east, and headed seaward, a crab boat glowed yellow and blue in sunlight as it traced a silver wake. Toward the middle of the Canal the creature moved ever-so-slow, like a wreck adrift. Waves were not yet breaking, but chop caused white furrows between crests. The fisherman shuddered. His storm gear, boots 'n all, were parked in the cabin of his boat. He figured that mister sun would last another fifteen minutes before dirty weather hit.

A low murmur came from the crowd as a logger made a miracle-type shot, then ran the table. The game of nine-ball, it should be noted, moves quick. It's possible to drop three or four games without getting a shot. The game asks for plenty of positioning, combinations, and not a few banks. The excited murmur came mostly from the crowd of Beer and Bait regulars, not from the butterflies who were otherwise occupied. Stinky stuff has a way of happening.

Because, arranged around the large room, poolers and wives and girlfriends sat at tables and sipped beer or pop. The women; secretaries, sales clerks, waitresses with rough hands, dressed in blue jeans and logging shirts, or ready-to-wear skirts and blouses. Hair was nicely brushed, tied back, or with bangs, or shoulder-length and swingy. Bottoms were narrow or broad, legs slim or chunky, shirt fronts abundant; but mostly, the ladies broadcast vitality; were alive. The Beer and Bait ladies watched the butter-flies, and the ladies were hostile.

The butterflies, with beetle-lady acting as choir director, pre-tended to pay no attention; but a two hundred dollar scarf might be dropped accidentally, or a diamond ring large enough to choke a snake might be twisted into plain view as a butterfly leaned for-ward, chin on delicately curved wrist.

Tension grew as rich guys watched the Beer and Bait ladies while pretending otherwise. Rich guys gave sideways glances that checked out nicely turned legs, or low cut blouses. The Beer and Bait ladies, in a less-than-loving attempt to communicate with butterflies, showed a little extra leg. Silent messages passed back and forth, and the messages were not kind.

The hustlers stayed out of it. Loners. Never sitting. Never congregating. They remained practically invisible except when shooting. The Beer and Bait players, though, watched rich guys checking out the Beer and Bait ladies. The Beer and Bait players started to get their backs up, a condition not advisable if a guy wants to win at pool.

The trouble being . . . a 'course, that it probably wasn't even a hustle, since rich guys are traditionally known to be horny. . . .

The fisherman watched the two kid bartenders. The kids picked up on the tension and asserted control. They were like a pair of twins, except one had curly dark hair, and one had straight blond; both with white shirts, bow ties, goldy-brass rings in their ears, and hands so deft they could make change whilst wiping bar, drawing beer; and all the time flipping bartender-type bull that tells each-'n-all just who controls the joint.

Mostly the bartenders flipped it at the Beer and Bait guys, because those were the guys who suffered. This early in the game guys were getting shed like mange. Wizardry romped as cueballs backed the length of the table, and as three-ball combinations became so common as to go unnoted. The level of play ran so high that ordinary players rose to the occasion, got hot, stayed hot, and lasted three or four games. Other guys who were very, very good, discovered that very-very-good was not good enough. Each time a team found itself eliminated, the players shifted from pop to beer, mutters, and excuses.

Meanwhile, the rich guy's secretary kept everything straight. She dressed to look plain, wore big eyeglasses to keep butterflies from jealousy, and spoke nicely, but with authority. She took no crapola from anybody, rich guys and bartenders included. The fisherman watched her, thought her the prettiest woman in the joint, and certainly the smartest. Then, thinking about women who were pretty, he searched the crowd for Bertha.

She stood in a far corner and looked onto the Canal. Bertha should be joyous at so many customers. Instead, she slumped. Bertha pretended to look at rising waves, but was actually stand-ing in a place where she could watch a weasel-type gent who drifted through the crowd. The guy was too scrawny to be a cop, but a stench of copness dwelt about him; something too observant, something official, something slightly smarty. He dressed in work pants and chambray shirt, both new. He wore pointy shoes. A real wrong guy.

The fisherman told himself that there would be cops. The scrawny gent kept close to where guys were side-betting, even made a few bets himself. Money passed back and forth, and pretty openly. A lot of money.

The guy was a plant for cops. A bust was gonna happen, it was gonna. The fisherman watched Bertha, then watched the hustlers. Hustlers were not stupid. They paid no attention to the guy. It figured then, that the hustlers knew about the bust. And Bertha was not stupid, but looked scared and helpless. Seeing her that way was a new experience for the fisherman. He wondered if it was new for Bertha.

Busted Hustles

From the Japanese Current, sometimes, a warm front seeps north as clouds command satellite pictures on TV. The screen goes gray, like old-time black and white, as clouds churn slow cyclonic motion. When that happens we get abundant rain, and those who love the forest fear the very soul of wind. Our Pacific Northwest is so wet that trees do not grow massive root systems. When soil turns liquid with rain, and wind arrives, giants crash across the forest, and into houses.

And, not often, but sometimes, a band of arctic cold sweeps south along the Canadian Rockies. It covers Washington, Oregon, Idaho, Montana; with smidgens left over for the Dakotas. Where warm clouds meet cold, snow forms; then ice. It's a time of unrest and fear as things happen that should not. Wind chooses a tree in the densest forest, wraps around the top, gives a little twist, and over-she-goes, though logic and physics say the tree stood protected.

Wind rages on the Canal as dreadful things appear. Water-logged sternboards of wrecks sweep to the surface, *Tinker Bell*, Seattle, *Junebug*, Port Townsend, *Plastic Lady*, San Francisco, *Joseph and Mary*, Portland; the stern boards still holding small chips of color; white or green or blue on dead timber.

Sometimes bones wash ashore, bones we hope are those of animals. And sometimes, in the fury of surf, in rain or ice, on water or

land, hideous things appear; sometimes unseen, but always unexplained because they should not be there.

Unexplained, and at the time unseen: at a fairy-tale house a
man shakes with palsy. His face reddens as if from stroke, then
bleaches fish belly white. He tries to form words, makes only
protesting moans and goes dumb. His hands cover his ears as
though he could trap consciousness. Sugar Bear claws at the last
remnant of awareness. Then his face goes blank, nearly lifeless,
inert, eyes dull, lips slobbering only a little.

Nor does one see a gray-haired woman, torn by grief, turn to
fury as trees shed branches that rattle to the forest floor. The
woman sobs and calls forth rain while wiping slobber.

And equally unexplained, a thing rises from the dunk site, red-
haired, permed, skinny, but jaunty as it strolls the road, hitches a
ride south with a discouraged pooler, and simpers only a little.

And, if no one sees, then maybe it is rain, or maybe the promise of ice; but probably it is the wind that scares everybody, even
fishermen, or maybe especially them. Plus, if a guy only sits and
watches, the scare-level rises quick.

At Beer and Bait the fisherman watched as the tow-truck kid ran
the table three times; then get whipped because his partner could
not, as the saying goes, bop a bull in the butt with a bass fiddle.
The guy was so bad he had to be a ringer, or else so good he
could shoot just awful and make it look natural. Either way, it
was a heist.

The kid's pride kept him silent. He did his work, stepped aside,
watched his chances slide down to subterranea, then gave an easy
smile and ordered a bottle-a-pop. When he looked at his partner he
did not sneer. He even smiled somewhat natural. Then he walked to
stand beside the fisherman.

"You did that well," the fisherman told him. The fisherman looked toward the Canal as sun faded behind clouds of darkest gray and the surface of the Canal turned sullen. "We could use a few more like you."

The kid stood silent, but the kid just glowed.

Tension in the joint crept skyward as butterflies, having aught to do but sip, made low and cutting comments beneath tight smiles. They watched their pet rich guys show off in attempts to impress Beer and Bait ladies, and the rich guys mentally cavorted. The fisherman watched the butterflies sharpen their claws (unusual in a butterfly) while they figured how much they could charge for rich-guy indiscretions. He felt almost sorry for rich guys, then told himself, naw, nope, uh, uh.

"There's gonna be a bust," the fisherman told the kid. "It's a question of do we get busted before, or after the fight."

"The jail ain't big enough," the kid whispered. "They can't bust everybody." The kid watched the guy who was too scrawny to be a cop, but who had to be a plant. The guy disappeared through the doorway, stepping into wind that drove everybody else inside. "It's about to come down," the kid said, "but it'll be a wash. I ain't done nothin'."

"We're in for a big hand of weather," the fisherman mentioned. "You may want to get out ahead of it." Wind had shifted and now blew from the east.

The kid grinned. "And miss the fights? It's not like I was never in jail before." Then he sounded worried. "If this kicks loose, get behind the bar." He said it casual so it wouldn't sound insulting. A good kid. Protective.

Sudden wind popped hard against Beer and Bait. The building did not tremble, exactly, but the gust caused tingles in a fisherman-style subconscious. The fisherman looked toward the Canal.

A crab boat ran a little too close to shore as whitecaps rose. The crabber put his helm to port and clawed into the wind and toward the channel. Odds on getting blown ashore seemed perfect.

Another gust hit. The gust held spatters of rain. Water ran on the windows of Beer and Bait, little streams flattened by wind as noon sky turned to gloaming. The fisherman told himself it was time to be elsewhere. Actually, past time. He watched the crab boat struggle and felt helpless. There wasn't squat anyone could do.

A pause. Silence. The click of pool balls stopped, and murmurs from the crowd drizzled away. The fisherman's ears proclaimed another mess even before he turned.

A small shriek rose, then faltered as figures appeared in the doorway. Unrest moved across the crowd in waves. A large sigh came from Bertha, and gasps from rich guys combined with fluttering from butterflies. The guys at the pool tables tried to play it cool, and all three guys shanked their shots.

In the doorway Petey stood bemused. Petey carried no cue case, wore no ball cap, thus presented no poolish threat. He took his time surveying the whole room, rich guys, butterflies, loggers, truckers and fishers, bartenders and other enthusiasts, plus hustlers. He watched benevolently, as if he owned each-'n-every one. He continued to watch as two smashingly gorgeous hookers stood on each side of him. The ladies were dressed most splendid. They looked over the crowd with experienced eyes, smiled in the general direction of rich guys, then headed for the ladies' can to fluff hair, repair makeup, and all that other girl stuff.

Bertha began to step forward. Petey looked her away. He loomed like a colossus, although technically Petey isn't tall enough to play the part. His dark hair glowed like a close-cropped halo in twinkly barlight, and his bald spot shone with rain. He stood like a championship wrestler at rest. Petey did not even look as the hookers disappeared into the ladies' can, although every other regular in the joint watched enchanted; except the fisherman who made mental notes . . . in case he ever had to write stuff down.

a. Beer and Bait regulars in shock, and most scared spitless. A ghost appeared among them. Some pale, some shaking, some gulping beer like it was medicine . . . at the same time Beer and Bait regulars watch gorgeous hookers: male regulars wistful/lustful, female regulars competitive/steamed.

b. Butterflies unimpressed by Petey who they didn't know, but terribly impressed by hookers. Butterflies sensing classy competition because their fifty-going-on-thirty-five was not as magical as twenty-five-going-on-twenty-six.

c. Bertha looking hopeful. Bertha looking jealous. Bertha looking ticked. Bertha with soft light in eyes, silly, mooshy, schoolgirl.

d. Other hustlers impressed. A bare nod from one, a tap of pool cue on top of shoe by another, while a third pinches nose and grins slowly, slowly. Hustlers recognizing a major hustle and approving.

e. Bartenders taken out of their game. Bartenders wondering whatever in the cotton-pickin' universe is going on.

f. Tow-truck kid not impressed but mightily amused.

g. Secretary business-like, checking player lists to see if anything amiss.

h. Daylight rapidly fading above dark water.

i. Rich guys recognizing hookers. Rich guys owning memories of cavorting with hookers at China Bay. Rich guys looking like they'd just been shot.

j. Petey arranging table, so-to-speak. Petey telling Beer and Bait regulars that all is okay. Petey telling rich guys that if a burn starts, there'll be many-a-blister on many-a-rich bottom.

"Bottle-a-pop," Petey mentioned, "strawberry if you got it."

A kid bartender practically tripped over himself fishing in the cooler. Petey strolled to a group of Beer and Bait regulars who trembled behind beer glasses. As he approached their table, which sat close to the fisherman, they stood, scrammed, and Petey rested. Mighty solid for a ghost. Sipped pop. Waited for hookers. Or maybe not. Waiting for something.

"Bust," the tow-truck kid whispered almost joyful, "and here I was, looking forward to the fights." He flipped bull so easily anyone could tell he was brave. "First time I was ever glad to see a cop." He looked toward Bertha. "She don't need a tore-up joint."

Sudden cold entered the room ahead of the first cop. It was winter cold, like the backside of November, not October. The fisherman watched as the cop came through the doorway and stopped. The cop looked around, then took up position beside the door.

A blast of winter wind hit windows and another handful of rain flattened then blew away. Every fisherman in the joint turned from the cop to watch the Canal, and every fisherman knew that winter had just announced the end of fishing season.

A second cop entered and took position on the other side of the door. No one would be allowed to leave.

Local cops. Not too bright. Leg breakers in uniform. Noises came from the front porch where the stamping of feet told of a convocation of cops. The fisherman wondered if the tow-truck kid was wrong. Maybe they could bust everybody.

"Gimmie a beer," the kid whispered to a bartender. "Not a can. A bottle."

"Don't," the fisherman whispered. "We've been set up, but don't. Something more is gonna happen."

A smarmy little guy, the guy who was a plant, slipped through the doorway slick as snot on a doorknob. He looked over the heads of the crowd. "Mr. District Attorney." he said. "Illegal gaming; and recess is over. Who runs this joint?"

Bertha stepped from the back of the room, and Bertha had glad lights in her eyes. Bertha had worried herself sick for a long, long, long time and finally had someone she could tussle. The fisherman watched with certain knowledge that the first time the punk touched Bertha the joint would explode. There weren't enough cops in the world . . . and besides, there was Petey.

Petey rested. As Bertha got near the guy Petey yawned. He tapped the tabletop with his fingers, said, "I got a better idea."

Bertha stopped. The smarmy guy turned his attention to Petey, and motioned to one of the cops. Petey watched the approaching cop, and Petey looked bored as a hundred sermons. He turned toward the rotund little rich guy who stood behind a pool table.

"What in sam hill were you and momma thinking?" he asked the rich guy. "You need a wolf pack and you hired puppies. Call 'em off." Only someone who was totally bored, or else a total hustler, could sound that disinterested. To the approaching cop, he said, "See ya."

The cop stopped. He looked at the smarmy guy. The smarmy guy shrugged, and looked at rich guy. Rich guy tried to look indifferent, but his face was flushed. He dropped his hands to his sides so no one could see them tremble. At the butterfly table the beetle-lady watched closely, but seemed tentative.

"Thanks anyhow," rich guy said to the smarmy guy. "Go away." He flushed even deeper as the hookers came from the ladies' can. The girls chose a table at the far end of the room where two loggers sat solid as stumps. The loggers, who in their wildest dreams had never been around such classy babes, blushed and found extra chairs. The hookers sat in communicating distance with the butterflies, who they ignored.

The butterflies watched the hookers, were puzzled. Of course, the butterflies had never nuzzled nectar at China Bay.

The rich guys were looking everywhere in the joint except at the hookers. The rich guys pretended total innocence.

"There's still a tournament," Petey told the crowd. "Do it."

Cueballs began to click. People who had been ready for a fight now had to get rid of adrenalin. The crowd grew noisy in spite of the tournament.

"Over here," Petey said to Bertha, and his voice was affectionate. At the same time he was obviously in no mood to argue. He watched the two cops follow mister smarmy. They stepped outside.

A burst of rain swept against the windows like waves breaking over the cabin of a boat. In Beer and Bait, in what had been an overheated room on a sunny noontime, chill entered from windows made cold by rain. Gloom lowered so that only the white of breaking surf showed the Canal still existed. If the creature was out there it could not be seen.

Bertha took one look at the hookers, like there was gonna be hell-and-hallelujah happening, then decided to go along with Petey's program. She came to the table. Sat.

"You too," Petey said to rich guy.

Rich guy didn't even hesitate. He only glanced at beetle-lady and pretended not to shudder. The rest of the rich guys cuddled up on the far side of the pool tables away from the hookers. Butterflies, still confused, took notes as another shovelful of rain flooded the windows.

In the rapidly cooling room rich guy had sweat on his brow. His tummy was the only normal thing about him, because fear and meanness caused his shoulders to tense. His face filled with anger. "You want something," he said. "So what?"

"You can buy those girls off." Petey kept detached and pretty quiet. "But, you can't buy them off here and now. The minute one of your boys walks toward them they'll cuddle up to him, and that starts a discussion group with the mommas." Petey glanced toward the butterflies and rubbed his bald spot, maybe for luck. "How much will that many divorces cost? Gimmie a figure."

Rich guy tried to set his anger aside. He was ready to deal. "You want something. What?"

"Ever since the Phoenicians invented money there's been only one answer to that question." Petey looked at Bertha. "I read that in book somewhere." He still sounded detached, almost indifferent, but maybe a little bit amused.

"What?" Bertha is not used to mystery-stuff. She is not used to being in the middle of conversations she doesn't understand.

"I got a lever," Petey told her. "We're talking facts of life." And, although he was talking facts of life, he couldn't bring himself to discuss hookers.

"You got hustled," he told Bertha. "That bust was a setup. This guy bought one of his pet gov-guys, and the gov-guy brought in cops. Cops would run people home. Tournament canceled. You were going to end up owing ten grand to the leader of the tournament at the time of the bust. Plus, you'd owe a big piece of the three grand registrations. You'd have to refund guys who hadn't had a turn at the tables. This guy never intended to pay a prize. He was gonna bankrupt you."

It was the absolute worst moment of Bertha's life. Probably. She sat breathing shallow, turned pale, then began to turn red. The shame. To be suckered like that. The shame. She caught a deep breath. "Why?"

"He wants the joint," Petey said. "This goes back a-ways. You wouldn't sell, and his boys could have upped their offer. But it's a game to them. He was setting you up where you'd have to sell. He's got big plans." Petey looked toward the group of rich guys. "They got blown out on the tables once before. That was a heist. This guy used the purple momma to open this up, because you wouldn't have bought in, otherwise. The other mommas didn't know." Petey watched the butterflies who were watching each other with lots of questions. He looked again at the rich guys. "After those boys got blown out the first time, anybody could figure they'd bring the mommas to the second joust. Because anyone could figure they'd show off with a fake win." He looked at rich guy. "Big mistake."

The fisherman, sitting nearby, told himself that rich guy had about seven and one-eighth seconds to make things right, because Bertha would pretty quick start to flame. The fisherman actually made a bet with himself and checked his watch. Then he noticed general movement toward the door. The outdoors guys, the fishermen and loggers and linemen, the men who understood weather, were bundling their ladies out and into the night . . . except it wasn't night yet, it wasn't even mid-afternoon.

"If you ever need a job," rich guy told Petey, "look me up." Rich guy, though totally ticked, could not control his admiration. "So what's it gonna cost?"

"I'm gonna miss this joint." Petey watched the rapidly thinning crowd, saw players bent over pool tables, saw butterflies perched on the bandstand and looking absolutely smashing from a distance. He saw a cluster of rich guys pretending to pay close attention to the pool tables. He saw hookers jiving a couple of uneasy loggers, and he saw hustlers packing up their cues; because hustlers may not know a lot about weather, but they know when a hustle is busted. "I bin thinking," Petey told Bertha. "There's a nice joint for sale in Tacoma."

Bertha looked the place over, looked at Petey with all kinds of personal questions, stuff that couldn't be asked except in private. "Why?" She looked at her bar like a thing already lost, her voice puzzled and sad.

It turned into the greatest moment of Petey's life. Probably. "It's time to cash out," he said gently. "I don't mean to tell you what to do, and there's stuff we've got to talk over." He paused. "This running the road gets to a guy. Being dead is a pain, but it was a cover for the hustle. These guys bought hustlers, but they couldn't buy me. I had to fix it where I wasn't a threat." He looked at rich guy, then back at Bertha. "He and his buddies own half the real estate for miles around. They own absolutely everything for three miles around you. They're putting in another housing project, plus they're buying the legislature. It's a matter-a-time until the road gets widened, and that much road construction means tons and tons of money. More than we would ever need . . . " he paused, blushed all the way from his hairline to his bald spot, because that "we" had slipped out. ". . . not worth the hassle," he muttered. "Take the money and run."

Bertha caught her breath, sharp, caught it again. That "we" had gotten to her. That "we", right here in the middle of a pool tournament, in front of lots of people; that "we" had come out in public when it couldn't be said in private. Bertha tried to remain normal. "How much?"

"More than enough. Enough for two joints, if needed." Petey reached in his jacket pocket and pulled out papers. "You can argue duress," he told rich guy, "but you'd have to do it in court which means it would be public." Petey laid papers in front of rich guy. "Take your time. Talk to your boys. If you try to leave, the hookers will get affectionate." Petey actually touched the back of Bertha's hand. "Dirty pool," he said, "but not as dirty as what they tried to pull." To rich guy he said, "A lawyer wrote that up. The promissory note is for thirteen thou. The other is a binding offer."

The guy looked it over. Whistled. "It's steep," he said calmly, "but do-able." He looked at Bertha. "You want to sell?"

Bertha, who had already forgotten pool tournaments, bar worries, wrecks, troubled friends, and a dead or dying cop, nodded. Bertha planned a wedding and a move to Tacoma.

"I'll be double-durn," the tow-truck kid said, "it's the bust that turned into ice cream." He touched the fisherman's shoulder. "I'm outta here. You want a lift?"

The fisherman, who had nowhere to go, and who could not protect those he loved, looked at a joint now stripped of hustlers, outdoor guys, their ladies; stripped of just about everyone except butterflies and hookers and rich guys, plus a couple bartenders and, a 'course Petey and Bertha who, it appeared, would soon be left alone.

"Sure," he said to the kid. "You're headed for Olympia. Let's go there."

Storm Surge

Until the kid turned it off, radio yammered breathless. The subject was a zone of weather hovering midpoint along the Canal. The radio guy made bad jokes, sparked and fizzed, then phoned National Weather Service. The lady at weather service came up with a big, "Don't know?" but that was okay. The radio guy didn't listen. Neither did the tow-truck kid. He had his hands full.

By the time the Dodge rolled a half mile south of Beer and Bait the road went black as the sky. Wind crashed and young cedars bent nearly flat while the tops blew out of young fir. The fisherman thought of the sea and told himself he had seen brighter midnights. Rain pulled power from darkness, and speed dropped to ten m.p.h. as the truck rocked and tried to blow sideways beneath the wail of wind. Wipers slowed under overflooding rain. Above barnyards, mercury lights peeked through darkness. They were tiny spots of blue in an eternity of night and rain. Occasionally an oncoming truck crept past, headlights blue and steaming. Headlights of the Dodge turned the roadway into a blue path between gray shoulders that lay like shrouds. Water crashed and tumbled in the ditches, rose, washed across the road, gnawed at the roadbed.

Twice the kid had to pull over. Twice the kid turned off the lights to avoid a rear-ender. The first time the kid had to pull

288

over because windshields went solid with rain. The second time he pulled over, fisherman and kid looked at each other, showed commendable calm in the middle of fear.

"I gotta stop. We weigh too much. The back end is rocking, front end is lighter." The kid kept his head, even if no one, nowhere, had ever been in rain so great a pickup bed filled too quick to drain. This was not land-based stuff. This kind of stuff happened on open ocean.

"Don't do it," the fisherman said. "Wait it out."

"I gotta."

"Then don't get on the lee side. You'll get blown away. Take my word." The fisherman felt the weight of age, the weight of helplessness.

"I gotta do it." Before he bailed from the cab the kid set the heater on high. When he jumped from the cab to let down the tailgate, the voice of storm screamed the high-pitched wail of Banshee, or even greater, a scream of Fury. The fisherman knew from the sound, more than the feel, that wind made up to sixty-five or seventy out there; and hurricane force is seventy-five.

The rear end of the truck lightened as the bed drained. The kid had pulled it off. When he jumped back into the cab, water flowed from him. The fisherman shrugged from his jacket as the kid stripped to the waist, and the heater blew like a champ. The kid huddled into the dry jacket. "Cold," he chattered. "Cold as a well digger's hindey."

Only once before, and that at sea, had the fisherman seen lightning in the middle of a snow storm. As they pulled back onto the road, rain turned to blown snow, nigh thick as a New England blizzard. Snow hit the wet roadway and turned to ice. Lightning crashed above the snow, blue, blue, wickering as wind dropped to fifty knots, then forty. When thunder boomed, the pickup recoiled from shock. Snow crossed the road, piled in the forest, and the Dodge crept across ice like a truck on tip toe.

The fisherman figured that in thirty minutes they had come under two miles. He figured, if the kid could hold on, they would drive out of the mess further south. The fisherman mourned his failings, and wondered if he should not be headed in the other direction; headed back toward Annie. Then he told himself this whole business really did run on rails. He just couldn't figure who had laid the track.

"Looks like folks gotta find a new joint." The kid's voice trembled, but his teeth stopped chattering. He stayed focused on the road, but needed reassurance.

"Small loss," the fisherman said, and found himself too overwhelmed to explain. He watched blown snow, watched a black sky cut with streaks of electric blue; lightning like symbols of fury, sorrow, dread. Thunder crashed like voices of ancient gods.

And a joint was a very small loss when thirteen cars, and maybe twenty people, were drowned; when a good cop, who was also a good man, lay dead or dying, and when another good man was insane; a good woman crazed with grief; and himself, old and helpless, driven south to safety. The loss of a beer joint amounted to zip.

And what good came of it? None. Except a kid was growing up and pointed right. But, maybe that would have happened anyway. Maybe.

"You ever feel like you're in the middle of something you oughta understand. And don't?" The kid's foot lay gentle on the accelerator. The pickup moved across ice like a slow dance, controlled, athletic, serene amidst blowing snow. Thunder boomed above the forest, and here and there, beneath flashes of blue, wide spaces appeared where a pathway of trees had blown flat.

"All the time," the fisherman admitted, "and I've got more information than you."

Snow drifted. The world turned white. As wind continued to drop the fisherman puzzled aloud, "I made a mistake. I kept looking at *things* instead of forces. That creature in the Canal is huge and ancient and sad. It's actually kind of friendly. But, then, there's something else out there and it's different. It's equally old, but it's shallow and silly and dangerous." Along the shoreline lightning crashed, cracked, and a big tree split and showered wind-blown kindling. If the truck window were open the cab would flood with ozone.

"I don't know what the dangerous thing is," the fisherman explained. "But I finally understood it isn't the dead guy."

"Looked pretty dead. Smelled extra dead. I think we're going to make it." The kid gentled the steering wheel. "First we had too much weight over the back wheels, now not enough. Things are skiddy." He watched road, figuring where road had to be, because the landscape was blank with snow. Only the flowing ditches traced a path.

"I thought I saw a war," the fisherman said. "I thought it was some big damn contest between good and evil. Turns out that was too easy." He watched the kid to see if anything registered. Hard to tell. At least the kid listened. "If I read history right," the fisherman said, "civilizations hardly ever die because of catastrophe. They die because they become trite."

"We are gonna make it," the kid told him. "This crappola is breaking up." A half mile down the road daylight appeared as snow thinned and wind dropped. The fisherman turned around in the seat and looked north. Behind them lay complete darkness, wind, storm, lightning, snow and ice. Behind them, in a small house, Annie must still be tending to Sugar Bear. Annie fought back, but against what she fought, she could not know. Nor, he told himself, could he; because he still didn't have it figured out.

"I thought the trouble had something to do with the Canal," he told the kid, "but any body of water, or any mountain valley would have served. It's a tussle between forces."

"Then why here?" The kid still paid attention, sorta, but truck speed picked up. The kid was eager to drive out of the mess.

"I don't have the foggiest notion," the fisherman admitted. "But, you've got to figure there's some kind of reason." He looked toward the shore. In gradually growing light the ripped and broken hull of a crab boat littered the beach. The bow had separated and lay twenty feet beyond the tide line. The fisherman shuddered, knew what decision the crabber had made, and admired it. The guy had known the boat was a goner, so he had not waited to be blown in sideways. He had opened the throttle and driven it ashore bow first. He no doubt saved his life but at the cost of a boat.

As the road cleared and daylight returned the kid picked up speed. The cab turned hot and humid. The kid rolled the driver's window but did not lower the heater. He was coming down, relaxing, tension coming off. "I don't know what I'm gonna do," he confided to the fisherman, "but I ain't driving a tow truck the rest of my life."

"Kind of figured that would happen," the fisherman told him. "I wonder what you'll come up with?" He knew the kid asked for advice and didn't need it. The kid just needed reassurance. "Whatever you do," the fisherman said, "I know it's going to be good."

"This truck is a hustle," the kid said. "Do you understand that? Because I don't. I just know I'm getting rid of this sucker."

"It's only a truck. The hustle happens when you think a truck is something else. The hustle stops when what you do, is more

292

important than what other people see." The fisherman remembered their talk outside Beer and Bait. "You already know that. You didn't get sore because you were set up at pool. Because a pool game means absolute zero."

"That is gonna save a heap of truck payments," the kid muttered, and it was clear that he almost understood. As the sky continued to lighten the kid no longer had to keep his gaze fixed on the road. He glanced at the fisherman. "When we get there, what?"

"Drop me downtown," the fisherman told him. "I can make my way from there." He doubted if he would ever see the kid, ever again. Unless, of course, more cars dunked; but somehow that part of the game seemed played-out. "And thanks for the lift."

Winter blew into the bright streets of Olympia where the Capitol dome stood lighted and glowing like an ideal of commonwealth; though beneath the dome anything tacky could be, and was, goin' on. Streetlights in the old part of town shone softly beneath cold clouds, while promises of warmth dwelt in the brightness of coffee houses, dry goods stores, and video parlors. The fisherman found himself dwelling happily on common things; women buying bluejeans for their kids, men leaning against bars watching ball games, kids carrying cornet and fiddle cases as they waited for buses. The fisherman watched a clean-shaven itinerant standing before a bakery window. The guy looked like a man who understands five-cent cotton and forty-cent meat. The itinerant turned, walked away, and he hunched inside a thin jacket. The itinerant looked vaguely familiar.

Since the state of Washington lies northerly in the latitudes, night came early apace. The fisherman ordered burgers in a brightly lit cafe, downed one, found he could not finish the second; a young man's appetites no longer fitting an old man's body. He found a public phone, called a cab. By the time evening news arrived on TV he had settled in one of those motels so beloved by golfers of the polyester persuasion. The motel parking lot, he saw, was peeing Lincolns.

Television flurried with breathless stuff labeled "breaking news" although it was clear the news had already broken and gone. The fisherman watched TV flacks discuss the fantastic—impossible—once-in-a-century—tragic—climate-climactic-catastrophe of weather along the Canal where an unexplained storm had taken out the road. Home video was remarked upon, and TV cameras offered views from helicopters, views of snow and ice, of blown trees, of a couple hundred yards of water where road once ran, and the tip of a yellow crane barely poking above waves. The flacks consulted their weatherman-in-residence. He consulted satellite photos, ouija boards, astrology, and came up with zilch-O. The TV flacks were as well groomed as any hooker.

What TV did not say, although it might have guessed, is that rich guys somewhere had just fallen feet-first into a bonanza. Now the new road would have to be built. The fisherman could actually feel the rich guys visiting their tailors, and ordering deeper pockets.

He told himself he should be angry, horrified, lamenting, concerned, or something. Instead he felt dull. He watched TV and realized that he and the kid had not been anywhere near the worst of the storm. They had driven along the fringes. At the center of storm, where the road was out . . . and if the fisherman judged aright, where the dunk site had lain . . . weather must have struck like the lighting bolts of Zeus.

He thought of Sugar Bear and of Annie. As winter wind

294

wrapped around the building the overheated motel room felt cold. He told himself to get some sleep. He told himself that being helpless meant a guy was not responsible for anything, except, a 'course, a guy could cry.

Day of Darkness

Dreams came and went and came again, heavy-footed and ruthless and crazed. He dreamed of Annie, of Annie's young smile disappearing into a cave of darkness where voices wailed. He dreamed of Sugar Bear, pounding and shaping glowing steel, and using the dead guy's forehead for an anvil. He saw the dead guy, a misshapen thing rising from the Canal, and the shape sang love songs of the dilly-silly-ditsy kind; stench and decay spreading from the dead guy to cover grasses and hang like clusters of moss from trees. He dreamed of the cop, stalwart, well-intended, idealistic sorta, and smart, but not smart enough. And the dream said there was no more cop, only something left over to fill a coffin. He saw Bertha and Petey, smiling, then frowning as they danced along the top of a bar while hustling each other. He saw his fishing boat blowing above the tops of trees, long lines sweeping the depths of forest and hooking varmints before it disappeared among clouds. And, he saw the bartender at China Bay; saw the bartender's face, calm, detached, immense, watching all of them, watching, watching . . . somewhat entertained, somewhat amused.

In spite of dreams he slept late, and woke surprised to find himself granted another day of life. He lay for long moments without moving. Mixed sunlight filled the windows. In the parking lot rich guys and butterflies bailed out of the motel. They had driven south because the road was out. Now they would circle north to Seattle, take a ferry, and return to the project. The rich guys walked with confidence. They had pulled one off. The two hookers, who at present were doubtless shacked up with a couple of badly shocked loggers, had caused no trouble for rich guys.

The fisherman rose, bathed, dressed, found breakfast. He walked morning streets beneath sun and cloud. He told himself that if a guy needed to hitch a ride north there was only one place to go. He set a course for China Bay.

The three goldfish at China Bay Taverna swim among ferns, and, like the old Chinaman in Mr. Wm. Yeats' great poem, deal with what is past, or passing, or to come. The goldfish fatten with the years, cruise lazily, and have been known to burp at exactly the right point in barroom discussions. On the day when the fisherman arrived, their lighted tank overlooked only one geriatric lad seated at the far end of the bar. He wore a black armband, and the hanky in his jacket pocket was black. This was the man who claimed a former career as a diplomat. When the fisherman sat beside him, the guy took a careful look, then motioned to the bartender. The motion was more of a command, than a request. The bartender produced a deck of cards and a board.

"It's a little known fact," the old guy said, "that in spite of English claims, the game of cribbage was actually invented aboard ships in the days of Alexander. It originally carried a name equivalent to our word, swindle."

"I believe it," the fisherman told him. "Why wouldn't I believe it?" The fisherman flexed his twisted hand. "You'll have to shuffle. But I can deal with my left hand."

"You'll get used to it," the old boy said. "I advise serenity. I caution against haste. You'll find that age has pronounced advantages, but they must be realized in methodical manner."

"How much?"

"Penny a point," the guy said, "but in order not to burden society, save back enough to cover your funeral."

"Your friend?" the fisherman asked about the ex-Navy guy.

"A true master of the bull flip." The old man sighed, touched his black armband, sincere, even somewhat sad. "We are not like to see his kind again." He looked around the joint, at pool tables and punchboards, at pictures of Athens street scenes, and Chinese cheesecake. "But bull lives on. It's a comfort in its way. Actually, a memorial."

Beyond the windows of China Bay the Canal lay calm as the mind of a monk. No hump moved beneath the water. Mixed sunlight came and went. The Canal beamed, then went sullen beneath clouds, then brightened beneath another smidgen of sun.

"It's gone," the old guy said. "What humped out there moved on. It tried to save lives, but only managed to twist cars. It fought against decay and lost the battle, but there will be other wars." He shuffled cards, pushed the deck toward the fisherman. "One need not ordinarily feel sorry for the dead, but those who drowned were emptied, neutered, turned into blanks. For that, one may have feelings."

For a long moment the fisherman felt more lonely than usual. He had come to depend on the creature, come to think of it as a sort of partner in what could only be called confusion-with-good-intent. Then he realized that his loneliness came because the creature had actually known what it intended, had not been confused.

The fisherman felt isolated, watched calm water, watched where gulls scavenged the tideline, and knew that he too had departed the scene. He could not pretend to himself that the storm had left him with a boat. He could not pretend that, insurance or not, he would buy another.

"You weep for a while," the old man said, "and then you laugh. Mostly at yourself. Once in a while you shake your fists at the gods, just to keep in practice."

From the back room came the sound of Lee cussing in Chinese. The bartender moved quietly behind the empty bar, arranging ashtrays and humming something classical. The bartender moved with the music, graceful as a girl, strong as a working man. Precisely placed chairs ranked around small tables. Cones of light illuminated pool tables. Floors glowed swept and clean; the place orderly, that through the day would descend to confusion and chaos.

The goldfish burped. The Dragon-Lady-red doors swung open and an itinerant entered. The fisherman looked up, looked twice, looked three times. He was actually surprised that he could still feel even mild shock. He dealt cards.

"I bring truth," Chantrell told the bartender.

"How cunning of you. Will you be using the parking lot today?" The bartender placed a can of pop and a barroom sausage before Chantrell.

"Thus doth the Lord provide," Chantrell told the bartender, "and you, his beloved servant."

"I'm actually a bartender." The bartender smiled, and turned away so Chantrell could wolf his handout with some dignity. From the stockroom Lee's voice mixed Chinese and English cuss words.

"Pearl of the Orient," the bartender said, "we're about to get company. Save back some curses. One must not run short."

Sometimes the bartender's eyes are blue, sometimes gray, but this day nearly black. The bartender looked the joint over, gaze benevolent. "A bully pulpit, the parking lot. Perhaps the mission of this joint is to supply souls for you to save." The bartender's voice sounded droll, but not unkind.

The fisherman discovered that he felt almost happy. Chantrell had made it. He had made it in about the way a guy would have to expect; clumsy, sort of dumb and awful sincere, but unstoned. The mushroom kid had moved up a slot or two.

"If you wonder too much about the Mysteries," the old man told the fisherman, "insanity becomes part of the package."

"What?"

"You are wondering if a small step forward is worth the attendant destruction." The guy chuckled. "I am very, very old, and very wise, and a helluva lot smarter than you. It pays to pay attention."

The fisherman glanced again at the Canal. "I make it to rain in five minutes."

"You see," the old man told him.

"That guy used to be a junkie," the fisherman explained about Chantrell.

"Perhaps he still is," the oldster mused, "there's all kinds of junk. On the other hand, it takes moxie to stand preaching in the rain." The old man moved pegs. "Needfulness clusters around joints. There's a sufficiency of needfulness."

"Is there such a thing as an honest hustle?" The fisherman remembered telling the tow-truck kid there was no such thing. "Maybe being mistaken, or even wrong, doesn't have much to do with being honest."

"It's something to think about," the oldster admitted. He glanced toward the Dragon-Lady-red doors. "What happens next may explain quite a bit." He shuffled and dealt.

A red-hair thing entered, simpering. Its hair was permed, and it exuded a light stench. It walked to the bar with all the ease of slime draining from a garbage truck. It looked the bar over, then took a seat beside Chantrell.

Chantrell stood. He looked at the red-hair the way a cop looks at drunken vomit. "There's things I'm not strong enough to handle," he told the bartender. Chantrell's voice was actually calm. "But I grow stronger every day." He moved toward the door. "Parking lot," he said quietly. "Grace is like rain. It can happen anywhere. Take my word."

"We're fresh out of strychnine," the bartender told the red-hair. The bartender watched Chantrell leave, watched rain begin to patter on the Canal. "You have certainly settled for a shabby incarnation this time," the bartender told the red-hair. "I thought you'd pick something attractive, something people would like."

"They like this," the thing said. "I gave it a lot of thought. This incarnation is actually perfect. It's that sort of time in history."

"Suppose I grant your point," the bartender said. "Which, of course, I do not."

"You may take my word about what losers like," the red-hair said. "I've been at this for a long, long time."

"As have I," the bartender murmured. "And sometimes the days move slowly." The bartender turned toward the back room. "We have among us a creature of urges and low desires."

Cussing flowered, then sparked, then threatened to blister paint. Lee came from the back room, gray shirt, orange tie, wrinkled face. "Didn't we just do this?"

"Time flies," the red-hair suggested.

"Hear what I say and trust it," the oldster whispered to the fisherman. "Every three or four centuries there's a meeting of

301

these forces. Every three or four centuries some nation begins to slide. When that happens you get this caucus. I am a superior diplomat."

"Incarnation or not . . ."

"Stay out of it," the oldster insisted. "You are truly helpless. That thing is a force. It can empty you as it emptied others. Lee and the bartender are forces. They play on a stage too big for your imagining."

"People are dead." The fisherman did not lower his voice.

The red-hair turned. "Death is not a thing I enjoy. Where necessary, yes, but death is not an object. My pleasure comes from damage, wounds, wreckage, broken and fractured things." The red-hair simpered. "I enjoy you, your ruptured hand, your age, your feeble indignation." The red-hair stopped simpering. "And now you must shut up."

"Are you not premature?" the bartender asked. "It took a goodly while for you to manifest this time. You were hardily opposed."

"Perhaps a little," the red-hair admitted. "Always before it's been a walk. But the stage has become bigger."

"Always before," the oldster whispered, "the battle lay within the heart of one or another nation. This time it's in the heart of the western world."

"One thing puzzles me," the bartender said. "Why here? Why manifest in this small and unimportant place?"

"The cities are already mine," the red-hair said. "They did it to themselves. But there are small pockets out here in the boonies where people stumble around and bump into each other. They aren't particularly good, or particularly bright, but they halfway try to take care of each other. They actually try to protect their worlds. I'm doing a mopping up operation, nearly meaningless, an amusement, actually. Most enjoyable."

Lee loosened his tie. "The next time we go through this you won't find me owning a joint. Next time through I'll raise mangos or cabbages. Or, maybe I'll seed clouds." Lee's scorn was so great the fisherman thought he could hear it sizzle. "The problem with a joint," Lee told the red-hair, "is there's too many guys like you . . . look the same . . . talk the same . . . " Lee wrinkled his nose. ". . . smell the same . . . and too stupid to zip their drawers."

"It's my specialty," the red-hair simpered. "Intelligence doesn't damage things, just lack of it." The red-hair snickered.

"Gimmie a time-line," Lee said, "then get the hell out."

"Be careful," the red-hair told him. "If it were not for me, folks like you would have no work."

"What a delightful idea," the bartender said. "Or, as Grandma used to put it, 'Land of Goshen'. . . or did she say, 'my stars and garters'." The bartender smiled broadly.

"There will now be negotiation," the oldster whispered. "Dreadfully boring. All about wealth and lack of it, ideas or lack of them, offers and counter offers. Lee will choose a new continent to bring to prominence. The bartender will work at protecting history. The red-hair will fake and giggle and hustle."

"I got nothin' to lose," the fisherman said, and knew he talked like a kid. "I could get in one good swing."

"You have everything to lose," the oldster whispered. "That thing is immortal. Go now, and wend your way; but take this with you: although a civilization dies, it does not mean that intelligence must. Thought and honor are that thing's enemies, and thought and honor are individual. You may remain strong in the midst of squalor. Protect your loves if you can. Protect their worlds if you can. Wend your way." The oldster moved pegs. "Crib," he said.

Epilogue

After heavy storms the forest seems to rise and stretch and shake like a dog waking from a nap. Branches of fir that sailed before the wind lie on the forest floor and arrange themselves in clusters. Cones continue to mature, and from the decaying clusters will eventually sprout new seedlings. No one knows how the branches manage this, but people of the forest know it is true.

And movement returns. The birds of winter, sparrows, of which there are more than twenty kinds, Oregon juncos, nuthatch, and chickadees emerge from sheltered spots where they have huddled against wind. They flit and putter about tops of giant trees where they pick seeds in the canopy. Sometimes a robin, who has failed to get the winter message, hops on the forest floor where there is movement of mice; while up and down the trunks of trees chipmunks whistle, chase, and chatter.

This, according to the poet, is /the forest primeval/the murmuring pines and the hemlocks/and this, according to forester and lumber magnate, is old-growth timber in which resides owl, cougar, bear, deer, goat, wolverine, shrew, and in which, from time immemorial humans have dreamed dreams, some shabby, and some of beauty.

And, after a storm, a hound may trot through a splendor of smells, because wind and water bring breakage. New sights

304

appear in old places. As Jubal Jim trots through the forest he pauses at the site of an ancient Indian village. Rain has flooded the slope, washed at roots of trees, tumbled shrubs and unearthed a variety of things.

Jubal Jim stops and sniffs a yellowing fragment. In this Pacific Northwest, through centuries, bone becomes soil but stone and ivory and teeth remain. This is a small tooth, certainly human, now cleaned by rain and yellowed by time. Jubal Jim makes water against a tree, moves on. There is something troubled in his gait, like a dog with arthritis, or a dog confused, or a dog unsure.

Like men and elephants, Jubal Jim is a creature of habit. He follows a familiar path. Where a tree has fallen he jumps over, stops to sniff among broken limbs or around torn roots. Insects are already about their business, burrowing, hiding, feeding in the rubble. Where the nests of mice or shrew are ripped away there remains a sense of departing warmth, though the nests, in fact, are cold.

Jubal Jim moves on, but with caution. At places along the path his belly lowers toward the ground. He crouches. Jubal Jim is brave, but tenuous in the face of change. He moves a bit more quickly as the roof of Sugar Bear's shop appears among the trees. Windows in the shop are dark. Blown cedar tips cover the roof. Jubal Jim moves forward into Sugar Bear's clearing, stops, momentarily confused.

The cliff, where in springtimes swallows were wont to dance, has disappeared. The cliff has become a slide, raw earth flowing beneath the sluicing force of rain. Where once stood a fairy-tale house, now lies a slope of mud and forest debris.

Crows fly above the clearing. A tree squirrel pokes its nose into the winter air, withdraws into its nest. The mud is nearly liquid, a field of mud above which not even a chimney shows.

Jubal Jim inches forward, sniffs, paws at the mud, and begins to dig. Liquid soil spatters behind him. The dug hole keeps closing as more mud flows in. Jubal Jim stops digging, Sniffs here, there, walks through mud. Gives voice.

The howl rises through the forest, deep, throaty, filled with sorrow, filled perhaps with anguish. The howl moves through trees toward the Canal. It is absorbed by forest and by the rush of water in a distant stream. Jubal Jim howls and howls.